San Marcos

1754~1946

Graphic by West King

Cherokee
Hawkins

Capt.
Lewis
Lawshe

Lawshe

Georgia
Lawshe

Woods

Laura Hoge

Woods

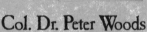

Peter Woods, Jr.

Col. Dr. Peter Woods

Wilton
Woods

PATERNAL

The Sam Houston Oak at Peach Creek

AF   Windle, Janice Woods
Win   True women

23293   9/06

DATE DUE			

GAYLORD M2

TRUE
WOMEN

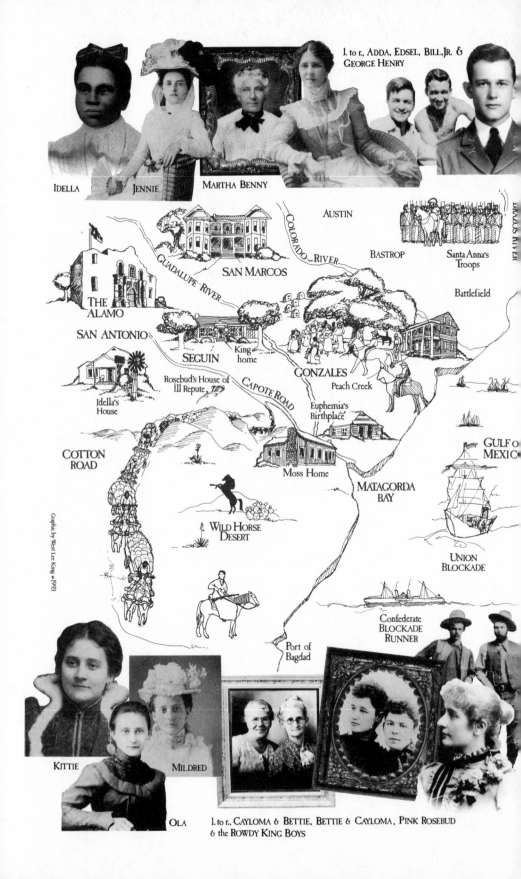

l. to r., ADDA, EDSEL, BILL, JR. & GEORGE HENRY

IDELLA   JENNIE   MARTHA BENNY

AUSTIN

COLORADO RIVER

BASTROP

Santa Anna's Troops

Battlefield

BRAZOS RIVER

SAN MARCOS

GUADALUPE RIVER

THE ALAMO

SAN ANTONIO

SEGUIN

King home

GONZALES

Peach Creek

Rosebud's House of ill Repute

CAPOTE ROAD

Idella's House

Euphemia's Birthplace

COTTON ROAD

Moss Home

GULF of MEXICO

WILD HORSE DESERT

MATAGORDA BAY

UNION BLOCKADE

Confederate BLOCKADE RUNNER

Port of Bagdad

Graphic by West Lee King © 1993

KITTIE   MILDRED

OLA   l. to r., CAYLOMA & BETTIE, BETTIE & CAYLOMA, PINK ROSEBUD
& the ROWDY KING BOYS

TRUE WOMEN

Janice Woods Windle

G. P. PUTNAM'S SONS
NEW YORK

G. P. Putnam's Sons
Publishers Since 1838
200 Madison Avenue
New York, NY 10016

Library of Congress Cataloging-in-Publication Data

Windle, Janice Woods.
   True women / Janice Woods Windle.
      p. cm.
   ISBN 0-399-13813-7
    1. Family—Texas—Fiction. 2. Women—Texas—Fiction.
I. Title.
PS3573.I517T78 1994   93-17982 CIP
813′ .54—dc20

Printed in the United States of America
1 2 3 4 5 6 7 8 9 10
This book is printed on acid-free paper.

*To my husband, Wayne E. Windle,
who always believed in the dream.*

*To my mother, Virginia Woods,
whose scholarship made it a reality.*

*In memory of my father, Wilton G. Woods,
whose love of history was the inspiration.*

From: Journal of the Reconstruction Convention
Austin, Texas, Dec. 7 A.D. 1868 Vol. 580
Committee minority report against woman suffrage

Sir: We, the undersigned, members of the Committee on State Affairs, after examining the declaration presented by Mr. Mundine on female suffrage, respectfully present this minority report, and unhesitatingly state that we are opposed to female suffrage; not because we think them of less capacity than men, but, forsooth, we think that by the very law of their nature they are transcending above the active participation in the government of the country, and because their native modesty and inborn refinement of feeling causes every TRUE WOMAN to shrink from mingling in the busy noise of election days. They are conscious that they exercise, by keeping themselves in their appropriate spheres, and by exhibiting all those gentle qualities directly opposed to the rougher sex in their capacities as wives and mothers, an influence mightier far than that of the elective franchise. We are opposed to it, further, because we believe that the good sense of every TRUE WOMAN in the land teaches her that granting them the power to vote is a direct open insult to their sex by the implication that they are so unwomanly as to desire the privilege.

We therefore believe that such a declaration should not pass this body of gentlemen.

Idella

Few places on earth could be as magical to a child as where the Guadalupe River bottoms cut deep around Idella's house behind Court Street in Seguin, Texas. It was forbidden, of course, to go there. Idella could talk with the dead and she lived very close to where water moccasins slept among the violets and where beneath great oaks certain uncertain creatures prowled in shadow. There was quicksand by the river that could swallow horses, even children whose bones we feared finding after hard rains, children whose last living moments we could imagine with terrible and fascinating clarity.

The Guadalupe River bottom was filled with little pieces of Eden and with danger and death. There were entire silver cities not unlike Byzantium down there, and crawdad civilizations, and rampaging Comanches. In the caves that rogue storms had dug were fortunes in gold the cruel Santa Anna had hidden before my great-great-grandmother Euphemia Texas Ashby King and her sister Sarah sent him flying in disarray back to the heart of his evil empire. But for all its mythic lure, it was thoughts of Euphemia that brought me back to the river bottoms and to the place where Idella talked with the dead.

Vivid stories of the women in my family had been passed down mother to daughter, grandmother to granddaughter, aunt to niece, and even father to daughter, for six generations: stories about the widows of the Alamo and how Euphemia nearly died in the Runaway Scrape and how her sister Sarah outsmarted the Comanches, stories about the women in my family who lived and loved and died in a river of time reaching back to the Alamo and Sam Houston. They were great epic tales of war and adventure, love and murder, violence and redemption. These remarkable lives had become a part of my own being, as real as the little Texas town where I was raised, as familiar to me as *A Child's Garden of Verses.* Yet, when I became a mother and I retold the old stories to my own children, citizens of a generation raised in the age of television, they would challenge me—"Is this true? Are these women real?" The question was a sobering one. For here were the lives, the flesh, the spirit that had shaped my own just as surely as a sculptor shapes clay. If their lives were not real, what did that say about my own journey through time? Would I be merely a myth to the children of my children?

Who were the daughters of Euphemia Texas? There was so much I didn't know about these women whose blood flowed in my veins, whose lives lay as prologue to my own. Were the tales embellished with the telling? Was Euphemia Texas really there when the Widows of Gonzales found refuge at Peach Creek and when Sam Houston's rag-tag army routed Santa Anna at San Jacinto? Could she ride and shoot like a man? And how did she manage to survive a life constantly plagued by war and violence, by wild Comanches and dread Republicans? Did my great-grandmother Georgia Lawshe really risk her plantation running the Yankee cotton blockade and did she help her children kill the Yankee officer? Did Aunt Sweet really fire on the advancing Yankee column from the balcony of their home? Was another of my great-grandmothers, Bettie King, really left alone all night as a small girl to protect the bodies of her dead friends from a pack of hungry wolves? And did that wonderful cast of characters really pass through their lives and their homes: Thomas Jefferson, Sam Houston, Santa Anna, Juan Seguin, the Queen of Tuckabatchee, Robert E. Lee, Teddy Roosevelt, the Comanche chief Iron Jacket, General Henry McCulloch, Pink Rosebud, Precious Honey Child, and Reverend Andrew Jackson Potter?

So I began my search for the daughters of Euphemia Texas. I revisited their homes and their graves. I pored through boxes of accumulated family documents and photographs brought out from under beds and down from attics. I interviewed surviving relatives, studied letters, diaries, maps, census records, death certificates, deeds, and land grants. I began to piece together an authentic version of the stories I'd heard as a child. In almost every detail, oral tradition and the historical record were identical. But the stories were incomplete, the characters somehow not as vivid as I had hoped. So I went back to Seguin, as an adult, to the Guadalupe, to find Idella who could talk with the dead and whose greatest gift was the finding of things lost.

When I was a child, I had the impression Idella was rich. At night we would see long black limousines parked by her house, hired by prominent people who wished to consult Idella but who also wished to remain anonymous. Her clients came from throughout the Hill Country and the High Plains, from as far away as San Antonio. It was said Idella's ability to see into the worlds of the future and past was unfailing. She could predict with absolute accuracy the month and day certain people would be married, well before a proposal had been contemplated, much less made. She could see details of a person's life as if she had lived it herself. Idella was a mystic, one of those rare beings whose soul floats free in time.

There was a raggedy old man named Peachtree who lived in the river bottoms not far from Idella's house. He was a hermit with long unkempt hair and terrible secrets, and he wandered down there by the Guadalupe with an owl on a chain. He had always lived in the bottoms, old as oak, and mysterious. It was rumored he had been taken captive by gypsies when he was a child, then abandoned in the bottoms where he was raised by a family of raccoons. Peachtree lived in a dugout carved into the riverbank. His home was surrounded by a rampart of old automobile parts, cast-off refrigerators, scraps of old wagon wheels, and a marvelous miscellany of rummage and junk he had rescued from the trash cans of Seguin. Some children swore there were caves behind his dugout, and tunnels leading from the river bottoms to the basements of old haunted houses. Peachtree was harmless, yet there was in his secretive manner the suggestion of a capacity for mayhem. Sometimes, at night, I would lie in bed and hear the mournful cry of the old man's owl, and I could tell by the sound where Peachtree wandered through the bottoms. Sometimes I could hear the owl over by Idella's house, and I imagined the black fortune-teller and the hermit talking together in the darkness, telling their secrets.

I walked eastward along the Guadalupe and hoped to feel Euphemia Texas and Georgia Virginia and Bettie King coming west. The river was the color of smoke and jade. It was deep by the shore and the sound the river made spoke its name— *Guadalupe, Guadalupe.* In the falling light I could see Idella's house, pineboard and tin, perched on the bank as though floating in a flood. Idella stood on the porch, a thin, dark reed, watching the river slide by on its way to the sea. I was still in the bottoms, in deep shadow, a long way from her porch, when I heard her voice.

"Miss Janice?" she called. It was as if I had never left and time was a myth. Her voice was soft and familiar, part of the sound the river made. "I was wondering when you'd come."

Idella hadn't changed. She was fragile yet beautiful, like old porcelain. She could have been the mother of a lesser pharaoh. Her skin was pale olive, nearly translucent. Her eyes were bright and gray and deep. She was very old now. Yet Idella had always been old. As I entered her house I felt again that curious blend of awe, respect, and fear I had felt as a child in her presence; a sense that Idella knew all the secrets of the universe. We sat at a table in her parlor and talked for a while about things remembered, about my mother and my mother's mother, and the passing of the years and how the town had changed. We talked of change and of things that never change; of Blue Northers and drought, wildflowers and the river, and how the land itself has remained much the same as it had been when Georgia's great cotton wagons went rumbling by or when Euphemia and Tildy saved their horses from the flood. It grew dark. Idella lit a candle and placed it on the table. Shadows moved like pilgrims along the walls. She took my hand and traced the lines on my palm with her finger.

"I see a lost child," she said. "But not in the way children are usually lost. Not in the woods or in the river. Something else. Something deeper. More like something lost in the rivers of time." She looked up from my palm, then into my eyes. "It's a dangerous thing to ask, Miss Janice. Not just to talk with the dead, but to bring the dead alive. Once you bring them alive they become part of you. Their pain becomes your pain. I'm not sure you want to bring all that suffering back into the world. All those dead children. Maybe you should let them rest."

"Can you tell me about Euphemia Texas? About Georgia Lawshe and Bettie King? Not just who they were, but what they thought and felt? What they dreamed?"

Idella sighed. "Do you have something of Euphemia's? A picture. A ribbon from her hair. Something I can hold in my hand."

"Yes."

For a moment she waited, expecting some mementos I might have brought. I could hear the harsh breath of cars passing on Court Street and just maybe an owl in the dark beyond the window. Then Idella smiled and reached across the table to touch my face. "Of course you've brought something of Euphemia's," she said, and she took my two hands in hers and held them as if I were a lost child.

"Now," she said and she opened my hands. "Let me tell you about Euphemia Texas Ashby King. Let me tell you where and who you are."

1

Euphemia Texas Ashby King

On the afternoon of March 13, 1836, the wind veered to the north and the early wildflowers began to move and flow like a great floral tide in the meadows. It had rained that morning as it had so often this strange spring season, and Peach Creek was beginning to overflow onto the wide skirts of the McClure land east of Gonzales. In the eye of the wind, dark clouds assembled in brooding undisciplined ranks, promising still more rain to a country that could bear no more without flood.

In the field behind the house, where orchards of wild plum grew by the creek, Euphemia Texas gathered a bouquet of blue-bonnet, wine-cup, and Indian paintbrush, and tried to remember the moment of her birth. It had been all of five years since she had come into this world. She tried to remember her mother, but the only image her mind would create was Mary, the mother of Jesus. She knew her mother was dead, taken away somehow by Baby Jesus to Heaven, supposedly a better place than Texas. Euphemia Texas was proud of her name and was certainly glad she had not been named Euphemia Heaven. Now her father had gone to Kentucky, wherever that was. She was abandoned for some reason she couldn't understand.

She began to feel the cold and started back toward the house, releasing the bouquet to the rising wind. She would pick flowers for her mother another time. Maybe tonight they could build one last fire, pass the evening telling stories of magic kingdoms and faerie children and orphans touched with the gift of bearing sorrow with grace. Then, for the first time, a curious thought touched her mind. *Maybe I'm just a story somebody made up and I was never actually born at all.* As she moved through the wildflowers, she repeated the thought over and over in her mind, trying to get just the right inflection, so she could test the idea on her sister when the time seemed right. "I don't think I was ever born." Although she could not know it at the time, it was a refrain that might keep her alive in the months ahead when all around her began to die.

As Euphemia came up from the creek bottom, she was surprised to see a crowd milling beneath the oaks and in the fields before the house. On the road from Gonzales, which crossed Peach Creek by their land and then wound south through the wilderness toward Victoria, Linnville, and the sea, there were more people than she had ever seen before. Normally, only a few peddlers moved along this road or secretive men on government business. Now the road was filled with travelers, mostly women and children, all heading for the great oak guarding the approach to her house. Euphemia knew the oak was old as the world. Its limbs were black, scarred by lightning and twisted by time and the wind. There were stories that Indians once camped beneath its shelter, and sometimes when Euphemia climbed up into its branches to sing lullabies to her cornhusk dolls, she could hear the ghosts of their children trying to sing along. The ghosts sang badly, and the notion that Indians could not carry a tune was one of the few prejudices Euphemia carried into her middle years.

Beneath the oaken patriarch, oxen now pulled wagons filled with furniture, bedding, and children. Mules and cows were led by women with muddy skirts and by Negroes with one eye on the road and the other on the approaching storm. Armed horsemen sagged in their saddles or sat before small fires, beards and flames whipped by the wind. Euphemia felt an unexpected tug of indignation when she realized their camp was ruining the garden of English peas and turnips she and her brothers Travis and William had helped plant just last week. What possible disaster could justify such rudeness?

Then she became aware of the sounds: soldiers calling their short, sharp imperatives; horses and wagon wheels screaming; women shouting at their children to stay close or to move away;

the first deep drumming of thunder to the north. Soon a strange crowd of women came, faces white and hard as chalk, some staggering along, calling their grief to the wind. "It's the widows of the Alamo," Euphemia heard a man say. "They're all dead. Colonel Travis, Bowie, the volunteers from Gonzales, every last one." There was a kind of morbid desperation to the scene, as if the people were running from some horror they knew flew faster than themselves, an approaching storm that would soon envelop and consume them. Euphemia Texas had had dreams like that. Maybe she would wake and all the people would be gone. Or they would wake and she would not be there.

From behind a grove of trees a white horse came. Its rider seemed brother to the oak, a man as large as any Euphemia had seen. He wore a feather in his hat, and as he rode toward the house she imagined he was a king forced to flee his castle by a superior evil force. The first drops of rain began to fall. The cold came down like the touch of a dead hand and the crowd seemed to moan, and then the black clouds hurled down a spear of bright yellow fire wrapped in a hammer-blow of sound. Euphemia ran for the house, and as she bolted through the door and up the ladder to the loft she knew the rider on the white horse was coming her way and would enter their house and their lives.

Inside, it was warm. Leviticus was tending a fire in the great fireplace. The coals glowed golden red in the dark room. The one small window was shuttered against the wind. The thick log walls muffled the sounds of the refugees and of the storm. Euphemia knew the roof was sound and would hold them safe because the oak shakes were split in the dark of the moon and would therefore last a lifetime. Behind her, in the gloom of the loft, were William, Travis, and her nephew Little Johnny, their eyes wide and aware, like owls waiting in the dark for day. Both her brothers were old; Travis was seven, William nine. Euphemia asked them what was happening outside. They told her it was war and they were going to join the army and fight Santa Anna. Johnny climbed to Euphemia's side and pressed his body against hers, as if for comfort from the storm. He was like a small oven, and Euphemia was sure he would keep her warm this cold night as they lay dreaming together like spoons in a drawer. From the half-loft where she and the other children slept, she waited for the arrival of the horseman.

Below was the rest of her family. Not her mother, who was in Heaven, or her father, who was in Kentucky, but her sister Sarah and Sarah's husband, Judge Bartlett McClure. Euphemia adored them both. They were bigger than life, like characters in a legend. Sometimes when she tried to remember her mother's face, it was Sarah's face she saw. Sarah had dark, dark eyes set wide apart and hair black as night. Her expression was constantly changing, sweeping from the broadest smile to frowns and scowls and back again in less time than it took to walk across the room. Euphemia could always tell what Sarah was thinking just by watching her face from moment to moment.

Sarah, now nineteen, had been a mother to Euphemia since their own mother had died. It was hard to imagine a real mother as extraordinary as Sarah: a beautiful woman who could ride like a Comanche and shoot as accurately as any man in Texas. *If only I could be as beautiful and as brave and smoke a pipe as gracefully as Sarah,* Euphemia Texas Ashby often thought. *Or if I could have a husband like Bart McClure, who is a judge and knows how to speak foreign languages and make friends with Indians, I would be the happiest girl east of San Antonio.*

Euphemia felt the tug of a vagabond sorrow that had troubled her sleep in recent weeks. Where were her father and her sisters? And why had they abandoned her to the war? She knew what they had said. But words didn't fill the emptiness she felt when she thought of her father's laughter and embraces and the smell of leather and tobacco he left in the loft when he had tucked her beneath the covers and kissed her goodnight. One day they had all been together, then the next day the family had come undone. Sarah had explained that their father had done what he thought was best for his children. When war between the settlers in Texas and the army of Mexico became inevitable, John Ashby decided he would move his family out of harm's way. First he would take his older teenage daughters, Mary, Jane Isabella, and Frances, to Shelbyville, Kentucky, where they would be enrolled in the Julia

A. Tevis Academy for Girls. Once safely established, John would return to Texas for the rest of them. In the meantime, they would remain under Judge McClure's protection.

As Euphemia had observed, and as Sarah had explained, there were three major problems with John Ashby's plan. The first problem was Euphemia's sister Mary, who shocked her family when she refused to go to Kentucky. Instead, she revealed she had fallen in love with John Smothers, a gentleman farmer nearly twice her age, and she would face the future, war or not, in his house and his care. The second problem was Sarah herself, who also refused to accompany her father. "This is my home," she had insisted, "and I'll stay and protect it as long as I can." So only Frances and Jane Isabella had gone with their father to Kentucky. The third problem with John Ashby's plan was that the war had come to Peach Creek sooner than expected and he had no time to return for Euphemia. He was still in Kentucky when the armies of Mexico and Texas began to march.

The fourth person in the room below was Euphemia's friend Juan Seguin. He called her *mi jita,* my dear little daughter. She loved his kindness and the way he always seemed dressed for a ball. Sometimes she imagined herself dancing with the dark and handsome Juan Seguin. He was from an old and aristocratic family—his father, Don Erasmos, had been born in San Antonio, and the Seguin family had been respected landed gentry in the area for nearly one hundred years. Euphemia often played with Juan Seguin's daughters, Antonia Ana and Teresa, and his son, José Erasmos.

There was the sound of heavy footsteps on the porch. Bart McClure rose, opened the door, and welcomed the rider of the white horse into the room. "General Houston," Bart said, "come into my house." He was a giant, and his body and his presence filled the room.

"So it's true?" McClure asked.

"The Alamo has fallen," Houston said. His voice reminded Euphemia of old thunder and sand. "Six days ago. Santa Anna is on his way."

Juan Seguin bowed and then shook hands with General Houston. "All were killed?"

"Travis. Bowie. Crockett. The entire garrison."

"None were spared?"

"A Negro named Joe and the Dickinson woman," Houston said. "Mrs. Dickinson said Santa Anna told her to spread the word that Anglo settlers should expect no quarter. He told her he intended to kill everyone between San Antonio and the Gulf of Mexico."

Euphemia wondered which of the two Sam Houstons had entered the house. She had heard the adults talking about them both. One of the two Sam Houstons was a man of heroic stuff, a general in Andrew Jackson's army, a Congressman and Governor of Tennessee. The other was a tragic figure, a man of great promise destroyed by his love for a young woman. The fact that such a man had been elected Major General and Commander in Chief of the Texas army had been the cause of endless debate. Naturally, Euphemia was drawn to this second Sam Houston, the wilderness recluse who had lived for years among the Cherokees, where he was known as Big Drunk. She could see something of both in the bearing of the man below; the man who could have been President of the United States and the melancholy wanderer who lived for so many years among the Cherokees.

"We have very little time," Houston was saying. "At dawn we fall back toward the Brazos."

"Couldn't we stand and fight?" McClure asked.

Euphemia wondered if the tightening of the tracery of lines around Houston's eyes was a smile. She couldn't imagine such a man smiling. "We can stand," he said. "But we have less than four hundred men. That's what's left of the Texas army, besides Fannin's five hundred at Goliad. No food, little ammunition. The best we have is a company of fifty Kentucky rifles who were on their way to help Travis at the Alamo. We could stand. But I don't think we'd hold a chance."

"So we retreat."

"We retreat. Back to the Brazos. Join up with Fannin and see what happens."

Houston led the others to a table, where he spread out a map of Texas. "Here's San Antonio and the Alamo. Only sixty miles to the west. Santa Anna is bound to be on his way. Our best hope is to fall back to the east into Anglo Texas. We should be able to pick up hundreds of Texas men along the way. The rivers here run north and south and will provide defensive positions. We'll send a message to Fannin to abandon Goliad and join us. That's five hundred more men. The Brazos River is a hundred and fifteen miles to the east. We fall back to there. Along the way we drill the men, build an army."

There was a silence then. A kind of gloom, substantial as a fog in the cabin. Euphemia had never been to the Brazos. What could be so bad about going there? It was certainly better than staying here and waiting for Santa Anna. Every child in Texas already knew that Santa Anna cut off the fingers and ears of his prisoners. She touched her ear and a shiver danced down her spine.

Then, Sam Houston squared his shoulders and there was no sign of Big Drunk in the room. "There are things we must do."

From her dark loft Euphemia listened to the desperate plan they made that night Sam Houston came to her house on Peach Creek. Sarah sent Leviticus to bring the Alamo widows and their children in out of the storm. Tildy, a young girl of eighteen who had been Euphemia's mother's slave, brought the strangers warm bread and water. They filled the other room with the smell of wet clothing and sorrow. Outside, thunder tumbled across the heavens.

Sam Houston ordered Bartlett McClure to leave at dawn for the Indian encampments to the east. He would negotiate with the chiefs to allow the army and the civilians safe passage. He would also try to find the Redlanders, the East Texans who came from Arkansas, and recruit them in the fight against Santa Anna.

Juan Seguin was to ride out to outlying settlements and homesteads and warn them of Santa Anna's approach. He was to watch for the Mexican advance and report back to Houston each day. The remnants of the army would move east in hopes of gathering additional volunteers along the way.

The usually composed Seguin had moved into the light of the fire and Euphemia could see he was struggling for control. When Houston paused, Seguin spoke. "I do not care to run your errands, General."

"Saving lives is no small errand," Houston said. "What really bothers you, Juan?"

"You seem to forget I was at the Alamo. All who were at the Alamo are dead. All but Captain Juan Seguin. How would you feel to be the only surviving officer of the Alamo?"

"I'd feel alive," Houston said. "Besides, Travis ordered you to go for help. You simply followed orders. It was an order that might have saved them."

"It's not so simple, General. I am a Mexican, yet I am a Texian. I will face suspicion. This land is my country, my ancestral home, yet I hear the whispers. I hear those who wonder if I would really kill my own people in battle. Sometimes I wonder if I know who my real people are."

Sam Houston moved to where Juan Seguin stood by the fire and he placed his massive hand on Juan's shoulder. "You're not the only one who hears whispers. I hear them every day. 'Can a man who has made such a colossal failure of his life possibly lead us to victory?' I hear the whispers. But I have a defense against all those doubts. I'll show you." Euphemia watched Houston take a ring from his finger. He handed it to Juan. "My mother gave me this ring. Read the inscription."

"Honor." Seguin read, then returned the ring.

"That's the only word that matters, Juan. I know you're a man of honor. There's no question concerning your courage or your loyalty. And right now I have need of an honorable man." Houston moved to the window and looked out at the storm. He motioned Juan Seguin to the window. "Look, Juan," he said. "There's my army. Poorly armed, undisciplined, demoralized. Most are hard-headed misfits who probably can't wait to disobey any order I give out of just plain meanness. Most of them aren't even Texians. Tonight I need people I can trust. I need a Texian. A man I can be sure of. You fought bravely beside Jim Bowie at Concepción. I thank God the Alamo spared you. I need Juan Seguin here."

Euphemia watched as the slight Juan Seguin seemed to grow taller. Once again, he bowed slightly from the waist. "I'll do what I can, General."

"What about the women and children?" Bartlett then asked. "We can't just leave them here. Sarah is in her seventh month." Euphemia thought of Santa Anna's approach and her hand moved again to her ear.

"We can travel together for a while," Houston said. "We are not that many. Yet, in a few days, as our numbers grow, the refugees and the army must part. The army must be unhindered, able to move quickly. I suggest the women and children make a run for the United States. Santa Anna won't follow them across the border."

"I've already sent my family eastward to the Sabine River," Seguin said.

"We could provide a small escort," Houston said. "But I'm afraid it must be very small."

"You've been all through that country, General," Bartlett said. "Once off the main trails, it's very bad country. It's almost wilderness. Empty. No place for women."

"What place in Texas is?" Sarah said. "We haven't exactly been living in high civilization all these years."

"Not only is that country wild, you'd have to stay off the blazed trails. You'd have to cut your own trails for the wagons. And those woods are filled with escaped criminals, runaway slaves, looters and people who would kill for a wagonload of goods."

"The rougher the country, the more unlikely the Mexicans will follow us in," Sarah said. "Maybe all those freebooters who would kill for a wagonload of goods are our best protection. They'd as soon have Mexican goods as a Texian's goods."

Euphemia could tell Bartlett was unconvinced. "I don't like it," Bartlett said, shaking his head.

Then Juan Seguin spoke. "I know Santa Anna. I have seen his butchery. Whatever lies to the east, beyond the Lavaca River, can be no worse than what approaches from the west."

"We can manage," Sarah said. "We'll take what we need and leave the rest. Travel light. If we make ten miles a day, we'll be safely across the border in about thirty days. There's plenty of game along the way. Don't worry about us. We'll be fine."

"The idea is to stay ahead of Santa Anna," Houston said. "We'll move generally eastward toward the Brazos. First along the trail from here to the Colorado. Then on toward San Felipe. I have no idea how long the retreat will be. Probably just long enough."

There was a pounding at the door. "General," a voice called. "Gonzales is afire!"

Euphemia, her brothers, and Little Johnny climbed down from the loft and followed the others outside. It was night now and the rain had slackened, but it was very cold. To the northwest, beneath the canopy of rolling ebony clouds, the sky was red as a sunset. For a moment the gathered crowd of soldiers and ragged refugees was silent as explosions hurled columns of fire above the embers of Gonzales. Some said the explosions were created by Santa Anna's cannon, and a cold throb of panic clutched the crowd. Then a soldier in buckskins said it was probably only kegs of powder left behind when someone had torched the settlement to keep it from falling into the hands of the advancing Mexican army. Euphemia wondered what it would be like to see your home burn down. She felt close to the orphans of Gonzales and the widows of the Alamo who had come outside to watch the flames consuming their homes. After all, she was an orphan, too. But she still had her warm house and her sturdy roof of oak shakes cut in the dark of the moon.

As the strange night progressed, Euphemia understood the grown-ups were preparing to flee. Leviticus was sent to bring the wagon around. Sarah and Tildy gathered bedding and warm clothing and the implements they would need for cooking meals. In tin buckets and wood boxes, they packed what food they could carry: crocks of meat and lard, cornmeal for making johnnycakes, dried beef and beans, dried peaches packed in chinaberry leaves, sorghum molasses, and salt, coffee, and two bottles of persimmon beer. A pot and a kettle and a skillet, spoons and forks were tossed onto the floor in front of the fireplace to be packed in the wagon. It didn't take long to gather what they would need on this adventure that history would remember as the Runaway Scrape.

Sarah moved about the house with a certain reckless grace.

Euphemia often wished she herself were so self-assured. But to-night, as she prepared to abandon her home to the advancing Mexican army, there was something in Sarah's manner, something about her eyes, that Euphemia had not seen before. Something ragged. Maybe she was merely tired. And she was carrying that baby around inside, one of the few things about her older sister that Euphemia found disgusting. Sarah paused occasionally, look-ing around at the confusion and clutter in the house, and she made that sound Euphemia so admired, part sigh, part oath. Among Sarah's best qualities, besides her physical beauty, was the way she could take the most ordinary words and make them into swear words just by using her voice. Sometimes she would curse in Spanish or French. And every now and then she would say words just like a man. At one point as they were packing, she sent William and Travis out into the garden to bury the large kettle and her clay pipes beneath the turnips. "That blasted Santa Anna! Bad enough to think of him cooking in my kettle but it's a damn sight worse if Santa Anna takes a notion to smoke my pipe!" Then she attacked the packing again with re-newed energy, filling the room with "thunderations," her long hair, having escaped its pins, flying around in the air like black fire.

Sarah sent Euphemia back to the loft to gather the children's bedclothes and all the clothes they possessed. Little Johnny, Euphemia's constant shadow, followed. When they returned, Sarah gathered them both in her arms. She felt Little Johnny's forehead with her hand first and then kissed his brow with her lips. "Hope you're not coming down with something, Little One. Not really the best time, you know, since we have to go on this little trip into the woods. I'll fix you some whiskey-honey-butter and that old fever will leave faster than a mule can bite the grains off an ear of corn."

While mixing Little Johnny's medicine, Sarah called Euphemia aside. There was that raggedness in her eyes again. "Phemie, I'm de-pending on you to take care of Little One. I want you to watch him like a hawk. Shouldn't be too hard since he goes everywhere you go anyway. There's going to be some bad times, Phemie. Everybody's got to do their job. And your job is Little Johnny. He can't do for himself. He's your responsibility, no matter what, come what may. Can you do it, Phemie?"

Euphemia Texas had never felt so proud, so important, so grown. "Damn right," she said. "I sure as hell can."

After gathering her long rifle, a pouch of bullets, powder horn and a pound or two of Du Pont powder, a knife given to her by Jim Bowie (God rest his soul), and then a whetstone and a hatchet, Sarah settled down with her pipe and began writing a letter in Spanish to General Santa Anna. "Dear General Santa Anna," she wrote. "I leave you my house to use until I get back. However, if I return and find you have burned my home, I will hunt you down, shoot you, burn your body, and feed the ashes to the pigs." The letter was signed, "Respectfully, Sarah McClure."

Soon came a gray and gloomy dawn. In the yard, Houston stood before his tent beneath the oak tree, issuing orders. Soldiers were stamping out their fires and forming up in undisciplined ranks. It was not raining, but the air was so thick moisture formed on their rifles faster than the soldiers could wipe them dry. More refugees had arrived during the night, their eyes haunted, their belongings sodden and covered with mud.

Inside, high in the sleeping loft, Euphemia, with Little Johnny sleeping by her side, watched Sarah and Bartlett through her secret crack in the loft floor. They were holding each other in that mysterious way. They moved, like dancing, for a long time. Then they were still. For a long time they held each other. Euphemia felt they were more like one person than two, and she thought she could have heard their whispers, except their lips were too close together and their kisses consumed them. Bartlett moved to the side of the bed and began dressing. Suddenly, he threw his boot across the room.

"It's just not right. Leaving you and the children like this."

"Of course it's not right. Nothing's right. Everything is upside down." There was silence again between them.

"How can I leave you, Sarah?"

"Quickly," she whispered, and she left the bed and moved from Euphemia's view.

* * *

Houston's men were gone and it was raining again. The column of refugees straggled eastward from Peach Creek toward the Lavaca River crossing. There were many women and children now, more joining as they moved eastward. Euphemia and the other children rode in the wagon. Tildy and Leviticus walked on either side of the oxen, urging them along, through mud that was often like knee-deep molasses. Sarah was one of the few in the column traveling horseback. She moved back and forth along the lines of strangers and stragglers, encouraging them to hurry, for sometimes it seemed the wind carried the sound of Santa Anna's trumpets through the brush. These were the same trumpets that had blown more than two decades before when so many had been shot, others beheaded and dismembered, still others hung from trees and balconies in San Antonio. The same terrible trumpets blew when the surviving widows were forced into the beds of soldiers and their children were publicly whipped. Many of the refugees flowing toward the Lavaca River that morning remembered the dismembered bodies left hanging from the trees. And they also remembered the young officer who had been responsible. His name was Santa Anna and now he was coming this way. His standing orders to take no prisoners were public knowledge.

Euphemia could feel the terror of the refugees. They were driven by their fear of Santa Anna, yet the heavy, tenacious mud made every motion painfully slow and ponderous and dreamlike. Along the way they began to pass chairs and chests of goods, pots and skillets and bundles of clothing cast away to lighten the loads on the wagons. Soon the rain began again and then hard fists of hail drummed down. The children climbed beneath the canvas, where the hail sounded like rifle fire and the howling of the wagon wheels filled the darkness.

When they reached the Lavaca River, they were joined by other widows and orphans of the Alamo. Mary Ann Kent rode horseback with her little daughter behind her. Margaret Hallett joined the refugees in her wagon with wooden wheels that often caught fire from friction. Blind Mary Milsap, another Alamo widow, and her six children joined the march, as did Minerva Hunt McGehee, her two children, and a Negro slave girl in their two-wheel cart pulled by two oxen.

Euphemia and Sarah were delighted when they were joined by sister Mary, who had at last been convinced of the wisdom of flight. Mary was one among many women who were pregnant. On the sixth day of their march, Sidney Kellog gave birth to her baby in the back of her wagon. The rain came down in rivers. The women held blankets over the mother and newborn child to provide at least some protection from the bone-chilling downpour.

By the eighth day, Euphemia noticed some of the women were barefoot, their shoes having been destroyed by the rough terrain and the constant slogging through mud. Most of these walking women were wives of men who had gone to join Houston, taking their family's only horse or pony with them.

One late afternoon, when their exhaustion eclipsed their terror, the column of women and children halted by a spring. Sarah returned to their wagon. Her face was flushed, yet the unsettled look about her eyes was gone. She seemed strong and alive, as if she intended to pull the column eastward by strength of will.

"How is Little One?"

"Warm. Asleep."

"Tildy is building a fire. We'll give him some hot cornmeal mush and some of that whiskey medicine. You'll also find some oak leaves packed by the medicine. Have him chew those."

From her place in the wagon, Euphemia could see Sarah begin to create some sense of order among the milling refugees. It was important to build shelters before night came. A group of women was organized to create places beneath the wagons and beneath tarpaulins and tents, even brush bowers, for those who had no wagon or shelter of their own. Another group of women volunteered to pool their food and cook for the group. Sarah asked another group, those known for their nursing skills, to check the wagons for sickness and to survey what remedies or medicines might be shared. Those women who were known to be accurate shots were recruited to hunt for what game could be found. There were plenty of rabbits and squirrels, even deer, along the way. The problem was not a scarcity of game, but a scarcity of ammunition. The ammunition must be saved to defend against

Santa Anna or outlaws or Indians or cougars or the bears which prowled the canebrakes by the rivers.

Euphemia watched Sarah gather the women she had selected to post as guards. They came back to the fire where Euphemia was warming Little Johnny's blanket. "We need more guards on the border of the encampment," Sarah said, "but we'll have to make do with what we have." Sarah drew on her pipe and looked out into the darkness beyond the fire. "The army is to our south and slightly ahead of us. So any threat will come from behind or from the north. We'll concentrate there. I'll go with you to your positions so I can tell your relief where you are. Let's go." The women moved off into the darkness, a place Euphemia was prayerfully glad she did not have to go.

"The army has Sam Houston," Euphemia heard one of the women say, "but we've got General Sarah McClure."

By nightfall dozens of small fires winked beneath the highwood where the refugees hoped to be safe from the rising creeks. Simple food was prepared and shared. On most of the fires water boiled for cornmeal. The fires seemed to carry the terror away, as if all bad things fear the flames of open fires. A strange silence settled over the woodland. But there was a sound that Euphemia had never heard before, a puzzling plural chattering muted by the moisture in the air. Euphemia listened to the eerie chorus, trying to identify what made the stillness so unsettling. Then she realized the sound she heard was children coughing, like the barking of a colony of squirrels. She held Little Johnny close and it was good that he felt so warm on such a cold night as this.

Euphemia was dreaming. She was riding Sam Houston's white horse, Saracen, across a field of buttercups. It was warm and the sky was porcelain. She was riding toward a place where she knew her mother would be, a grove of willows by a stream. When she arrived, she dismounted and she and Saracen walked toward the willows, where she could just make out the form of a woman. She dropped Saracen's reins and as she began walking forward she heard hoofbeats and men shouting. "He's here! He's here!" The shouting grew louder. "Santa Anna's here! There's no time to take anything. Just go! Go!" Confusion erupted. Women screaming, rushing with their children into the darkness. Gunfire. The horses of the strangers scattered the fires, stirring blizzards of yellow sparks.

Not quite sure she wasn't still dreaming, Euphemia found herself running, with Travis and William, into the woods. She was terrified, but somehow comforted by the thought that she would soon awaken or soon resume her dream. When she was some distance from the wagon, she stopped and turned back. She could see horsemen throwing things from the wagons, then setting them on fire. Silhouetted by the burning wagons, she saw a familiar figure and her heart was an anvil falling. "Little Johnny!"

All thought of dreaming was hurled cruelly from her mind and she was running, fighting, scrambling through the mud and briars and undergrowth, back to the wagon. As she climbed into the wagon, a rider ripped the canvas tarpaulin from its place. He leaped from his horse onto the wagon to search through their belongings, casting aside the things they had so carefully packed for their trip. Suddenly he came toward Euphemia and she wondered why a soldier of Santa Anna's army would be so fair and would have such yellow hair. He was so close she could smell the liquor on his breath and she could see the scar beneath his eye. Little Johnny came bounding into Euphemia's arms and she tried to push him behind her out of the way of the man with the scar and yellow hair. They stood there on the wagon, the man and the two children, and the moment seemed to Euphemia to extend into a lifetime. It was as if she had known the man all her life and she had somehow always known he would come to bring his evil into her life. "You kids hiding gold or somethin'?" he said. He reached for Little Johnny and Euphemia struck at his face with all her strength. The man laughed and grabbed Little Johnny again. Then, miraculously, as Euphemia was looking into his face, the top of his head seemed to explode and she was covered with blood. In a flash Sarah was there, holding her, holding little Johnny, wiping the blood from her face, humming a tuneless melody as she did when she was very happy or very angry.

All the looters escaped but the one Euphemia would always think about with a certain sense of proprietorship. It was her looter who had been wounded in the wagon. The bullet had cut

a furrow along the top of his head. The women tied his hands behind his back and dragged him into the firelight. Sarah asked one
of them to bring bandages for his wound.

"Why bother? We ought to just shoot him." It was a woman
named Maggie Boles, one of the hunters.

"Nobody got hurt or killed," another woman said. "We got
most everything back."

"Burned our wagon," Maggie Boles said. "That's about the
same as killin' us. Same as killin' my children."

"I saw at least six of them," another woman said. "We let this
one go, they might try again. Then again, we shoot him, that
might make them think twice."

The man said nothing. He merely lay in the firelight, eyes half
closed, as if the discussion involved some stranger in some other
place. Sarah also was silent. Euphemia wondered what Sarah was
thinking. The women seemed to be growing more angry. Those
who were urging the death of the outlaw were gaining force.
Surely, in a minute, Sarah would bring the women back to their
senses. After all, Sarah was their general and generals were often generous to fallen enemies. It was always that way in the
stories Bartlett told by the fire on winter nights at home in Peach
Creek.

"Shoot him. Look, he don't even care," Maggie Boles said.
Euphemia agreed the man seemed unconcerned. Every once in a
while he would look up at the women and then off into the
woods, as if bored. Curiously he looked up at Sarah.

"You're the one shot me this much," he said. "You oughta
have some say." Euphemia thought she saw just a hint of emotion
in the man's eyes. Or was it scorn?

"I can't say do it," Sarah said, and Euphemia was glad.

"He didn't burn your wagon," Maggie Boles observed in a
voice as steady as if she were discussing the killing of hogs, not
a man.

"And I can't say don't do it," Sarah said. "If he'd burned my
wagon, I'd shoot him."

Euphemia closed her eyes. She'd already seen the man shot
once that night. She wondered if he would go to heaven and that
made her think of her mother and if it was possible she had ever

been born. The sound Maggie Boles made with her gun didn't seem loud enough to put out a life as mean as the one Euphemia's looter had.

The days went by. The women and children moved eastward through rain and bitter cold that caused their clothes and blankets to freeze during the night. So difficult was the terrain, on some days they were able to progress less than three miles.

When they reached the Colorado, the refugees overtook the army. It took them all several days to cross the rain-swollen river on Beason's Ferry. Once across, Houston had the ferry burned.

On March 26, after thirteen days of struggle, the refugees and the army parted again. Sarah led the women and children toward the United States border at the Sabine River. In the middle of the night, having left the army's campfires burning to confuse the enemy scouts, Houston led his army southward.

The march and the suffering continued. The refugees had first crossed the Lavaca, then the raging Navidad, the Colorado, and now they moved on toward the Brazos. Five thousand women and children were in the column now, pitiful battalions of the dispossessed. Small groups of refugees from settlements and towns to the north joined the original refugees struggling slowly eastward. On the twenty-seventh of March, they met a group from Goliad. A dozen women and children accompanied a wounded man who claimed he had fought with Colonel Fannin and his men before they had surrendered to an overwhelming Mexican force. As the women cleaned and redressed his wounds, he told them the fate of Fannin and fully one-half of the Texas army that remained.

"Me and a bunch of others went with Captain Ward to Refugio to help the settlers who were running away from the Mexicans. Well, we got caught in the open and them that wasn't killed hid in the swamp. Up at Goliad, things got hopeless for Fannin and he had to surrender. The Mexicans got all them prisoners and they formed them up in three columns and they marched them a little way out of town. Then they just shot every one of them. One right after another. They shot Fannin in the head and he fell with the others in a common grave."

A sound rose from the gathered women that seemed half curse and half prayer, half human and half beast. It was the sound of the many women who had just learned they were widows, that their husbands' lives had been extinguished, their voices stilled forever in the massacre. The sound grew in intensity and in its rage and anguish. Only a few women had gathered around the wounded soldier and only a few had heard his actual words. Now the news spread, like a fire in grass, and the sound of mourning led from one group of women to the next and to the next. Some one hundred of the women among the refugees now were widows of Goliad.

In all, 390 men had been massacred at Goliad. Houston had expected Fannin's five hundred. Only a handful had escaped to find their way to where Houston would make his stand, if he would make his stand at all.

The anguish of the widows of Goliad seemed to touch the will of the others. The resolve of women who had suffered with such courage since the beginning of the trek seemed to weaken, to falter. Euphemia heard talk of staying where they were. "We're going to die anyway," she heard one woman say. "Let's just stay here and get it over with."

In the late afternoon, Euphemia, Sarah, Mary, Maggie Boles, and a few other women were sitting by Sarah's fire. They discussed the lethargy, the strange mood that had taken over the women since the Goliad survivors had brought their terrible news.

"It's only natural," Sarah said, drawing on her clay pipe. "Most of us are just plain worn out. You can just take so much."

"And those poor women from Goliad," Mary said. "They thought they were suffering all there was to suffer. Then something far worse comes along."

Sarah looked out at the women resting on the ground by their wagons and fires. They seemed like something left after a cyclone. "We've got to do something. They're giving up. I can feel it in the air. And it's spreading. It's like a fever of defeat. If we don't do somethin', it's gonna infect everybody."

A group of women approached the fire. They were gaunt, red-eyed, their motions slow and methodical, their heads bowed.

"We're going home," one of the Goliad women announced. The words hung above the fire like an epitaph.

After a long silence, Sarah said: "That's the worst thing you could possibly do."

"What could be worse than what's already happened?" the woman sobbed. "If it's going to happen it might as well happen at home. We're going home to bury our husbands."

Mary rose from the fire and embraced the Goliad widow. "We know how you feel," she said. "But we have to stay together. All the way back to the United States border if we have to."

Euphemia looked at Sarah, wondering how she would react. What kindness, what gesture of love would Sarah offer these women who had lost so much? Sarah looked at the weeping woman, and her neighbors who had also just learned they were widows. She saw many had already gathered their belongings to leave. Then Sarah looked back at Maggie Boles and she nodded. Maggie Boles rose from the fire, moved to her wagon, and returned with her rifle. "I want you to look close at the end of this gun," she said. Her eyes were hard, her hands white on the dark steel. " 'Cause that's where the bullet will come out if anyone tries to leave this camp. Now stop being stupid and go get some sleep. We're makin' tracks east in the mornin'. And I'll shoot anyone who says or does otherwise."

One by one, the widows of Goliad turned and walked back to their piles of belongings.

As the migration of Texas widows and orphans and refugees struggled toward the safety of the United States, a sense of despair seemed to envelop them like a cloud.

Soon the children began to die. On some nights a bone-chilling cold would follow a day of rain. Nothing ever was dry or warm. The babies died of pneumonia or exposure in their pathetic shelters of sticks and cloth. Sometimes the children would be fine one day, and the next a raging fever would rise rapidly and strike them down. Their bodies would become rigid and convulsed and they would die almost before anyone knew they were sick. Some of the younger and weaker ones seemed to just give up, as if tired of being so cold and so hungry for so long. The possibility of an epidemic of some deadly fever was as terrifying as the Mexican army. It had only been four years since the Year of the Big Cholera, when hundreds had died in Austin's colony, and the towns of Brazoria and Velasco had been devastated.

The mothers, often led by Euphemia's sister Mary, did what they could with what remedies they had at hand. Mary was gifted in the preparation of potions of herbs and oakbark tea, rice water or broth made with the dried linings of chicken gizzards, but still the children continued to die one by one. Each was wrapped in a cloth and a prayer was read as they were lowered into the ground. Euphemia felt the saddest things about these small funerals were the graves. The children had died because they were cold and wet, and now they were placed in graves of mud half filled with water. Some even floated for a moment before the earth and water closed around them. Euphemia wondered why Baby Jesus needed all this company.

In spite of their leaders' efforts to inspire and cajole, the sense of hopelessness persisted. Each new group joining the march had a horror story to tell, of atrocities, of fallen fathers, sons, and husbands. The horde moved on toward the east. The trail was too small for so many refugees and Sarah assigned shifts of trailblazers to hack away at the wild briars that barred their way. The rain resumed and the women were forced to walk through waist-deep bogs. Often Euphemia saw younger women carry the sick and elderly through the deeper quagmires. At times the horses and oxen became so deeply mired in the mud that the women had to pull their animals free with ropes.

On the afternoon of March thirty-first, the first refugees reached the Brazos River. Some of the people who had come to Texas overland had seen the river before. "But never like this," they said. It was enormous, a raging torrent, wide and awful, filled with whirling eddies and fallen trees. Euphemia was sure they would never be able to cross such a river. She thought they would have to wait there for Santa Anna to cut them down like the soldiers of Travis and Fannin. She even began to prefer that thought to the prospect of crossing that cold, wide river.

Sarah, Maggie, and the other women of the Gonzales group began to build rafts. Their axes rang on the water elm and cypress trees that grew in the bottoms. Others, with oxen, dragged dead trees that had already fallen to the riverbank. Using rope and vine and rags tied together, they bound one log to another. A wagon was disassembled and the boards were nailed across the logs to form a floor. But it was just one raft and there were thousands of people to ferry across. They cut down more trees for additional rafts. Sarah's axe was never still. She and the other women worked long into the night. It was a race against time. How far behind could Santa Anna be?

As dark fell, Euphemia began to doze. The sound of the women's axes was comforting. It reminded her of the sounds at home when Bartlett McClure cut wood for winter fires. She curled herself around Little Johnny, his body warm against her own, closed her eyes, and slipped into sleep.

Euphemia was awakened by the cold. It was still dark, although there was a steel-gray rim around the horizon to the east. Euphemia wondered why she was so very cold, and then she knew. She became aware of a kind of dread so deep and dark and horrible that the weight of it began to press her down. She thought her chest would cave in and then she would be pressed down into the center of the earth where Hell was sure to be. But Hell would be cold. The fires of Hell were lies, she knew, told by preachers who had never been there. She wanted to go to sleep so that she might wake to a different reality. So Euphemia held her dead nephew for a long time, until the sun rose cold and barren. Some women came to tell her that Sarah had lost her baby, stillborn while she was cutting trees in the night. Then they saw what Euphemia held. They had to force her arms apart to release Little Johnny from her embrace. She didn't cry. But it was a long time before she stopped screaming.

They wrapped the bodies in a tarpaulin and they placed Little Johnny and his infant sister in the ground, in a hole that Leviticus had dug. Sarah lay in the bed of the wagon and she and Euphemia Texas watched as Leviticus and the widows of the Alamo, of Gonzales and Goliad, covered the bodies with earth. "Sure are a lot of dead children," Sarah said. "When all this is over, I swear

I'm going to take these two little ones home. We'll come back here and get them. Have a proper burial back where those oaks are at Peach Creek. We'll build a fence around their graves." Then she began to cry.

At last Euphemia began to cry too. But there were no tears, just the sound and the contractions around the eyes and the awful aching inside. Sarah held Euphemia close. "Baby, it's not your fault. You did everything you could. Little One just wasn't supposed to make it over the Brazos."

"I feel so bad," was all Euphemia could say out loud, as Travis and William tried to comfort her. But inside, silent demons bounded around like dark dervishes, making her feel dizzy and nauseated. Then she was sick, violently. Sarah tried to pick her up, but pain drove her down again. She called Tildy to clean Euphemia and put her into the bed and cover her with a blanket. "No fever," Tildy said after feeling Euphemia's brow. "She's just done in. Too much for a little girl."

Sarah sat taller in the wagon and looked back at the grave. "Goodbye, Little One," she whispered, and then she turned and saw Leviticus staring at her. His eyes, too, were filled with tears. "He's all right now, Leviticus."

They waited there in the mud by the grave of Sarah's two children, surrounded by lost widows and orphans and strangers. Exhaustion and an hour of unaccustomed tears had drawn dark moons beneath Sarah's eyes and her hair was caked with earth. For a moment she looked very old, but she was not quite twenty.

"What are we gonna do now, Miz Sarah?"

She looked at the graves of her children, then at the Brazos, then at the desperate company of women waiting for her to lead. "We're going to get across this old river," Sarah said, and she called Maggie Boles to her side.

Euphemia slept for most of three days. Sometimes she would half wake and she would feel the cold and remember Little Johnny and she would pray to sleep forever. The soft blanket of sleep would enfold her again until the cold, gray cycle of sorrow returned. There were times when the voices of Maggie and Sarah would enter her dream as they planned a strategy to defeat the river.

"Suppose the first raft does make it across," Maggie said. "The current's gonna push it way downstream. So the problem is, getting the raft back over to this side to take another load."

Maggie shook her head. "What if we strung a hawser across? Like a ferry. And we pulled the rafts across, unloaded, then pulled the raft back for another load. Problem is, how do we get the hawser across without being swept halfway to the Gulf of Mexico?"

On the fourth day after they buried Little Johnny, Sarah woke Euphemia with a kiss. "It's time," she said. "Time to get on with what we've got to do." Sarah kissed Euphemia once more and then pulled away the blanket. "I want everything in this wagon tied down good. See to it, Phemie."

Euphemia felt the cold like a blow. She could hear the voice of the river. When she looked out from the wagon, some women were putting out their fires and others were launching a raft in the backwaters. As Euphemia looked out at the river, a huge up-rooted tree swept past. The Brazos actually seemed to boil. It was as if all the rain that had fallen in the past weeks had rushed to this single channel to find the sea. At the edge of the river, Sarah and Maggie Boles were securing a rope to a horse.

"It's the best horse we've got," Sarah said. "Young and strong."

Maggie asked the horse's name.

"Dancer," called Minerva McGehee. It was her horse.

"Wish his name was Swimmer," Maggie Boles said, as she swung into the saddle. She rode to the riverbank and then along the backwaters searching for the best place to cross. Euphemia noticed a group of women at the river's edge had carefully coiled the rope so it would not become tangled as it was pulled across the swollen stream. Then, as if she was going for a Sunday ride, Maggie walked Dancer into the backwater. The women moved closer to the river. They came out from behind wagons and trees and formed rows along the water's edge. Every eye was riveted on the horse and rider as they moved slowly into the river. The water was now to the horse's belly, and Euphemia could tell the animal was confused and frightened, not quite sure what was expected. Maggie encircled the horse's neck with both arms and then the current gripped them and Dancer was swept off his feet. At first, horse and rider moved rapidly downstream, the horse constantly turning its head toward the safety of shore. Euphemia could see Maggie fighting for control, willing the horse to fight the river as she had willed the widows of Goliad to continue their journey to the east. Sometimes Maggie and Dancer would completely disappear, hidden by logs or trees or simply forced under the surface by the strength of the current. The women crowding on the bank would sigh and scream and lean their bodies against the stream, then shout with relief and encouragement when horse and rider would appear again, moving slowly toward the center of the maelstrom.

Suddenly they were gone. The current had carried them out of sight. The women grew silent. Only the angry voice of the river could be heard. No one moved. The women stood, still as statues, gray as marble. Euphemia noticed that all the color of their garments had been washed away by the constant rain. She wondered how long the women would wait and if maybe, in some future time, people would come here and find the statues by the river and wonder who carved them and why their expressions were so desperately expectant. Then, there was a stirring among the women and someone shouted she had seen something move on the other side. The women rushed forward and some were even pushed into the shallows by those behind. It was something moving, Euphemia could see. Horse and rider on the other shore, coming north, moving into plain sight. Maggie and Dancer had made it across and Maggie was now securing the line to a stout cottonwood on the far shore of the Brazos.

Once the pilot line of horsehair was secure, the women pulled a larger hawser across the river. Then the crossing began. It took four days to move the people, animals, wagons, and supplies across. Not a single life was lost. The Brazos had been conquered.

After they crossed the Brazos, they found the country alive with rumors about Sam Houston's retreat. The women who joined them now asked when Houston was going to stand and fight. There were stories that his rag-tag army was in disarray, officers threatening to desert because of Houston's refusal to engage the enemy, men abandoning their posts to help their families flee the Mexican advance. Houston was urged by his officers to stand and fight, but he continued to retreat, turning north again.

In his pursuit of Sam Houston, Santa Anna burned more towns. Harrisburg was torched. More refugees took to the road back to the United States border. As the women passed, some said the exhausted, angry remnants of Houston's army were trapped. But on the afternoon of April 21, 1836, more than a month after the first of the refugees had left Peach Creek, they heard the voices of the Twin Sisters, Houston's two iron cannons, boom out across the flatlands at San Jacinto.

The refugees had come to the end of their journey. Starving, weary to the very soul, their resources of will depleted, when they heard the gunfire, they simply stopped. They could go no farther. They would share the fate of Houston's soldiers who stood with their backs to the San Jacinto River.

The land was awash with flooding and dark bayou and patches of flat sodden prairie. If there had been a hill, Sarah and Euphemia would have climbed it to view what they knew would be history in the making. There was no hill, but they were close to the battlefield and they tried to piece together what was happening from the sounds they heard. "Now we'll see which way the cat jumps," Sarah said as the sound of music, drum and fife came drifting across Buffalo Bayou.

"What's that they're playing?"

"It's not for little girls' ears, Phemie. It's called 'Come to the Bower.' "

"What kind of song is that?"

"A not very nice song."

"What are they doing now?"

"Sounds like Houston's advancing. Listen ... muskets. Galloping horses. Now bugles. The Mexican buglers. That means Houston has attacked first." The idea that Houston was on the offensive swept through the refugees like a fresh wind. They had been retreating so long. Then they heard the Twin Sisters again. The wounded man from Goliad had heard the voice of cannon before. Booming, then howling as nails and broken horseshoes were hurled at the Mexican lines. "They're shootin' nails and horseshoes, 'cause nothin' can kill more men quicker. A ball will only kill one man. Nails will kill twenty at once."

The staccato reports of the long rifles picked up cadence. "They're running now, charging." Chaos. Shouts, the roar of rifles, screams of horses and men, oaths hurled at fate and at Santa Anna, the wailing of trumpets, and then the battle cry of the Texians like words given the power of a blade. "Remember the Alamo! Remember Goliad!" It was a great chorus of voices, an anthem of anger and desperation and revenge. Then, almost as quickly as it had begun, the battle was over. The Mexicans had surrendered. Euphemia and Sarah moved through pastures of the dead. Hundreds of Mexican soldiers twisted in grotesque positions lay bleeding into fields of thistle poppies and rain lily. The refugees, many of the women and children, walked among the bodies. Euphemia Texas felt she was walking among the dead of a faerie tale. In a moment, when she and Sarah were swept into the embrace of Bartlett McClure and they were by Sam Houston's side, she had no doubt she was a faerie child plucked alive from a legend, certainly not born at all. There was the long, dangerous journey, the victory won, the knight and his lady reunited with their strong, good king who was wounded, but alive, his reign secure. When Houston recounted the battle to Bartlett and told him that 630 of the enemy had been killed while the Texians had lost just two men, it didn't surprise her. It was the expected outcome when your cause was just and good. Bartlett explained that the Mexicans had not set out a single sentry and Houston had planned the attack when the enemy was taking its siesta. General Santa Anna was in his silk tent with a beautiful mulatto girl named Emily Morgan, a woman the soldiers were already calling the Yellow Rose of Texas.

Then Euphemia saw Saracen, Sam Houston's great white stallion. He lay on the ground as if carved there from stone. An awful wound in his breast spilled onto the grass and patches of star phlox. As she walked through the dead soldiers to where the horse lay, she knew she was walking out of the story she had lived into something else. Maybe she had been born after all. Maybe she was real. *Lots of things can happen in stories,* she thought. *But never, ever, do they find the king's white stallion dead.*

It was the first day of May, 1838, nearly three years after Houston's victory at San Jacinto. Euphemia and Sarah rested on the only hill for miles around, a modest knoll of sweetgrass and bluebonnets, rising to the east of Woman Hollerin' Creek. They watched their horses graze and looked down, in the far distance, where Leviticus and the other hands were sweeping the rows of yellow corn. Beyond the fields, the graves of Sarah's children lay sheltered by a canopy of oaks. The day was warm as a hand, the air fragrant, fresh and ambrosial. Euphemia was thinking how fine it was to have a brand-new republic named for her, an honor given only a few, like Amerigo Vespucci and Simón Bolívar. Sarah breathed a small cloud of smoke and pointed her clay pipe toward the place on Peach Creek where the new house would be.

"Down there," Sarah said, "by that grove of wild plums, will be the grandest house this side of New Orleans. Tall white columns and everything."

"Can I try your pipe?" Euphemia asked.

"May I," Sarah corrected.

"May I try your pipe?"

"Of course not!"

"You smoke."

"You're not me," Sarah said. "Times are going to be different now. It's time for change."

"Like what?"

"Like smoking tobacco, drinking whiskey, and talking tough and all the other rough edges of our lives. I keep thinking we're a civilized people living like rabble. For two years now we've had a proper republic with a proper president. Well, maybe Sam

Houston isn't exactly proper, but he is a president. So it's time we lived in a proper house and lived proper lives. Did you know we Ashbys once lived in a castle? In England. It was built by King William I, William the Silent. A huge castle, made of stone, with towers and battlements. Our ancestors lived like royalty, even entertained Mary Queen of Scots. So what are we doing living in a log cabin?"

"And smoking tobacco," Euphemia added.

"I'd like to build a place that's beautiful," Sarah continued. "A place where life isn't so hard and mean. Sometimes I think we're just squatters in Texas, just biding our time, waiting for the next bad thing to happen. Maybe it's time we put down some roots. Made plans for something good to happen for a change. We're so busy just surviving, we don't have time to be human. Look at Bart. He's a very cultured and educated man. A good lawyer. Speaks French and Spanish. I'm sure he'd be at home in any of the courts of Europe. We have friends out here in the wilderness who could name all the kings of England, in order, and tell you who poisoned each, and debate Aristotle and the Free State and recite whole passages of 'A Midsummer Night's Dream.' But what good does that do you when you live like a savage? Like some kind of Stone Age people."

A chimera of smoke ghosted from Sarah's lips and Euphemia was amazed at how gracefully Sarah held the pipe and how naturally it seemed to belong in her hand. She could almost understand why the Indians believed smoke was a living thing, a messenger between the things of earth and the world of the spirit.

"I'm too wild to change how things are. I've had to be these last few years, to survive. But you can. You can change this world. Soften the edges of our lives. Somebody has to civilize these men of ours. If we left the Republic up to them, there'd be no schools, no churches, nothing really enduring. We'd just have four things. We'd have duels and dreams and war. And the fourth thing we'd have is politics, a kind of substitute for the first three."

"What can I do?" Euphemia asked. "How can I change things?"

"Grow up to be a woman," Sarah answered.

"But I'm just a little girl."

"Well, you're an apprentice woman," Sarah said. "You know, Phemie, there was a time when a whole lot of the old gods were women. They were worshiped as the creators of our world. The givers of life. But there's more to giving life than having babies. Sometimes I think I've tried all my life to be something I'm not. I tried to be a man. I thought that was a way to make my life count for something. But I was wrong. Men may be stronger, but there is power in being a woman."

The sun grew warmer, and Euphemia remembered the times when she thought she would never be warm again. The long march that ended at the battlefield of San Jacinto. The terrible feeling of not knowing if their home would still be there when they returned or if Santa Anna had burned it as he passed. She remembered the joy of seeing the log house still there by the creek, stripped and gutted but sound and dry. The beds had been built into the wall and so had survived. Euphemia had helped Tildy and Sarah take the old bedding sacks outdoors to dump out the corn shucks and Spanish moss. "I'd die before I'd sleep on a mattress Santa Anna shared with Lord knows who!" Sarah had said, as she boiled the ticking in a large black iron pot of lye soap. After the bedding sacks were clean and dry, Euphemia, William, and Travis filled them with clean moss from the woods and they helped wash down the walls and beds to get rid of the accumulation of bugs.

Euphemia had been terrified there would be some new reason to leave their home. Sometimes in the middle of the night she would wake after dreaming she held Little Johnny's cold body in her arms. She knew Sarah and Bartlett were worried about her. Once she heard William tell a friend that his sister never smiled. When she was alone she would practice smiling, but the reflection in Sarah's mirror always looked back at her with mournful, even frightened eyes. Euphemia had decided she had lost all her smile somewhere on the banks of the Brazos or in the field where Saracen died.

On nights of full moons, a number of nearby homesteads were attacked by Comanche raiders. During the 1830s, both Mexican and Anglo settlers had been steadily moving into the traditional lands of the Karankawas and the southern Comanches. The

Cherokees, Kickapoos, and Creeks, forced from their eastern lands into Texas, were being pressured once again to move. When Texas became a republic and waves of new settlers began to immigrate, the Indians fought to stem the tide. Sam Houston negotiated a treaty with the Karankawas and their raids ceased. Houston also pressured the Congress to guarantee Cherokees title to their Texas land. The bill was voted down, yet the Cherokees decided not to make war on the government headed by their old friend. In spite of all Sam Houston's efforts to avoid conflict between Anglo settlers and the Indians, Comanche raids continued. In 1838, a band of twenty-seven Comanches led by the notorious renegade warrior Tarantula raided the Tucker place, just a few miles from Peach Creek. They cut the skin from the bottom of Tucker's feet and forced him to walk on burning grass. Then they scalped him and hung him from a tree. Earlier, William Cotton and John Hayes, neighbors of John Ashby, had been cutting poles for a corn crib when a stray band of Comanches caught them and hacked them to pieces.

Now the raids were increasing. A band of thirty Comanches struck the Lyons home, about eighteen miles from the McClure place. After each raid, a posse was hurriedly organized. The farms and homesteads around Peach Creek became armed camps. Usually the killings were revenged in kind. So many Indians were killed that the raiding parties began to carry away white women and children to replenish the tribes. It was the very worst nightmare of any child Euphemia's age, and almost any unusual noise she heard in the night was surely the whisper of Tarantula's moccasin on the ladder to the sleeping loft.

Now, as Sarah and Euphemia watched their horses graze on the hill above Woman Hollerin' Creek, Sarah's eyes followed something moving in the near distance to the west. When she spoke it was through lips that barely moved. "What you must do right now, Phemie, is look at me and listen very carefully to every word I say."

Surprised, Euphemia looked into Sarah's face and couldn't imagine why this beautiful woman would want to be a man, even though she herself wished to be a man almost every waking hour.

But surely not Sarah. Then, she noticed the steel in her older sister's expression, and she knew something was terribly wrong.

"I want you to get up and mount your horse as if you didn't have a care in the world," Sarah said, "then I want you to ride like lightning toward home, 'cause there's Comanches coming up from Woman Hollerin' Creek. Take the south trail by the graveyard."

"What about you?" Euphemia asked.

"I'll lead them to the ravine. I don't think they can jump across and I think I can." Euphemia stole a glance toward the Woman Hollerin', but could only see the heat now beginning to rise from the earth, the simmering mirage of the prairie. "Now go. Quickly. And ride."

Euphemia Texas walked to her horse, fighting the impulse to run, listening for the whispering flight of arrows and wondering if they would pass right through her body or stick in her bones and muscle. She prayed they would pass on through, first to God and then to all those female deities who were the givers of life. Then she was in the saddle, her heart pounding, the horse flying away toward where Sarah's children were buried beneath the oaks. Back on the brow of the hill, Sarah stood her ground before six hard-charging Comanche warriors. She was waving her arms to hold the Indians' attention and shouting what Euphemia could only imagine was Shakespeare.

Euphemia looked back again to see that the Comanches had chosen to ride for Sarah, who turned and hurtled down the hill toward home. She was riding high on the horse's neck, the Comanches following like a single monstrous animal, all hooves and horns and feathers. The warriors had long, slim, feathered spears. Two wore buffalo cap headdresses, another a tall silk hat, the savage haberdashery of the plains. It was a tableau from a dream. They flew along the brim of the hill, perfectly silhouetted on the horizon. The sound of the chase crossed the distance like a whispered conversation.

The breathing of her own horse and the pelting of her thoughts were louder than the thundering hooves and howling Comanches. The distance diminished the danger. Euphemia watched them flying, almost gliding across the rolling prairie, seven people bound by the chase, moving in slow motion, more poetry than peril. Occasionally Sarah would turn in the saddle, look back, then ride on toward Big Elm Draw, a deep, wide ravine separating the McClure homestead from no-man's land. The Indians didn't gain on Sarah, nor did they fall behind. Euphemia thought for a moment it was a game they were playing, no harm meant, just something playful to do on a fine spring morning.

As Sarah approached the ravine, the Comanches were still in hot pursuit. She fastened the reins under her leg, wrapped her arms around her horse's neck, and then she and her horse left the ground, as if pulled skyward by a puppeteer. Over the ravine they flew. How long horse and rider remained airborne, Euphemia would try to remember in days to come. It seemed hours, lifetimes. It was an event that spanned the ages of mankind. On one side of the ravine was the past, on the other the future. The Comanches had stopped at the edge of the ravine, apparently afraid their ponies could not fly as well as Sarah's midnight mare. After a while, Sarah descended from her ride through the winds, the horse's front feet just catching the far edge of the ravine. Then, scrambling, they were up and across and safe. Sarah turned and Euphemia was almost sure Sarah was laughing. The Comanches watched her ride away and the one with the tall silk hat raised his spear in salute. The warriors rode back toward Woman Hollerin' Creek. Sarah turned her horse toward where the great white house would be.

Not many days after their encounter with the Comanches, Euphemia Texas fell desperately, everlastingly in love. She had often heard of the Kings, a legendary family of lawyers, planters, Indian fighters, and adventurers, who came to Gonzales after the town had been burned during Sam Houston's retreat to San Jacinto. Now they were headed into the wilderness to build a new town, a new life, in the new Republic. It was the kind of adventure she would expect of this family of bigger-than-life individuals who seemed to live with more flair and exuberance than ordinary souls. The Rowdy King Boys, they were sometimes called. Now Henry Brazil King had brought his betrothed, Ma-

hala Day, to be married by Judge Bartlett McClure. There were
no preachers along Peach Creek, no churches except the brush arbor where the Baptist missionary circuit rider sometimes held services in the intervals between Comanche Moons. Certainly there
were no ministers up on the Guadalupe where the Kings were
bound. So Bartlett McClure, after what seemed a rather lengthy
search, found and dusted off the old Bible they had brought from
Kentucky and Sarah began preparations for the wedding feast.

At first, Euphemia noticed the Rowdy King Boys were not at
all the boisterous, disorderly cutups their reputation had led her
to believe. Henry Brazil King was very reserved for a rowdy.
Like the other King brothers he was very tall. He moved with a
grace and dignified bearing that reminded her of Juan Seguin. She
could imagine him in the stirrups of the stallion he rode when the
brothers drove a herd of fine horses all the way from the Cum-
berlands to Texas. His eyes were set wide apart, still his dark eyebrows nearly touched, like a hedge, Euphemia thought, across his
wide, intelligent brow. Of all the brothers, he seemed most serious. There was something in his eyes and in his good, strong
laughter that suggested to Euphemia he just might be able to
muster a touch of rowdiness if the time and the mood were right.

Although the second brother, John Rhodes King, had been a
riverboat captain, he reminded Euphemia of a preacher. He was
tall and angular, and seemed to love to hear the sound of his voice
rolling like the lower notes of an organ from somewhere deep in
the caverns of his chest. Half of what he said was conversation
and the other half quotes from the Bible to verify, illuminate, or
quantify what he said in the first half. When they all prepared to
sit down for their first supper together, John Rhodes King urged
his brothers to wash before the meal and Euphemia heard him
quote and expound from the Gospel of Saint Mark. "Except they
wash their hands oft, they eat not," he said, and then launched
into the importance of washing pots and cups. He said such a
thing might not appear important, but the teaching was in the
Good Book right next to the Scripture demanding we honor our
father and mother. "Therefore," he said, "if we do not wash our
hands, we dishonor our parents and are guilty of breaking one of
the Ten Commandments." Euphemia was amazed at his ability to

find in God's word a point to be made for all matters large or small.

In both the older King brothers, Euphemia sensed contained and secret strength. It was an attractive quality, as if Euphemia could see and know only what the brothers wished her to see and know. Yet, it was the third brother who made Euphemia Texas feel so strange and happy and miserable. And he wasn't even there.

How often it seemed they mentioned this William, youngest of the Rowdy King Boys. He was a center to every story they told of their exploits. They wove their tales of mischief and adventure, and when the climax came, in would ride William to save the day or to astound with his daring or his audacity. William rode with his two older brothers on the first weeks of their drive before returning to Kentucky to close up the family business. When rustlers cut a dozen horses from their herd and headed into Arkansas, it was William who circled around and caught the rustlers, burned their clothes, and tied them stark naked to trees along the trail to Fort Smith. It was William who insisted they bring their dog Old Peaches along on the drive. Along with the horses were a number of cows, including one that had a growing hatred for Old Peaches and never failed to lunge at the dog when it came near. One evening, as it was growing dark, they passed a black tree stump by the side of the road and the cow, thinking the stump was Old Peaches, attacked that stump and "her senses were knocked clear across the Red River." John Rhodes and Henry Brazil King loved to tell stories about William's dog Old Peaches.

When they all got the itch, it was William, they said, who decided to cure it by sitting in a pan of whiskey. When they came upon a band of starving Cherokees, it was William who gave them the milk cow, much to the relief of the Indians and Old Peaches. When they passed the wagon train of settlers moving west, it was for William the girls changed into their Sunday best on Tuesday. "He'll be coming through before long," Mahala said, "just as soon as he can finish up in Kentucky. And you'd better watch out, Phemie. He'll take one look at a pretty thing like you, and before long your daddy'll have to find that old dusty Bible again."

In her mind, a portrait of William King began to take form. He was more handsome than his older brothers. He was even more handsome than Juan Seguin, more handsome than Bart McClure or Sam Houston. He was very tall and he had eyes that were wild, yet kind, and a smile that would melt Arctic ice. She imagined dancing with him as she had once dreamed of dancing with Juan Seguin, and she could actually feel the strength in his arms. The intensity of her feeling for this mental image surprised and puzzled her. *Do I need love so much,* she wondered, *that I must create someone to love me in my mind? Or is it just the excitement of the wedding? A time to think such thoughts.* But it felt very good, this secret romance with a beautiful stranger, and she held it close, like a promise waiting to be kept.

The Kings were in Peach Creek three days and it was a joyous time. They talked about the new town they would build in the wilderness. It would rise at the remote Ranger camp of Captain Callahan and Matthew Caldwell, on the Guadalupe River where deep, clear spring water flowed through groves of walnut and pecan trees. They talked about new beginnings and the future and the lives they would have. They talked about the passing of power in the new Republic from Sam Houston to Mirabeau B. Lamar, who was elected President of Texas in 1838 on a platform of Texan greatness and future glory.

One afternoon the Rowdy King Boys brought musical instruments from their packs—a fiddle, a fife, and a Jew's harp. With Leviticus scraping the rhythm on a cotton hoe with a case knife, they created the most beautiful music Euphemia had ever heard. Bartlett's voice rose clear and deep as they sang everything from gospel tunes to the impolite choruses Euphemia had first heard Sam Houston's soldiers sing when they had made their charge at San Jacinto.

During the evenings, Euphemia would lie in the loft listening to the adults talk of the Republic and the chances of avoiding another war with Mexico. There was no money to pay the army, there was no money at all. The Republic of Texas was merely a scattering of farms and settlements, without industry, roads, or even real schools. To the south was the might of Mexico, a nation humiliated by its defeat at San Jacinto, consumed with a need to redeem both its national pride and its territory. Mexico refused to recognize the independence of Texas. It seemed only a matter of time before war would engulf them again.

"If we're to remain free," Henry King said, "we'll have to throw in our lot with the Stars and Stripes. As much as I'd like to see the Republic endure, we just can't survive on our own."

They talked about how the Mexicans were making alliances with the Comanches, turning them against the Texans who had invaded their lands, encouraging them to make raids against the isolated settlements. They talked about the renegade Tarantula. Euphemia thought the awful sound of the name was almost like seeing one, hairy, heavy, and black.

"His name is actually Pia-war-rah," Bartlett said. "But the Mexicans call him Tarantula for obvious reasons. He's poison. One mean Comanche, in his tall black hat. We've had run-ins with him before. He calls Sarah 'Brave Squaw.' "

"That was Tarantula chased Phemie and me home," Sarah said. "We outfoxed him, though."

"He's a bad one," Bartlett said. "About as bad as they come. Even the Comanches are afraid of him, don't trust him. He and his band have been camped over at the Woman Hollerin' for some time now. At night we have to chain our horses just in case."

"We could drive him away," Henry said. A picture blossomed in Euphemia's mind of the dashing William King riding hard and fast and fierce against Tarantula's band of renegades.

"Frankly, I want to avoid trouble with the Comanches," Bartlett said. "Few bands attack without provocation and I sure don't think we ought to provoke."

"Well, Tarantula came after me and Phemie," Sarah said. "And I sure don't remember provoking anybody."

"He's an exception. But we can't make our whole policy with the Indians based on a renegade band. Somehow, we've got to work toward a general peace. If we keep killing Indians, Indians have no choice but to keep killing us."

"President Lamar certainly doesn't feel that way," John said. "He says to anybody who'll listen the only solution to the Indian problem is total extinction or expulsion."

"That's why we need Sam Houston back as president," Bartlett replied. "Too bad he was restricted to one term in office. He knows the Indians better than anyone in Texas. He knows how they think and he has their respect. We need old Sam Houston to lead us out of trouble one more time."

The day of the wedding, the sky and the clouds were the color of a cameo and pale clouds drifted lazily above a counterpane of green forest and meadow. Earlier in the week, Leviticus and the Rowdy King Boys had taken to the creek bottoms after a wild boar to barbecue for the feast. At dawn, Bart rode out after wild turkey, which would be broiled and served with honey. Venison, aged in the spring house and marinated in a sauce of onions, carrots, parsley, thyme, bay leaves, and whole cloves, was larded and prepared for roasting. Euphemia collected fresh sweet onions from the garden and roasting ears from the crib. There would be pudding and pound cakes and to drink there would be mustang grape juice, black coffee, corn whiskey, and wild plum wine.

The homestead was astir with activity. And all day, as she went about her chores, Euphemia thought about the day she would marry William and become Euphemia Texas Ashby King. At one point, early in the afternoon, she went to her secret place by the creek. She lay down in a bed of clover and watched a soaring hawk sign its signature in the air. She knew, beyond doubt, she had never been more happy. *There is no pain anywhere in my body or my mind,* she thought. *I will remember this moment forever.* And then, a strange gray thought passed behind her eyes. "If I am so happy," she said aloud, "why don't I ever smile?"

Bartlett McClure performed the wedding ceremony with elegance and dispatch, shocking most who were present by reading a passage, perhaps at random but probably not, from the Song of Solomon. Euphemia closed her eyes when Bartlett got to the part about breasts like two young roes feeding among the lilies. When she opened her eyes, her face aflame, she could tell Sarah was barely hiding her outrage and the Rowdy King Boys were on the edge of an avalanche of laughter. Judge McClure, as serene and composed as ever, read on about the honeycomb lips of the righteous. Then he pronounced Henry and Mahala man and wife and the wedding feast began.

Among the wedding guests was the Lockhart family and their fifteen-year-old daughter, Matilda. Although they lived many miles apart and Matilda was a few years older, the two girls were fast friends. On occasion, they had attended school together, when classes were held in area homes. Euphemia's first memory of Matilda was how she carried her lunch to school wrapped in corn shucks. Matilda was a quiet and reserved child; however, when she was called on to recite, especially from Aesop's Fables, her spirit would seem to catch fire. She would lend each animal a separate personality and the children would be mesmerized by her talent. When the class sang "Geography," a song that embraced the names of the oceans, islands, mountains, and rivers of the Western Hemisphere, Matilda's voice gave even the most wearisome archipelago an air of mystery and romance. Matilda's secret dream was to be a ballerina, like the beautiful Fanny Elssler who was then taking Paris by storm. Euphemia loved Matilda for her secret dream and her forbidden knowledge of an exotic, gleaming, golden world beyond the wilderness. But she was often saddened by the absolute impossibility that a girl who brought her lunch to school wrapped in corn shucks would ever make her way to the ballet companies of Europe.

Matilda had long, golden hair that reached an inch or two beyond her waist and reminded Euphemia of corn silk. Her eyes were blue and she had dimples, even when not smiling, that Euphemia envied almost to the point of sin. For such a young girl, she seemed extremely womanly to Euphemia. Matilda's body had the same combination of softness and strength that Sarah had and that Euphemia imagined she would never herself achieve, through either exercise or prayer. Euphemia had one night, in a moment of weakness, prayed for breasts. For the next seven nights she had prayed for forgiveness. Not only did Euphemia believe Matilda was beautiful, but she believed she was a kind of missionary of beauty. It was as if she carried beauty around and she broadcast it, here and there, like seeds, into the lives she touched.

"Before this day is over, I'm going to teach you to smile," Matilda said. They were walking hand-in-hand through the wild plum trees along the creek. "First, you have to think of something very beautiful."

Euphemia thought of Saracen. She looked toward the Sam Houston oak where she had first seen Sam Houston's horse appear like something from a legend.

"Are you thinking of something?"

"Yes." She closed her eyes and thought about Saracen as hard as she could. She saw the horse against the shades of her closed eyelids, white against the black. Then she saw the blood and the horse lying dead on the field, and she began to cry. She sobbed and her body shook as if she were freezing cold and she didn't know exactly why she was crying but she couldn't stop. Matilda gathered her into her arms and pulled her down into the grass by the creek. "Shhh," she said, again and again, until Euphemia grew still and silent.

Matilda sat behind Euphemia and began to braid her hair. "I know you had a hard time, Phemie. I know bad things happened. But they're gone. They're in the past. They don't exist anymore. What you need to do is think new thoughts. You need to redecorate the rooms of your mind. Rearrange the furniture. Paint the walls."

"What color?" Euphemia wiped her nose on the hem of her skirt.

"Well, look around. How about the blue up there, and some white like the clouds? Think about what you told me about William King and what it would be like to be marrying him today. Think about love. And think about me. If you're unhappy, it makes me unhappy. Put me in your redecorated rooms. If you love me think of me and I'll make you happy."

"I'm sorry," Euphemia said.

"Good girl. Now look at me." Euphemia turned, sniffed, and again wiped her nose. "Now think of me. Think of how much I love you."

Euphemia actually felt Matilda entering the rooms of her

mind. She actually saw her going from room to room throwing open the windows, filling the rooms with fresh, cool air.

"Now, silly girl, smile."

Euphemia could see in Matilda's face her own smile reflected.

"Now if you'll just practice a few hours each day, I think you'll get the hang of it."

That night, after the wedding supper, the Rowdy King Boys and Leviticus created a jubilant carousel of hornpipes, jigs, and reels. The floor was cleared for dancing and the sound of clattering, shuffling feet was so loud it eclipsed the melody of Henry's fiddle. The room became alive with sound. Euphemia felt this must be what it would be like to be inside a guitar or a drum. The air pulsed with the rhythm of Leviticus's cotton hoe percussion and the shouts and laughter of the guests. Bartlett and Sarah whirled in a spinning pattern of buckskin and taffeta. Henry laid his fiddle aside and he and his bride shuffled and double-shuffled and "cut the pigeon's wing." Euphemia and Matilda watched the adults dance late into the night. There were pirouettes of lantern light upon the walls and on faces reddened by fine corn whiskey and by what seemed to Euphemia something near hysteria.

Late in the evening Bartlett approached Matilda and Euphemia and asked Matilda to dance. They whirled away like the porcelain dancing figures on Sarah's music box. Then Henry King moved from the floor to where Euphemia stood alone by the door. He was smiling and he held out his hand in invitation. Euphemia's first reaction was dread that she would run away or that she wouldn't. She would rather die than dance. Her second reaction was bliss because, in her mind, it was William who took her hand, and she didn't run and she didn't die—she danced. Unlike what she had feared, she felt as graceful as Sarah or Matilda. She felt grown and alive and beautiful. Her feet seemed to know exactly where to go as she and William turned and whirled across the floor. She felt the rooms of her mind overflowing with the music and motion and promise of the wedding dance. She knew she was loved and she knew, as she danced, she was smiling.

In the night, when the house was dark, Euphemia was awakened by voices and fragments of laughter. By her side, Matilda said, "It's the shivaree. Come on."

The two girls crept from the loft and out into the yard where Bartlett and the unmarried King brother had gathered a strange miscellany of cowbells and tin pans and every conceivable thing that could make noise. Euphemia noticed they were quite unsteady. Then, after Bartlett made a sweeping, exaggerated count of three with his arm, they began to howl and shout and pound pots together and raise a mad orchestra of sound that would surely wake the dead if not the groom. The revelers lighted a torch and Euphemia and Matilda retreated farther into the shadows at the edge of the forest. "What is it?" Euphemia asked.

"Shivaree. It's just a prank they do on a wedding night," Matilda answered. "Just to torment the groom on his first night in bed with the bride."

The men called for Henry to come out and make an appearance. "Once I heard they stole the groom and threw him in a pond," Matilda said. "He got pneumonia and died."

"But why?" Euphemia asked. "Why would they make all that noise? Why steal the groom?"

"To interrupt what they're doing," Matilda answered. "You know. They're together, in bed together, you know, naked together, for the first time."

Henry King refused the invitation to come out and be stolen and thrown in a pond, and soon the men grew tired of their prank and they went inside. The light of the torch was gone and the night closed in like a shroud. The girls waited for the house to grow still so they could climb back to the loft unseen. There was a coolness in the air and a small wind cut through their nightgowns. An owl called from the darkness. Then a wolf off somewhere howled defiance at the night sky.

It was then Tarantula stepped from the shadows, his nearly naked figure towering, his face a garden of scars beneath his tall silk hat, his eyes like poisoned wells. He looked at them, first at one girl and then the other, as if he were trading for meat. Then he turned and moved back into the dark woods.

* * *

In the months following the wedding of Henry King and Mahala Day, Sarah McClure was consumed by plans for the new
house. She made sketches based on memories of the family home
in Kentucky and the other great houses of the Old South. She
had once seen The Hermitage, Andrew Jackson's stately home in
Tennessee, with its great towering columns and manicured gardens, and she was convinced that something just as grand could
be built in Texas. Euphemia never tired of hearing Sarah describe
the new McClure estate which would rise from the wilderness at
Peach Creek.

"My house will be frame, not brick like The Hermitage, and
when you first see it rising from the oaks it'll remind you of a
Greek temple. There'll be double porches across the front and the
whole structure will be white as a cloud with Doric columns two
stories high. And on the third floor, there'll be a ballroom with
gilded mirrors where we can dance 'til dawn. There'll be a music
room with a crystal chandelier and a parlor where one day all the
family portraits will hang."

There would be no need to send to Philadelphia or New York
for furniture or even to New Orleans. All the furnishings would
be the creation of their own personal master craftsman, John
Ashby, their father. In his letters from Kentucky, where he was
waiting for Frances and Jane Isabella to graduate from the Julia A.
Tevis Academy for Girls, John Ashby had promised to work on
the new house. Few craftsmen in the South were as skilled, and
the furniture he had created over the years was as fine as any that
graced the houses of Natchez or Richmond. Black walnut chests,
dropleaf tables with oak and pecan inlays, a great huntboard
banded with burled walnut where Bartlett and Juan and maybe
even Sam Houston could drink their whiskey from silver goblets
after hunting panthers out by Woman Hollerin' Creek.

Now they were coming home. The letter had arrived on the
stage. Euphemia's sisters Frances and Jane Isabella, who had fled
from Santa Anna, and her father, who had abandoned her to the
enemy, would soon return. It had been barely three years since
she had seen them, but it seemed nearly forever.

"It won't be long now," Sarah often said. They would
try to imagine how far their father and their two sisters had

progressed on their voyage down the Mississippi to the Texas coast.

Euphemia Texas had a difficult time picturing her father's face. When she tried and the image would emerge in her mind unclear, like a reflection in flowing water, she would be touched first by guilt, and then by a kind of hollow pain. What kind of person could not remember her own father's face? But then, he abandoned her, left her to suffer the terrible Runaway Scrape. What kind of father would do that? Why would he take Frances and Jane Isabella out of harm's way and leave her to face Santa Anna? How sad for a girl with a living father to feel like an orphan. Several times Euphemia asked Sarah why her father hadn't taken her along to New Orleans.

"Well, you see," Sarah would begin, "Isabella and Frances were of an age when they were in particular danger. When there's a war, girls their age are sometimes hurt by enemy soldiers. And sometimes men like Papa aren't very good takin' care of little girls. He thought I might take care of you better than he could."

Such conversations were always profoundly unsettling and she would be left more confused than ever. They would generally end with Sarah insisting John Ashby loved all his daughters equally. "Whatever he did," she said, "he had good reason. Your turn will come. Besides, there's no use stewing over such things. What's done yesterday is dead and buried. There's no time to worry about things you can't change. What we can change is tomorrow."

"Did Mama die having me?"

"Of course not, Phemie. She just died."

"I think she died having me," Euphemia said. "That's what I think. I think that's why Papa left me behind."

Sarah pulled Euphemia to her and enfolded her in her arms. Euphemia flowed into her sister's embrace, letting her body go limp as the doll with the painted china face. "Listen to me, Phemie. Look at me." She held Euphemia away and looked into her eyes. "Our mother died because, for some reason I don't understand, God needed her with him. Remember, he loved us so much he left us a gift. The most important thing in the world. He gave us a life. He gave us you."

"A trade? One mother for one baby?"

"Phemie! That's nonsense."

"Was she alive when I was born? Did she know I was there?" It was the first time Euphemia had expressed these thoughts aloud. Was there an instant before she died that her mother was aware of her baby? Did she see her or hold her? Or was she only thinking about her pain? *Or,* and Euphemia shuddered at the thought, *maybe she was already dead when I was born.*

"I'm going to count three now, Phemie. And when I've finished I want you to put all these thoughts out of your mind. Life has a way of stoning us. But blast if I'm gonna supply the stones. Neither should you. Now go wash those tears from your face and stop thinking nonsense!" She embraced Euphemia and kissed her forehead. "Now I'm about to count. You ready?"

"I'm ready."

"Now when I say three, you'll only think good thoughts." Sarah began to count. "One, two . . . three."

Euphemia decided she wouldn't talk about these things again. How could anybody know how she felt, anyway?

As the weeks passed, each morning Euphemia would walk to the road and picture the stage rumbling through the ford at Peach Creek and then stopping beneath the oaks in front of the old house. Then the doors would burst open and her family would emerge in a swirl of motion and color. Frances and Jane Isabella would descend from the stage like flowers falling from a basket, each surrounded by rainbows of silk and taffeta and satin and Chinese embroidery, the newest styles from the salons of New Orleans. Her father would be in a ruffled shirt and a black velvet suit and he would wear red-topped boots with silver spurs. She did not think it strange they would arrive in anything other than traveling clothes nor did she wonder why this image of her father was curiously similar to her mental picture of William King, the youngest of the Rowdy King Boys. Each day she grew more and more excited about the arrival of the family she had never had.

As the days went by, actual work on the new house began. A wandering carpenter named Jean-Baptiste Beauchamps, formerly of Orleans, France, who claimed to have completed a series of restorations on the château at Chambord, was hired as house-wright. He was a flamboyant yet able worker, and he provided marvelous entertainment for Euphemia as he cut down oak trees with his felling axe and then chopped them up on the spot for posts and beams. Euphemia watched as Jean-Baptiste showed Leviticus how to square and trim the beams smooth and straight with a broad axe and how to cut mortises and tenons for joints. Each of the prefabricated timbers was stamped with Roman number codes to facilitate assembly, a practice Jean-Baptiste claimed was a craft tradition from medieval times. Leviticus was soon working without supervision, drilling holes in the timbers for trunnels and preparing the frames for assembly. One evening Jean-Baptiste asked Sarah if she minded that he was teaching the slaves his trade.

"Why on earth should I mind?" Sarah replied.

"Some planters in the South discourage the development of such skills among slaves. In order to be a housewright or carpenter or cabinetmaker, you must learn symbols and formulas. It's only a small step away from learning to read. Most people don't want their slaves to be able to read. Puts too many ideas in their heads."

"That's ridiculous." Sarah dismissed the whole subject with a wave of her hand.

As the finished timbers were moved to the building site next to the old house and the stone foundations were cut, Sarah began to accept the fact that her new house might not be as grand as she had dreamed. There would be no fluted columns nor Carrara marble mantels, no wrought-iron roses on the gallery rails, no imported French wallpaper with murals depicting the travels of Ulysses. With few exceptions, everything required to build and furnish the house would have to be obtained by barter or made on the site. There was no money to import nails, so Bartlett hired a blacksmith from Gonzales to make what nails they needed. The blacksmith cut the nails from flat iron stock, then hammered the heads by hand. He told Euphemia nails were so valuable many pioneers moving west would burn their old homes so they could reclaim the nails for building their new houses in the wilderness.

The days went by in a whirl of activity and anticipation. Sarah and Euphemia imagined the ship that carried Frances, Jane Isabella, and their father had entered Matagorda Bay and they were stepping ashore. During the days, they observed the building of the house as if they were attending an operetta written, choreographed, and orchestrated by the indefatigable Monsieur Beauchamps. He was a living machine of energy and motion, always seeming fully in command.

One morning, when Bartlett was away and Jean-Baptiste was supervising the carving of roofbeams, Euphemia was helping Sarah set up the loom for weaving. On previous mornings they had spun the cotton thread on a spinning wheel and had carded the cotton that would eventually go into the warp and woof of their homespun. Euphemia heard the horses complaining behind the house.

"Horses sure are fussin'," Euphemia said. "Must be Mr. Beauchamps stirrin' 'em up."

As Sarah rose to check on the stock, Jean-Baptiste burst through the door. "Indians out there!" He was pale and trembling. Euphemia saw General Sarah McClure coolly take her rifle from its rack and Euphemia followed her to the window. When she looked out toward the back she could easily see the Comanches. They were in plain sight, five horsemen, sitting still as stone statues on their mounts. They were all nearly naked. They wore only breechcloths but, oddly enough, carried parasols. When Euphemia first saw the Indians, she thought no real danger could come from naked men carrying parasols. Then she realized the parasols must have once belonged to women settlers and she felt fear creeping, like mercury, down from her mind into her body, making her limbs heavy and slow to move. Among the riders was the huge familiar figure of Tarantula. He was somewhat apart from the others, watching the house. In his tall silk hat he seemed to dwarf his pony. When he saw Sarah at the window he shifted his position on his mount and seemed to grow even taller. Euphemia thought his scars might have rearranged themselves into a smile.

"It's Tarantula," Sarah said, moving back from the window. "After horses?"

"Or women. Probably knows Bartlett's gone. Lots of Indian children died from the pox this year. They need women to give 'em more children."

"What'll we do?" Jean-Baptiste asked.

"We run 'em off," Sarah removed a revolver from the mantel and gave it to Euphemia. She took a second rifle from the rack and handed it to Jean-Baptiste. "Looks like they've already been raidin'. They got themselves some parasols. Just hope they haven't got the women that owns 'em."

The carpenter began to tremble again. "I've never fired a gun in my life," he managed to say. "Let's just lock the doors. Maybe they'll go away."

"Look," Sarah said. "You don't have to shoot the gun. Just look like you might." Sarah showed Jean-Baptiste which end to point at the Comanches and how to hold the rifle on his shoulder. "Phemie, you stay here. And you, Beauchamps, let's go see what they want."

"I'd rather stay here."

"Either you go out there with me or count the seconds until I shoot you myself." Sarah pushed the rifle barrel into the carpenter's middle. "Take your choice."

At first, Euphemia thought Jean-Baptiste would faint, he was that pale. But he straightened his shoulders, sighed, and followed Sarah to and through the door.

Euphemia watched Sarah and Jean-Baptiste move into the dog trot and then out into the harsh sunlight behind the house. They walked a few yards toward the Indians, then stopped. Euphemia covered Sarah from the window. Tarantula tipped his hat. It was a horrible gesture, a nightmare neighbor come to call. For what seemed hours, Sarah, Beauchamps, and the Comanches stood facing each other, not thirty yards apart, easily within range of the rifles they carried. The faces of all the Indians but Tarantula's were shaded by their parasols. There was not a word spoken. Yet, some instinct within Euphemia told her Tarantula had come for Sarah.

Suddenly, Jean-Baptiste turned and ran toward the house, his shirttails flying like broken kites. Sarah didn't turn to watch the carpenter flee. It was as if the man had never existed. She turned and faced the Comanches. She stood her ground, staring back at Tarantula, as if daring them to move closer. Then, as Euphemia watched spellbound, Sarah did a remarkable thing. With her rifle, she drew a line between the mounted Comanches and the house. It wasn't a long line, but it was obvious she had marked a boundary between them. When she had drawn the line, she moved back to her position behind it and she stared back at Tarantula for a full five minutes. Then, she turned and she walked slowly to the house, never once looking back at the Comanches. It was an act as brave as any Euphemia had seen. As brave as Maggie Boles's ride across the Brazos River. It was as if the Comanches were dismissed. One by one they closed their parasols and rode away. The last to leave was Tarantula.

That night the Comanches killed a few calves they found wandering in the fields, but they stayed beyond the boundary Sarah had drawn. Throughout the night they remained near, and in the moonlight Euphemia could occasionally see Tarantula's tall black hat moving in the brush. Sometimes he would move into the clear and stand defiantly, watching the house. Even though Tarantula stood some distance from her window, Euphemia could feel his menace. She remembered his awful eyes as they bored into hers and then Matilda's that night of the shivaree. When she had thought about that moment since, she had decided it was as if Tarantula was making some kind of choice between her and Matilda. Toward midnight, the Indians moved away, leaving a dreadful silence behind.

The night seemed interminable, a long slow slide toward light. They kept the house dark, and Sarah and Euphemia, rifles ready, moved from one window to another, watching for any movement, listening for any sound, that would signal the presence of Tarantula and his band. Jean-Baptiste had withdrawn into himself, too ashamed to talk. Sarah told him to take up a position by the east window, and to his credit he remained there all night, watching for shadows in the moonlight. To pass the time, Sarah whispered to Euphemia about her plans for a music room and how maybe the piano from their home in Kentucky could be shipped to Texas. "I would like to hear music out here," she said, and sighed, her rifle across her knees. Within the little house in the middle of the wilderness there were dreams of Beethoven, while out in the darkness the Comanches butchered stolen meat.

When morning finally came, it appeared the Indians were gone. The horses out back were still. As soon as it was fully light, Sarah told Jean-Baptiste to go. "I don't want you in sight one minute longer."

"I can't just go!" he said. "They might still be out there!"

"Well, if you go, I admit, they may still be around and you might get shot. But if you stay, you'll be shot for certain." Euphemia had always marveled that the angrier Sarah grew, the more calm she became. There was no anger in her voice, yet Euphemia could see fury in her eyes. "So make your choice, Mr. Beauchamps," Sarah said. "Their bullets or mine."

Jean-Baptiste Beauchamps left Peach Creek within the hour, his work on the house unfinished, perhaps to return to the safety of the Loire, where in the château of Francis I he would never sense the dreadful silent tread of moccasins.

When Bartlett returned, he brought news that Comanches had raided the Lockhart place. They had killed two boys and had carried Matilda away. They had been picking mustang grapes when the Indians came. Matilda's sister, Drusilla, who was not taken away, said it had happened so quickly and she had been so frightened, she knew no other details.

Bartlett and the Texas Rangers Ben and Henry McCulloch organized a search for Matilda. After several weeks of tracking down renegade bands, they killed a number of Comanches but were never able to find the missing girl. When Euphemia would think of Matilda, and she did nearly every waking moment, she remembered how grown-up her friend was and she knew she had been taken to breed children to replace those who had died of the pox. She wondered if she had been taken by Tarantula. The attack on the Lockhart place had been only a few weeks after his band had appeared at Peach Creek. All the terrible stories about captives filled what Matilda had called the rooms of her mind. Girls skinned and boiled alive. Children butchered. For weeks the images tormented her dreams and she hoped her dear friend, who wanted to be a ballerina, was dead.

* * *

One morning, nearly a month after the disappearance of Matilda Lockhart, a letter from John Ashby arrived on the stage from New Orleans. The letter was dated the second of June. At last they were on their way home. Their ship was due to arrive at Matagorda in mid-June and from there it would be a 125-mile stage ride to Peach Creek. Bartlett calculated the voyage from New Orleans, with fair winds, could take as little as ten days. Then, allowing two or three days to arrange for a stagecoach, they'd make it to Victoria the first night, and then Cuero to spend the second night. They'd spend two more nights in inns along the road and then the seventh day they'd be in Peach Creek.

"So they could be here as early as the nineteenth of June."

"That's only ten days away!" Sarah said. Euphemia felt something heavy turn over in her abdomen. There was a tingling in her fingers, almost as if they were asleep, a feeling somewhere between small pain and pleasure.

Euphemia was standing in the road, as she had each day for nearly a week, imagining her family's stage coming over from the coast, when suddenly the image became real. First she heard the horses, moving fast, sensing the oats at the end of the road. Then she saw the yellow cloud of dust their hooves cast into the summer air. Then she saw the horses, emerging from the distance, growing larger, the coach swaying and lurching behind like a dirty animal chasing the horses along. Now, at last, there would be a real family. She would no longer be an orphan. She could feel her father's arms around her, the roughness of his face against hers, and the strength of his arms as he lifted her high and threw her into the air.

Euphemia watched the coach grow closer. She remembered those high-hearted moments when she was wrapped in her father's laughter and his arms. "We have survived," she thought. "The Ashbys have survived Santa Anna and the Comanches and all the worst things war and the wilderness can deliver. Now there will be family." She rushed to where the stage stopped beneath the Sam Houston Oak and waited for two strange girls to climb down to make room for Frances and Jane Isabella and her father.

Yet, except for the two strangers, the stagecoach was empty.
There was no tall man in a ruffled shirt with a black velvet suit
wearing red-topped boots and silver spurs. Just two strange
young ladies, covered with dust from the road, who could not
stop crying as they told how their father had died aboard ship for
hardly any reason at all. One moment he was fine, the next he
had terrible hiccoughs, then the next he was gone. They had
buried him at sea, in Matagorda Bay, fed by the waters of the
Lavaca River near where Euphemia's mother lay.

In the winter of 1839, the capital of the Republic of Texas had been moved to a new site on the Colorado River called Waterloo, a town that soon would be renamed Austin after the Father of Texas, Stephen F. Austin. Although it was already a rather large town, home to some nine hundred citizens, to the people of Peach Creek, Austin seemed terribly remote and distant. Now, as Christmas approached, Mirabeau Buonaparte Lamar and Sam Houston and all the representatives of the people suspended their political wars to return home to celebrate the birth of the Prince of Peace. It had been anything but peaceful in the new capital of the new Republic of Texas. The Texas Constitution limited the President of the Republic to one term, so when Houston's term as president had been up, Lamar had run against two other candidates, both of whom committed suicide during the campaign. When elected, Lamar increased the public debt, showed open hostility toward Mexico, and pursued an aggressive policy against the Indians. Houston and his backers were four-square on the opposite side of all these important issues and they looked forward to the elections of 1841, when Sam Houston would run again.

At Peach Creek, the families were intent on other things. Euphemia helped Sarah sew bright new holiday bunting for her tiny son Joel, born the previous summer. Jane Isabella gathered the unlikely ingredients for syllabub, a mixture of wine, eggs, milk, and spices, a Christmas libation for the ladies. Fannie, who preferred the more formal name of Frances but would be called Fannie the rest of her life, stayed away from the kitchen because, as she said, "Sarah's pipe smoke offends my sensibilities." Instead, she spent most of her time dipping snuff, with her little finger pointing skyward at what Euphemia felt was an impossible angle, and officiating at the morning and evening sessions of prayer she had instituted on the first day of her arrival.

Unlike her sisters Euphemia, Sarah, and Jane Isabella, who were slender, Fannie was rather stout. She rolled when she walked like a ship at sea. Jane Isabella was slender, even graceful. She was constantly concerned about decorum, insisting Euphemia should act more like a lady. Even though her newly arrived sisters were scornful of Euphemia's ability to ride and shoot, Euphemia could tell they were impressed when she pitched her Bowie knife so accurately it pierced an empty snuff can from twenty feet away.

Although her sisters' backgrounds were entirely different from her own, so refined and protected from the realities of the frontier, Euphemia sensed a growing respect building among them. She and her sisters seemed to complement each other, the way the left hand complemented the right. Perhaps, together, they could become whole, she thought.

The fifth sister, Mary, who had married old Mr. Smothers and had been with them on the Runaway Scrape, declined an invitation to spend Christmas at Peach Creek. Sarah had begged her to come be with the family and had done everything but make the day's ride to Mary's place on the Lavaca River and drag her away.

"It's because of Old Man Smothers," Jane Isabella said. "He won't let her come. I even think he locks the door at night."

"Problem is," Sarah said, "he didn't want a wife, he wanted a servant."

"Serves her right for running away like that," Fannie said.

"Well, I wish she could come," Euphemia said. "I sure do wish she could come."

As the guests began to arrive from the neighboring homesteads and were warmly welcomed by Bartlett and Sarah McClure, the girls could scarcely have imagined they would see a man shot dead before midnight and that Jane Isabella would vow to marry the killer.

The Christmas season on Peach Creek began with the terrible caterwaul of dying hogs. Although it was a necessary part of life, Euphemia hated the violence of the winter hog killing, the sticking and gutting and boiling. Every time there was a hog killing, all the best parts—the hams, the shoulders, the tenderloin—were saved for the family. The slaves were given what was left, such pieces as the tongue, ears, tail, feet and ankles, skin, stomach, and intestines.

"Isn't it amazing how they prefer those awful parts, chitlins and cracklins and all?" Jane Isabella said, as they watched the slaves divide the meat. Over the years, on so many homesteads and plantations, the slaves got the leavings or didn't eat meat at all. And so it was on this Christmas, when the great round of suppers, parties, and dances was in full swing. Euphemia again felt an almost physical pain in the clockworks of her conscience. Even though Leviticus and Tildy and the others were treated with kindness, what would Jesus say about holding people in bondage? Holding them in ignorance? Euphemia could see there was something terribly wrong.

Euphemia looked beyond the arriving guests to where Leviticus and the other slaves were cutting the Yule log for the parlor fireplace. The day was cold and the breathing of the men struggling with axe and saw formed a cloud of mist in the brittle air. It was as if the slaves were dancers frozen in a kind of nightmare ballet, their lives, their every motion, choreographed by others. And they couldn't run away to escape the cruelty because to run away was to always be hunted or fall victim to the Comanches, who hated Negroes as much as they hated white people. Euphemia grew angry as she heard Jane Isabella and Fannie speak disrespectfully to Tildy in voices that were sharp and mean. "I'll never have slaves," she told Jane Isabella, when Tildy was out of hearing. "It's wrong. If I live to be one hundred, I'll never have slaves in my house."

Jane Isabella looked up from her tub of syllabub and said, "You'll think differently when you grow up and have your own home. How could we get all the work done?"

Euphemia looked at the sister she had finally come to know and she wondered why they should be so different. It was as if they were born of separate parents, as if their minds were shaped by different worlds.

Euphemia loved Jane Isabella, admired her beauty and intelligence and the air of sophistication she wore like a graceful gossamer gown. At dinner, Jane Isabella could carry on a conversation about most anything and she would lace her language with words even Sarah didn't know. She always dressed as if she were on her way to the most important engagement of her life and she wore her fashionable outfits with the natural grace of a dancer. Yet, Euphemia often felt her sister lived only on the surface of her world. She didn't seem to see beneath the expected and the ordinary, where true but troubling things could be found. It almost seemed that school for women in Kentucky had refined away what was important, had prepared her for a world that was not real. It was as if Jane Isabella were a gifted actress cast in the wrong play. *Sometimes I think I'd be happier if I didn't think so much,* Euphemia sighed.

Christmas dinner at the McClures' was a feast for the senses. Beneath decorative festoons of wild holly and brilliant possum haw berries was a beautiful and bountiful banquet of stuffed turkey and wild duck, sweet potatoes and plum pudding, pies and cakes and sweetmeats, whiskey for the men and syllabub for the ladies. After dinner gifts were exchanged. There were exquisite handmade dolls and brightly painted rocking horses for the children. The slaves were tossed pennies and candies and compliments. Then, as the sun began to fall behind the oak trees, everyone went outside for the fireworks display.

In the womb of the night, a great fire had been set. Its flames flowed and leaped skyward and touched the skirts of darkness with shattered shards of light. It reminded Euphemia of the night Gonzales burned, when they had begun their flight from Santa Anna with the widows of the Alamo. There was something about the brightness of the fire that made the surrounding woods seem darker, more mysterious and primeval. Euphemia wondered if her friend Matilda Lockhart was alive, out there somewhere sitting before a fire like this, watching the swaying dancers in the flames.

The people gathered around the fire, laughing and singing, the firelight reflecting from their glasses of whiskey and from their eyes filled with the moisture of joyous celebration. Hog bladders from the last hog-killing time were brought from the smokehouse. The bladders had been filled with air, tightly tied, and hung up to dry. Now, the young people tied the air-filled bladders to sticks and with great ceremony they threw the bladders on the fire, where they exploded like the Twin Sisters cannons of San Jacinto. *What a long way we are from Bethlehem,* Euphemia thought. She couldn't chase the vague sense of sadness she always felt at times of celebration when everyone else seemed so happy.

Among Sarah and Bartlett's guests that night were Ben McCulloch and his younger brother Henry. Both had been involved in the search for Matilda Lockhart earlier in the year. Ben, who had once killed eighty bears in a single season, had come to Texas just in time to command a cannon at San Jacinto. Henry had joined him in a surveying partnership a year later.

Both men were slight of build, with light hair, blue eyes, and high intelligent foreheads. Jane Isabella confided to Euphemia that Henry McCulloch was what she most wanted for Christmas.

Having just returned from serving on the first Texas Congress to assemble at the new capital, the older McCulloch's mind and conversation were filled with political news. He talked about the battle for influence being waged between Sam Houston and his conservatives who wanted peace, and Lamar and his radical expansionists who pursued a more warlike course.

Politics and war seemed strange topics for a Christmas celebration and Euphemia was surprised the women expressed such strong, often harsh opinions. Someone reminded them that the little town of Walnut Creek, where the King family had settled, had just that summer been renamed Seguin, and an argument arose as to whether it honored the old patron Erasmos Seguin or the son Juan. Euphemia was shocked to hear a neighbor woman say: "I don't know why they would name their town after a Mexican. Why not after someone like Matthew Caldwell or Bartlett McClure or Ben McCulloch! We know what side they'll fight on when war with Mexico comes." *What a foolish woman,* Euphemia thought, but held her tongue. She knew that without Juan Seguin and his courage during the revolution, they might all be dead.

As the evening passed, Euphemia noticed that Henry McCulloch was constantly at Jane Isabella's side. After the fireworks, when the party agreed to move on to a neighbor's place for dancing and further revelry, Jane Isabella and Euphemia rode in Henry's wagon, the horses rushing through the darkness, the night gathering momentum like a runaway stage. When they arrived at the small log home, guests crowded into its single room. Some of the men took up instruments and the dancing began. Jane Isabella and Henry became a single whirling image, one body instead of two. They reminded Euphemia of china dancing figures cast together, joined forever. Fannie held herself somewhat aloof, as if she were serving notice to the frontier boys she was refusing their invitation to dance before it was even tendered.

Hardly had the first few tunes tumbled from the fiddles, when first one couple and then another stopped dancing and turned toward the door. Then the wail of the fiddles wound down and Euphemia could only hear the hard, fast breathing of the dancers. Standing unsteadily in the doorway were the two men. Although they were standing in shadow, Euphemia recognized them at once. Colonel Alonzo Sweitzer was obviously drunk and had his hat set at a fighting angle. He was partially supported by his friend Reuben Ross. In the new, strange, charged silence, Sweitzer called out Ben McCulloch's last name. It had the sound of a rifle shot.

Everyone in the room knew the story of the feud between Ben McCulloch and Colonel Sweitzer. When the Texas Republic had been founded, Ben McCulloch had become a candidate for Congress, representing the settlements of Gonzales, Cuero, and Walnut Springs. His opponent was Alonzo Sweitzer, a man of considerable refinement, educated in the East. Sweitzer had challenged McCulloch to a debate. He was certain that with his classical education he would have an advantage over the backwoods Indian fighter from Tennessee. Ben McCulloch, a man of action rather than of words, declined to debate.

A few days later, after Sweitzer had been drinking, he called McCulloch a coward and campaigned against sending a coward to Congress. The voters, by a wide margin, chose McCulloch. Within hours of Ben's victory, Sweitzer, again in his cups, announced with high melodrama that McCulloch was "a sneaking skulker," an insult that caused Ben to challenge Sweitzer to a duel. This time, Sweitzer backed down and Ben publicly called Sweitzer a black-hearted cowardly villain. Sweitzer sent his friend

Reuben Ross, an excellent shot, to duel McCulloch in his place. A meeting was arranged, rifles at forty paces. Ross fired and the bullet wounded McCulloch in the arm. Although Ben McCulloch had lost the duel, Sweitzer's honor had been far from restored. He was, in fact, humiliated.

All this was in the minds of the guests when the music stopped and the drunken Sweitzer said: "Well, Reuben, what a colorful place we've found. It seems we've happened onto a house of yellow dogs and scarlet women."

After a stillness as loud and shattering and alive as any Euphemia had ever heard, Ben McCulloch replied, "Ladies, if you will retire to the kitchen, we will protect you from further insult."

Henry McCulloch helped guide the women and children into the kitchen, a small separate building to the rear of the house. He closed the door and darkness black as blindness filled the room. Euphemia could hear Henry's footsteps fade from the door and muted voices arguing, rising and falling. Pounding footsteps again and the loud, drunken voice of Colonel Ross. "It's the Christmas season, a time of sharing. We only want to have a dance or two with the town harlots."

At that moment, the door to the kitchen was wrenched open and Euphemia was aware of the foul whiskey breath and the silhouette of Colonel Ross in the door. Behind him, in the light of the house, she could see Henry McCulloch raise his pistol and fire. She was amazed that fire actually came from the barrel of the gun, and she even thought she saw the bullet as it came directly toward where she stood. The explosion filled the room with dreadful sound, and Ross's body was thrown toward the crowd of women. He dragged them down as he fell. He died at their feet without uttering a word. Then there was silence again as the women disentangled themselves from the weight of the bleeding corpse. After the gunshot, the first words Euphemia heard were Jane Isabella's, whispered in her ear. "I'm going to marry that man," she said, and she removed Colonel Ross's lifeless arm from around her waist, rose, walked to Henry McCulloch's side, and took his hand in hers.

*   *   *

Euphemia Texas named her horse Saracen. Bartlett had purchased the horse as a Christmas gift from Senator Sterling Robertson, of Nashville on the Brazos, one of the finest judges of horseflesh in the republic. All his horses were named after characters in Sir Walter Scott's novels, including the great Arabian stallion Black Douglass. Robertson had called the horse Ivanhoe, but in memory of Sam Houston's fallen stallion, Euphemia changed his name. Saracen, like the horse after which he was named, was milk-white and stood nearly fourteen hands tall. He was beautifully formed with a long, graceful neck, a wide forehead, and eyes that Euphemia thought expressed all the wisdom of the world. She just knew there was an intelligence trapped within Saracen seeking release, and it was this inability to tell her what he knew and felt that made his eyes so sad.

Not long after the first Yule log had burned itself out and the women were beginning to plan their spring gardens, Euphemia and Saracen rode out past the wild orchards and beyond Big Elm Draw to the hill above Woman Hollerin' Creek where she often went to dream. It had been weeks since Comanches had been reported in the area, yet she felt just a touch of danger in the cold winter wind. But she knew no Indian pony was a match for Saracen. She moved down low over Saracen's neck and whispered for him to fly and he carried her beyond the hill above Woman Hollerin' Creek and high into the realm of fantasy. Euphemia imagined she and Saracen had won the top prize at the *Houston Telegraph and Texas Register* spring horse races and she had been honored at a ball the evening following the race. Everyone was there, even Juan Seguin and José Navarro, the two most elegant horsemen she knew. She danced with William King 'til dawn and then when she raced again the second day, she won again.

Although there was no race and no ball, only a sprint across the prairie and a wild ride after wild hogs along the bogs of Elm Slough, there was a prize. It was the joy of feeling the wind rush by and the power of the animal she rode and the freedom of submission to motion. *I wonder how much of life is in our minds,* she thought. *The race is imaginary, but the running is real.* Euphemia had always loved riding, ever since Sarah had lifted her into a saddle almost before she could walk. Neither Sarah nor Euphemia rode sidesaddle, as was customary for most ladies of the day. They rode astride, like men. "Only mermaids ride sidesaddle," Sarah had said more than once.

It was when she returned home to Peach Creek that winter day that Euphemia heard Matilda Lockhart might be alive. Euphemia was stunned. She laughed and cried and prayed that God would forgive her for ever wishing her dear friend dead. One emotion followed another, like waves against the shore. She was happy, then terrified that Matilda might have suffered the terrible things others had in the camps of the Comanches. Bartlett had just returned from San Antonio where Texas Rangers and three Comanche chiefs had spent several days negotiating a treaty. "The Comanches are in a vise," Bartlett explained. "They have the Apaches pressing them on the west, the settlers to the east. I think they want to relieve the pressure on the east so they can concentrate their warriors against the Apaches."

"What about Matilda?" Euphemia asked.

"The chiefs said they would sell us all their white women. They indicated there might be as many as fifteen. I think we can assume Matilda is among them."

Sarah was aghast. "Sell them! How can you buy or sell human beings?"

"It's not exactly unheard of," Euphemia said softly. She was surprised and relieved neither Sarah nor Bartlett caught her meaning.

One early morning in March, when the wild buffalo clover and primrose began to bloom, Jane Isabella, Fannie, the two boys, and the infant Joel were left with Mary on the Lavaca River. Euphemia, Sarah, and Bartlett began the long, hard ride to San Antonio. The chiefs had agreed to reconvene at the Council House where they would turn over all their captured women to the Rangers. Euphemia would stay at Juan Seguin's house on Commerce Street to await the possibility Matilda might be alive and would be released as promised by the Comanche chiefs.

In their two-horse wagon, Bartlett riding at their side and sometimes ahead, they crossed Elm Slough and then moved east toward the Old River Road that would take them the eighty miles westward to San Antonio. It was a great adventure for

Euphemia, the longest journey she had made since the Runaway Scrape. She especially loved the river crossings—Mr. Reece's ferry across the San Marcos and Mr. Dehill's ferry across the Guadalupe.

Mr. Dehill had spanned the Guadalupe with a cable, secured on both sides to deep-rooted cypress trees. As they boarded, the passengers paid their thirty-cent fare. Euphemia decided if she were a man she would operate a ferry service and become rich beyond measure. The water was swift and there was a sense of danger as the ferryman pulled the log raft across. The buggies and horses and slaves with their bundles rocked and swayed in the passing tide. Once across, they all struggled up the muddy slope onto the Old River Road, a trail cleared through the wilderness just wide enough for wagons to pass. The trees had been cut close to the ground, but the stumps remained and occasionally a wheel would climb a cypress or a blackjack stump. Then the wagon would lurch and Euphemia would imagine she was in a storm-tossed ship at sea.

The way west was a mosaic of beautiful yet constantly changing vistas. Along Burris Creek they passed through a dark thick woods of post oak and hickory and pecan. There were panthers in the shadows of that wood, she knew, and ring-tailed cats and wolves and bear. Then they would emerge from the woodland onto the wide, rolling plain, where God spread a blanket of rain lilies and widow's tears and bluebonnets across the sunlit prairie for their wagon to cross. Near Capote Peak, a lonely little mountain rising like a surprise from the flatland, she saw a small herd of deer. From a grassy meadow by Santa Clara Creek a flock of cardinals took wing, maybe a hundred or more, like a crimson wind above the grassland. Each creek they passed had a personality so individual Euphemia felt she would remember each forever—Tortugas, Polecat, Geronimo, Santa Clara, Cibolo. The Santa Clara was soft and feminine, while Cibolo Creek, with its steep banks and rocky bottom, was more like a man. Polecat Creek was a mean-spirited trickster and filled with quicksand and snakes. Geronimo Creek was clear and cool as the eyes of an angel. The Tortugas Creek scarred its bed with ripples of sand.

As they approached San Antonio, the woodlands gave way to

rolling slopes of chaparral and the tough little mesquite, a graceful tree that reminded Euphemia of a peach tree with thorns. They crossed the Salado Creek, then came to a rise and San Antonio lay before them, sleeping by its river, an oasis in a desert of chaparral under the spring sun. Out there, somewhere near, was her friend Matilda. What would she be like, she wondered, after a year with the Comanches?

Somehow Euphemia had expected San Antonio to be more impressive than she found it to be. In her mind she had pictured Seville or some Spanish city with great walls and towers and battlements. But the town was little more than a village of old adobe and reed thatch. Most of the people she saw at first were Mexicans, most of them descended from Indians converted by the fathers of the San José Mission. There was a certain lazy melancholy about the town. She had expected guitars and castanets. Instead she heard the bleating of sheep and the sad call of the San Fernando Cathedral bell and the song of wind in the cottonwoods along the river. Even the Alamo was a disappointment. A building already famous for so much rage and valor and sorrow should have towered above the earth like the walls of Jericho. Instead the ruined and broken walls were overgrown with vines and weeds.

They crossed the beautiful little San Antonio River, a stream clear as liquid blue crystal, before passing through neighborhoods of white plastered houses with bay windows and balconies. Bartlett told them these were the homes of Germans who had immigrated to the city. Euphemia was amazed how different they were from the blue and yellow adobe houses of the Mexicans and the American houses with their white picket fences. *How strange it is that people can be known by their houses,* she thought. *The German houses are solid and austere. The Mexican houses are covered with passionate colors and are surrounded by fences to keep their animals in. But the Americans build fences to keep animals out.*

The Council House, where the prisoners were to be traded for salt, whiskey, and guns, was a stone building adjoining the jail at the corner of the Main Plaza and Market Street. The courthouse complex, once known as the Casas Reales, was more than a century old. Euphemia quickly calculated the courthouse was older than almost anything she had ever seen, except, of course, the Sam Houston oak beside her house. She realized some of the buildings in San Antonio had been old even before the United States had become a country.

Soon two Comanche scouts arrived to inform the Rangers that the main body of Indians was on its way. The scouts rode horses painted with colorful designs, squares, circles, lightning patterns, and crimson imprints of the human hand. Along came a ragged assembly of women, children, old men, and warriors, as undisciplined a caravan as Euphemia could imagine. It was as if a whole village had suddenly decided to stop whatever they were doing and come to town on a holiday. There was about the parade a strange combination of menace and domesticity. The Indians made no sound as they walked; the children seemed transfixed by the alien world they were entering, neither afraid nor overly bold. People in the street stood still as stone as the Indians passed by. *If I were a painter,* Euphemia thought, *I'd capture this scene forever, two worlds passing, both in full flower.* She knew somehow this passing would never happen again. A young boy passed, not much older than Euphemia, and as their eyes touched she wondered how he would fare in the years to come. Euphemia had an unexplainable, almost overpowering urge to nod, to catch his attention, and with some gesture, indicate she recognized he existed, was alive and walking upon the earth God made.

Among the Comanches rode thirteen chiefs with their buffalo helmets and feathered finery. Towering among them, wearing his tall black hat, was Tarantula. Riding close behind, her arms around a warrior's waist, was Matilda Lockhart. She was alive.

As Tarantula and Matilda moved toward where Euphemia stood by the courthouse wall, she began to see how horribly her friend had changed. The initial elation she felt at seeing Matilda alive turned to something cold and dark and awful. At first, from a distance, all Euphemia could see was skin and hair and bones. Although Matilda sat erect on her horse, her eyes focused on some distant point in space or time. She was frail and emaciated and her hair was like an explosion of wet yarn clinging to her neck and shoulders. Then Euphemia could see that her arms and face were covered with burns and scars and sores. Euphemia felt ill and had to hold on to the wall to keep from falling, because as the procession passed close by, Euphemia could see that Matilda's nose was gone.

The day grew hot. The cottonwoods were still. The Comanche chiefs and Texas Rangers moved into the Council House with what remained of little Matilda. The main body of Indians, including the women and children, settled down in the courthouse yard as if it were their own and they were going to camp for the summer. A company of troops remained outside on guard. At the gates, the people of San Antonio gathered to see the ferocious tribe that had walked peacefully into their midst. Boys climbed the walls and into trees to see their enemy in repose. Soon, the Indian boys were shooting arrows at rocks and then at coins placed as targets by some of the Americans. One of them was the one Euphemia had seen and been so strangely attracted to earlier. She wondered if he had known Matilda and if he had been involved in her torture.

Euphemia was numb. The thought of confronting Matilda, which had filled her with such joy before, now consumed her with dread. What could she say? What could she possibly say? And what if she would faint or get sick at the sight of the poor disfigured girl? Euphemia was terribly ashamed and she wanted to run from the courthouse and ride away from this world of violence, where little girls' noses were burned off and where people were unspeakably cruel to each other. She would pack her things and ride with Saracen to a better world, maybe to New Orleans, where she would enter a convent to pray for the perfectibility of the human heart.

Soon the heat of the sun pushed people down from the walls and trees, and a stillness settled on the courtyard. The Indians and the Texans waited, while inside the Council House the chiefs and Rangers negotiated. Euphemia wondered what kind of negotiations they could possibly be. How could salt, guns, and whiskey take away Matilda's scars? Then, as Euphemia was beginning to think the day would last forever, there was a sound like pumpkins dropping from a wagon. Soft explosions coming from within the adobe walls of the Council House. Then she heard muted shouts. Euphemia looked into the eyes of a nearby Indian woman holding a child, and she saw the fear blossom there like a poison flower. She and the woman realized, at the same time, the sounds that now grew louder were rifle fire and war whoops.

Immediately, the Comanches in the courtyard, shocked, surprised, and confused, rose like startled sparrows to scatter in all directions. Some attacked the soldiers outside with knives and others rushed through the gates and out into the city. A few chiefs stormed out through the doors of the Council House and were shot as they ran. The Indians fled through the streets, between houses, pursued by Rangers and troops. The panicked guards in the courtyard fired into the crowd at the escaping Comanches, killing both Indians and whites. Screaming people were running first one way and suddenly the other. Those trapped in the courtyard rushed to the gates, where some were crushed in the press of bodies. The air was filled with terror and the smell of gunpowder. Euphemia saw a huge Negro woman threatened by an Indian making his escape toward the river. She had gathered a covey of white children beneath her skirts, then, raising a heavy stone above her head, she hurled it at the approaching Indian, who dodged and hurried on. A number of Indians escaped into a small stone kitchen house. After it was set on fire, the Indians ran from the flames through smoke and were shot. Euphemia stood transfixed, watching the massacre as if it were the end of the world. Swiftly Bartlett lifted her into his arms and she was soon carried from harm's way.

Later Euphemia would hear that sixty-five Comanches had come to San Antonio that day. Twelve chiefs, eighteen warriors, three women, and two children were killed. Twenty-seven women and children and old men were taken prisoner. Six Texans were killed. Three Indians escaped. Tarantula was not among the dead or among those locked away in the old stone jail. Matilda Lockhart was free. All this, Euphemia thought, for a little girl who wanted to be a dancer.

"It was a thing destined to happen," Bartlett said, seeking to explain the massacre to the family and to himself. "There was so much hatred in that Council House. I tried. But there was noth-

ing I could do." Bartlett told them the Indians had failed to bring
in all their white prisoners, as agreed. The Indians were then told
some of their chiefs would be held until all the white captives
were brought in. The Indians objected. "I don't really know how
it started. There was little Matilda right there before us. Someone
just couldn't control their anger at what they saw. At what the
Indians had done to her. A soldier fired. It just began."

"I want to go home," Euphemia said that night, as Sarah
mended a skirt torn in the flight from the Council House.

"You must first see Matilda," Sarah replied. "She's your
friend."

"I can't face her! I don't know why, but I'm afraid. I know
it's wrong, but I can't. After seeing her with them, I just can't."

Sarah's needle paused. She put her sewing down, wiped a tear
from Euphemia's cheek, and took her two hands in her own. "A
bird can't fly so far its tail won't follow," she said. "If you leave
before seeing your friend, the hurt of that will follow you the rest
of your life. Every time you're alone with your thoughts, maybe
even years from now, you'll remember you ran away from something important. And in Matilda's quiet times—and she will have
many in the years to come—what will she think of you?"

"It could have been me," Euphemia whispered.

Sarah picked up her sewing again. "But it wasn't you, Phemie.
So thank God and then go do what's right."

After Matilda had been questioned by the Rangers, she had
been taken to the home of a local doctor. He had tended her
burns, given her a thorough physical examination, and put her to
bed. Euphemia moved to the closed bedroom door, pushed it
open, and passed through. Matilda was in bed, covered by a sheet,
her face turned to the wall. Euphemia moved to her side, stood
looking down at the pitifully diminished form beneath the sheet,
gently sat down on the edge of the bed. "It's Phemie," she said.
There was no answer. From the jail came the wailing of Comanche widows mourning their dead.

For a long time, Euphemia sat looking at the girl in the bed,
waiting for some response, some sign of recognition. Quietly she
took off her shoes, slipped beneath the sheet, and took Matilda in

her arms. The warmth reminded her of Little Johnny and how they would lie together like spoons in a drawer before he died in her arms that night so long ago. Her hands touched Matilda's scars. They felt like walnuts and some like the cord used to tie cotton bales, hard and mean. At last Matilda turned and they held each other very close and they both began to cry. They cried for a long time and then, very quietly, Matilda began to whisper. "I could never sleep. They would wake me by putting hot coals in my nose or touching my breasts with heated arrows."

"Shhh, don't talk," Euphemia said. But words held inside too long came rushing out, like steam escaping a boiling pot.

"I was the chief's woman, his breeding animal. They didn't kill me because he wanted another son and I was good at herding their sheep. Maybe I was an amusing pastime. They liked me because I wouldn't plead and grovel and because I hated them so completely. Some of the children who cried they carved to pieces, a little at a time. It would take days for their screams to end. Sometimes they cut off the bottoms of their feet and made them walk until they died. Some they roasted alive. But I wouldn't cry. So I was his woman and his animal. And I'll always be his woman and his animal 'til I die."

"You can sleep now," Euphemia said.

Matilda began to cry again. Between sobs she said, "I couldn't cry before because they would have killed me. Now I don't think I can ever stop." Euphemia held Matilda, kissed away the tears that flowed downward across her scarred face, and held her close. Hours later, the doctor came and took Euphemia away.

In May, a few weeks after Euphemia and the McClures had returned to Peach Creek, the Great Comanche Raid of 1840 began. A war party of one thousand warriors moved through the wilderness between the San Marcos and Guadalupe Rivers on the west and the Colorado on the east. In an effort to avenge the death of their chiefs in the Council House massacre, the Comanches and their allies—Cherokees, Pawnees, Kickapoos, and renegade Mexicans—swept from the Hill Country in a huge 300-mile swath southward toward the Mexican border.

For a few days, the Indians moved unnoticed. Then, as they

attacked travelers and isolated homesteads over and over, their movements were discovered and once again the people of the Republic prepared for war. Captain Ben McCulloch assumed command of the force that gathered at Big Hill just beyond the McClure land, the rise where Euphemia and Saracen often rode to enjoy the view from the highest place Euphemia had ever been. It was here that Euphemia had decided there was something magic about mountains. The Indians were said to believe the high places of earth were holy and it was in the mountains they held their vision quests. Maybe Big Hill was closer to God and that's why she was drawn to its heights, even though it was merely a rise in the endless solitudes of the prairie.

Now the Texans gathered at what some called McClure's Hill to renew the seemingly endless round of killing that was so much a part of life on the frontier. McCulloch's force was comprised of one hundred men. In all, some six hundred Rangers and armed settlers would set out to subdue the Comanches and their allies. From her window at Peach Creek, Euphemia could see their figures moving in the distance. As she watched the men of Gonzales and Lavaca set up camp for the night on her special hill, she thought again about riding away with Saracen to a convent, away from killing and hate. She wondered what kind of rules they had about keeping horses in the holy orders of New Orleans.

Once again, the house at Peach Creek seemed empty. In fact, houses throughout Texas were filled with the strange and melancholy absence of men. Sarah seemed angry as she prepared the house for siege. "Why is it men always have to go off to war?" she muttered. "They go off and we stay here where the hard part is."

Euphemia helped the slaves bring kegs of water in from the creek, water both for drinking and for fighting fires that flaming arrows might kindle. They brought in dried meat from the smokehouse, dried corn from the crib. Sarah checked the iron hinges on the shutters to make sure they had not rusted through and could be closed against arrows and spears. She and Euphemia cleaned the rifles and pistols, molded bullets, sharpened knives, and laid out a store of powder and ammunition where it could be reached at a moment's notice. Euphemia was amazed at their calm. She decided they prepared for war with the same quiet confidence they prepared their gardens in the spring. When she mentioned her observation to Sarah, her sister agreed. "If it isn't the Comanches, it's the Mexicans," she said. "Going to war is so common, we've learned to say goodbye without tears. It's like Bartlett was going out to hunt wild hog."

Early the next day, Euphemia rode to Big Hill with some dried fruit Sarah had prepared for the expedition. There she learned of the attack on Victoria, a settlement to the south only a day's ride away. The Indians had surrounded the town and had burned and robbed houses and stolen some 1,500 horses and mules. The rider who brought news of the Victoria attack reported that Mrs. Cyrus Crosby, a granddaughter of Daniel Boone, had been captured, and when her child had cried it had been speared before her eyes. Euphemia thought of Matilda.

Then, the men were gone. Bartlett and a small force headed for the Lavaca River settlements to make sure Fannie, Jane Isabella, and the others were safe. McCulloch and his men picked up the trail of a war party heading south with about a half-day's lead. Euphemia and Sarah were alone with the slaves and their guns and their thoughts. Sarah opened a shuttered window and peered out toward the creek. She said: "We pride ourselves on conquering, on taming the wilderness. But I'm not sure the wilderness isn't winning. We're not civilizing this place. It's making us more savage."

The Comanches arrived at high noon. The band had broken from the main force and circled back to Peach Creek. Their horses cast no shadows. They came from the creek bottom boldly, perhaps thirty riders, moving fast, bright ribbons and calicoes woven into their horses' tails, streaming like regimental colors behind them as they rode toward the unfinished frame skeleton of Sarah's new house. Several of the Comanches waved cigars in the air. Others were draped in yards of cloth or coats plundered from nearby Linneville homes. Another rider exploded from the forest dragging a featherbed with holes cut in the ticking. Each time feathers would fly, the Indians would yell and laugh and attack the featherbed with their lances.

"Oh, God," Sarah said from the window. "They've got Tildy."

A mounted Indian dragged the slave girl into view. She was struggling against a rope tied around her neck. She would run behind the horse for a few feet before falling, then twist and drag along the ground until she could fight to her feet again. They took her to the big house and tied her arms to one of the beams which had been so carefully carved by Jean-Baptiste Beauchamps and his workers, and then tightened the rope so that her feet barely touched the ground.

"They're within range," Euphemia said.

"Don't fire. They're too many. Just wait and we'll see which way the cat jumps."

Soon cattle were driven to where the Indians had gathered at the new house. Some of the Comanches had climbed up into the beams and were silhouetted against the radiant cloudless summer sky. They tied the front legs of a calf together so they could lift and suspend it from the beam next to Tildy. Its howls and bawling seemed almost human. Then the Indians stepped back from the calf, pacing off distance, and with much yelling and posturing they turned and let their arrows fly. The calf grew silent, twisted, and was still, the feathered shafts of arrows pointing toward its heart. Now only Tildy's screams could be heard. The Indians moved to the calf and slit its body with their knives. Entrails slid to the ground at Tildy's feet. The Comanches began pacing back from the slave girl and the dead calf, selecting new arrows from their quivers as they prepared for another round of target practice.

Sarah moved from the window. "Stay here, Phemie. Here's what you've got to do." Sarah placed both her hands on Euphemia's shoulders and looked into her eyes. "I'm gonna go get Tildy. I want you to take the rifle and move to the door where you've got a good shot. If things go badly, I want you to shoot Tildy and next shoot me. After that you've got to take the pistol and kill yourself." Euphemia was shocked that Sarah could say such unspeakable things with so little emotion. "I'm sorry, Phemie. Just remember Matilda and do what you have to do." Sarah hugged her quickly, then was gone.

Sarah moved from the door, stepping out into plain view of the Comanches. The two pistols strapped to her waist remained in their holsters. She shouted once to attract their attention and began walking toward Tildy. For a moment, the Indians watched in amazement as Sarah walked toward them. The Comanches began to laugh and a boisterous discussion erupted, with much pointing and gesturing. Sarah continued to walk, as if she were on a Sunday stroll. One of the Indians drew an arrow from his quiver and took aim—the arrow flew and Sarah fell to the ground. Euphemia knew Sarah was dead and the world had ended. But Sarah moved, pulled herself erect, and limped forward again, an arrow in the flesh of her leg.

When she rose, the Indians made a sound, not unlike a kind of song, almost gentle, a plural expression of wonder. Again they fell silent, as if Sarah's motion forward toward certain death had woven a spell or reminded them of something noble deep in their mythology. She walked like a person dragging a stone with her foot, always forward toward Tildy. Soon she was within the circle of Comanches, moving slowly, defiantly, painfully toward the slave girl. The Indians remained silent. Just as she reached the girl, she stumbled, fell, lay still, and the spell was broken.

The Comanches howled and rushed forward. Roughly, she was stripped of her guns, tied, and suspended from the beam next to Tildy. As the Indians stepped back to their firing line, it was apparent to Euphemia what would happen next. But what wasn't so apparent in those lightning-quick moments was what Euphemia should do. She surveyed the options. She could rush outside to Sarah's aid only to be killed or captured or tortured like Matilda Lockhart. She could try to run and hide in the creek bed. She could stay to defend the house and kill as many Indians as she could. Or she could obey Sarah and do the unthinkable. It was a mental process that took no more than a few agonizing seconds. She picked up the rifle, moved through the door into the harsh shadowless light of noon. There was a ringing in her ears, like great bells. She would have been afraid except for her rage and an unfathomable sorrow. Then, as she raised the rifle, something incredible happened.

He came from the forest, a figure so large, so menacing, he

seemed someone imagined in a nightmare. Even from a distance Euphemia could see the canyon scars which marked his face under his tall black silk hat. He rode straight to where Tildy and Sarah were hanging. As he came forward the other Comanches parted. He held up his hand and they grew silent. He dismounted and as he walked toward Sarah he drew a knife not unlike the one Jim Bowie had carried when he visited Peach Creek before the Alamo. The sun caught the edge of the blade and hurled a sharp piece of light back into the sky. Tarantula looked back at the house once, stepped forward, raised his knife, and cut Sarah down. He lowered her to the ground and with one swift, power- ful movement, he pulled the arrow through her leg. And then, more slowly, he bound the wound with mistletoe and crushed mescal. When the leg was bound, he stood, mounted his horse, and signaled the others, and Tarantula and the Comanches turned to ride away. He looked back at Euphemia once, held her eyes for a long strange moment, and he was gone.

On the afternoon of August 15, 1840, the women of Peach Creek watched Ben and Henry McCulloch, Bartlett McClure, and the men of Gonzales ride back from one of the greatest Indian battles of the western frontier. Over a thousand warriors had been engaged at Plum Creek, some forty miles to the north. Eighty Comanche chiefs and warriors had been killed in a crushing defeat. Never again would the Comanches pose a major threat to the towns and settlements of central Texas. Now, two days after the battle, the men returned, crossed the creek and the parched midsummer fields, passed the Sam Houston Oak, and moved into the yard. There did not seem to be much joy in their victory, Euphemia thought. Where were the waving banners and the songs of triumph?

Sarah and Euphemia rushed outside and Bartlett was soon in their arms, his clothes covered with a mixture of blood and dirt. He seemed exhausted. "I don't ever want to do this again," he said. "I'm through with killing." Euphemia wondered what awful things he had seen or done to make victory so hollow.

Only one Texan was killed. Among the two dozen wounded was Henry McCulloch. By nightfall, the McClure house at Peach Creek, which had always served as an inn for travelers through central Texas, had the appearance of a field hospital. As the men returned, wounds hurriedly tended at the battle site were freshly washed in the clean water of Peach Creek. Bandages were changed using strips from Sarah's bedding. Some of the men wore clothing so torn by battle that Bartlett's wardrobe was raided and depleted.

Among the returnees was a Russian physician named Dr. Weideman, who had been sent to Texas on a scientific expedition by the Tsar. He had interrupted his scholarly pursuits to fight the Comanches. Now he changed the dressing on Henry's wounds, which he claimed were not serious and for which he prescribed Brazos Tonic, a concoction containing opium and whiskey, believed to prevent complications such as "chronic ague or enlargement of the spleen."

Dr. Weideman also treated the arrow wound in Sarah's calf. It was swollen, slightly discolored, and hot to the touch. "I'm afraid you'll never be able to dance a gavotte," he said, as he prepared a hot poultice of cornmeal and chewed tobacco. Then, from his leather kit, Dr. Weideman removed his dreaded scarifactor, a small box containing twelve spring-loaded blades, used for bleeding. After Sarah's skin had been washed with milk, Dr. Weideman placed the box just above the elbow and tripped the spring. The blades pierced a vein and a dark thread of blood began to flow. "Hold this cup to catch the blood," Dr. Weideman told Euphemia. "I have something for you to see."

In a moment, Dr. Weideman returned with a large leather valise that matched his doctor's bag. "Now, ladies and gentlemen," he said, "for years I have been exceedingly anxious to secure such specimens as these. And I have you gentlemen to thank for the opportunity. Without your victory at Plum Creek, I couldn't have obtained these magnificent specimens." Then he opened the valise and showed the contents all around. Euphemia was stunned and then sickened when she saw the valise contained two severed Indian heads. "I also selected two entire bodies, one male and one female, which I have boiled and shall preserve as skeletons."

Leaning heavily on Euphemia's shoulder, Sarah pulled herself to her feet. "Dr. Weideman, I think your talents are needed elsewhere."

"But madam, I haven't finished your bleeding."

"Yes, you have, Doctor." Sarah took the cup of blood from Euphemia's hand and poured it into Dr. Weideman's physician's bag. "Here's some more blood to take back to the Tsar," she said. "Now, take your trophies and get out!"

The silence Dr. Weideman's departure left in the room was heavy and oppressive. "What a sad bunch we are," Sarah said. "All shot up and sick. Sick of body and sick of heart. People kill-

ing and people dying and to top it off we have to suffer that Tsar-
ist maniac!"

Bartlett moved to Sarah's side and eased her into a chair.
"Things will change," he said. "I promise."

That night, when the house was still, Euphemia could hear
Sarah and Bartlett talking in their room below the sleeping loft.
She didn't try to listen, as the two lay together in their bed. The
voices just came uninvited to her ears. Sarah told Bartlett about
the Comanche raid on their house and Euphemia thought she was
much less brave in the telling than in the event itself. Then
Bartlett told how bravely the Indians had fought and how, in the
heat of battle, some of his men began to mutilate the Indians.
"They were taking scalps. I saw one young boy from Walnut
Creek. Couldn't have been over fifteen. He was in a kind of rage.
He killed this Indian up close, with a knife, and then he began to
take his scalp. Only he didn't know how. He just kept hacking
away, but he was makin' an awful mess of it. Then I saw all our
neighbors, good people, keep on killing even though the Indians
were beaten and ..." Bartlett sighed and was silent.

"I know," Sarah said.

Five days after Dr. Weideman left Texas with his "magnificent
specimens," Jane Isabella Ashby and Henry McCulloch were
married. A few months earlier, a jury had found him innocent in
the murder trial leading from his Christmas night shooting of
Colonel Reuben Ross. "He was saved from the Comanches and
saved from the gallows," Jane Isabella said, "but no force on earth
could save him from me."

The trial had become more of a social event than a murder
trial. It filled the Gonzales County District Court to overflowing.
It also became a stage for the dramatic and highly visible courtship between the defendant and the defense's star witness. Jane Isabella's testimony was a highlight of the trial. She described the
terrible events of that Christmas night with clarity and what
Euphemia thought was just the right balance of outrage and hu-
mility, especially when she described the "liquor-laden breath of
that beast who was insulting the ladies." The jury returned a
unanimous verdict of "not guilty" and Henry and Jane Isabella's

love was sealed by the sound of Judge Hemphill's gavel as the jury was dismissed.

Not long after the wedding at Peach Creek, Euphemia and her family were invited to the San Geronimo Ranch of Don José and Margarita Navarro. The *estancia* was famous throughout central Texas for its annual fandangos, gala social gatherings with music and dancing long into the early morning hours.

Euphemia was fascinated by José Antonio Navarro. As she urged Saracen through the bluebonnets toward the *estancia,* she pictured the imposing man in her mind. He had pure white hair swept back from his wide forehead, ending in rich, full curls at his collar. Don José was slight of build, yet his presence completely filled any room he entered. Although he treated Euphemia with courtesy and kindness, always showing interest in her activities and thoughts, his expression rarely changed from its mask of melancholy. His eyes were Oriental and mysterious and sad, as if he were mourning for a lost child or a lost world. He was a living, breathing mystery and the more Euphemia learned about him, the more mysterious he became.

From Bartlett she had learned Navarro was the son of a Corsican adventurer, a former colonel in the Spanish army, who had come to the new world to search for gold and silver in the mines of Chihuahua. He had then resigned his commission and married Josepha Ruiz, a beautiful girl of noble descent. The son, José Antonio, had become a lawyer, scholar, and statesman and a great friend of Stephen F. Austin, the Father of Texas. He was one of the three Mexicans who signed the Texas Declaration of Independence in 1836. The odd thing that fascinated Euphemia most was his preference for the color white. She had often seen him dressed all in white, riding a white horse, with his white hair flying in the wind. No wonder the families who lived on his land called him "the White Dove."

Euphemia could hear the music from some distance. They came to a rise and there below, among mesquite and Osage orange, the white adobe walls of the *estancia* rose from the bank of Geronimo Creek. The *hacienda* was large and low, embracing the earth with its cool, clean walls of silver and chalk. Beyond the walls were the smaller houses of the families under Don José's protection, small fields of corn, and corrals for stock, and beyond were lands that seemed to reach to the ends of the earth. Bartlett had told Euphemia Don José was probably the largest landholder in Texas. He had ranches in five counties and his *estancia* on the Geronimo was home to fifteen families who worked the six hundred horses and five thousand head of cattle.

At the center of the Navarro *hacienda* was a large, shaded court where Euphemia could see people already gathered. Among them the silvery figure of Don José moved like a ghost among his guests. She passed by a great bell suspended from a wooden frame, through a tall archway, out of the shimmering heat into the cool, civilized world of the White Dove.

The house of Margarita and Don José had always been a sanctuary to Euphemia. Everything within was smooth and old and enduring. It was a house that would surely last forever. There was a richness and elegance about the rooms, yet everything within them was simple, furnishings woven or carved from wood or shaped from clay or fashioned from the abundant gifts of the earth. Yet, in this house these simple things seemed lifted like treasures above the ordinary things that surrounded Euphemia's life.

The Navarros and Juan Seguin's family were among a constellation of respected and influential Mexican families who had been granted great estates in the wilderness lands of northern Mexico. Many of these families had made their homes in these far outposts of the Mexican empire for a hundred years or more. Many, such as Navarro and Seguin, served as legislators in the Mexican government. They were loyal citizens, who loved their motherland, yet had often fought for reforms. Juan Seguin and his father had called for a provisional government to replace Santa Anna long before the Anglos even thought of rebelling. It was men like Navarro and Seguin who had actually fired the revolutionary spirit. Would their loyalty be with their mother country to the distant south or here, in Texas, where their roots had been planted and their children had been raised? It was never in doubt. Nearly all of the *rancho* families had cast their fortunes with Sam Houston and the Texans. Navarro was a true hero of the Revolution.

As the evening progressed, Euphemia became aware of a strange undercurrent flowing unseen among the guests. There were hushed conversations in the intervals between dances and a kind of forced conviviality. The talk centered on her friend Juan Seguin: his ranch had been attacked, his cattle killed, his property destroyed, and his family threatened.

"Surely it was the work of vandals," Sarah insisted.

Don José shook his head. "No. I know there is an organized attempt to drive Juan and his family out of the country. Ever since he was elected Mayor of San Antonio, vigilantes have been killing his cattle. Rumors have been planted that he's a spy for Santa Anna."

"How can that be?" Sarah wanted to know. "How can they say things like that?"

"There's a new kind of society evolving in Texas," Bartlett answered. "Thousands of newcomers are flooding into the Republic, people who weren't here when Juan was fighting by our side in the Revolution. And now that Mexico is rattling her saber again, poised for a new invasion of Texas, the newcomers mistrust any Mexican, even those Tejanos who've lived in Texas all their lives and fought for independence."

"But why Juan Seguin? Why not the others?"

"I feel the mistrust and resentment, too," Don José said. "I think Juan is more vulnerable. He's so different . . ."

Sarah picked up his thought. "What you mean to say is he's resented because he's educated, sophisticated, powerful. He has all the qualities his opponents lack. They're just jealous because he's the kind of man they can never be."

"Perhaps," Don José said. "But it's serious. The hatred is real and Juan is very sensitive. San Antonio is essentially a Mexican city in the center of Texas. Juan has resisted a takeover by the newcomers. He represents the Tejanos old guard with its ties to Mexico. The Anglos have a new vision for the old city. They simply want him out."

"What will he do?" Sarah asked.

"What can he do?" Don José asked in turn.

"I know Juan Seguin," Bartlett said. "He'll fight back. And I wouldn't want to be in his way when he does."

Later in the evening, when Euphemia was alone with Jane Isabella, she was rocked by her sister's opinion of the Seguin situation. "Isn't it exciting?" Jane Isabella said. "Juan Seguin, a traitor."

"A what?" Euphemia almost shouted.

"Well, that's what Ben and Henry say. They say he's a Mexican spy. After all, he is a Mexican and Mexico is our enemy. It's just simple logic."

Euphemia could no longer hold her tongue, the words came spilling out, breathlessly, out of control. "You don't know Juan Seguin! None of you do. You were safely in some finishing school and your husband was back East somewhere while Juan was fighting to free this country from Mexican tyranny!"

"I didn't mean ..." Jane Isabella began.

"Well, don't say what you don't mean. I was there. I know Juan Seguin. Ask Henry McCulloch where he was when Juan Seguin returned to the Alamo after the war to bury the remains of the dead heroes."

The sisters stood looking into each other's eyes. Then Jane Isabella looked away. "You shouldn't yell at me like that," she said.

"You shouldn't spread lies," Euphemia answered, and she turned to walk back into the beating heart of the fandango.

Euphemia was so angry at the sentiment expressed against Juan Seguin that she decided to become a spy herself. At first, as she moved among the guests, listening to the conversations, it was a game. But then she realized the people invited to the Navarro home were some of the most important people in Texas. These were the people whose actions created the ebb and flow of political power, whose lives shaped the times. Maybe she could gather information Juan Seguin might use against his accusers. She learned that Don José had wanted this year's fandango to be particularly festive, because he had been assigned a difficult mission by President Lamar. Accompanied by a group of teamsters, traders, and adventurers, he would leave the next week for Santa Fe. Officially, it was a trade mission. The real motive, however, was to persuade the people of Santa Fe to renounce Mexican authority and join forces with Texas.

It would be a dangerous mission, Euphemia learned. The

country between San Antonio and Santa Fe was largely unex-
plored. There were few water holes, many hostile Indians, and
Mexican army units were rumored to be patrolling the area. As
she passed another group, she heard some women talking about
the time Santa Anna had been a guest in Margarita Navarro's
home. Euphemia could tell from the texture of the whispers and
the women's expressions that something memorable had happened. But when she drew near, there was a pause, as if what they
had to say was not meant for a young girl's ears.

As the evening grew late and the guests began to leave,
Euphemia realized she hadn't learned anything Juan Seguin
would find useful. Her career as a spy might have flowered had
she not fallen asleep among the Navarro children in a room filled
with moonlight and the echo of guitars. Don José had carried her
into the bedroom himself and had said goodnight. His voice was
velvet, his eyes, as always, sad. It was the last time she would see
the White Dove before he was cast into Santa Anna's dungeon.

Once again Euphemia and Sarah rode toward Geronimo
Creek. More than three months had passed since the fandango.
Nothing seemed changed. The Navarro sheep still grazed like
clouds in grass turning brown in the dry summer sun, just as they
had when she had last passed by on Saracen. The land still
reached to far horizons made indistinct, almost dreamlike, by
shimmering heat and mirage. The six Navarro children were gathered beneath the mesquite and Osage orange shading the patio
listening to a tutor describe in three languages the world beyond
their land. The stone and adobe house and the cool courtyard
looked as if they were an actual extension of the earth, an old but
living thing that had been there since time began.

As she looped Saracen's reins around the branch of a mesquite
tree, Euphemia thought about how central the Navarros and the
other Tejano families were to the spirit of Texas, how very much
they belonged. It was terribly wrong that Juan Seguin was being
driven away by fools and thieves while Don José Navarro had
been thrown in prison by a dictator.

Margarita Navarro had asked Sarah to help her compose a letter to the dictator Santa Anna. Euphemia remembered the last let-

ter Sarah had written the general, threatening to hunt him down and feed him to the pigs if he were to burn her house. *How small the world is,* Euphemia thought. The President of Mexico had been in the Navarro homes and in the house at Peach Creek. He had received a letter from Sarah and now another from Margarita Navarro. Yet this time the letter was not a threat, it was a plea. A plea to spare the life of the White Dove, who was chained in the depths of Mexico's darkest dungeon.

The Santa Fe expedition had gone terribly wrong. As the group had approached the city, they had been taken prisoner by Mexican troops and marched to Veracruz fortress. Navarro was confined to the terrible dungeons of San Juan de Ulloa. On special orders from Santa Anna, he was chained to an iron ring in the floor of his cell. Most of the Santa Fe prisoners were released and returned with news of Navarro's fate. Because Santa Anna considered Navarro's signing of the Texas Declaration of Independence an act of treason, he condemned Don José to death. However, he commuted the sentence to life imprisonment. Santa Anna offered amnesty if Don José would renounce Texas. Navarro refused and was again chained to the cell floor.

The basic draft of the letter had been written by a lawyer, but Margarita knew Santa Anna personally, had entertained him in her house, and was aware of his enormous ego. The two women rephrased the letter to appeal to his vanity. Euphemia thought it sounded a touch flowery. Surely a man who possessed the ability to achieve such absolute power, not once but several times, would see through such flattery.

"How does this sound?" Margarita read: " 'What humane act could be impossible for Your Excellency? Happily, the whole nation has exalted Your Excellency to the highest rank of power and the voice of Your Excellency is omnipotent. Why, then, should we not hope to be heard and to be favored? We believe that when the great and powerful bring content and happiness to those in distress, then they themselves experience their happiest moments and can proudly reflect upon their dominion. The many public and generous acts of the incomparable heart of Your Excellency assure us that Your Excellency acts on principles.' "

"Well," Sarah said, "it makes me sick."

"But he really believes this kind of adoration. He believes he's loved by the people."

"How about this," Sarah offered. "If you grant our petition, we would praise forever Your Excellency. And if you don't, we'll hunt you down and feed you to the pigs."

"Sarah! This is very serious," Euphemia admonished.

"So am I, Phemie," Sarah answered. "Deadly serious. There are two graves behind my house. Santa Anna killed my children just as surely as if he had done it with his own hand."

"Do you think the letter will do any good?" Euphemia was doubtful.

"There's always been a rivalry between Santa Anna and our family," Margarita answered. "I think Santa Anna has always felt threatened by the prestige of Don José and the Navarros. And especially by my family, the Garzas. And he remembers that time when he was asked to leave our house."

"What did he do?" Euphemia asked.

"Nothing that would surprise you. He made improper advances. Something you would expect of such a man. Now he has his old adversary in his power. He has what he wants. And at last he has a Garza woman groveling at his feet, writing this humiliating letter. After all these years, he finally has a Garza woman in his power."

"But he doesn't really," Sarah said.

"Of course not," Margarita said, as she signed the letter with a flourish. "But for the moment he does have Don José in prison. And I'll do whatever I have to do to get him out."

In the spring of 1841, Anglo settlers came flooding into the frontier along the Guadalupe River. Euphemia could see the country changing. The old *rancho* culture of the Navarros and Seguins was being forced out by the land-hungry immigrants from the east. Farmers, storekeepers, laborers, adventurers, planters plagued by worn-out land and potential bankruptcy moved west in legions in search of the prosperity that had evaded them in the East. Driven from the heartland by the Panic of 1837 and the promise of cheap land and a new life, the immigrants brought with them cotton seeds and slaves and dreams of a new order.

Navarro was in a Mexican prison and Seguin was fighting a losing battle against vigilantes and economic ruin. He had invested in land deeded to him by Anglo businessmen and they were calling in their notes. He had been driven from his home and had fled into Mexico because he had felt the lives of his wife and children were threatened. But when he arrived in Mexico, a country he had fought against in the Texas Revolution, he had been immediately arrested and thrown into prison. With their two great leaders in disarray, the Tejanos, the old masters of the land, were in retreat. The new masters were the Anglo planters, a strange blending of gentleman and yeoman farmer, who were transplanting the plantation system from the Old South to the Texas frontier.

In the spring of 1842, Santa Anna sent a force of one thousand men north across the Rio Grande. It proved to be merely a show of force. Then, in September, General Adrian Woll and another thousand men invaded Texas, capturing Goliad, Victoria, and San Antonio. Thirty-five Texans died at San Antonio. Sixty-seven prisoners were taken, including every Anglo male in the city. Suddenly the roads were filled again with people fleeing Santa Anna's army.

It was difficult for Euphemia to believe history was repeating itself, and she had visions of another forced march through the wilderness. She made up her mind to stand her ground this time. The Mexican Army remained in San Antonio for a few days, then, with their prisoners, they turned back toward the border. Once more the Texas militia mobilized. The Rowdy King Boys, Henry McCulloch, and the Texas Rangers fought skirmishes with the Mexicans as the superior force moved south. At Salado, a portion of Woll's force was trapped in a brushy bottom and about one hundred Mexicans were killed. After the battle, Henry McCulloch returned home with news that shook Euphemia to the very soul.

"He was there," Henry said. "I saw Juan Seguin with my own eyes. In the uniform of a Mexican cavalry officer."

"There must be some mistake!" Sarah said. Euphemia could hardly breathe. She felt as if something enormous was pressing down on her chest.

"There's no mistake. Some of Woll's prisoners say they saw him in San Antonio. And I certainly saw that miserable traitor at Salado."

Euphemia remembered how just a few years before the family had accompanied Juan Seguin to Walnut Creek for a ceremony held in his honor. The highlight of the day had been the renaming of the town from Walnut Creek to Seguin. She remembered how proud she had been when he had ridden through the town square acknowledging the applause of the crowd. How could things have changed so much? What could make a man change from patriot to traitor in just a few short years? If Henry had seen Juan Seguin at Salado in a Mexican uniform, it was because men like Ben and Henry McCulloch had driven him to it. And then there was another possibility. Euphemia looked at Henry McCulloch now and she wondered if he would tell such a lie.

Texas was changing. The great *estancias* of the Tejanos were being replaced by the slave-driven economy of King Cotton. Along the roads, great wagons moved in caravan from the cotton gins to ports along the Gulf Coast. Loaded with a dozen bales, each weighing four to six hundred pounds, the ox-drawn freighters would struggle along toward Port Lavaca, Matagorda, or Quintana, making merely ten to fifteen miles a day. At night, when the caravans would pause by the road near her house and the oxen would be turned loose to graze, Euphemia could hear their bells casting melody into the darkness. Toward morning, Euphemia would hear the curses of the drivers and the crack of whips as the caravans began to move again.

Since she had been injured by the Comanche arrow, Sarah could no longer ride without pain. Euphemia would either ride alone or, with increasing frequency, with Bartlett, during those periods when he was not out chasing Comanches or bandits with the Texas Rangers. Once they rode by a vast field where rows of slaves were scraping away weeds and grass from the small cotton seedlings.

"Cotton is the way of the future," Bartlett said, as they listened to the song of the workers and watched a child passing a gourd of water among the slaves. "There's more than ten thousand slaves in Texas and more coming every year. Old Jim Bowie brought in some of the first of those slaves when he was an agent for Jean Lafitte. I think one of the reasons why Navarro and Seguin and the other *rancho* families are being driven out is because most of them don't care for slavery. Mexico outlawed it in 1820. I believe a lot of Anglo planters believe leaders like Navarro and Seguin want to outlaw slavery in Texas."

The road passing Peach Creek was now filled with immigrants who had come by ship from New Orleans to Galveston or Indianola and now made their way northward to Seguin and the good land along the Guadalupe. The McClure place, with its fresh water, great spreading oaks, and wide inviting porch, had always been a stop for the stagecoach. Quite often travelers stayed the night before resuming their difficult journey. At first, when the sojourners were few, Sarah entertained them, if not lavishly, with courtesy and a sense of Christian duty. When she would hear the sound of wagons and horses outside, she would quote Deuteronomy. "Remember the stranger, the fatherless and the widow that they may be within thy gates and be filled."

Although the new McClure house was large and white and rose from the land like the beautiful imposing houses of Virginia and Mississippi and Tennessee, it was free of the ornamentation of the great estates of the Old South. But it was wonderfully commodious, and accommodation on the frontier was in great demand. As the months passed and more and more visitors came by, Bartlett found his supply of Kentucky whiskey was fast diminishing. Sarah and Tildy found themselves constantly at the fireplace, turning the spits and basting the venison or turkey on which guests would dine. The McClure place became famous for its coffee and loaf cakes, which Euphemia made with scandalous quantities of butter churned in the great oak keg on the back porch.

Sarah felt trapped, a prisoner of her guests. "I really don't know how many strangers, orphans, and widows God wants me to remember," she finally said.

"We can't turn them away, can we?" Euphemia asked.

"I suppose not," Sarah replied. "But they're eating us out of house and home. We've got to do something."

"Why don't we charge them for bed and meals?" Euphemia said. "There's plenty of room."

"It's not exactly what I had in mind for my life," Sarah said, as she limped with a load of linens from one guest room to another. "Somehow I didn't think I'd end up a crippled innkeeper."

By happenstance the McClure house, that vision of splendor and elegance Sarah had carried in her mind for so long, that symbol of graceful and civilized living in a savage and hostile land, became one of the first inns in the region. Euphemia's life was filled with the tales of strangers, people on the move in a new land. When Euphemia listened to these newcomers to the world she had always known, she wondered if they weren't talking about some foreign land. How innocent and romantic their dreams were, as if they wandered through a tale told by Sir Walter Scott. They were embarking on epic adventure, heroic characters in a legend, on an odyssey to a province created in their minds. The McClure table became a theater for dreamers. Euphemia wondered what they would do when they encountered the brooding loneliness of the land and the bitter cruelty of the seasons and the savage heart of the times. *How like children they are,* she thought. Sometimes she felt like a very old woman, the world's oldest child.

One day Euphemia rode Saracen out toward Woman Hollerin' Creek. She rode alone, because Bartlett had been rangering to the south and wasn't expected home until the morrow. When she left Peach Creek, the air was warm and light as the breath of a muse. Early wildflowers splashed the hills with the colors that fleck the iris of the eye. It was good to be away from the good humor and zest and indomitable optimism of the strangers. She wondered why they depressed her so. When she watched a wagon moving in the distance, its wheels rumbling like the memory of thunder, she realized it was headed somewhere. There was a purpose to its movement, a sense of destination. The travelers at her table were enlivened by a sense of motion through time and space. Where, then, was her life headed? What would she become? Would she live out her days at Peach Creek listening to the illusions of wanderers, watching Sarah and Bartlett grow old? Her face grew crimson as she remembered the time she had watched Sarah and Bartlett make love on the night the Runaway Scrape began, and she wondered where the man was that would share her nights. She thought of William King and she tried to imagine how it would be. A strange fever spread from her blush, and she felt unsteady and uncertain, as if she were standing at the door to something both terrible and wonderful. She tried to determine if she was elated or depressed, but found the line between the two wavering, insubstantial as fog.

Then a cold wind walked across the meadow. The wildflowers closed upon themselves and a darkness spread across the hills like the shadow of evil wings. Saracen grew skittish and pawed the earth, impatient to run before the northern winds. It was a Norther for sure, one of the great storms that wheel unexpectedly into Texas, their freezing winds and rain consuming warmth and light and life. It was in such a storm that Stephen F. Austin had died in 1836. So Euphemia rode for home, her strange fever diminished by a cold rain that soon turned to sleet.

For three days the storm raged. On the third day they found Bartlett. Like Austin, he had been claimed not by iron, but by ice. He was buried in the little graveyard beneath the oaks. The Texas Ranger, patriot, Indian fighter, attorney at law, judge, lover and mate of Sarah Ashby, was dead. Once more Euphemia Texas, the world's oldest child, was an orphan.

Shortly after Bartlett McClure died, Sarah returned to Kentucky to settle the McClure estate. The great old house in Peach Creek was closed. As Euphemia and Sarah discussed the estate, Euphemia realized for the first time she was a woman of property. When her father had died, he had left each of the children a share of the Ashby Grant. Euphemia had received one-seventh of the total homestead, some 295 acres on the west side of the Lavaca River. She had also received one-seventh of Tildy, which often filled her with shame. In her own mind, she had long ago set her one-seventh free.

With the house at Peach Creek closed, it was decided to send Euphemia to Rutersville, a boarding school about three days' ride away. It was named for the Methodist missionary Martin Ruter, who'd died raising funds to establish the new college. The objective of the school was to provide a wholesome environment for young people, away from the "ardent spirits and gambling and temptations" of the time. There were nearly sixty students, only four of them girls from Gonzales. The young ladies were to be instructed in the social graces as well as the skills and knowledge required to be a good wife and mother. Among these skills were penmanship, botany, logic, Latin, Greek, French, and calculus.

On the first day Euphemia attended Rutersville College to learn how to be a lady, two boys were found dead on the Matagorda-Bastrop-Ector Road, only a few miles from the school. The boys had been killed and mutilated by Indians, scalped, their hands cut off, their hearts hacked from their bodies. That night, her first night ever to be so alone, she sat in her room, surrounded by the books that would provide what was called a "thorough English education." On the table by her bed was an enormous volume of Plutarch's *Parallel Lives*. As the search for the butchers of the schoolboys progressed outside her window, Euphemia browsed through the names of those ancient Greek and Roman lives Plutarch described. Where were they now, she wondered. Where were Fabius and Pericles? Where were Lysander and Alexander and Bartlett McClure? Where were Little Johnny and Sarah's unnamed baby? Where was John Ashby and where were her mother and the looter they had shot on the way to San Jacinto? Euphemia knew these lives were fading away, becoming unclear in her mind. But the *Lives* of Plutarch she would commit to memory. It was necessary if she were to become a good wife and mother. She was alone in a roomful of irony. Alone with death and with Plutarch. Alone as she had never been before. She wanted to ride away. But where could she go? And, besides, it was dark and she was afraid of the Indians who had cut off the hands and cut out the hearts of her classmates.

Euphemia had never felt she made friends easily. She was more comfortable around adults than with people her own age. Poor Matilda Lockhart had been the only person she had ever let know her secret heart. The boys at school were strange beings from another planet, only slightly related to the species that had given her family Travis and William. These young men had voices that careened strangely between octaves, had the long, clumsy legs of newborn horses and hands big as pie plates. She couldn't imagine speaking to one of these creatures and she quickly grew adept at avoiding them in the hall.

In a few days, she saw that the other girls were also feeling homesick and alone. They were from small rural communities in the surrounding counties, and as the weeks passed, much to her surprise, she found that she had things in common with the Rutersville girls. She had always thought her life was unique, that no one else on earth had felt her sorrow or her pain. Now she began to see that others on the frontier had seen as much of life and death as she had. She became friends with these girls, although not really close. The only really close friend she made at Rutersville was a teacher named Annie Forbes Franklin. Euphemia was drawn to her because Annie Franklin was the opposite of the women Rutersville College was established to create. In short, Annie Forbes Franklin was no ordinary lady.

Euphemia had first taken notice of Annie Franklin at the Rutersville celebration of San Jacinto Day on April 21, the most cherished of Texas holidays. At Rutersville, it featured a banquet and parade, a reading of patriotic documents, a recognition of veterans, and a presentation by the Rutersville Debating Society. Annie Franklin was a sponsor of the debating society. The presentation was not a debate in the strictest sense. Rather, the Society had prepared a series of patriotic speeches on the issue of a renewal of war with Mexico. And in these turbulent, dangerous days, with Santa Anna back in power and the dogs of war growling, the San Jacinto Day debate took on special significance.

A wooden platform had been raised on the large green next to the school, where on other days the boys marched against a phantom Santa Anna and drilled with wooden rifles. Patriotic bunting was festooned around the back of the platform, including the tattered remnants of a flag Georgia volunteers had brought to Texas and had flown over the fortress at Goliad. Crowning the platform was the Lone Star flag of Texas, a huge banner sewn by the young ladies of Rutersville, including Euphemia, who felt no little pride as she watched how beautifully it rode the wind. Families from the surrounding county had come to spend the day in celebration of Texas Independence and a crowd of nearly one hundred had gathered to hear the speeches.

Euphemia had been surprised, then intrigued, to see a woman on the platform. Political involvement, unlike penmanship and Plutarch and the sewing of flags, was not considered a necessary skill for the good wife and mother. Because Annie Franklin's opinions were so passionate, she had forsaken her role as sponsor and had become a participant in the presentation. Annie Franklin had auburn hair that would not stay pinned but flew as wildly in the wind as the Lone Star flag. Her skin was almost as white as Don José's riding coat. When she rose to approach the podium, there was a decided bounce in her step, almost as if she were dancing. When she spoke, Euphemia was amazed that her voice could achieve such volume, yet seem to be cast out to the crowd with so little effort. Euphemia was captivated by this beautiful woman who seemed so self-assured and articulate. Then, as Annie Franklin moved past her introductory remarks, Euphemia recognized that a central figure in the speech was her old friend Juan Seguin.

Annie told of Juan Seguin's terrible ordeal, how his home had been attacked, his property vandalized, his livestock stolen, and then in the dark of the night vigilantes had killed his wife's brother. Seguin had no choice. With his family, he had fled to Mexico, where he was promptly arrested. When he had returned to Texas, some believed he was in the uniform of the invading Mexican army. Was it true? Was he justified? Was he a traitor? Newcomers to Texas believed he was the Benedict Arnold of the Republic of Texas. But not Annie Forbes Franklin.

"No man has done more to defend the cause of freedom in Texas for all Texans than Juan Seguin," Annie Franklin argued in a strong, clear voice. "Yet, because he was Mexican, he was made the foreigner in his native land. He was driven from his home. In order to save the lives of his wife and children he fled to Mexico. And when he got to Mexico, a country he had fought against in the Revolution, he was immediately arrested and thrown into prison. His family, without support, was destitute. The Mexican authorities offered Juan Seguin a choice. Either he served Mexico or he would be turned over to the Texans who wished him dead and his family would be left to starve. What choice did he have? He had to do something to save his family and to stay alive. All his options were horrible."

Annie Franklin then read a letter Sam Houston had written to old Erasmos Seguin, Juan's father. " 'I pray, Sir,' " she read in her clear clarion voice, " 'that you will not suppose for a moment that I will denounce Colonel John N. Seguin, without a most perfect understanding of his absence. I rely upon his honor, his worth, and his chivalry. He is as pure a patriot as any in the land.' "

Annie Franklin's speech stirred the crowd that was already fired by the spirit of San Jacinto Day. But most had had enough of Mexico and Santa Anna, and many were not too happy with Sam Houston, whose efforts were aimed at making peace with Santa Anna, not war. When Annie Franklin continued her argument, hecklers tried to shout her down. One of the hecklers, a well-dressed gentleman, was standing next to Euphemia. "Seguin is a traitor," the man shouted. "He should be hanged." Euphemia was enraged. She had seen the letter Juan Seguin had written in December 1835, warning of a Mexican invasion. It had been delivered to Peach Creek by Ancilo Vergara and Andres Barcona. *Without Seguin's warning,* Euphemia thought, *this pompous fool next to me might be standing in Mexico.*

She tried to think what Sarah would do if she were to confront such a man, for Sarah did not suffer fools easily.

Annie Franklin resumed her argument. "I'm certain Seguin was a spy for Sam Houston. He still serves Texas. Show me one person, including the great Ben McCulloch, who can say they saw Juan Seguin raise his hand against a Texan. No one doubts Juan Seguin was with Vasquez and General Adrian Woll, but in the service of Texas, not Mexico. He killed no one. He harmed no one. Juan Seguin is just as much a patriot as any Texas Ranger alive or dead."

The man next to Euphemia was sputtering his outrage. "If you weren't a woman . . ." He was too angry to finish.

"If you were a man," Annie Franklin replied, "I might listen to your opinions." Euphemia looked up into the face of the heckler. Above his flowing silk cravat, his face was red and alive with fury, almost the color of his velvet coat which she supposed was the latest fashion from New York. As she looked down at his feet and at what appeared to be thin dancing pumps, Euphemia was struck by the notion that newcomers from the East were always more vocal than others in their desire to appear patriotic. True Texans took patriotism for granted and lived their convictions rather than shouting them in public display. Euphemia calculated the heft of her copy of Plutarch's *Lives* and decided the volume weighed about six pounds. She calculated the thickness of the heckler's dancing pumps and determined they were little more substantial than paper. Then she took aim and dropped all forty-nine of Plutarch's parallel lives, from Aemilius to Themistocles, on the gentleman heckler's toes.

The next few moments were rather a blur of sound and motion, dancing velvet, and high horrible howlings she had not heard since the Comanches attacked Peach Creek. From the podium, Annie Franklin caught her eye and bowed, just a small recognition of Euphemia's bold stand for truth and justice and reason. Euphemia had not only made a friend for life, but she had also discovered the relevance of the classics to contemporary politics. Although she would never resort to guerrilla politics again, she was reminded that being a wife and mother might not be the passive role society was being so careful to prepare her for at the college of the missionary Ruter.

Euphemia spent a very happy year at school in Rutersville. It was not so much her time in class she valued, but the hours she spent with Annie Franklin, in her room or in long walks along the green or by the stream that flowed below the school. They talked about ideas and life and philosophy, about what made people the way they are and why. Annie wondered aloud why truth and politics were imperfect strangers and why people were so blind when it came to issues like slavery. For the first time, Euphemia heard a woman challenge the right of men to preside over human society. Sarah had railed against the plight of women, but she had never laid the blame for that plight at the feet of men. Annie charged that men would do anything to retain their power. "No one," she said, "who holds absolute power can be trusted to willingly give it up. Even a small part of it. If women want liberty, they'll have to steal it when men are looking the other way."

With the other students, Annie was very serious and severe and guarded. She was not at all reluctant to express her sometimes outrageous opinions, but she was careful not to reveal anything of herself or her deeper feelings. In Euphemia's presence she seemed to relax and to open herself, even reach out for a soul she felt might have been fashioned from the same stuff as her own. For a long time, Euphemia was confused about their friendship. After all, there was a significant difference in their ages. But after she had known Annie for a month or two, it became easier for her to allow herself to be loved by this fascinating woman, this kindred spirit, this young mother she had never had.

When Sarah returned from Kentucky and the house at Peach Creek was reopened, Euphemia did not mind leaving school, but she was terribly reluctant to leave Annie. They vowed to remain in each other's lives and then, both in tears, they parted.

Euphemia had come to think of happiness as a kind of pen-dulum. It would swing toward you, all bright and polished and gleaming, and then just about the time you reached out for it, the pendulum would swing away again. But in the years after Rutersville, she seemed to hold on to the pendulum for longer than ever before. She was sad that Juan Seguin had been dishon-ored and that Don José Navarro was still in a Mexican prison, but she was embarking on years she would remember as some of the happiest of her life.

Soon life at Peach Creek resumed its rhythms. Once again, the stagecoach brought guests for the night. Other travelers came by horseback. Sarah, Fannie, and Euphemia spent their days looking after the needs of their guests. In the evenings they would gather on the front porch to enjoy the breeze, drink the good whiskey Sarah had brought back from Kentucky, and en-gage in long, often passionate, political discussions. Sometimes, congressmen would stop at the house as they rode to and from the seat of government in Austin. One of these guests was a newly elected congressman from Gonzales, a man named Charles Braches.

Born in Prussia, Charles Braches was a scholar, a musician, and a man of rare personal magnetism. He had a long face, wide at the forehead and narrowing down to a pointed chin, with dark, deep-set eyes. He was tall and thin as a willow. His most remarkable feature, Euphemia believed, was his hands. They were large and long and moved gracefully in the air when he spoke. Euphemia had never seen such expressive hands. Sometimes she thought they had a language of their own, and would continue to speak even if Braches grew silent. Before coming to Texas he had been headmaster of a literary and music school in Mississippi. Euphemia remembered Braches as one of those who had come home with Bartlett after the battle of Plum Creek. She had been fascinated then with the idea that a foreign-born scholar who had studied and taught classical music would have found himself in Gonzales, Texas. Now it was Sarah who was fascinated as Braches captivated his listeners with stories of a world beyond the hillsides and prairies of Texas. In the soft Texas night, on the wide front porch of the Peach Creek house, his strange musical voice was a loom weaving magic. One night he told them about the "glass harmonica."

"Every schoolchild knows Benjamin Franklin was a printer and publisher and statesman," Braches began. "But in Europe we also knew him as the inventor of the glass harmonica. It consisted of twenty-four glass bowls, of graduated size. The bowls were mounted on a long spindle and suspended over a trough of water. A pedal mechanism was used to moisten and spin the bowls. To play the harmonica, you merely touched the rotating bowls with your finger and a musical tone was produced. Franklin's brainchild was very popular in Europe. Mozart, Beethoven, and Haydn all wrote compositions for it."

"I don't think such a thing could be," Sarah said. "Surely that's just a story."

Braches pretended to be hurt by Sarah's skepticism. "Then we'll just have to reinvent the harmonica," he said. "It is no less than Ben Franklin's reputation we must defend." Euphemia and Tildy were sent to gather bowls and other apparatus from the kitchen and from the barn, and the construction of Franklin's glass harmonica began. After spilling gallons of water and laughter, even breaking one of Sarah's mixing bowls, a primitive instrument was completed. And much to their amazement, the freshman congressman from Gonzales spun the bowls and a Bach sonata wheeled into the night.

In addition to wagons of furniture and seven more slaves, Sarah had brought several fine horses back from Kentucky. Euphemia's days were consumed with the care of the horses and long rides with Saracen into the surrounding countryside. And when she would return to Peach Creek she would often find Sarah orchestrating some new improvement to the house or to the grounds. A combination garden and orchard was established with quinces and pomegranates and plums and beds of roses and pink crepe myrtle and yellow jasmine climbing white fences. Fields of corn and cotton that had been neglected when Bartlett died once again stretched green and golden from the house. Never had Sarah seemed more alive. Then, one day, when Euphemia and Saracen came riding home from the hill above the Woman Hollerin', Euphemia saw a freight wagon standing before the front door. Sarah directed the slaves as they unloaded a magnificent rosewood piano that had been shipped up the Colorado to La Grange and then overland to Peach Creek. There was only one person Euphemia knew who could play such an instrument. It seemed very clear it was just a matter of time until the music of Mozart and Beethoven and Haydn would spill out into the yard and under the oaks where Sam Houston had begun his journey to San Jacinto.

It seemed Charles Braches was fascinated by everything God had placed in the world of men. For the boys, Travis and William, their new friend's interest in flying machines held them spellbound. In a trip to England, Braches had met Sir George Cayley, a Yorkshire baronet who had spent his life and much of his fortune developing what he called an ornithopter. "The original design," Braches explained, "was conceived by Leonardo da Vinci." Braches then sketched a strange machine with wings. "Some of the machines actually flew through the air carrying a man along. Sir George's coachman was usually the man at the controls of the machine. Once, after gliding down a steep hill on the machine and coming to a jarring stop, the coachman dusted himself off and walked angrily back to his master. 'Sir George,' he said. 'I wish to give notice. I was hired to drive, not fly.' "

Sarah and Charles Braches spent more and more time together, usually with the children trying to command his attention. Then Euphemia noticed the two were managing moments alone. She could tell they were becoming more than friends. The only time Euphemia heard cross words between them was when Braches agreed to help the boys build a flying machine for flights from the top of the barn to the pasture. Sarah had said if boys were meant to fly "they'd have been born with feathers."

Seven years after the Runaway Scrape, on Texas Independence Day, the widow McClure and Congressman Charles Braches were married. It was March 2, 1843, the year Sir George Cayley invented the helicopter. In Alabama, that same year, another acquaintance of Charles Braches entered politics as a delegate to the Democratic State Convention. His name was Jefferson Davis.

After the wedding, Euphemia had been invited to stay at Jane Isabella and Henry McCulloch's home at Mill Creek, near Seguin. It was an obvious effort to provide the newlyweds privacy, yet Euphemia couldn't help feeling like a vagabond orphan once more. She spent much of her time that summer riding Saracen and dreaming and wishing she could talk with Annie Franklin about the thoughts and feelings that accompanied her through her days and nights.

Sometimes she was surprised how much she missed Bartlett. She would remember moments she had shared with him when he was like a father to her. It seemed the men in her life were destined to disappear, like badly written characters in a play.

This was a summer Euphemia would always remember as the Summer of Fannie. Euphemia had long felt she was an outsider when it came to her sisters Fannie and Jane Isabella. Now that Jane Isabella was married and busy in her new role as wife of a rancher and Texas Ranger, Euphemia spent more time with Fannie, who was also spending the summer at the McCullochs'.

At Big Hill was the prosperous ranch of Roderick Gelhorn, a German immigrant like Charles Braches, who had come to Texas some years before. He was a large man, with blond hair and clear blue eyes. His strong, bold features could have been carved from marble. Henry McCulloch said Gelhorn had been a Von Gelhorn in Germany, a nobleman and cavalry officer who rebelled against his fellow officers, took the family inheritance, and sailed for America. Here he dropped the "Von" from his name and started a new life in the new world. Gelhorn and Henry McCulloch became good friends. Soon, to everyone's utter amazement, the handsome bachelor nobleman fell in love with one of John Ashby's daughters.

One day that summer, the McCullochs, Fannie, and Euphemia rode to the Gelhorn place. Euphemia, as always, was immensely impressed with Gelhorn. Not only did she find him to be handsome and appealing, but he spoke with an accent that made her think of a prince in a faerie tale. There was also something mysterious about his background, his family, and his rebellion against the officers of his regiment. After establishing his ranch, he had returned to Germany once to visit his family. As he was walking down the street, members of the royal family rode by and Gelhorn was ordered to dismount, move off the road, and remove his hat. Gelhorn refused. He said he was an American now and he would take off his hat to no man. Now this former officer, nobleman, and rebel was entertaining his friends in his house on the American frontier, playing a Mozart sonata on an enormous, elaborately carved Empire piano from Austria. Perhaps the most remarkable thing about the visit was that their host seemed unable to tear his eyes away from Fannie Ashby.

At first, Euphemia thought she might be mistaken. But as the afternoon passed into evening, his special attentions to Fannie became obvious. How, Euphemia wondered, with some feeling of disloyalty toward her sister, could such a prosperous, elegant, handsome man be so taken with her plump, rather plain big sister?

After the autumn harvest it was time for Euphemia to return to school. Euphemia begged Sarah to let her go back to Rutersville and to Annie Franklin, but Sarah felt a school closer to family would be better. She decided on the one in Seguin, which had been established by a Methodist circuit-riding preacher. It was considered one of the best schools in Texas, better even than the larger ones in San Antonio. Jane Isabella arranged that Euphemia board during the week at the home of Dr. Joseph Johnson, physician, Guadalupe County Commissioner, and part-time schoolmaster.

Although she couldn't explain exactly why, she loved the little three-room frame schoolhouse and its teacher, Mrs. Elizabeth

Ann Thompson. It was like an island tucked away from the real world, a place where a girl could hide away for awhile and abide in a province safer and more refined than the raw frontier world of woods and prairie. Although there was an enormous difference between the Rutersville and Seguin schools, something about Mrs. Thompson made Euphemia eager to walk those few blocks from the Johnsons' house each morning. Mrs. Thompson, unlike Annie Franklin at Rutersville, was one of those women easily recognized as a teacher at first glance. She was a graduate of the famous Georgia Female College, the first college created solely for the education of women, and she was the first woman teacher in Guadalupe County. Yet what impressed Euphemia was the range of Mrs. Thompson's activities. Besides teaching school, she kept her home, raised her seven children, and managed their plantation when her circuit-riding preacher husband was away saving souls. With their many slaves, she raised cotton and operated a profitable cloth mill as well. It was said more than a thousand head of cattle grazed on their lands. It amazed Euphemia that Mrs. Thompson could care for their slaves, their mill, and their thousand head of cattle, and still have enough energy left over to make learning an adventure.

It was from Mrs. Thompson, and her astronomy class, that Euphemia first grew aware of the magic of the night sky. Once Mrs. Thompson read the class a passage from Ovid. "Though all other animals are prone and fix their gaze upon the Earth," Mrs. Thompson read, "God gave to Man an uplifted face and bade him stand erect and turn his eyes to heaven." At night, when all in the little town of Seguin were asleep, Euphemia would walk out beneath the jewelry of the night sky and she would wonder why a woman so sensitive to the magic of the world would have enslaved human beings plant and pick her cotton. It was almost as unjust as God having created Saracen in such a way that he could not easily gaze at the stars.

As much as she enjoyed school in Seguin and her week-long stays in the sophisticated little town on the Guadalupe River, Euphemia loved the weekends best. When class was over on Friday, she would pack a bag, saddle Saracen, and ride out across the prairie toward her sister Jane Isabella's place on Mill Creek.

And it was on one of these weekend rides that she came face to face with a deadly beast and the youngest of the Rowdy King Boys.

It was a day of golden sunlight and heavenly fragrances, an April afternoon as fine as the first day God made. Wildflowers were scattered everywhere and clouds wandered the sky like white-robed pilgrims. The road from Seguin to Mill Creek was not really a road at all. It was merely a blazed trail following the contours of the hills, through creek bottoms and along the paths animals had made on their way down to their watering places. Euphemia was about five miles from Seguin, not far from Beard's Mill, when she heard the sound.

At first, she thought she heard a child crying on a ledge above Baer Creek, a thin wail borne upon the wings of pain or some awful sorrow. Then the wail grew into a scream, a terrible yowling explosion of sound, and Saracen bounded away as the panther leaped from the ledge onto the horse and rider. Time and motion and sound became all confused, and Euphemia was rocked with bolts of numbing fear. Suddenly, or after an eternity, Euphemia found herself watching a small spider spinning a web between two blades of grass. When she awoke she was on the ground, her arm pinned beneath her, pain spreading like acid spilled from the tips of her fingers to somewhere behind her eyes. The pain was so terrible, she decided it didn't matter where the panther was, and she closed her eyes and waited. When she felt the breath and heard the breathing and knew the moist touch of an animal's mouth, she screamed until the pain put her to sleep, and she slept while Saracen continued to nuzzle her face with his own.

The next hour was like a series of disconnected dreams. In one dream she was being carried up a hill in the arms of a stranger, or was it her father or the ghost of Bartlett McClure? She was in his arms, like a child, her face against his chest. He smelled like leather and firewood. Once she opened her eyes long enough to see his face. She saw it wasn't her father at all, but some young man, about twenty-five years old, with blue eyes and hair the color of corn silk. Then she awoke in the Beard house, in a bed, and the Beards were gathered all around, and Dr. Johnson was rolling down his sleeves. The young man with eyes as blue as the sapphire brooch Jane Isabella often wore was brushing her hair from her eyes.

"Who are you?" Euphemia whispered.

"William," the young man answered. "William King."

"Did you kill the panther?" Euphemia asked. Her pain was not so insistent as it had been. In fact, she felt a certain sense of well-being, as if floating in warm liquid or in William's eyes.

"You must have frightened him away," William said. "But you broke your arm. It's fixed now. Gonna be good as new."

Dr. Johnson looked at his watch. "The Beards have invited you to stay here and rest for awhile. In a day or two when you feel able, I'll come around and bring you home."

Euphemia wondered where home was. Not Peach Creek or Mill Creek or Seguin or Beard's Mill. *Maybe I'll be shuttled around, passed from one family to the next, for the rest of my life.* The thought made her eyes fill with tears and she began to cry. *Is it the pain or the fear of the panther or being alone among strangers that makes me feel so empty?* Or maybe it was because she had met the man she had dreamed about so long, the man she had actually fallen in love with in her mind. Now she hurt too bad even to smile at him or even thank him for saving her from the panther, if he did save her from the panther. She preferred to think he did.

Here was the great love of her life, smelling of leather and firewood, his hand brushing a lock of hair away from her eyes, actually touching her brow, and all Euphemia could do was cry like a child. "I want to go home," she said. "Please somebody take me home."

Euphemia remained at the Beard home for three days. The first day she remained in bed, her head upon down pillows, looking out a window toward Capote Peak. Each day William King came by to pay his respects. At each dawn Euphemia would begin to count the minutes until she would hear the sound of his horse and his call of greeting to the Beards. It was a little like waiting for Christmas morning and the sounds of church bells at midnight on Christmas Eve. One morning, before William's arrival, Euphemia asked Mrs. Beard about the panther.

"What really happened? How did William find me?"

"Well," she said, "there are two Williams around here. William King and my son William Beard. They're good friends and have done some rangering together." Mrs. Beard was fussing about the bed, fluffing up the pillows, and tiny feathers rose in the room like faerie wings suspended in sunlight. Then Mrs. Beard's arms dropped to her side and she seemed to somehow grow smaller, older. "My son is in prison now. In Mexico. Santiago Prison," she said with a sigh, and then brightened. "But about the panther. Must have chased you some way and then you fell. William King was here after news about my son. He heard you scream and went down there where the wild greens grow. There you were on the ground. Then William saw that panther. They're all around here all the time trying to get at our pigs. Well, William shot the panther and then carried you up here. I reckon that panther would have hurt you if William hadn't been around."

On the second day, William and Mrs. Beard carried Euphemia onto the front porch. For a good while, William and Euphemia were alone, looking out at the oak motts and the wide fields of Texas. Sometimes they didn't speak for long intervals, but Euphemia was comfortable in the silences. She could feel his presence and she thought maybe, if she tried, she could hear his thoughts. "What a beautiful place this is," Euphemia said. The words just flowed, like truth, and she was a little surprised at the deep feelings they expressed. "I suppose there's nothing in the world more lovely."

William turned and looked directly into her eyes. "No," he said. "I've never seen anything prettier than what I see right now." He looked at her a moment longer, smiled almost shyly, then looked away toward the horizon. Euphemia was suddenly aware of her heartbeat and she hoped desperately William couldn't hear its thunder. *Did he mean what I think he said?* She wished she could have the moment to live again so she could examine it more closely. How did he look when he said it? What was the sound like? How did his lips move when the words passed into the air? *Could it be that I am pretty? He didn't say beautiful and if he did I know that would be a lie.* Jane Isabella was beautiful. Annie Franklin and Sarah were beautiful. But pretty? Euphemia couldn't recall ever being called pretty. She was the ugly duckling, the orphan wanderer, the foundling, the sad mysterious stranger who lived in the shadow of others' lives. Then she recalled the story about the ugly duckling that became a swan. She felt strong and happy and graceful. Euphemia thought, *How fortunate I was to have encountered a panther and broken my arm.*

After a while, after she had thoroughly savored William's compliment, she asked about William Beard. He told her the story of the Mier Expedition.

"It was Christmas Day," he began. "About two hundred Texans were under the command of Colonel Fisher. He led his men against a force of three thousand Mexicans in a little town below the Rio Grande called Mier. The battle lasted seventeen hours. They say it was the bloodiest battle since the Alamo. There were bodies everywhere. People dying. Finally, the Texans left alive stepped forward and laid down their arms. William Beard was one of them."

Euphemia recalled Mrs. Beard's apparent grief when she mentioned her son. "Mrs. Beard said he was in prison." Euphemia thought again of Don José, still locked in one of Santa Anna's dungeons, too.

"I don't think so. There's this thing Santa Anna does called Diezmo. It means every tenth prisoner is executed. There were a hundred and seventy-six prisoners so seventeen had to die. A jar was filled with a hundred and seventy-six beans. Seventeen of them were black. Those who drew the black beans were shot."

"And William Beard?"

"He wrote a letter about it. Told how brave the men were. How they appeared unconcerned and went up there to draw those beans as if they were drawing rations."

Euphemia waited. She could feel William's loss. After a pause, he continued.

"In the letter he didn't say what color bean he drew," William said. "But he didn't come home. I don't know if he died or what. I just figure he must be dead." Then William took a letter from his breast pocket. "William Beard and I had another friend named Robert Dunham. He joined up to go down there with your brother-in-law Henry McCulloch." William unfolded the letter and he began to read.

" 'Dear Mother. I write you under the most awful feelings that a son ever addressed a mother for in half an hour my doom will be finished on Earth, for I am doomed to die by the hands of the Mexicans for our late attempt to escape the'—there's a word here I can't make out—'then, of Santa Anna that every tenth man should be shot. We drew lots, I was one of the unfortunate. I cannot say anything more. I die I hope with firmest farewell. May God bless you and maybe in this my final hour forgive and pardon all my sins.' There's something more here I can't make out. Then he signs it, 'Your affectionate son, R. H. Dunham.' "

Euphemia's eyes were filled with tears and she wiped them away with her good arm. "I'm so sorry," she said. "It's so terrible and I'm so sorry."

"The letter just came. He sent it to me," William said. "He wanted me to take it to his ma."

William refolded the letter and returned it to his pocket. Euphemia felt her hand drawn to his as if it were a bird returning to a nest. It seemed the most natural thing in the world, as if they had known each other all their lives. "Your hand's all wet," he said.

"Tears," she said. "I can't help thinking about his mother. Children shouldn't ever die before their parents."

"I've got to deliver the letter today."

"Stay a while longer."

Once again they were enveloped in a soft counterpane of silence. His hand moved upon hers, his fingers tracing the contours, feeling the flow of her pulse, then holding tight. "I should have been there," William said finally, his voice flat and hollow. "I served with the rangers when Vasquez invaded San Antonio. But I didn't go south to Mier. I should have been with my friends. I should have drawn from the jar."

"Then you wouldn't be here. I would have been killed by a mountain lion. We wouldn't have met."

He turned to look at her and once again she felt suspended in the soft blue light of his eyes. "We would have met," he said. "No matter what. There's no other way for things to be."

At that moment, Euphemia knew she was in love and that love was real, though not devoid of sorrow. Euphemia Texas Ashby was sixteen years old.

In 1845, the Lone Star flag of the old Republic was lowered and Texas became a State of the Union. Sam Houston, who had replaced Lamar and had served a second term as President, had fought for annexation, a policy urged by his old comrade-in-arms Andrew Jackson. The southern and western states were for annexation. The northern states were against, primarily because Texas would add another slave state to the Union. They called Texas a pauper wilderness. Sarah and Charles Braches had favored annexation. Like Houston, they believed that Mexico would never let them live in peace and that union with the United States was the only way Texas could survive.

On February 19, 1846, Anson Jones, who had replaced Sam Houston as President of Texas, lowered the Lone Star flag at the capitol in Austin. "The Republic is no more," he said, as tears streamed down the faces of the Texas veterans. The Republic of Texas had been two weeks less than ten years old. Soon Abraham Lincoln would run for Congress and Major Robert E. Lee would leave for his Mexican campaign and his wounds at Chapultepec. It was the year Andrew Jackson died. The White Dove, José Antonio Navarro, rode triumphantly back into Texas and into Euphemia's life. Euphemia thought it was high irony that Navarro was the only native Texan present at the convention that ratified annexation of Texas into the Union.

José Antonio's return was occasion for a huge *fiesta* at the Navarro *estancia*. Guests included nearly every living soul Euphemia knew, including Annie Franklin, much to her delight, and all the Rowdy King Boys, including the youngest. Since that spring day William had saved her from the cougar, their friendship, their love, had grown. They were together nearly every weekend at the McCulloch ranch and during the week at the Johnson home, in Seguin. Euphemia continued her studies with Mrs. Thompson. She wrote to Sarah faithfully and Sarah's return letters reflected a life of growing affluence and civility. Of course, Sarah and Charles Braches were among the guests at Don José's homecoming fandango.

Don José had lost a great deal of weight and there were shadows in the hollows of his eyes. In spite of that, Euphemia thought he was as dashing as ever in his white cape, welcoming guests while at the same time supervising the unloading of trunks filled with classics he had purchased at the bookstores in New Orleans. Everyone was eager to know how the White Dove had escaped from the dungeon where he had been held for four years and where he had been tortured by Santa Anna.

Navarro simply smiled and evaded the questions with characteristic courtesy and grace. He would only say he had escaped by boat to Cuba and then to New Orleans. Euphemia decided that a man who dressed all in white, rode only white horses, and spoke at least three languages fluently should be excused the small rudeness of secrecy. In the absence of an explanation from Don José, there were as many tall tales told about the escape as there were guests. Of all the wild and wonderful stories told, including one in which Don José severely wounded Santa Anna in a duel, Annie Franklin's theory seemed most probable to Euphemia.

"Santa Anna had Navarro at his mercy. First he tried to get Navarro to renounce his loyalty to Texas. He probably was offered all kinds of incentives. But Don José refused. He would be a patriot even if it meant his death."

"He was under a death sentence," Euphemia said. "Why wasn't it carried out?"

"That would have created a martyr. Santa Anna couldn't afford that, but he couldn't let him go. And I think the Navarro family knew of something Santa Anna had done so distasteful it would ruin him if it became public knowledge."

"Margarita Garza Navarro knows," Euphemia remembered. "But she won't tell. Something that happened long ago. It had to do with, well, some terrible indiscretion."

"Anyway," Annie continued, "I think Santa Anna allowed Don José to escape. He made it possible for Don José to get away, gambling that it would buy the silence of the Garza and Navarro families, yet he would not appear to be capitulating. No other explanation really makes any sense to me."

As Euphemia watched the guests, most of whom she knew, she was astonished by the behavior of a small, severe young woman she had not seen before. The woman was emptying glasses of liquor into the large earthen pot in a corner of the parlor. She would wait for a guest to put his drink down, then she would remove the glass, pour out its contents, and replace the empty glass. When Euphemia asked Annie Franklin about this extraordinary performance, Annie merely laughed and took Euphemia's hand and led her across the room to meet Ann Penn Ireland.

Ann Penn Ireland, like Annie Franklin, was a political activist in a time when activism was not perceived as an appropriate activity for the ladies of the South. She was very slim with dark hair parted precisely in the middle. There was something birdlike in her manner, and her movements were rapid and nervous. "You wouldn't believe what's going on in Europe and in the East," she said, after explaining that emptying liquor from the glasses of imbibers was a way of living her convictions about temperance. Later in life, when her husband was governor of Texas, she returned cases of wine to the supplier just hours before a state dinner.

"Women are taking their reform policies into the streets," she continued. "Women are advocating for the vote, for the repeal of discriminatory laws."

Later in the evening, William asked Euphemia to dance and she remembered how she had danced with his older brother so many years ago when she was a child. Now, as a woman, she whirled away the night in a carousel of waltzes, quadrilles, and reels. There was a strange mosaic of sounds, rhythms, and harmonies from both the Old World and the New. One moment the gifted hands of Charles Braches would hurl Beethoven from the Navarros' grand piano, then the next moment the Rowdy King

Boys, with their fiddles and banjos, spoons and old tin pans, would pound out the rustic folk songs of the Republic. Then from Margarita Navarro's guitar would weep tears of sound, Andalusian melodies of exquisite sorrow. All night Euphemia and William danced, and when the first loom of light eased in the east windows, they were still moving to the music and to the beat of their hearts.

Outside, the air was crisp and fresh and Euphemia could see Navarro's great herd of horses ranging on land surveyed by James Bowie back before the Alamo. The mares and their young foals, descendants of Spanish horses brought to the New World by Franciscan fathers, were moving silhouettes across the horizon. "One day I'd love to raise horses," Euphemia said.

"It would be a fine life," William agreed. "And profitable. There'll always be a need for good horses as long as there's evil in the world."

Euphemia turned, shielding her eyes from the first fierce rays of the sun rising behind William's shoulder. "What's evil got to do with horses?"

"Well, as long as there's evil like Santa Anna and the Comanches, there's gotta be war. And if there's gonna be war, men are going to ride to it and fight it on horseback. And generally the people with the best horses are going to win. That's the way it is. That's why Genghis Khan and Alexander the Great conquered the world. They had better horses."

"I wouldn't want my horses to go to war," Euphemia said.

"A man told me once how to capture wild mustangs," William said, as he watched the foals dancing along the hill. "There's thousands of mustangs out there, free for the taking. If they're in the clear, you can noose them with a lasso. But if they take to the woods, what you do is crease them with a bullet. A good marksman can knock a mustang down with a ball just under the mane at the center of the neck. The wound soon heals and you've got yourself a horse."

Euphemia turned away. "That's terrible."

"Well, I didn't say I'd do it." William's blue eyes laughed. "That's just how the man told me it was done."

"I'm going to have horses one day. The finest horses in Texas. Saracen is the start."

"Well, you're going to need a few things first," William said. "You're gonna need a ranch and some land and a house to start with. And you're probably gonna need a man."

"You know perfectly well there are three women right here in town have their own cattle brand." Euphemia was mildly irritated. "Duly registered and everything. One of them happens to be your own mother. There's no reason I can't run a horse ranch by myself." Now she was more than a little irritated. "And I won't need slaves and I won't need men! Besides, I already have property. In my own name."

"Well, I'd say then you sure will make somebody a fine catch," William said. "All that property. All those horses. All that sass." William smiled; at least she thought he smiled, for she was blinded by the sun and didn't see him bend to kiss her, only felt his lips touch hers. "A man sure could do worse," he said as he straightened, and the memory of his lips on hers would linger for days.

Each Sunday during the years Euphemia attended school in Seguin, William's mother, Granny Rachel Boyd, a devout Methodist, taught Sunday School classes under the oak trees along Walnut Branch in Seguin. Granny Boyd was a strong, vocal, yet fair-minded woman whose opinion had the power of law.

Granny Boyd's Sunday School classes were not nearly as exciting as the prayer meetings Euphemia sometimes attended in the brush arbor near Peach Creek. They began on Thursday and ended in a great explosion of fervor and hysteria on Sunday. She remembered the charged night, bonfires and torches, children sleeping on pallets oblivious to the passion and shouting and singing of hymns, hard log benches, shouts of "Glory," warnings of hellfire and damnation. She remembered how little Matilda Lockhart had loved the drama of these strange unknowable nights of mystery and glory and dread. It was theater, pure and simple. Occasionally, someone in the crowd would begin to wail and moan and then shake and jerk and contort. They said such people had been touched by God, yet Euphemia thought it more likely they had been visited by demons or bitten by scorpions. As for hell, it didn't impress Euphemia at all. She had been there once when Little Johnny died in her arms on the way to San Jacinto, and again when she heard Matilda Lockhart had gone to bed one day and had lain there hurting 'til she died.

Granny Boyd was constantly campaigning for a new church building. "How can the town grow without a church!" she would say, and then, with a wink, blame most everything on the Texas Rangers. "I swear this town has more Texas Rangers than you can shake a stick at. Just about the time we start to make some progress, off they go chasing Indians or outlaws, real or imagined."

In spite of the constant absence of male citizenry caused by the obligation of rangering, the little town grew. Soon there was a courthouse. No longer did the District Court have to share the oaks with Granny Boyd's Sunday School. Not only log houses but fine concrete houses in Greek Revival style spread out from the center of town. On her way to school from the Johnsons' house, Euphemia passed Neill and Baxter's blacksmith shop, and several mercantile shops filled with velvet, silk and satin, ribbons and lace. There was a new post office, a tree house with a ladder which was taken down at night by Caledonia Baxter, the postmistress. Along the roads a few carriages could be seen among the horses and wagons.

Finally, Granny Boyd prevailed and the Methodist Church was built facing Market Square. At first the congregation was too small to afford a full-time preacher but relied on circuit riders from various Protestant denominations. Granny Boyd had once warned Euphemia never to be caught out with a preacher after dark, "because they have roving hands." Ever since, Euphemia had never been able to look at a man of the cloth in quite the same way she had before Granny Boyd's revelation.

The church became a center of community life. Not only did the Methodists meet in their new frame building, but Baptists, Presbyterians, and Episcopalians filled the congregation to hear any preacher who came to Seguin. Here, on Market Square, was the town's political forum and the heart of the welfare system.

While the men would discuss whether California would be admitted to the Union as a free or as a slave state, the women would decide how they should follow the Scriptures teaching the need to care for widows, orphans, and strangers.

For the first time, Euphemia saw the kind of stability Sarah had always wished to establish, a sense of community that transcended the need just to survive. Here in the church, the people of Seguin began to deal with issues involving the quality of community life. They began to look toward the future. In the camp meetings Euphemia had attended with Matilda Lockhart, the focus had been on immediate and individual salvation. Who knew where death lurked, how soon the dark horsemen would come riding by? Now the community looked beyond the immediate and the personal. There was time to grow, to develop the community institutions and social services that would make the town prosper both materially and spiritually.

When the men of the town built the church, there was at first no fence surrounding it to keep animals out of church property, so free-roaming pigs would gather beneath the building where it was cool away from the sun.

One Sunday, as Euphemia was listening to the visiting preacher, trying not to think about his hands, she felt she could hear William King's thoughts. She glanced to the side of the church where the men sat separated from the women. He was looking at her, handsome as a knight, his gold hair parted in the middle, his eyes painting her with their azure light. She knew, somehow, that he was thinking about marriage. It was incredible but she knew it was so. He was asking her to be his wife. It was certain. The message was coming through the air from his heart to hers.

Euphemia began to feel terribly strange. Her skin began to tingle and she had an unbearable need to scratch. Could this be love? She noticed a tension in the room, glassy, transfixed, strained expressions frozen on the faces of the congregation as people shifted in the pews. Then, from beneath the floor, she heard the contented grunt of a pig, answered by another, and she realized the entire church had been infested with fleas. After an eternity, the sermon ended and the worshipers rushed from the church to the privacy of their homes. Later, as William helped Euphemia and Granny Boyd to scrub the building with boiling lye and to burn pans of sulfur beneath the church, Euphemia Texas answered "yes" and William knew the question.

In the year 1850, the year Jefferson Davis first urged secession of the South from the Union, Euphemia Texas Ashby and William King were married in the newly disinfected Methodist Church of Seguin, Texas. Everyone she loved was present. All the Ashby sisters, Sarah, Fannie, Jane Isabella, even Mary was there, apparently having escaped the unwelcome protection of old Mr. Smothers for once. Granny Boyd was in her usual place on the front pew on the women's side of the church. Tildy was seated in the Negro section at the back.

As Euphemia marched into the church on the arm of her brother Travis, she could not help but think of those who were not there. When she saw William's eyes, the moment of strange sadness passed. He was standing at the front of the church, like a god or something carved by Michelangelo. She thought how she had loved him longer than she had known him, maybe before she was even born.

The ceremony was performed by the Reverend Young of San Antonio. He wore an enormous black frock coat and spoke with a strong German accent. He had just recently changed his name from Jung, for the same reason Roderick Gelhorn had dropped the Von in his name.

"Who giff dis vumen in marriage?" Reverend Young asked. Euphemia couldn't help but notice his hands.

"I do," said Travis.

"I do," echoed Sarah in her strong fine voice and Euphemia was swept with a special fondness for the sister who had been so long her mother.

After the wedding vows had been spoken, the Reverend Young preached an interminable sermon on "luff as der fruit of der spirit" and then, at last, William and Euphemia, Mr. and Mrs. King, led a procession to Henry and Mahala's place where a wedding feast had been prepared. William had killed a young steer that Henry and John R. King had barbecued for the occasion.

Granny Boyd and Mahala had prepared potatoes, beans, and collard greens. Tildy had baked the wedding cake.

With as little delay as courtesy allowed, William managed their escape, and he took Euphemia to the little two-room log house he had built above the springs at King Branch. Finally, at age eighteen, Euphemia Texas had come home.

The first few months Euphemia lived in the little log house on the hill above the springs were like stories told of someone else's life. Perhaps the pendulum that so regularly cut a swath of pain through her life had broken from its mounting, had fallen and shattered beyond repair. She felt supremely happy and her life was as fine as fiction.

Each day she rose at daylight, even as the mockingbirds and cardinals began their morning symphony. She walked out to the horse pen to feed Saracen and the two Kentucky-bred mares William had brought to the marriage. She paused to watch the earth fall away to reveal the sun, a point of view regarding daybreak she had learned from Mrs. Thompson and Galileo. As the light improved, she gathered eggs to prepare for breakfast. Granny Boyd had given her three laying hens and a rooster as a wedding present. "This way you'll always have egg money," Granny Boyd told her, as if she did not know that Euphemia was a woman of property. After breakfast with William, surrounded by bird songs, the comforting conversation of the horses and hens, and the fine rich aromas of earth, she would plan her day.

She had learned something of running a household from Sarah, but her sister had servants. Sarah did more riding and shooting than baking and cleaning. Euphemia had some help from Tildy, who had been a sort of wedding present from her sisters and brothers and who lived in quarters behind the house, but Tildy also had no mother and all she learned at Peach Creek had been from Sarah. *How do you learn to be a wife and mother,* Euphemia thought, *when you have no mother?* She smiled as she thought about how the teachers at Rutersville believed reading Plutarch could help you clean and bake and mend. It was as if they believed you could learn how to make chicken soup, and soap, and hominy from old dried corn, from the more domestic passages of Shakespeare. In the end, it was Granny Boyd who took her under her wing and helped her make order out of the potential chaos of daily life. "Happiness is getting things done," Granny Boyd liked to say.

To the mild surprise of Granny Boyd and most of the Seguin citizenry, William King, the youngest and wildest of the Rowdy King Boys, attacked married life with steady and serious resolve. It was a side of his personality he had until now kept hidden from view. Even his heroics at the Battle of Salado, when William and his brother John had stolen a cannon from under the nose of General Vasquez, had been more of a prank than a deed of serious intent. His new, more mature demeanor was credited to the influence of Euphemia, the small, lovely girl who so rarely smiled.

William was elected the first Guadalupe County Tax Assessor and Collector. He became active in the town's new Masonic Lodge and in the newly organized Sons of Temperance, an organization devoted to something he had never been in his younger days. For sums ranging from one dollar to several hundred dollars, he began buying up property in and around town. His brother John, the first Mayor of Seguin, joked that William might well buy the whole town before he was through.

One morning, after William had finished breakfast and Euphemia had begun to clear the table, he brought up the subject she had dreaded from the moment she realized he was amassing a small fortune in land. "It is a matter of practical economics," he said. "If we are to compete, we must consider hiring slave labor."

Euphemia folded her hands in her lap and looked up into William's eyes. "I will not have slaves in my house or on our property."

"I don't mean buying slaves," William said. "What I'm suggesting is hiring slave labor. There's a difference, Phemie."

"Not much. There is a moral question. It's not right."

"You know I wouldn't mistreat these people," William continued. "In fact, they would probably be better off with us than with their owners."

"William, I'm sure that's true," Euphemia said quietly, adding firmly, "but I will not be a party to slavery." She knew William was subject to difficult pressures concerning the slavery question. Of Seguin's 986 residents, about one-third were slaves. She knew the numbers, because William had signed the 1850 Census which counted 301 slaves in Seguin. As in most Texas communities, only about one-third of the white people owned slaves, but they were those who held political, social, and economic power. For a community leader like William King not to own slaves led to suspicions that he was an abolitionist. Even a hint that he would, by word or act, seek to undermine the institution of slavery could ruin William in business and in politics.

"There must be an alternative," Euphemia said.

"There are some white people willing to work, new immigrants, mostly. But monthly wages for a farm hand are about nineteen dollars, more than two hundred dollars a year. And those people won't always work as hard or as long as a hired slave."

"You do agree with me on the issue of slavery."

"I would not bring a slave from Africa," William said. "I wouldn't buy a slave from the auction block. But these people are here already. They need someone to feed them, to take care of them when they're sick, to give them a roof over their heads. They're here. I can't wish them back to Africa."

"Some things are right, some things are wrong. Sometimes we know the difference."

William stood and moved behind Euphemia's chair and he put his hands gently on her shoulders. "I don't want you to be offended, but there's something I need to ask." His fingers moved on her shoulders, a kind of massage, as if to ease an anger he knew would come. "What about Tildy?" he said. "She's a slave."

The muscles of Euphemia's shoulders tightened beneath William's fingers. "She's like family."

"She's your slave, Phemie. You and your sisters inherited her, like any other property, from your father. She lives in quarters behind our house. Does your washing and works in your garden and will probably care for our children. As far as I can see, you have one more slave than I do."

Euphemia felt herself grow smaller. How unfair truth was. How difficult it was to live an honest life. There was nothing to say. She rose, moved from under William's hands, and left the house. She and Saracen rode as far and as fast as they could, until she began to feel the pressure in her belly. Euphemia wondered if the pain might be shame or a child. She knew how shame felt, but as for a child, she would have to ask Granny Boyd. First she would go to the courthouse and draw up papers to set Tildy free.

"Why would you want to set that girl free?" the lawyer asked. "What would she do? Where would she go?"

"She has money she's earned over the years. She can buy a place to live in. Or I'll give her the house she lives in. She's good with horses. She can raise horses."

"I still don't understand why?"

"It's a matter of conscience."

"It's also a matter of law. To free a slave is against the law." The attorney rattled his papers but Euphemia was listening to the sound of hammers building the new newspaper office that would challenge the views of the pro-Democrat *Texas Mercury*. She had read in the *Mercury* an editorial railing against the increase in the number of free Negroes coming to Texas from Louisiana. It called for selling them back into slavery if they didn't leave the state. But Euphemia thought that was merely the position of a mean-spirited editor, not the law of the State of Texas. Then the lawyer read her the section in the Seguin town charter prohibiting blacks, slave or free, from purchasing property.

"Even if it wasn't against state law to free slaves, it's still against the law for them to own property in Seguin. What I would advise," the attorney said helpfully, "is a clause in your will. You can reward faithful service and obedient and submissive conduct with freedom at your death. At that time, although she couldn't stay in Texas, she could leave the state. She could even go to Liberia." There was a moment of silence. "I might also add," the lawyer continued, "the very thought of what you wish to do would be abhorrent to most of your neighbors. The practice of manumission is a disservice to those who cherish the institutions of our society. It's also a disservice to slaves who are inherently unsuited to freedom."

Euphemia rose, thinking that Sarah would surely shoot this fool down in his tracks. "I appreciate your advice," she said as she rose. "But I'd appreciate it more if you'd draw up the papers. I want Tildy free now. Please do find a way." Then, as she moved to the door, she added: "Surely there are other lawyers in this town who can handle my affairs if you can't." *As long as I'm a slaveholder,* she thought, *I might as well also be a blackmailer. Happiness is getting things done.*

Euphemia did not talk to Granny Boyd about her pregnancy right away. A new life was growing inside her and she wished to hold this miracle secret for awhile, to savor the wonder of it alone for a small private season. Sometimes, when she and William prepared for bed or lay together listening to the gathering night, she felt ashamed that she was hiding this gift they were giving each other. At breakfast, when William railed against Sam Houston's refusal to support secessionist views, she would nod her head while dreaming of names and miniature dresses and hands so small they could not encircle her finger.

One morning, as she was trying to imagine how it would feel to have a child at her breast, William stopped his political monologue in mid-sentence. "Euphemia," he said, and she realized he had caught her in the rare act of smiling. "If there's anything Sam Houston is not, it's amusing."

As the days passed and Euphemia began to get comfortable with the idea of being a mother, she became aware of a disquietude lingering somewhere in her mind. The reality of childbirth began to disturb her private reveries. Burned into her memory was that awful stormy night that Sarah miscarried and Little Johnny died. How odd that birth and death were stored in adjacent compartments in her mind. She had heard the women talking of "oceans of pain" and "suffering beyond bearing." At a quilting with Granny Boyd, she had heard one woman say that she went down to death's door to bring her son into the world. Another said her child nearly killed her as he tore his way into life. Euphemia had thought at the time, *How can something so wonder-soft and wonder-small and helpless and exquisite cause so much pain?*

It was also apparent, as Euphemia settled into the rhythm of life in the little town, that many women spent their entire lives preparing to have babies, having babies, or recovering from a delivery. There were women in town who had seven children or more. Constant and recurring pregnancy, confinement and recovery. What an enormous toll it must take on their time, their bodies, their energy, and their dreams. Being a wife and mother, Euphemia decided, had its darker side. It was a dangerous, debilitating, fearsome, painful, often deadly profession.

After she told William, Euphemia told Jane Isabella about the coming child. Jane Isabella promptly told all of Seguin. Once Euphemia's secret was out, the little house above King Branch became a whirlwind of concern and preparedness. Sarah and Charles Braches brought a wagonload of baby clothes and toys from Peach Creek.

William was ecstatic and constantly underfoot, eager to make Euphemia's confinement as pleasant as possible. When he became more and more insistent that she stay close to the house and avoid exertion or drafts or any ventures out into the perilous world, Euphemia began to understand why they called these long months a period of "confinement."

As the time when Euphemia would be "brought to bed" came near, Granny Boyd and William began to disagree on whether Euphemia's delivery should be attended by a doctor or a midwife. Granny Boyd, of course, felt she was far more qualified than any doctor possibly could be. "How can Dr. Johnson know what it's like having a baby! Only a woman can know what a woman has suffered or is suffering. A midwife was good enough for me and my mother and her mother and that's good enough for Euphemia." William argued that modern physicians had ways of managing the birth process, of making it safer for both mother and child—new kinds of forceps to hasten the delivery and chloroform to ease the pain. "Why deny Euphemia these things?" he asked. But Granny Boyd stood her ground. "The birthing bed is a woman's world, and we don't need some male bungler standing around with his implements and ignorance."

At one point, when Granny Boyd was occupied with church matters, William made an appointment for Dr. Johnson to examine Euphemia. William was told to leave the room and Euphemia was amused, yet relieved, when Dr. Johnson performed the pelvic examination discreetly, by touch beneath her skirt, his eyes never once leaving some faraway point on the horizon. It was apparent to Euphemia that the world needed women doctors, but it was an unlikely possibility, because there would be little time to train or to practice between babies.

One early morning in 1851, Euphemia heard the rain crow. Even though she knew the rain crow was invisible, or at least gifted in the art of avoiding human eyes, she dressed and went outside to see if she could find this legendary bird that foretold the weather with such unerring accuracy. Although the sky was blue and clear, she knew it would storm before the first stars could be seen in the night sky. There were other ways of foretelling the weather. You could tell from the sound of the hooting of owls and the conversation of tree frogs and by how snails crawl upward to the tops of weeds to avoid the possibility of being washed away by flood. She followed the call of the rain crow down into the Guadalupe bottoms. Except for the rain crow, there was absolute silence. Apparently the frogs and the owls disagreed with the crow, signaling dissension among the prophets. Euphemia recalled with a chill that Tildy had said the rain crow was so dependable there was only one thing that made him wrong. Sometimes the rain crow couldn't tell the difference between storm shadow and death.

Euphemia was in the bottoms when her pain began.

The women gathered. Dr. Johnson was not called. With her strong, hard hands, Granny Boyd anointed Euphemia's hips and groin muscles and thighs with olive oil; Euphemia was locked in a dim, bewildering hall of pain, suspended between joy and dread.

They named the child Mary Jane King. She lived a few months, then died. The pendulum had come swinging back with terrible velocity.

*   *   *

For months after her baby's death, Euphemia had dreams about her mother, nightmares of cruel and bitter clarity. In her dreams she saw herself being born and her mother being taken by God's angels. She would wake and wonder why, as an adult, that it was she who had survived and her child who had been taken. She wondered if God had found a unique way to punish the sins of his children by making them survive those they loved. She supposed God was punishing her for some forgotten transgression. God had a reason for everything, yet she could find no sin in her life that would merit such terrible punishment. She had decided to kill a person once, had come within a few seconds of taking human life when the Comanches had threatened to kill Sarah before Tarantula saved her. Could the decision to kill be as sinful as the act? And, then, is to kill in defense of someone you love a sin at all? She prayed to be forgiven her forgotten sin. As the months passed and the terrible pain and grief began to fade, she realized God's reasons were unknowable and the child's death had been a part of the natural order, not unlike the death of a rose or a star.

The passing years brought new life to their home on Court Street. First George, then William, Jr., then Henry were born. Before the birth of each, Euphemia prayed almost constantly to be forgiven whatever sin she must have committed to cause her to survive the death of so many loved ones. She hated herself for these dark feelings and would try to "redecorate the rooms of her mind with good thoughts," as Matilda had once advised. Then she would remember Matilda was dead and she would sink into another deepening melancholy. But when the hour of her children's births arrived, and her family gathered around with their strong love and their strong hands, the blessed events passed without visitation by death's angels and were remembered only vaguely, like dreams.

When George was first placed in her arms and she saw his almost holy perfection, she began to cry. She cried for joy and thanksgiving, so many tears that Tildy said she was surprised there wasn't a rainbow in the room.

Euphemia never had known she was capable of such love. She would hold each of the soft, warm creatures to her breast and wonder if any happiness could eclipse these moments of union between mother and child. She marveled at the beauty of God's most cherished gift and she was terrified by its vulnerability.

With each child, she was at first terribly overprotective. At the slightest sound in the night, she was up and holding the baby in her arms. She wanted to do everything for the children herself and would shoo Tildy or Granny Boyd away when they offered to help, hold, bathe, rock, or feed the infants. It was only through exhaustion that Euphemia would, at last, allow her family to help her with the babies. Finally, after each child was about six months old, Euphemia would be teased into being a rational mother with normal reactions to her babies' needs.

When Henry King's wife Mahala Day King died, William and Euphemia adopted her three-year-old daughter, Kittie. The home was filled with the music of children and Euphemia became lost in a labyrinth of domesticity. She arose at five and went to bed long after dark. She was wife, mother, teacher, housekeeper, business manager, hired girl, laundress, seamstress, dairy maid, cook, nurse, gardener, water carrier, wood splitter, and field hand. These were also the years when she became one of the county's most serious horse breeders.

Ever since Bartlett McClure had given her the stallion Saracen, she had dreamed of raising fine horses. Saracen was now at his prime and Euphemia, assisted by Tildy, bred him to some of the Navarros' magnificent Spanish mares. Don José Navarro had bred a number of Paso Finos, descendants of the Spanish horses of Andalusia brought to the New World by the Conquistadors. These beautiful animals were noted for the smoothness and naturalness of their gait. Don José had also been experimenting with crossing the purebred Spanish horses with the wild mustangs of the plains. The result was a horse with astonishing speed over a relatively short course.

Ever since she could remember, Euphemia delighted in riding Saracen as fast as his heart and legs could take them. She had dreamed of racing at the many tracks springing up around the state. There were two horses in Texas reputed to be faster over a quarter mile than any Thoroughbred or Arabian. One was called Steel Dust, another Old Shiloh. Euphemia vowed to have such a

horse herself one day and it would become the most famous
horse in Texas. In the meantime, she began to build a small herd
based on the sons and daughters of William's Kentucky mares,
Saracen, the Spanish horses of Don José Navarro, and the wild
mustangs that roamed the grasslands. In 1854 the Red River Telegraph Company introduced the telegraph to Texas, and soon
folks said Euphemia's horses were so fast they could outrun a
rush telegraph message going downhill.

So completely were her waking hours filled with the children,
the home, and the horses that the time, the days, the months
passed as fast as thought. *Where has my life gone?* Euphemia
wondered. *Am I that same little girl who was gathering wildflowers the day Sam Houston came to Peach Creek?*

It was Ann Penn Ireland who brought the news that Sam
Houston had at last been saved. On November 19, 1854, shortly
after the birth of his child Andrew Jackson Houston, the hero of
San Jacinto had waded into Rocky Creek, near Independence,
Texas, to be baptized by the Reverend Rufus C. Burleson.
Euphemia was not sure why she felt such a sense of relief, almost
as if she had been somehow responsible for Sam Houston's many
sins.

Skirting dangerously close to the sin of gossip, Ann and
Euphemia had discussed the sin and salvation of Sam Houston.
They explored the mystery of his first marriage to the beautiful
Eliza Allan and they talked about its tragic aftermath. He had
been Governor of Tennessee, just a campaign away from the pres-
idency, when his bride had left the wedding bed and returned to
her father. Sam Houston had resigned as governor and left the
civilized world for a long exile in the forest. He had never told a
soul what had happened between him and Eliza. There had been
stories that Houston had an open, running sore of unmentionable
cause that Eliza "could not abide when he came to her in his na-
kedness." Ann Penn Ireland felt it must have had something to do
with demon rum, the imbibing of which to her was the funda-
mental sin. Euphemia preferred to believe the romantic tale that
Eliza must have been in love with someone else and was unfaithful to her husband, if only in her mind.

"Then what?" Ann asked.

"Well, she told him about this other person and Sam was angry. Probably flew into a rage."

"Then what?" Ann Penn Ireland did not like loose ends.

"She was frightened and she ran away."

Ann, who had once claimed her allegiance was to "the Democratic Party, the Methodist Church, and the Penn family, in that order," was not a woman who lost many arguments. "He was probably drinking," she said. "If not, it was certain he was thinking about drinking, a greater sin than actually drinking because it precedes it. If a sinner didn't think about drinking, he would never do it at all."

Euphemia wondered why she felt such allegiance to Sam Houston, a man she had seen only a few times as a child. Perhaps it was because his life had been filled with such pits and valleys, such enormous swings from the depths to the heights. She also saw him as the embodiment of the Texas experience. It was almost impossible to think about Texas without thinking about the towering figure of the general who had won independence, the president who had led the Republic into the Union. He was the people, what they had been and could be.

It was after the birth of her third child that Euphemia began to sin herself, her thoughts taking her in dangerous directions. She took a long hard look at her life and she began to want something more, something beyond the endless drudgery of her days. She thought of Matilda Lockhart and her dream to be a ballerina. In the evening, she read the world news in the *Gonzales Inquirer* and the *Christian Advocate,* or browsed in the *Washington Union* or *New Orleans Picayune.* She read about the Paris World's Fair. A brave woman named Florence Nightingale was saving lives in a place called the Crimea. Beyond the Guadalupe River was a wondrous world with lives of purpose and adventure and heightened meaning.

Euphemia found it difficult to talk about these things with Fannie or Jane Isabella. Somehow she felt they wouldn't understand. Their lives had been too different from her own. She thought about writing Sarah, but feared that strong woman would find Euphemia's longings a weakness that must be eradicated like weeds in a garden. Ann Penn Ireland, although a close and good friend, was a woman of action and did not often take the time to explore the more subtle mysteries hiding beneath the surface of things. And so Euphemia wrote Annie Franklin. In her first letter she mentioned how much she missed their talks and how she wished there was someone she could talk to now. Euphemia waited anxiously for a return letter from Annie. It didn't arrive. But Annie Franklin did.

Annie Franklin moved to Seguin, to teach at the new Female Academy. She stayed at the Johnson home and Euphemia was a constant visitor. For three days, while Granny Boyd watched the children, Euphemia and Annie Franklin talked. Sometimes they walked down in the Guadalupe River bottoms or along King Branch, the small creek behind Euphemia's cabin that had been named for the Rowdy King Boys. Euphemia expressed her feeling that there was more to life than being a wife and mother and keeping the home.

"If we are given life," she said, "doesn't it seem that we should experience as much of it as we can? We should collect experiences in the same way some people collect butterflies."

Annie Franklin listened with the absolute understanding that made Euphemia love her so. "Life is a basket to be filled."

"What if life is over and the basket is almost empty? That would be a terrible sin. God wove it for us, gave it to us, and we don't use it. I'd be awfully mad if I were God."

"Then fill your basket," Annie Franklin said. "Get involved in politics. I know you hate slavery. Fight against it. Or join Ann Penn Ireland's fight against demon rum. Help me fight for women's rights."

By the time Annie Franklin left, Euphemia was fired with a new resolve to make things right. She vowed to get involved in the issues that were raging on the political scene. Then she would look in on her sleeping children and she would be filled with such love, such an overwhelming sense of well-being, that she would forget for a while her hungers of the spirit.

Sam Houston came to Seguin in July of 1857 to campaign for Governor of Texas. Euphemia walked to the Hollamon home on its hill above the Guadalupe. Houston made an impassioned speech beneath the oaks and elms of that great estate. The old general wore a linen suit and behind him Spanish moss wept down from the oaks and Euphemia felt the touch of the ending of something. She was shocked that Sam Houston seemed so old. He was still a towering figure, but his hair above his broad brow had turned white. His eyes were deeply hooded and he was bearded now, his chin strong and square. Euphemia noticed he carried a long staff, perhaps to ease the pain of his wounds when walking.

But what startled Euphemia most about the event at the Hollamon home was what the great Sam Houston was forced to defend himself against. He was called a traitor and a coward, and someone charged that he had eaten opium before the Battle of San Jacinto. She was further amazed, even enraged, to find there were hecklers in the crowd who sometimes tried to shout the old general down. *How is it possible,* she wondered, *that this great man could be treated with such disrespect!* Here was a man who had almost been President of the United States; a man who had commanded the victorious army of Texas, was the Father of Texas Independence, and had twice been President of the Republic. He had served two full terms as a United States senator from the State of Texas and was now running for governor. Maybe there were some unsavory things in his life: his disgrace in Tennessee, his time among the Indians, his drinking. Euphemia knew the opium charge was merely political invention and skulduggery. The insane idea that he was a coward and a traitor was based on his opposition to the mounting sentiment in the South to break away from the Union. No one would ever convince her that Sam Houston was not a great and good man.

Some visitors from nearby San Marcos, guests of the Hollamons, seemed not at all impressed with Houston's performance. She recognized Dr. Woods, his wife Georgia, and their beautiful daughters, who seemed to be flirting with every man in sight. They seemed so refined and self-assured, as if born to great wealth. They were relative newcomers to Texas, having come from Mississippi with all their silver and a caravan of slaves long after the hard days of the Texas Revolution. Sam Houston had created the country they inherited. And now, it seemed only their obligations as guests kept them from joining the hecklers. And it was all because Sam Houston wished to preserve the Union.

Euphemia Texas remembered when she'd first seen Sam Houston, under the oak at Peach Creek riding like a king on his great white horse. Now it appeared he was at the end of his reign, his banners tattered, his blue-checked linen suit a kind of mockery. Today he was an angry old man, limping on his San Jacinto leg, railing at liars, a candidate with no party, no organization, and no campaign funds.

Again someone from the audience called out the word "Traitor!" Again Euphemia felt her face grow hot with anger. Houston limped forward and glowered. He seemed to grow larger, a towering figure waving his staff at the crowd. "Sam Houston a traitor to Texas!" he cried. His voice was thunderous. "Was it for this that I bared my bosom to the hail of bullets at the Horseshoe and rode into a bullet at San Jacinto—to be slandered in my old age as a traitor?" It was a moment Euphemia would never forget. The crowd grew still, as if ashamed, and old soldiers wiped tears from their eyes.

Old Sam came close, but he lost the election by about three thousand votes. It appeared his long public career was over. He went back to Washington to complete his Senate term and fight for the preservation of the Union. In a speech to the Senate, he said: "I was defeated. But I am very much obliged to my state, for they have not disowned me in beating me—they have only preferred another."

At the close of his speech he summarized his convictions about the South and the Union. "Ought I not to love the South? Yes, sir, I cherish every manly sentiment for the South; and I am determined while I live in it, none of the fraternal bonds which bind it to the Union shall be broken."

No, on the eve of the Civil War, politics whirled around the communities of Texas as never before. Among these rising tides in the years following Sam Houston's visit to Seguin was a strange and troubling movement called the Knights of the Golden Circle that began to sweep through the South and Texas and Euphemia's parlor in Seguin.

One evening, at a dinner party, Euphemia overheard her husband talking with Ben and Henry McCulloch about the formation of their "castle." When she asked about it, the men became oddly and ineffectually secretive. Later Ann Penn Ireland explained that castles were local units of the Knights of the Golden Circle, a secessionist, anti-abolitionist organization created by a brilliant and ambitious novelist named George Bickley.

"The man has a real problem with reality," Ann said. "He takes such ideas as states' rights, the Monroe Doctrine, and manifest destiny and stirs it all up into a kind of Southern Manifesto stew. The idea is to extend slavery not only by seceding from the Union but by creating a whole new Confederacy—a great Golden Circle—that would include Cuba and Mexico. The man is absolutely mad. But he's winning converts by the thousands."

"Why would anybody fall for that?" Euphemia felt a touch of disloyalty, or was it embarrassment, as she now realized William King and Ben McCulloch must be followers of the "absolutely mad" man.

"I think people are tired of politicians in the North telling them how to live their lives. There is a genuine states' rights issue. Slavery makes it an economic issue. The established order in the South can't survive without slaves. And in Texas, Bickley appeals to our longing for the romantic days of the Republic. Bickley is actually creating history using the same techniques he would use writing a novel. We are simply fictional characters living in Bickley's twisted mind," Ann concluded.

A few days later, Euphemia confronted William about the Seguin "castle" of the Knights of the Golden Circle.

"It's a means to an end," William began. He well knew Euphemia's position on slavery and he chose his words carefully. "There is no other outcome to the tensions between the North and the South but secession. I feel that strongly. We can no longer submit to Northern insolence and Northern outrage. Theirs is a different world from ours. Why should we force people with such contrasting beliefs and ways of life and cultures into a union that is not acceptable to either side? We must go our own way. Each state must be sovereign and independent. The Knights of the Golden Circle is simply a way to galvanize public support for secession."

"But Bickley believes this new nation—this new Golden Circle—should include Mexico. But Mexico opposes slavery. Surely you don't believe in an invasion of Mexico to force slavery into that country too?"

"Of course not!"

"Do you want war with the North?"

"I accept war as a possible consequence of secession."

Euphemia listened to the late afternoon traffic moving down Court Street. There were buggies now and carriages, instead of the old heavy wagons of previous years. Delicate creations, light and graceful, and their pace quickened now, the soft clatter of hooves hurried as if to reach home before dark. How the town had changed and grown.

"You know," Euphemia finally said, "I think men do want war. Yes, deep down, men actually love war. There is some kind of primal attraction, something in the blood, that makes men actually need war."

William looked up from his papers, letters he was writing to the castles in New Braunfels and La Grange and San Antonio. "You may be right," he said, a response Euphemia recognized as the one he always made when wrong.

"I've seen it all before," she said quietly. "I saw it at Peach Creek. I saw it in the war against Santa Anna and in the war against the Comanches. And I can see it now. There'll be uniforms with buttons polished bright as mirrors. Flags and banners waving. Parades with all the young girls saying tearful goodbyes. Speeches about courage and patriotism and sacrifice. I don't know. Maybe women love war, too. We urge it on you, I suppose."

William was writing now. Euphemia could hear the whisper of his quill. "William," she said, "listen to me." The whisper ceased and even by lantern light she could see the blue of his eyes. "I love you, William. I will love you until the hour of my death. But I tell you this. If you go to war, I won't cry and I won't see you off." She stood, moved to his desk, and kissed his brow. "And if you go, I won't say goodbye. I'm sick to death of death." When Euphemia Texas left the house, she slammed the door so hard something glass fell to the floor and broke. She recognized the sound. It was the sound a flint arrow makes passing through a window.

To the west of the Seguin courthouse they built a platform for the most beautiful of the daughters of the Confederacy. Just as Euphemia had predicted, there was a brass band playing "Dixie" and "Bonnie Blue Flag" while Company D, composed of the young men of Seguin, marched in review before pausing to receive from Miss Mattie Jefferson the flag the company would carry into battle. The flag had been made from remnants of dress material by the ladies of Seguin. It was a stirring moment and in spite of herself Euphemia was moved, especially when she heard the young girls singing "When This Cruel War Is Over." *How strange,* she thought, *to sing about the ending of a war that has hardly begun.*

This was the second time Euphemia had stood at a courthouse watching Confederate soldiers march out of town. Her brother Travis Ashby had organized the first company to leave Gonzales. They had been presented a flag by Miss Lou Scoggins. After the banner had been presented and Captain Ashby had gracefully accepted, the company marched to San Antonio for training. Now, as Euphemia listened to the cheering and watched the schoolgirls reach to touch the arms of the soldiers as they passed, she wondered, *Would men play war if women simply refused to attend the game?*

William King and other members of the Seguin Castle of the Knights of the Golden Circle had recently returned from San Antonio where they had captured the arsenal of the United States Army. The skirmish took place a few months before the South had fired on Fort Sumter, a bombardment that the Seguin Knights insisted was the second engagement of the War Between the States. Ben McCulloch and his force of volunteers had marched to San Antonio to force the surrender of Major General David Twiggs, thereby denying the Union the weapons, ammunition, and stores housed in the Alamo city. The army headquarters had been a scene of utter chaos. McCulloch's raiders, the red insignia of their fraternal order blazing from their coats, had filled the streets, firing into the air and riding and marching in various disorderly directions among the curious and amused residents of the city. The Union forces had surrendered their arms to McCulloch and departed without a single shot fired in anger. One of the Knights, however, did drop a double-barreled shotgun from his horse and it discharged, wounding seven men and two horses.

As the strange drama unfolded, a young officer assigned to the Texas frontier named Robert E. Lee passed through San Antonio. He was on his way to Washington after being recalled by President Lincoln. His father had been Henry Lee, the brilliant "Light-Horse Harry," hero of the Revolutionary War. Colonel Robert E. Lee had fought under General Winfield Scott in the war between the United States and Mexico after Texas joined the Union. Winfield Scott called the young colonel "the greatest military genius in America." When Lee arrived in San Antonio, he was shocked to see the milling masses of McCulloch's men. It was reported that his eyes were filled with tears when he said: "Has it come so soon to this?"

Euphemia learned that Robert E. Lee and Sam Houston were close friends with shared Unionist sympathies. Lee had argued there could be no greater calamity for the country than the dissolution of the Union he had served to defend for so many years. "Secession is nothing but revolution," he said. But his loyalty to Virginia was absolute. He would do what his home state would do. When he left San Antonio after the Alamo debacle, William King heard him say: "When I get home I think the world will have one soldier less. I shall resign and go to planting corn."

When Lee arrived in the east, Lincoln offered him field command of the United States Army. Lee, as a matter of conscience, refused and joined the Confederates.

Soon the men of Guadalupe County were gone again, to places called Etham's Landing and Seven Pines, Gaines Mill and

Manassas. After setting his affairs in order, William King followed the McCullochs to war with the Union just as he had once followed them into battle with the Comanches. Once again, Euphemia and Tildy were left to deal with the farm and the horses, the children and the land.

As the months passed, each day became a struggle to survive. At one particularly low point on the home front, Euphemia paid her boys' school tuition with eggs, butter, and bacon, a tender far more potent than Confederate dollars. Euphemia remembered how she and Sarah and Tildy had kept the Peach Creek homestead together during the Comanche wars. The feeling of *déjà vu* was so powerful she half expected to see Comanches come riding up Court Street, dragging featherbeds and yards of fabric from their horses. But the only dreadful thing to ride up Court Street was the coach that brought the mail. It would emerge from the hollow beyond the creek and life would freeze, as if suspended in amber, as the women would wait for the coachman's horn to break the silence with word from the living and news of the dead.

When William had announced his decision to go to war, Euphemia had been angry and then had been ashamed of her anger. He had reminded her of the first time they had been together, after Euphemia's encounter with the panther, when he had told her about the death of William Beard. "I can't avoid this conflict like I avoided the Mier Expedition," he had said. "I can't just keep letting my friends fight my wars for me."

Just as women have done since man's first war, Euphemia helped him gather the things he would need, sewed buttons on his uniform, and showered him with love enough to last as long into his absence as possible. And she did not follow through on her threat not to say goodbye. The departure had been tearful and she was surprised by the actual physical pain she felt as she watched him ride away, like a small boy off on some mysterious mischief.

Sometimes, at night, when the horses were quiet and the stars filled the night sky with their jewelry, Euphemia would try to reach for William with her mind. She would pour her thought toward where he must be and then would listen to the night for a response. An owl might answer or a wind walk through grass. But sometimes, she was sure, William's thought would come pouring back. She absorbed the substance and she would drift in it as in a quiet pond. There were no words in these communications, simply an awareness that they were together, that they were touching across the distance. "Be safe, my love," she would say and then she drifted in the stream that told her for the moment he was.

One night, as she was talking with William across the miles, the stars began to fade one by one, as if a dark shroud was being drawn across the sky. A cold wind whipped dust and tatters of cotton from the fields. Great heavy drops of rain exploded on the porch. For one horrible moment, Euphemia thought something had happened to William, then reason returned and she rose to close the windows against the coming storm.

Bright lightning pulsed and twisted in the clouds. Rivers of rain thrashed the roof and filled the night with an orchestra of sound. The wind howled and Euphemia could actually feel the house move and tremble in the gusts. Then, above all the sound that filled the night, she heard another, the rumbling, groaning sobbing sound the river makes when it has gone mad with flood. Tildy came into the house in a rush of rain and lantern light. "The horses!" she said, and Euphemia followed her into the fury of the night. Euphemia knew there was no William to help her now. If she was to save the horses, she would have to do it herself.

The creeks were rising fast, overflowing into the bottoms where the horses were kept. Euphemia could see their eyes, white and wild, as they screamed and splashed in circles through the drowning grass. She knew they would never leave their familiar lot and they were going to drown unless she and Tildy could lead them to safety. The thought of losing the horses filled her with dread and with strength. She gathered her skirts and tied them in a knot at her waist. With arms raised, with their lanterns high, Euphemia and Tildy waded out into the flood. They both knew if they could catch the old mare, the others might follow.

They called the horses by name and the wind carried their calls away. It was raining so hard it was difficult to tell where the boundary was between flood and storm. The current clutched at

Euphemia's thighs and pulled her down. The lantern went under, then Euphemia felt herself rolling and falling, being swept beneath the feet of the terrified horses. She grasped at a tree and stood. If she let go of the tree, she was lost. In the staccato fire of the lightning, she saw Tildy moving toward her, holding to the mane of the old mare, reaching for her, struggling through the flood. Euphemia grasped the mare's mane and they fought their way to higher ground, the other horses following as they outran the angry water.

Exhausted, trembling with the cold, they sat with the horses, talking to them, touching them, through the night. By first light, the storm had passed. Leaning on each other, Tildy and Euphemia watched the morning come.

Among Euphemia's greatest fears during the war years was that the Confederate Army would requisition her horses. As it was, she had to sell a horse now and again to get cash. But if the men needed the horses to replace those killed in the war, what could she do? She could not very well refuse when a good horse might mean the difference between life and death for a soldier. But she resented the possibility that all she had worked for could be taken away. She remembered telling William so long ago that she did not want her horses to go to war. She even considered taking the horses somewhere to hide them from the army. But a herd of horses is a difficult thing to hide.

One day the stage brought a letter from Sarah's son Joel with news that his uncle Roderick Gelhorn, an officer with Terry's Texas Rangers, had been wounded at Shiloh. "It is severe," he wrote, "and might end his life." Fannie waited in agony for further news, Euphemia often at her side. Weeks later the stage brought Roderick Gelhorn home. He had been spared from the enemy's guns, yet was a casualty of a mysterious and recurring fever that plagued him the rest of his life.

In January, 1863, Travis wrote a letter that Euphemia found especially moving. At this time, Travis and Joel were serving together with Terry's Texas Rangers in Tennessee. "It was so strange," he wrote. "We rode into town at daylight. The enemy had gone, but they had left the stores fully stocked. With winter coming on, it was a chance to get warm clothing. There is something about Shelbyville that reminds me of Gonzales and the folks here have a way of speaking that sounds like my family in Texas."

Within a month, the stage brought a letter from another soldier serving in Terry's Texas Rangers. "Thursday we made a circuit to the rear. We destroyed 120 wagons and brought off another fine cannon. Our losses in these six days of fighting was estimated at seven thousand. We are now wearing the blue coats of the Yankees we captured. But I regret to say that Lieutenant Joel McClure was killed on Christmas day."

Roderick Gelhorn drove Fannie, Euphemia, and Jane Isabella to Peach Creek to be with Sarah. When they arrived, Sarah's great white house was already filled with friends and neighbors. For four days the house was filled, yet strangely silent, as Sarah struggled with the notion her son was dead. Sarah had lost seven children over the years and Euphemia marveled that she didn't just curl up and die of grief. On the third day after news of Joel's death had arrived, Sarah shocked her sisters by releasing a cloud of smoke from her pipe and announcing that Joel was alive. "If he was dead, I'd feel it and I don't feel it." Euphemia was terribly saddened by Sarah's denial.

On the fifth day after news of Joel's death arrived, the stage brought word that he was terribly wounded, yet had survived. His uncle Roderick Gelhorn loaded a wagon and began the long journey to the front to search for Joel and bring him home.

The stagecoach horn sounded the roster of the dead. Ignatius Johnson. James Whitehead. Andrew Erskine. William Davis. James Butler. George Longstreet. Seguin's young men had marched so brightly past the grandstand filled with the fairest girls of the Confederacy and had accepted with such pride the banner sewn by the ladies of the town. Now so many lay in the earth like the heroes of the Alamo and the martyrs of Goliad. Then, at Pea Ridge, General Ben McCulloch, the man who had fired one of Sam Houston's Twin Sisters cannon at San Jacinto, was killed. *Death writes a cruel, yet efficient summary,* Euphemia thought.

By early spring, as the bluebonnets were beginning to suggest that there was still life and beauty in the world, Roderick Gelhorn returned to Peach Creek. Sarah watched as the slaves lifted Joel from the wagon and carried him into the house. He lived long enough to tell his mother goodbye. "Now Joel is dead," Sarah said. She had seen it for herself this time. She had lost eight of her nine children.

Two more hard years passed before the stage brought news that no more dead boys would be buried in cold far-away fields. Lee had surrendered at Appomattox. The old Texas Ranger Rip Ford, with a company of teenage boys and old men, fought on against the Yankees in South Texas for a month or more. When he learned of Appomattox, Rip Ford still refused to surrender. Finally he was convinced to simply exchange courtesies with the enemy and fade away. The Civil War was over. Euphemia thought it was ironic that a war so profane and so savage would be ended by an exchange of courtesies.

After the war was over and William had safely returned, Seguin was placed under the military command of Major General J. J. Reynolds and a Union garrison was established on Live Oak Street. During the Reconstruction years, General Reynolds ruled the city. He appointed city officials, purged jury rolls of Confederate sympathizers, destroyed Confederate money, seized Confederate property, and rigged such local elections as were held. He also imposed a heavy property tax, ostensibly to pay for the expenses of law enforcement. William and Euphemia could not pay the taxes on their land. Euphemia had not lost her horses to the flood or to the war. Yet after the war she lost many of them to the tax collector.

Hatreds and tensions between the people of Seguin and the encampment of Yankee soldiers constantly flared. The presence of the camp was salt to the wounds of Confederate veterans. The occupying Yankee soldiers resented the fact that life for their defeated enemy was returning to normal, while they were still serving far from home. Seguin escaped some of the chaos and lawlessness that plagued other Texas communities after the war. Here no bands of discontented and desperate veterans demanded pay for their four years of service; no angry crowds looted commissary stores. The rumors that San Antonio and Houston and other towns were being sacked and burned by Federals were not so often heard here in Seguin. At the end, eighteen men of Seguin's Company D had stood outside the courthouse at Appomattox when Lee surrendered his sword. For these and others in town, the war would not end quickly, certainly not in their lifetime. Occasionally young boys taunted Yankee soldiers and the boys would be chased and, if caught, beaten. One old black man, Sol Jefferson, a friend and fishing companion of Euphemia's sons, was hanged by his thumbs for twelve hours as punishment for "sassing" an occupation officer.

Since the Yankee encampment was so near her house, Euphemia feared for the safety of her children. They had to walk past the soldiers to get to school. So Euphemia and William worked out a plan that would accomplish two goals. William took the boys out of town and out of trouble. They went south to the Wild Horse Desert to find horses to replenish the stock they had lost to the Yankee tax collector. She reminded William not to capture the horses by shooting them in the neck, the process he had described to her so long ago. It was then, while William and the boys searched for wild mustangs in South Texas, that Euphemia was able to obtain the son of one of the most famous horses in Texas.

Not far from Seguin there lived an old Indian fighter and Texas Ranger named William Fleming. When he came back from fighting in the Civil War, he bought a stallion that two local women had hidden from the Yankees and the dreaded tax collector of Governor Davis. In order to keep the horse out of sight they had it chained in a thicket. The horse had been chained so long that his feet were deformed and he could hardly walk, much less run. But it turned out that the stallion Billy Fleming had purchased had been sired by a horse named Shiloh and foaled by a daughter of the famous Steel Dust. The horse was called "Old Billy," the greatest and fastest of those extraordinary horses they were just beginning to call quarter horses because of their speed over a quarter-mile track. Old Billy would sire many great racers in the coming years.

In the dark of one night, as General Reynolds and the Yankee soldiers were sleeping, Euphemia and Tildy rode Saracen and

Euphemia's favorite Spanish mare to William Fleming's place where they bred the mare to Old Billy. Months later, a colt was foaled, and they called it Dancer after the horse that swam the Brazos River in the Runaway Scrape. With Dancer's legendary breeding, Euphemia was practically assured that, at last, she would have the fastest and finest horse in Texas.

In the aftermath of the war, Euphemia found herself once again drawn to the exhilarating and mystifying world of politics. Her friend Ann Penn Ireland's husband, John, was deeply involved in local politics and was considered to have a bright political future. Often Ann, Euphemia, and Annie Franklin would meet at one of their houses to work on their quilts or to card cotton while discussing the troubling politics of postwar Texas. The tensions left by the war were not restricted to those between the defeated town and the victorious Federals. As the nightmare memories of battle began to fade, the returning Confederate veterans and their families began to settle into social camps based on their prewar sympathies. There were those who, like Sam Houston, had voted to maintain the Union and there were those, like Henry McCulloch and William King, who had voted for secession.

So strong were these divisions that Ann Penn Ireland predicted they would become the basis of Texas politics until "Kingdom come or until a Presbyterian becomes governor, whichever comes first." In 1866, delegates from throughout the state, including John Ireland, gathered at Austin to attempt an orderly reentry into the Union. They argued still about the issues of the state's right to secede, the abolition of slavery, the right of free blacks to vote. They also argued about public education and ways to hasten economic recovery from the war.

But it was the Reconstruction Convention of 1868 that galvanized the attention of Euphemia, Annie Franklin, Ann Penn Ireland and the other politically aware women of the town. At this convention, a formal attempt was made to include a woman suffrage clause in the new Constitution for the State of Texas. The movement for the rights of women, which had been stalled by the Civil War, was gathering momentum throughout the country. Susan B. Anthony's efforts to organize a national Equal Rights Association to protect the rights of both blacks and white women were well known in the towns and cities of Texas. On the surface, there didn't appear to be any organized woman suffrage movement in the Lone Star State. Yet beneath the surface, in the parlors and bedrooms of Seguin and Austin and San Antonio, a subtle, yet pervasive, advocacy was being pursued. No longer could women remain silent and inactive. When John Ireland and the other delegates returned to Austin in 1868, some carried a draft of an article providing the right of suffrage for both sexes.

The declaration was introduced by T. H. Mundine, of Burleson County. After an unsuccessful effort to table the bill, it was sent to the committee on State Affairs. The committee report in favor of woman suffrage was a glowing and eloquent tribute to the virtues of womanhood. At one point, the committee report read: "When the Blood of the Savior was poured out upon the Mount, she (woman) was the last to linger about the Cross and the first at the Tomb of the Resurrected Lord." Euphemia said it was the "splendacious" language that probably defeated the declaration. Ann Penn Ireland added: "It's hard to vote in the affirmative when you're sick at your stomach."

One night, after a small gathering for supper, when John Ireland and William and the other men left the room, Annie Franklin read the minority report against woman suffrage out loud. The women waited until the men left so their husbands would not hear the howls of laughter always generated when the report was read by women. When she was sure the men were gone, Annie Franklin, in a deep and sonorous voice, read the following: "We are unhesitatingly opposed to woman suffrage ... because of their native modesty and inborn refinement of feeling which causes every true woman to shrink from mingling in the busy noise of election days.... We are opposed to it further because we believe the good sense of every true woman in the land teaches her that granting them the power to vote is a direct open insult to their sex by the implication that they are so unwomanly as to desire the privilege."

The true women laughed, off and on, into the night until they were taken home by their confused and resentful husbands. The male conversation, over cigars, had not been nearly so amusing. The incident was especially disturbing to the men because it was well known throughout Guadalupe County that Ann Penn Ireland almost never laughed and Euphemia Texas almost never smiled.

As the years passed, Euphemia began to wear the little town of Seguin like a comfortable old coat. Her troubling discontent seemed behind her, those times when she yearned for horizons beyond the banks of the Guadalupe. No longer did she wish to rush away like Florence Nightingale to save the Crimea or the world. As she told Ann Penn Ireland, "There's plenty to save right here in Seguin." Once as she walked through the town, the sun warm on her face, the sound of children's laughter in the air, she noticed, with a kind of delicate shock, that the frontier was gone. Here, in Seguin, was a whole different reality than the one she had known as a girl. *Where is Tarantula?* she would wonder. *Where are the buglers of Santa Anna's army? Where is Jean-Baptiste Beauchamps, the cowardly carpenter?* It seemed just a moment ago that her world was filled with danger and death and violence. Now, somehow, in spite of the terrible War Between the States, maybe in some strange convoluted way because of it, the frontier had become what Sarah had always wished it to be. It had become civilized. Euphemia and her circle of friends, who now called themselves the "True Women," often talked about the illusive nature of the concept of civilization.

"In the old days," Euphemia Texas observed, "when Seguin was a kind of oasis in the wilderness, it was easier to forgive or overlook the wrong people do. When you're trying to survive, you just don't have time to observe such niceties as justice and truth. But now, the more civilized we become, the less patience I have with injustice and ignorance and fools."

"It's becoming almost impossible to suffer fools gladly," Ann Penn Ireland added—as if she ever had.

One thing that can be said about the True Women during the years of Reconstruction, they did not suffer fools gladly. When the occupation forces tried to make the Methodist Episcopal Church of the South reunite with the Northern Methodist

Church, Ann Penn Ireland and the other True Women led a campaign to build a new church. "I'd rather have a Southern brush arbor than the finest Yankee church in the world," Ann Penn declared to all who would listen. The new church was an act of defiance led by William King, chairman of the committee. But at the heart of the rebellion were Seguin women who refused to suffer fools gladly. The True Women gave from their egg money and put on dinners to raise money to fund the new structure. In later years, they would challenge the all-male leadership of the Methodist Church by defiantly organizing the Women's Missionary Society at a bold midnight meeting.

Euphemia and the True Women also came to be active in a quiet effort to improve the lot of the former slaves. The Reverend Leonard Isley, a Baptist missionary from Bangor, Maine, established the school for freedmen on Vinegar Hill in the west part of the town, and the True Women helped him as best they could, collecting used books for his school's library.

Over the years Euphemia had earned respect from the Negro community. Her convictions against slavery were well-known among her intimate friends, and every Negro person in town knew about them too. Before Texas won independence, some free Negro families had obtained land in the area from the Mexican government. Oppressive laws of the Republic and, later, of the state of Texas severely limited their freedom. Negroes could not own property or even buy or sell goods without a white sponsor. After she had tried to free Tildy, Euphemia paid more attention to these laws. She decided to "stand in" for the Negro farmers living near the Kings' properties, vouching for them when they bought and sold their livestock. She was pleased to find one thing she could do to help those with even fewer legal rights than herself.

During Reconstruction Euphemia showed her newly freed neighbors how to obtain farmland at reasonable cost, by applying for state homestead lands. She read over all their contracts to make sure they were not being cheated. She and William even stood for their credit at the stores until their crops came in and they paid their bills.

As she worked to help black families, Euphemia sometimes

heard the whispers of those who believed the white people of Seguin should keep to their own. Because Euphemia was from an old landed Texas family, the criticism remained veiled and indirect and Euphemia continued to follow her conscience.

Euphemia was glad that Sam Houston hadn't lived to see these terrible times of the Reconstruction years. He had died in 1863, perhaps grieving for his Union as he watched the Confederate troops march past his house in Huntsville.

Now the Texans were ruled by grim, often drunken soldiers in league with corrupt political hacks. Because of his service to the Confederate cause, William King was not allowed to vote. It galled him to see illiterate blacks, recently arrived immigrants from Germany, scalawags, and carpetbaggers lining up at the polling places to vote for people unworthy of a place on the ballot.

For William King and almost every other Texan, the most important thing on their minds was to rid their communities of the Yankee presence. As long as the Federals were garrisoned in their towns, the poison of their presence would infect any and all attempts at self-government or efforts to rebuild their institutions, their towns, and their lives. However, the men of Seguin were in hopeless political disarray. The old resentments between Unionist and Secessionist were as alive and pervasive as they were before the war. Neighbors were separated by walls of prejudice. Many Texans stood on the Conservative Republican side of the wall, while others stood on the Liberal Democrat side.

If Reconstruction were ever to be ended, if the war was ever to be over, if Texans were ever to reestablish control of their own government, someone, somehow, had to break down the wall that divided one neighbor from another. For any kind of effective political reform to occur, there had to be a fusion, a new kind of alliance between the Conservative Republicans and the Liberal Democrats in Texas. In Seguin, when Euphemia was preparing for her fortieth birthday, the forging of that new alliance between political enemies began. And it was the True Women who fanned the flame.

One day Euphemia received word her friend Elizabeth Douglass was extremely ill. She and Ann Penn Ireland spent an entire day preparing meals for the Douglass family. At suppertime they carried the soup tureen and other covered dishes the few blocks to the Douglass home. Together they would sit with Elizabeth through the night, care for her children, and take charge of the household chores. When Euphemia and Ann Penn Ireland arrived, they found that another old friend of Elizabeth Douglass, Polly Gordon, was already there. The mood in the sickroom, which would have normally been warm and caring and supportive, turned cold as a Blue Norther. Polly Gordon's husband was a Conservative Republican. Although he had served in the Confederate forces, as a matter of conscience, he had voted against secession. William King and John Ireland were Liberal Democrats, and they had fervently campaigned for secession from the Union.

Now the women had come together to care for a sick neighbor. Elizabeth had chills and fever. But Dr. Johnson was out of the county. Under the circumstances it was natural for the women to rally around and help Elizabeth out. In uneasy silence, Ann Penn Ireland soaked a towel in ice-cold water and then wrapped it around Elizabeth's neck. Euphemia searched the kitchen for the large-mouthed bottle of quinine and then heated water in the kettle. Polly Gordon gathered quilts and blankets to be used later to sweat out the fever. All this in silence, eyes averted, the air charged and heavy and oppressive. In the quiet of night, as Polly and Euphemia sat on either side of Elizabeth's bed, keeping the wrap cold and moist, their eyes met and held.

"This simply has to stop," Euphemia said. "What are we becoming? It's time for us to mend fences." Euphemia rose, moved around the bed, and put her hand on Polly's shoulder. They looked down at their sick friend and for a moment watched her struggle against the fever. "It's time for this war to be over," Euphemia said, and Polly Gordon clasped Euphemia's hand with her own.

When she returned home the next day, Euphemia gave William an ultimatum. "It's time you men put away your childish loyalties! We lost the war; now we can't lose our old friends, too. You men were so all-fired eager to start this fool war, why don't you have the gumption to stop it?" The True Women spread the word throughout Seguin. Polly and Ann Penn Ireland and Euphemia and the wives and daughters talked from sunup to sundown to convince the Seguin men that they must reach some kind of compromise. Little by little, something happened among this small group of neighbors. Soon the leaders of Seguin, with their vastly differing political beliefs, announced what history would later call the Fusion Convention, an alliance between Conservative Republicans and Liberal Democrats that sought to hammer out a legitimate political order in Texas. The first meeting was held in Seguin. The Rowdy King Boys were there. Henry McCulloch and John Ireland attended. It was a grass-roots movement for stability and order that spread throughout the state.

In 1870, a statewide Fusion Convention was held in Austin and the first unified attempt to create a new Texas Constitution was begun. It would be four years before Reconstruction would end. A painful nine years after Appomattox, the political war would finally be over. And the spirit behind the movement toward peace was kindled by a group of women gathered around the bedside of a sick friend in a little town by the Guadalupe River.

For the first time in her forty-three years, Euphemia Texas Ashby King would know what life was like in a world without war.

One autumn morning, as Euphemia and Dancer rode through the mist rising from the Guadalupe bottoms, she heard the ringing of a sledge on steel and the guttural oaths of strangers. Then she saw the heavy wagons, gaudily painted the colors of firecrackers and green apples. Rising above the meadow was a canvas tent, a huge tattered autumn leaf cut from cloth the color of earth. The wagons carried the legend: "John Boothway's Wild West Show." Euphemia had heard of such shows, which traveled from town to town, bringing the legends and lies of the "real West" to the East. Perhaps the most famous of these spectaculars had been established a few years earlier by Buffalo Bill Cody, featuring sharpshooters, rope-spinners, wild Indians, and beautiful, daring Mexican señoritas.

John Boothway's show was a small, sad version of the same melodramatic fare so popular in the big cities back East. As she watched the old tent rise, Euphemia was sure many of the workers probably doubled as stars. Posters promised two grand and complete performances each day, rain or shine. The posters also promised a defense of the Alamo, a Texas Ranger shootout, a "gorgeous" trick rider who could out-ride and out-shoot any man, and a savage attack by the last great chief of the Comanches. As Euphemia watched the workers struggle with the canvas and the wagons and the stock, she felt suddenly very old. *I'm already part of history,* she thought. *The life I led is already becoming myth.*

That afternoon, Euphemia rode Dancer to the meadow. There was a chill wind blowing through the river bottoms and music drifted from the grandstand, the same kind of brass band that had sent the boys off to war now welcoming children and dreamers and a whole new generation of people who would forever wonder if their origins were real. There was a good crowd. Not nearly so many as came last Sunday to hear the sermon of the Reverend Andrew Jackson Potter at Mill Creek, but then Andrew Jackson Potter could be more entertaining than all but a few Wild West shows. Euphemia wasn't sure why she decided to attend the performance or why she wanted to attend alone, without William. Maybe she wanted to indulge the child in herself, unobserved.

And there it was, her life unfolding beneath an old torn tent the color of earth. The band cast bad brass into the air, the announcer's voice roared and rose and fell as the marvels of the Old West and of Euphemia's life passed through time and the autumn afternoon. She saw the widows of the Alamo and heard the sound of Santa Anna's trumpets and Sarah leaped across the canyon and turned to laugh at the pursuing Comanches. Matilda Lockhart's ruined face and the blood of the looter passed before her eyes and she felt the blood of Colonel Reuben Ross in her lap. Here was a carnival of violence and danger, daring and death. And, then, as a grand finale, the Comanche chief was surrounded and killed by Texas Rangers. Slowly the Comanche chief died a death of elaborate and pitiful ceremony and the show ended. Euphemia found herself crying.

The next morning Euphemia returned to the meadow. It was a reverse of the earlier morning, for now the tent was coming down and the wagons were being loaded for departure. Dancer's breath made small white clouds in the cold morning air. Euphemia waited for the wagons and the horses to pass. First came the riders, looking very mortal and ordinary in the light of day. The wagons came and passed, their huge wheels whispering through the fallen leaves. Then came the last great warrior of the Comanches. Tarantula was walking, his huge body bent now, his eyes deep within his scarred face seeming to look inward. The power of his presence had diminished. His great arms, which had once held the power of life and death over those she loved, now hung at his side like meat. He, too, seemed mortal and ordinary in the light of time. Euphemia touched Dancer's flank and he stepped forward. Euphemia felt the eyes of the circus people, astonished, curious, as she stepped into Tarantula's path. The old renegade stopped. Slowly he looked up into Euphemia's face and after a moment there was a glimmer of recognition in his eyes. "Brave Squaw Child," he said.

The circus people watched as Euphemia dismounted and handed Tarantula Dancer's reins. "You shouldn't walk," she said. "Take the horse." Then she turned to the circus people and to the few from town who watched. "You see I have given him the horse." Then she turned and moved back toward the quiet, tranquil streets of Seguin.

Idella

It had begun to rain. I could hear the raindrops independently as they played their melody on Idella's tin roof. Another candle had burned down, adding towers and spires to the castle of wax on the table by the old woman's elbow. She seemed to be sleeping, hardly breathing, a part of the darkness and the river and the spiral glide of time. Outside the Guadalupe accepted the gift of the rain with silence, and I wondered how a night so still could hold such quick and sentient memories. The night breathed life. I felt Euphemia and Sam Houston and the Rowdy King Boys and Tildy at the window, a presence real as the rain, yet when I turned to look there was only shadow. I looked at Idella's still form and I wondered if she really did possess the power to speak with the dead. Her eyes were closed.

"Where are they now?" I asked. It was the same questions Euphemia had asked so long ago, a question I would ask only of Idella and on a night like this, filled with ghosts and rain and candlelight.

Idella opened her eyes, and they were clear and white as the eyes of a child. "They're all here, Darlin'. Euphemia, Tildy, Tarantula, and all the rest. Lookin' on and watchin' how things come out." Idella sighed then and smiled. I could tell she was tired. "It's late," she said at last. "Maybe it's time you went on home. I know you're not afraid of the river like some." Then she laughed, a sound in complete harmony with the rain on the metal roof. "Oh, I've seen you down there at night smokin' your cigars like a man."

Idella closed her eyes again and she seemed to look inward through the gray veil of the years. "I see you and Mary Telva Fischer and Faye Blumberg and Anne Baer and that Parker girl taking the car keys out of Mary Ann Fritz's mother's purse and leavin' the slumber party. Night dark as this. Rollin' that car whisper quiet down the drive and into the street, so Miz Fritz can't hear. Then startin' the car and flyin' off down Milam Street and down dirt country roads and then down below the cemetery by the river. I see all you girls down there in the river bottoms in your baby doll pajamas scarin' yourselves half to death. All you girls so innocent and new and filled with the power of youth."

I was absolutely amazed that the dark secret of Mrs. Fritz's car keys had been revealed. "Idella, how ..."

"Darlin', there's nothing about this country I don't know. Between old Idella and Peachtree and Pink Rosebud and Softshoe Willie, the only secrets there have ever been in this part of Texas are the ones God keeps. And we're makin' a little progress on those."

"But Pink Rosebud, Peachtree, they're all dead."

"Of course they're not, Darlin'. Everything that was ever here on this earth is still here in some form. Everything that will be is here now. Nothing goes away, it just changes. Euphemia is as alive now as a star or a rose or the river."

I left Idella standing on her porch, the rain falling like a lace curtain from her roof. She waved and called a name I hadn't heard in twenty years. "Goodnight, Queenie," she said. And I could hear her laughter like bells in the temple of the night.

The night was warm. I walked by the river and the rain washed away the years and I felt cleansed and alive and as new as the night I was named Queen of the Guadalupe County Fair. Idella had remembered the nickname inspired by that event. There were a number of important women in the mid-fifties— among them Lady Bird Johnson, Queen Elizabeth II, and the four Seguin High School cheerleaders—yet few celebrities were presented honors as prized, as esteemed as that bestowed on the Queen of the Guadalupe County Fair. I was a candidate of the Seguin Conservation Society and had entered the contest primarily to please my mother. Surely I had no chance of winning, for I was barely sixteen and the Fair Queens before had all been high school seniors or even freshmen in college. Yet, on that September night, as I stood on a platform erected in the center of the rodeo arena in my green silk suit and three-inch heels, to my great wonderment and surprise, I became the youngest Guadalupe Fair Queen in history. For a week I reigned over the rodeo and presented blue ribbons to those who entered champion hogs or sheep or lemon meringue pies. On a night like this, after I had been given the Queen's bouquet and had danced with a rodeo bullrider whose boots had heels as tall as mine, we left the fair in a convoy of red pickup trucks to dance the dirty bop, smoke cigars, and drink Lone Star Beer from long-neck bottles in the parking lot behind the White House Drive-in.

It was on a night like this that Jackie Schmidt and Peggy Parker and the other True Women of our generation committed what is still sometimes remembered as the Great Guadalupe County Tractor Outrage. In a small Texas town like Seguin, masculine symbols abound. They are so obvious and blatant—things like pickup trucks with gun racks in the cab and in the back gangly hounds sliding around in the truckbed—that they disappear like the trees in the forest. But of all the things in Texas solely and purely the province of men and denied to women, none possess exclusivity as do the products of such companies as John Deere, International Harvester, Ferguson, or the Tractor Division of Ford Motor Company. The tractor is an inviolate male symbol, unprofaned by the touch of woman's hand. At some time in our youth, we realized a strange fact about men and tractors. No man, farmer or rancher, ever removed the keys from his Ford or John Deere. When he finished his plowing or grading, he simply turned off the key, left the tractor in the field, and walked back to the house.

Texas is full of fine tractors out in the field with their keys dangling in the ignition. Surely no man would stoop to steal another's tractor. It would be a rare crime, punishable, perhaps, by hanging. What the farmers and ranchers of Guadalupe County could never have perceived in their wildest imagination was that girls might come in the dark of the night and drive their tractors away and hide them in the river bottom. And this is what the True Women of Seguin did in a series of raids that puzzled Police Chief Willie Hoffman and the men of Seguin for several months. Every boy in town was brought in for questioning and each swore an oath of innocence. For a while, the inquiry focused on Peachtree. Of course, it never would have occurred to them that girls could have been responsible for the tractor outrage. In time, the perpetrators went off to college, the tractors remained undisturbed in the fields, Peachtree retreated to the river bottoms, and the case was closed.

I returned to Idella's house once more the following night. Again, she met me on the porch above the river and we went inside for another session with the spirits. She had promised to tell me about the murder of the Yankee and about my great-grandmother Georgia Virginia Lawshe Woods and about her daughters Cherokee and Sweet and the war that wouldn't end, and about Captain-Reverend Andrew Jackson Potter, who carried a six-shooter in one hand and the Good Book in the other.

My great-grandmother Georgia lived most of her adult life in the Hill Country town of San Marcos, Texas, a community a little more than fifteen miles from Seguin. Although she and Euphemia met several times, in their lifetime they were unaware their blood and spirit would mingle in the generations to come. When I tried to define the relationship of these two matriarchs, the thought that they only became blood kin after their death and with my birth was staggering to me. Their relationship would exist only through me and by my children and grandchildren; a compelling example of how our lives can be played out long after our own curtain has fallen.

"How did you know Georgia?"

"Everybody knew Georgia. She was a beautiful woman. Rich. And smart as can be. Back during the War Between the States she outsmarted the Yankees and got even richer running the cotton blockade."

"Is it true about how she killed the Yankee?"

"We'll see, Darlin'. We'll have to look and see."

When I tell the story of Georgia to my children, they always urge me to hurry up and get to the part about the Yankee captain and the killing. But of all the characters in Georgia's life, the one that intrigues me most is the Queen of Tuckabatchee. I've always wondered if it's true she and Georgia's grandfather were lovers and Indian blood flows in our veins. So many women in our family are named Cherokee. In the old pictures it's not difficult to imagine Georgia as an Indian princess. To this day, I have relatives who insist it's true, and others who refuse to talk about

Georgia because they *suspect* it's true about old Benjamin Hawkins's earthy dalliance. I asked Idella about the Queen of Tuckabatchee.

"That's a long way back, Queenie. A far piece for a body to see."

Idella looked out toward the river for a moment and then closed her eyes. I could feel the gathering of forces in the half light. "Now, Darlin', let me tell you about a life called Georgia Virginia Lawshe Woods."

2

Georgia Lawshe Woods

Georgia Virginia Lawshe saw the rock coming for what seemed hours before it actually hit her forehead and she had ample time to consider why a nine-year-old girl would be stoned by a crowd.

She was walking along a road between her home on the Flint River and Francisville, Georgia, on this day in 1836, when she saw a heavy wagon lumbering toward the ferry. Pulled by two oxen, the wagon was loaded with furniture and bedding. A man was driving. A woman holding an infant sat beside him. Here and there, in the clutter of household belongings, Georgia could see other children of the family she now recognized as the McGregors. Orin McGregor and his family had lived on the Flint River since the days Georgia's grandfather, Benjamin Hawkins, had been Indian Agent to the Creek Nation. McGregor's mother had been a full-blooded Creek, his father from the Highlands of Scotland. They had farmed the land south of Georgia's father's farms and had been good neighbors. Now, it seemed, the rumor she had heard for several weeks had come true. The McGregors were being driven out of town. The soil was deep and rich and there were too many "civilized" people who wanted the land and the "savages" must make way for the new social order.

As the McGregors approached, Georgia could see their slaves walking along behind the wagon. Behind the slaves came a noisy group of men holding rifles and boys carrying stones and canes cut from the swamps and riverbanks. Georgia could feel the menace rising from the crowd and she supposed most of the grown-ups had spent the day in the Francisville Tavern where a sign hung reading: "No Dogs, Pigs or Indians." As the wagon passed, Georgia lowered her eyes. She felt it would be somehow an invasion of privacy to see the terrible humiliation and rage and help-lessness that must surely be reflected in the McGregors' faces. She stood by the road, her head down, feeling ashamed of what was happening to her friends the McGregors. Only when she heard the sound of the wagon wheels fading did she raise her eyes.

It was then she saw the rock coming, turning slowly like a small dead planet. Suddenly, she was on the ground. She sat for a moment in the dust. There was very little pain, yet her head felt large and heavy, and when she reached to touch her forehead, her hand came away red with blood. She tried to focus her eyes, but tears and a strange gray fog clouded her vision. She heard the approaching boys and the two words they shouted over and over again. "Squaw Baby! Squaw Baby!" Then Georgia was aware of being lifted into the air and carried away. "You forgot one of your dirty little squaw babies, McGregor!" Then there was laughter. Georgia marveled at how clear her hearing was. She could hear the laughter of her attackers note by note, a sound like the raucous calls of baritone birds. And she could hear McGregor whisper, "Those swine!" as he placed her in his wagon, climbed back aboard, and drove away from the laughter and stones toward the river.

Once the McGregors had taken her home and had moved on west toward their uncertain future, Georgia's mother, Cherokee Lawshe, gathered her up and swept her into the house. As her mother washed and dressed the wound, Georgia watched her closely. She wondered if all the talk in town was true and her mother's mother had been a woman of the Creeks. There was even a name for this mythical grandmother. People said she was called the Queen of Tuckabatchee. Now Georgia looked at her mother and she wondered if she was looking at the daughter of the Queen of Tuckabatchee standing there: long, shining, raven hair, high cheekbones, skin the color of copper and firelight, something graceful, yet wild and untamed in her bearing. Only her startling blue eyes confused the image. But of course Benjamin Hawkins had blue eyes. Why would her grandfather have named her mother Cherokee if she was not the daughter of an Indian queen? Georgia knew that Benjamin Hawkins had lived among the Indians in the wilderness for nearly twenty years.

Here was a man of passionate instincts, an intimate friend of Thomas Jefferson, a worldly man educated at Princeton, who spoke several romance languages fluently. He had been appointed by George Washington as Indian Agent to all the tribes south of the Ohio River, and he had come to the wilderness out of duty. He stayed because of love. He grew to love the Creek people, and for sixteen years he did what he could to save them. It would be only natural if he had loved a woman as completely as he had loved a people. That was what the people in town said. Cherokee Lawshe was an Indian. And the Lawshe land was very rich.

When she first heard the whispers, Georgia had secretly hoped they were true. There was something wonderfully romantic about being the granddaughter of a queen. Now, Georgia looked at her own bandaged face in the glass and she compared herself, once again, with her mother. She had the same wide-set eyes, the high cheekbones, the straight black hair, the blue Hawkins eyes. Georgia looked into the glass and at the blue-green bruise that was spreading out from the bandage above her eye. For the first time she felt the shock of what had happened on the road to Francisville. The glass reflected a small, dark Indian princess as she began to cry.

"There, there, sweetheart," her mother said, gathering her once more in her arms. "It's over now." Georgia's face pressed against the soft comfort of Cherokee's breast, and she thought of the way people had described the Queen of Tuckabatchee as "full-breasted." Georgia lifted her face until she could see her mother in the glass. "Who are you, Mama?" she asked, wiping tears from her eyes with the back of her hand. "Who am I?"

Georgia looked back at the house. Her father, Captain Lewis Lawshe, had built it when he had come back from fighting with Andrew Jackson in the Red Stick wars some twenty years before. The house stood on the crest of a small hill far from the road, a low white structure completely surrounded by a wide porch. Sometimes Georgia pretended the porch was the deck of a great sailing ship moving on an endless green and rolling sea. She would stand on that deck and imagine she was on a voyage to a distant, exotic land, like Siam or Texas. When she and her friend

Joanna Troutman played and dreamed on that porch, they often set course for the far, fabled province of Texas. She was fascinated by Texas, and knew, somehow, she would go there one day. Georgia's cousin Joseph Hawkins had gone to Texas with a friend named Stephen Austin. He had returned with wonderful stories of how Austin had purchased the schooner *Lively* and they had sailed up and down the Texas coast selling provisions and farm supplies to the settlers. That was the ship Georgia imagined when she paced the deck of her porch. Cousin Joseph said he had purchased hundreds of acres to establish a large plantation at a place called Matagorda Bay, and he tried to persuade her father to purchase land on the new frontier. But Captain Lawshe replied they had land enough, cotton fields and forests that seemed to embrace all of central Georgia.

From the road before the house, a path turned toward the Flint River. It led through a field with grass so high she and Joanna could cut secret tunnels through its thick cover, and even make rooms where they were completely hidden from the world. Georgia passed through the field and over a rise to where she could see the river below. A steamboat carrying cotton moved southward, bound for the Gulf of Mexico, its twin stacks breathing ash and soot into a sky blue as Cherokee's eyes. Beyond the river was the road to New Orleans the McGregors had taken before they turned westward somewhere in Alabama. The thought of the McGregors reminded her of the dull ache above her eye. She began to run toward the small cabin above the river where Josiah and Tobe lived, where she would find out once and for all who she was.

Josiah was waiting for her as she approached. He was very tall and very black and to Georgia seemed old as the earth. He had been a slave of Benjamin Hawkins way back when the family still lived in North Carolina. He had come to Georgia as a boy and had been with Hawkins in the wilderness until the old Indian Agent died. He was now Cherokee's slave, but he had a special status. Although he had not been freed by either Cherokee or her father, he did not live on the Lawshe property like the other slaves, but in a small cabin he had built by the grave of Benjamin Hawkins above the river. The old man's job was to tend the grave and to make sure it was not disturbed by the enemies the Indian Agent had left behind. Josiah lived there above the river with a Creek woman named Tobe.

Tobe came out of the cabin when she heard Josiah call a welcome to Georgia. She was a small woman who moved very slowly, as if her heartbeat was not as tightly wound as most. Even her speech was slow, her eyes dreamy and sad. In the Creek language, her name meant "I Have Lost." When Georgia had asked her what she had lost, Tobe just smiled her mysterious smile. "When I find it, I'll let you know." Georgia thought Tobe often talked in circles, but she loved her and was never more comfortable than when she and Tobe and Josiah were alone together on the little cabin's porch above the river.

Georgia often wondered if they loved each other, the old black slave and the woman of the Creeks. They were so peaceful, so still, even their voices were soft. Georgia was certain that between them they knew all there was to know of her grandfather, her family, and the Queen of Tuckabatchee. Sometimes she thought Tobe's name should be "Woman Who Knows," for she seemed very wise in the ways of her people and the land.

"It's true," Josiah said. "She was a beautiful woman. I was there when she came to Mr. Benjamin. He was in bed with rheumatism and I was reading him a passage from Cicero. He often had me read from his library, especially when he was ill or too tired to make the effort himself. I was reading Cicero and this woman presented herself at his bedside." Georgia had seen the small classical library in Josiah's cabin, books left to him when his master died. "She was not a queen, exactly. But she was a very special person and highly regarded by her people. Queen was as close as our English language could come to describing her."

"The Tuckabatchee were keepers of powerful things," Tobe said. "Keepers of the seven sacred plates that were given them by the Master of Breath in the time before time."

"Master of Breath?"

"That is the spirit you call God."

Josiah looked up toward the grave of Benjamin Hawkins, then continued. "It was no small thing . . . An alliance of two special people from two different worlds. The woman said she would be proud if he would take her into his house and his bed. She said if he took a young girl into his house or his bed as well, she wouldn't like it, but she wouldn't object. I remember she said she wouldn't be able to love the young girl, but she wouldn't abuse her either." Georgia noticed Josiah was smiling at the memory. Tobe was also smiling.

"You're teasing me," she said, smiling herself.

"No, Little One," Tobe said. "We're not teasing you."

"It's just that life is a strange thing to live," Josiah said. "And those were strange times."

Josiah continued. "I know Mr. Benjamin was tempted. I wasn't always around, but I know Mr. Benjamin was attracted to the woman. They were often together. Once he even asked me to recite for them, a sonnet, it was." Josiah's face brightened with the memory and he began to laugh. "I'm sorry, Little One. But you have to understand that your grandfather was a statesman. He was a master negotiator. And it seemed to me he conducted his affair with the Creek woman in the same way he would negotiate a treaty. Once I overheard them discussing how their children would be raised. She insisted her children be raised in the Indian way and so her brother would be responsible for them. Your grandfather insisted he would see to the education of his children. It was a problem never resolved. So they were never married."

"But he did marry," Georgia said.

"Yes, I was there," Josiah replied. "It was late in his life. He thought he was dying. He married Miss Lavinia Downs."

"Then he wasn't married when my mother was born?"

"No. He was not."

"Not in the Christian sense," Tobe added. "He was married in the Indian way, which is just as sacred to the Master of Breath."

"Then, when he thought he was dying, he called a Moravian minister and asked him to perform a Christian ceremony. There was another slave named Philemon. Mr. Benjamin had educated him like he had educated me. Philemon was always preaching to the other slaves. The Moravians were angry because they wanted to be God's exclusive messengers. Mr. Benjamin was angry too, exasperated really, because he had spent years giving Philemon an education and now he was wasting it all on foolishness, or so Mr. Benjamin said. He had little patience with religion."

"When death is at the door," Tobe said, "you do not curse the lock."

"So we all gathered at his bedside, and the Moravian spoke the words that made Miss Lavinia and Mr. Benjamin man and wife."

"Then he died?"

"He got well. I think he was more embarrassed than thankful."

"Tell me about Lavinia."

Josiah did not answer immediately. He looked out at the river. "Your grandfather was a great man. He was the kind of man born for the assemblies where ideas are discussed and exchanged. He was a man who loved company, who loved the sound of voices and the touch of other personalities. He probably should have spent his life among his friends James Madison and Jefferson. He even named your uncle Madison and your aunt Jeffersonia, after his two friends. But he came here. He was alone in the wilderness, with only the company of soldiers and slaves and the Indians for sixteen years. He loved to teach. I think one reason was that he wanted companions with enough knowledge to discuss things with him. So he taught me to read, and to speak precisely and correctly as you hear me speaking now. He tried to civilize the Creeks by teaching them to live and think as he did. All this, I believe, because he was lonely."

"And what of Lavinia?"

"She cleaned his house. Washed his clothes."

"My people called her Woman Painted White," Tobe said. "She was like a slave, but she was not."

"Jeffersonia was born after my grandfather and Lavinia Downs married?"

"That's right."

"My mother was born years earlier, before they married?"

"Yes."

Georgia looked directly into Josiah's eyes. "Then why does my aunt Jeffersonia look like a woman painted white and my mother Cherokee look like the Queen of Tuckabatchee? And why did people throw a rock at me and call me Squaw Baby?"

"Life is a strange thing to live," Tobe said.

"Please don't talk in circles!"

"You are the daughter of Cherokee Lawshe. She is the daughter of Benjamin Hawkins, one of the greatest men who ever breathed."

"We called him 'Beloved Man of the Four Nations,' " Tobe said.

"So be proud of your blood. You are named for this land. Be proud of your name—Georgia, daughter of Cherokee. Granddaughter of the man who would have saved the Creek nation, had the Master of Breath given him time. I doubt if more can be said."

"But that's no answer. I don't understand." Georgia searched their eyes.

Tobe held up her hand. "The answer," she said, "is in your name and in your blood and in your heart." Then Tobe began to sing. Old Josiah reached down and took Georgia's hand. "Would you honor me with this dance, Miss Georgia?" He pulled her to her feet and laughed her confusion away, and Georgia and Josiah danced to an old tuneless heathen hymn there above the river not far from the grave of her grandfather.

Captain Lewis Lawshe was waiting for Georgia on the porch when she returned. He was a small man, yet muscular, and his erect bearing made him appear larger than he was. Georgia was often shocked when she saw him standing next to a tall man. Even at a distance she could see how his fine yellow hair flowed in the wind and how he was constantly brushing it out of his eyes, a mannerism he affected even indoors, out of the wind. Now he was pacing and she knew she must be in trouble. An almost physical rush of fondness enveloped her and she ran up onto the porch and into his arms. He embraced her and kissed her. Then a frown pulled his eyebrows down in the middle. Georgia could tell he was trying to be stern. She never understood why others called her father gruff and aggressive. In her presence, he was always loving and gentle.

"We were worried," he said. Georgia could see her reflection in his emerald eyes. "It's not safe to be out running around like some wild animal. Promise me you'll never leave our land by yourself. There are plenty of slaves to go with you. Ask Mose or Jack. Promise me now." He hugged her again and they moved inside. He failed to notice that she had not promised.

By the time the supper dishes had been cleared away, Cherokee followed her husband into his study, where he ritually enjoyed a solitary pipe and sherry. When she closed the door behind her, Georgia was surprised, because the study, at this hour, was her father's private and personal domain. It was not the family custom to interrupt the Captain's evening reveries. There had been very little conversation at the table, and Georgia sensed there were things unsaid between her parents, things they preferred to keep secret from young ears. *Well,* Georgia thought, *there are too many secrets around this place.* She moved to the hall and made herself comfortable by the door to the study, where she could hear what was said within.

"I think we should wait," Georgia heard Cherokee say. "All this will pass."

"It won't pass. It will get much worse. Everything your father spent his life trying to prevent is happening. Mobs are taking their land. The Creek families are being driven from their homes, their houses burned, their livestock stolen, their crops destroyed. And it's all within the law. People like the McGregors are being driven out and forced to the west."

There was a long silence behind the door. Georgia tried to imagine her mother's reaction. What would be written in that face of copper and firelight?

"Now the Creeks are fighting back. In Alabama, just across the Chattahoochee, warriors are gathering and raids on white settlers have begun. Many Creeks who've chosen to fight have moved south to join the Seminoles. You know that Andrew Jackson won't rest until every Indian in Georgia is gone, one way or another."

"So you would sell our home?"

"Better to sell it now than have it stolen later."

"But that can't happen!"

"Look what happened to Georgia."

Again, there was a silence behind the door. Georgia knew her mother was not crying, because she had never seen her cry and couldn't even imagine it now.

"My father thought he was saving the Creeks," Cherokee said after a while. "I'm glad he didn't live to see how wrong he was. He thought he could teach them so they could become a part of the United States. Teach them to farm, to be blacksmiths and carpenters. To live and think like the whites. He thought they had to change to survive."

"He did teach them, Cherokee. He just didn't understand the hatred and meanness of his own race."

"He took away the warriors' weapons and gave them plows and books. He took away their ways and their anchors to the earth and to time, even their names. Now they're powerless. Those who chose his way are being driven from their homes. Those who resisted my father are the ones who just might survive."

"No, those who fight the whites will be exterminated. Your father knew that all along."

"So, you would sell our home."

"Move west. Find new land in Mississippi or even Texas. I'm ashamed to see what's happening. Let's start out new."

Georgia moved away from the door and out to the porch. She stood on the deck, looking out into the night toward Texas. After a while, it almost seemed the house moved and groaned upon the seas of night.

In the year 1836, news came to the state of Georgia that the Texans needed help in their fight against Santa Anna and the armies of Mexico. In Macon, more than $3,000 was collected to help outfit Georgian volunteers who planned to join the Texians in their fight for liberty. One evening, when Georgia was staying a few days with her friend Joanna Troutman, she met a number of these dashing young volunteers. Joanna's father owned the Troutman Inn in Knoxville, Georgia, an hour's ride from the Lawshe farmhouse. Joanna, who was seventeen, fell absolutely in love with a handsome lieutenant named Hugh McCloud, who had recently graduated from West Point. McCloud and the other young men filled the Inn with an exuberant and infectious spirit of adventure.

"I wish we could go with them," Georgia said.

"Yes, let's run away to Texas. Join the fight against Santa Anna."

"We could stay with Papa's old friend Sam Houston."

"You stay with General Houston, I'll marry Hugh McCloud."

"Maybe we could dress up like soldiers. You be a drummer girl, I'll be the flag bearer."

"What flag will you carry? The Stars and Stripes?"

"Not if they fight in the Texas army. I'll have to carry the Texas flag. But I'm not even sure they have one."

"Then we'll make one," Georgia said, and the girls began to create the first flag under which Texians fought in their revolution against Mexico.

It was Joanna who came up with the design, a lone blue star on a field of white. The cloth had been salvaged from several of Joanna's silk petticoats. On one side of the flag, they sewed the words "Liberty or death." On the other side appeared the phrase *Ubi libertas habitat, ibi nostra patria est*—"Where liberty dwells, there is my country."

On the morning Lieutenant McCloud and the young volunteers left for Texas, they mustered on the square in front of the Inn. The new flag was presented, stirring speeches were made, and they rode away, Joanna Troutman's undergarments unfurled at the head of the column.

Three mornings after Lieutenant McCloud headed for Texas, Georgia's father sent Josiah to escort her back to the Lawshe plantation. Rather than ride directly home, the Captain and Cherokee had agreed she could spend a few nights with Josiah and Tobe at their place by the river, a treat that was one of Georgia's greatest joys.

That night they built a fire outside the cabin and Tobe told the old stories of her people. She told how bears had once been keepers of fire but had let it burn dangerously low, and the Master of Breath took fire away from the bears and gave it to the Creeks. "Now the fire burns low again," Tobe said. "It has been taken from us and given to the white man."

Late in the night, after they had been silent for a long time, Tobe asked Georgia to go with them in the morning to visit the most holy place of the Creeks. "You will see something there you will remember all your life," she said. "And you must never tell a soul what you've seen."

"Why?" Georgia asked. "Why would you let me know your secret?"

"Because of your blood," Tobe said.

Just after sunrise, when the sky's brilliant palette to the east had begun to fade, Josiah, Tobe, and Georgia began their journey. They rode in Josiah's old wagon, pulled by a mule. The wagon rocked gently, the wheels made almost no sound. Tobe sang her tuneless song. Georgia smiled at Josiah, and he said, "It is a very good day to be alive."

They followed the Ocmulgee River, first through elms along its bank and then through great stands of pine along the hills. Somewhere, out of sight, Georgia could hear the sound of an axe cutting firewood for the boilers of the riverboats. Suddenly Georgia recognized a familiar site—through the trees, she could see in the distance the watchtower of Fort Hawkins, the fort named for her grandfather.

"I've been here," she said. "Lots of times. What could be so secret?"

"You have looked with your eyes," Tobe said, as they passed the abandoned fort. "But have you really seen?"

The path led into a place that seemed to swallow them up in a secret province of leaf and sunlight and silence. Yet there was a sound, like bees, a humming, that rose and fell on the small wind that wound through the mounds towering like great topless cones on either side of the path.

"What's that sound?" Georgia asked.

"It is the voice of the ancient ones. The ones who came before," Tobe said. "They are in council. Deciding what should be done."

Georgia felt she had stepped into another world. The temple

mounds rose on all sides, substantial as earth itself, yet somehow shaped of spirit and dream. It was like being in church, yet she was outside beneath the sky. There seemed to be no human presence since they passed Fort Hawkins, yet she felt life all around. She wondered why she had never felt all this before when she had looked at the mounds from the fort. It was as Tobe had said. She had looked, but she had not seen.

"What is this place?" Georgia asked at last. "It's beautiful."

"This is the place we first remember. Our first people came here maybe one hundred lifetimes ago. They came from the west and when they found this place of plenty they stayed. They built villages and temples. For two thousand years they took sturgeon from the waters of the Ocmulgee and took deer from the forests. They lived and died and were buried here beneath our feet."

"Where did they go?"

"We Creeks are what became of them. We are still here. Our hearts beat their blood."

They moved deeper into the mounds. Then, suddenly, an Indian carrying a rifle stepped into their path. He nodded at Tobe, then stepped aside. She led them to an opening in one of the mounds. Josiah removed a saddlebag from the wagon and took Georgia's hand. They entered the opening and passed into a low tunnel cut into the earth of the mound. Inside it was cold and dark, and Georgia held more tightly to Josiah's hand. Then, ahead a dim light grew brighter and brighter as they moved deeper into the earth lodge.

The tunnel opened into a large room where some twenty people were gathered around a central fire, mostly men but several older women, too. They were dressed in bright ceremonial clothing of calico cotton and long colorful sashes of dyed wool and yarn tassels. The glass trade beads woven into their headbands reflected the firelight like jewels. When Tobe, Josiah, and Georgia entered the room, the council fell silent. Tobe placed Georgia before her and put both hands on her shoulders. "She belongs," Tobe said. "It is the child of Istechote lige Osetat Chemis te Chango." The others made room for them to sit.

For a long while, the Indians talked in the language of the Creeks. Josiah whispered to Georgia that they were the elders of the Tuckabatchees and they were deciding whether to stay or to begin the long, hard journey westward to Oklahoma. An old man finally held up his hand. Josiah translated what he said. "We who all burn the same fire and speak the same tongue will take our last black drink in this nation, rub our traditional plates, and begin our march. We will put out the old fire and never make or kindle it again until we reach the Mississippi, there never to quench it again."

Then Tobe opened the saddlebag Josiah had carried for her. She removed the seven sacred plates of the Tuckabatchee. They were made from thin strips of copper and brass, the largest plate nearly two feet wide. They were as old, Josiah whispered to Georgia, as anything on Earth or in Heaven. Tobe carried the plates around the fire to the chief, who accepted them with tender care, as if they were glass and might break. "Tobe has kept the sacred plates hidden," Josiah whispered again. When the plates had been passed and rubbed, shells of black drink were passed. The chief drank and then sang the black drink note, a high wavering tone that lasted until his lungs were empty. The shells filled with the black drink were passed around the circle three times. Finally Tobe extinguished the sacred fire and a two-thousand-year-old bond to Earth and to Heaven was broken forever.

By May of 1836, news arrived that the Texans, with the assistance of the Georgia volunteers, had defeated General Santa Anna at a suddenly famous place called San Jacinto. Captain Lawshe's old comrade-in-arms Sam Houston had been the victorious general. Houston had personally written Joanna Troutman a letter expressing thanks for her support. He wrote that Joanna's flag had flown above Fort La Bahia, in Goliad. After the flag had been partially destroyed in a storm, remnants of it had been carried by Georgia volunteers throughout the war.

Along with the letter, Sam Houston sent a silver coffeepot that had belonged to the defeated Santa Anna as a token of his appreciation. "Do you know the secret about Santa Anna the afternoon before the battle?" Joanna asked Georgia shortly after the gift arrived. "They say General Santa Anna was in his tent with a high yellow woman, a Texas patriot, who volunteered to . . ." She leaned forward and whispered in Georgia's ear, and Georgia jumped back and shrieked with laughter. "She didn't!"

"She did! In his tent. All afternoon. Santa Anna was so tired, he couldn't fight." Both girls again howled with laughter. "Just imagine," Joanna said. "I'll go down in history. I've got the silver coffeepot from which the high yellow woman served Santa Anna coffee in his infamous tent."

"And your undergarments flew above battles that made Texas free," Georgia added, and the girls were lost in another avalanche of laughter.

By summer, Captain Lawshe had set in motion his plans to migrate west. He had heard of a plantation that was for sale in Water Valley, Mississippi, and he had begun to test the market for his holdings in Georgia. By the end of 1836, more than fourteen thousand Creeks had been driven from the state, and eager settlers poured onto the lands they once held. Most of the Creeks left peacefully. But a few were dragged from their homes and beaten, and were then held in crudely built stockades. There they where stalked by starvation and disease before being forced to march westward. They followed the same route the Cherokee nation called "The Trail Where We Cried."

When it became apparent they would move, Cherokee Lawshe decided to set old Josiah free. "Let him live out his days with Tobe," she said. "He can read his books and take care of my father's grave." Captain Lawshe agreed with his wife's decision.

Georgia begged to be the one to carry Josiah the news and to her great joy her parents agreed. She was filled with happiness for her old friend and admiration for her mother, as she flew from the porch and ran through the field and along the path leading to the bluff where Josiah's house stood above the river.

When she was alone in the high grass where she and Joanna had made hidden cities, a sadness came like a dark bird to settle on her heart. It occurred to her that freedom for Josiah meant she would never see him again. She would go to Mississippi—Tobe and Josiah would stay. In an instant of terrible regret she almost turned back home to ask her mother to reconsider. Then her face burned with shame that she would deny her friend what he most wanted in this world. Filled half with joy and half with sorrow she breasted the rise that led to the cabin, and then stopped short. She wondered why all the horses were coming, why so many, and why they were coming so fast.

There were five horsemen in all. Strangers. Quickly, Georgia moved from the path into the tall grass where she could not be seen. Quietly she slipped through the grass to the shed behind Josiah's cabin. She could clearly see the horsemen at the door and hear them shouting to Josiah to come out. Georgia felt a strange tension in the air, a sense of impending doom.

Josiah emerged from the cabin. He was so tall he had to bend at the waist to come through the door. *Everything will be all right,* Georgia thought. *Look how big he is, and strong, like a tree.* Then she heard a sound like two pine boards slapping together and Josiah fell to the ground and lay still. Two of the riders dismounted, kicked at Josiah's still form, then entered the house. They came out dragging Tobe by the hair. When Tobe saw Josiah, she tried to fight her way to his side, but the men were too strong. Georgia realized there were no shouts, no curses or words spoken. The men moved with silent purpose, as if they had known exactly what they would do when they came. Then Georgia felt an almost overwhelming anguish, as she saw what the men were doing. She grew dizzy and light but she willed herself to keep the darkness at the edge of her vision from completely closing in on her mind.

The men dragged Tobe to a tree. One tied a rope around her neck and another threw the other end of the rope over a branch. Tobe had stopped fighting. She stood tall and still as the riders struggled with the rope. Georgia thought she saw Josiah move. Did she imagine it? He was still again. Georgia prayed for a miracle. She prayed the branch would break or lightning would strike the riders dead or God himself would see the horror of the moment and come down in a fury. But the rope was now positioned and Tobe was jerked into the air and Georgia howled and screamed as Tobe danced and twisted and then was still. At the sound of the screams, the riders turned and moved toward the shed. Georgia was still screaming when Josiah rose unnoticed and with one powerful arm broke one rider's neck while taking his rifle with the other. He shot the man holding the rope and Tobe folded to the ground. That was the last Georgia saw before the darkness closed in.

Josiah dug Tobe's grave just a few feet from where his old master was buried. "He'll keep her safe," Josiah said when he selected the site. Georgia felt she should be helping him with the grave, but she had never been so tired. It was as if heavy stones were pressing her into the same ground where Tobe now lay sleeping. Josiah put down the shovel and sat down beside Georgia. Then she remembered why she had come.

"My mother says you are a free man. She's prepared the papers."

Josiah sighed, his eyes on Tobe's grave. "Freedom," he said. "So I am a free man. What good is freedom to me now?" Georgia laid her head against his shoulder and grasped his great arm with her two hands.

"Where will you go?"

"Maybe south. Some of the Creeks are joining up with the Seminoles. Since I'm a free man, I suppose I'll have to fight for that freedom."

"I wish I were dead." Georgia's words just tumbled out.

Josiah turned. "Never wish that!" he said. "You are in enough danger as it is. Those men who killed Tobe would come after you too if they thought you were part Indian. Wish to stay alive, whatever you wish. And stay close to the Captain. He'll know what to do."

Josiah took her hands from his, rose, and walked to where he had left the shovel. Then he walked slowly to the place by the river where he would bury the five white men he had killed in his first act as a free man.

It was the year the great Seminole chief Osceola died and, in Georgia, two groups of Americans began a long passage toward the western frontier.

From the good lands around New Echota, Springplace, and Red Clay, the Cherokee families were arrested and driven by bayonet into stockades. The Cherokees and what remained of the Creeks were loaded into hundreds of wagons. At the sound of a bugle, the wagons began to roll. There were no blankets, no shelter from the sleet, snow, and cold. Four thousand men, women, and children perished along the way in the winter of 1838.

Within months of the Cherokees' departure, another wagon train moved from Bibb County, Georgia, across the iron-red clay of Alabama, and into the deep pine forests of northwestern Mississippi. It was the first leg of another movement westward.

Georgia's most enduring memory of this journey was the graves of the Cherokee children lining the banks of the Tennessee River and the abandoned farms in northern Alabama where land speculators and common thieves were carting off the belongings of Americans that Congress had voted to strip of all rights. The Treaty of New Echota, ratified by Congress in 1836, had ordered the removal of all Cherokees. As the Lawshes traveled westward, they could see that the removal had been on schedule.

As the Lawshe family and their large company of slaves moved through Alabama, Georgia saw two white men in fine dark suits driving a wagon loaded with furniture and household goods, rapidly, as if pursued by ghosts or guilt. As the wagon of plunder passed by, it lurched and a painting sailed like a wing to the ground. An Indian girl Georgia's age looked back from the picture in the road. She was holding a white bird in her two hands lightly, yet firmly enough that the bird would stay. Georgia thought it was the most beautiful painting she had ever seen. She asked her mother if she could have the painting of the girl with the bird, and they stopped and placed it in the wagon. It was elegantly framed and there was a small brass plate at the bottom of the frame where the title was engraved. "Child Holding Bird," it read. She wondered where the girl in the painting could be and if she were grown now and walking somewhere ahead along the Trail of Tears.

The land that Captain Lewis Lawshe and Cherokee purchased with the proceeds from her inheritance was a little community called Water Valley south of the Yocono River, on the Great Stage Route from Nashville, Tennessee, to Jackson, Mississippi. The four hundred acres in the newly organized county of Yalobusha, in Mississippi, had been the home of the Choctaw and Chickasaw people until the Treaties of Dancing Rabbit Creek in 1830 and Pontotoc in 1832, in which the two tribes gave up the last of their lands in Mississippi. With the departure of the Indians, settlers began to stream onto the land between the Yocono and Yalobusha rivers. The settlements of Water Valley and Coffeeville, Oakland and Washington rose from the forests. Where there had once been primal silence, now the sound of hammers building stores and saloons and churches could be heard.

All the rivers and creeks around Water Valley had Indian names. Georgia thought about how the Indians had gone and had left the names of things behind. *It's the only way we know they were here,* she thought.

As their new home was being built, the Lawshes stayed at the hotel kept by J. D. Mathews in the little town of Washington, two miles north of Water Valley. Each morning Georgia rode out to the construction site, on a high knoll overlooking the fields and pasture and the distant Yocono River. The homesite reminded her of Josiah and Tobe's place above the Flint River, and her remembrances of her old friends kept her company during those first weeks in Mississippi. The house grew rapidly, almost an exact copy of their house in Georgia, with its low hipped roof and wide porches lined with white columns all around. Shuttered French doors joined the porches to the inside rooms and the house was open to winds from all points of the compass, all the holy directions of the departed Choctaw and Chickasaw. From the porches, Georgia soon learned, you could see both the rising and the setting of the sun, and the night sky was a splendor of stars and distant silver worlds. The slaves built their own small houses below the brow of the knoll. Georgia thought the little slave homes looked like hatchlings of the larger house on the hill. Other slaves lived in rude cabins in town, and were hired out to clear the canebrakes and dense forest to make way for more houses and farms. Soon the new Lawshe plantation was producing crops, and bales of cotton moved across Mose Perry's Yocono River ferry and on toward Chickasaw Bluffs and then down to New Orleans on the great Mississippi.

For Georgia the move to Water Valley was like a page turning in her life. One life had ended with Tobe's death, the new one was a blank page on which she could write whatever she wished. She believed that life in Mississippi would be like a stage stand where fresh horses were obtained for riding on west. She would make the best of life in Mississippi before she set out to fulfill her destiny in the far Republic of Texas.

At Mrs. Judith Bryant's Female School she made many good friends, including a number who attended Mr. F. A. Brown's Male School. She was disappointed to discover that the parents of her new friends had different traditions concerning how much freedom young women should be allowed. While Georgia had permission to wander freely anywhere, her new friends seemed like prisoners or indentured servants who would only be freed upon maturity.

Her friends' parents were quick to notice this wild, dark child lived such an unconventional life, almost devoid of rules and restrictions. If it had not been for Georgia's excellent manners and her infectious exuberance, they might have warned their children against her. Instead, with only slight apprehension they welcomed her into their home and into the lives of their children.

By her fourteenth year, Georgia was generally regarded as the prettiest and most popular girl in Water Valley. That autumn, in the Cherokee month of the Black Butterflies, Georgia went to a late afternoon supper at the McKie family's plantation on Swann

Lake. All her friends were there, dressed in their newest, most elegant gowns. She could feel the eyes of the young men follow her every move. Then, suddenly, from among the swans that graced the McKies' garden, there came a honking, thrashing white apparition. It headed straight for Georgia, who turned and ran, skirts flying—the most beautiful girl in Water Valley pursued by a rogue goose. She fell ingloriously, twisting her ankle, soiling her dress with green stains and her soul with black humiliation. The doctor came and touched her ankle with both his hands and the pain flew away, vanishing completely. It was sorcery. She fell immediately in love with this strong, good man with the healing touch. His name was Dr. Peter Cavanaugh Woods, and he held her ankle and her eyes for so long and with such eloquence that even Georgia blushed.

Everyone in Water Valley considered Georgia and the young physician a match made in heaven. Yet Georgia was puzzled because it seemed everything about them was opposite. *How,* she wondered, *could our love last when we are so different from one another?* Peter was an established physician and community leader, Georgia was only fourteen. He was patient and soft-spoken, she was volatile and unpredictable. Dr. Peter was a creature of logic and order, Georgia lived by whim and happenstance. But each time they were together, Georgia could feel some magic force pulling them, binding like a silken cord.

One day Peter told Georgia about a dream of his, and she thought she would die with joy. Peter told her he had always wanted to go to Texas. It was then she asked him to marry her. He accepted at once.

Dr. Peter Cavanaugh Woods and Georgia Virginia Lawshe were married the next year. Georgia was only fifteen. It was, according to the *Herald Water Valley Democrat*, the grandest wedding ever held in Yalobusha County. Many of Peter's family members were there, including his mother and his brother, Captain Pinckney Davidson Woods, a prosperous local merchant. But the most exciting guest was Georgia's uncle Madison Hawkins, Cherokee's brother, who came all the way from North Carolina to see his favorite niece marry.

Madison had always been a mystery to Georgia. One day he

would drift into their lives and a few days later would drift out again. But for the time he was in their home, he filled it with laughter and adventure that lingered for months. Georgia loved her strange, lively uncle and there was no one except Dr. Peter whose company she enjoyed more. Madison had never married, and he lived alone in the great family plantation house in North Carolina where Benjamin Hawkins had lived before he became Indian Agent. Georgia couldn't imagine why a man who loved company so much would live alone or why he had never found a woman to share his life and his laughter. Like his father, Benjamin Hawkins, Madison had red hair, freckles, and brilliant aqua-blue eyes. Unlike his father he was a bit heavy, with a round, almost childlike face and merry eyes. For a heavy man he moved gracefully and was light on his feet, yet his clothing, while expensive, was always rumpled and out of fashion. Even though Madison seemed always cheerful, Georgia thought she noticed something almost haunted in his expression. She wondered if he might be ill. There were times, at the height of laughter, when he would be gripped by a spell of coughing. At one such time Georgia glanced at Dr. Peter and caught the momentary concern in his eyes.

But the most intriguing mystery Uncle Madison brought to Water Valley was the two handsome women slaves and the small child that traveled with him in his entourage. One was a dark woman in her late thirties named Mahalia Hawkins. Another was Georgia's age, a beautiful, light-skinned girl known as Martha Benny. The little boy was called Jim. When Georgia asked why she was called Martha Benny, she said her name was Martha Benjamin, for Benjamin Hawkins. Georgia flushed with irritation that a slave girl would be named for her grandfather. The most conspicuous thing about Martha Benny was her eyes. They were blue.

Both Mahalia and Martha Benny stayed in the big house throughout the few weeks of the wedding, helping with the many celebrations, parties, and receptions that were the focus of the Water Valley social season. Georgia wondered about Martha's blue eyes. Maybe Madison was not the confirmed bachelor he appeared to be. Could it be this young Negro girl was her first cousin? Whenever she had a chance she studied Martha Benny unobserved, and there was a definite resemblance to her own image in the mirror. Both were dark. Georgia's skin was more olive, while Martha Benny's skin had a dusky, golden tone. Both had delicate, regular features, yet Martha Benny was larger, more solidly built. Georgia had straight black hair but Martha Benny's curled into tight ringlets.

After the wedding, Georgia and Dr. Peter moved into a bright, new bungalow on the edge of town. It was large enough for Peter to have his practice on one side of the house, while Georgia reigned supreme in the rooms on the other side. Captain Lawshe had given them the house as a wedding gift. He had also given them thirty slaves, who remained on his plantation but would be available when Dr. Peter's practice became established and they could build a proper house in the hills above the valley. Both Dr. Peter and Georgia knew they would never build a plantation house above the town, because it was just a matter of time before they moved to Texas. It was a secret they shared between them. Georgia knew the Captain and Cherokee would be hurt to know they planned to move, away from family and Water Valley. One of the most troubling things in Georgia's life was realizing she must tell her mother she was going away. She need not have worried.

On a spring morning, shortly after Georgia and Dr. Peter were married, Cherokee Lawshe died giving birth to a stillborn child. She was buried in the cemetery on the knoll behind the house. Georgia had felt this kind of grief before, a numbing, crushing sorrow that became a towering rage. Just as she had hated the men who had killed Tobe, she now turned her anger on her father. "It's no less than murder," she told Peter, who had tried in vain to save Cherokee's life. "It's mean and vicious to impregnate a woman my mother's age. He might as well have shot her with a gun. Either way a woman's going to bleed to death." During the funeral Georgia was unable to look at her father, and each time their eyes met she would turn away, blaming him for her mother's death.

In the months following Cherokee's death, Georgia's anger began to subside, but she continued to feel a grief so powerful it made her physically weak. One night, when she lay sleepless by Peter's side, she felt him stirring. "You awake?" she whispered.

"Umm," he said.

"I don't know what's wrong with me," she said.

Dr. Peter rolled over to face her. "What's wrong?"

"That's it. I don't know. I always thought I'd be able to handle something like this. But it's pressing me down. It's like I feel the earth pressing down on my mother's grave. It's like I'm down there in the dark, not her."

"You feel grief. That's what it's like."

"When does it go away, Peter? I want it to go away."

"It will go away when you come to terms with who you're grieving for."

"My mother, of course."

"I venture that it is your father that's at the heart of your grief," Peter said. "Not your mother."

By midnight, as she listened to Dr. Peter's steady breathing, she began to feel the anguish her father must be feeling. Georgia reviewed in her mind all the times she had recognized the love her mother and father felt for each other. She remembered gestures and secret messages of adoration passing back and forth between their eyes. She remembered how they had treated each other with a gentle and constant courtesy and how they had seemed to lift each other's mood. She thought of the love she felt for Dr. Peter and she remembered how helpless and lost the Captain had seemed on the night Cherokee died. What terrible pain he must have felt to bring such a strong man down.

At first light, Georgia slipped out of bed, dressed, saddled her horse, and rode out to the Lawshe house on the knoll above the valley. It took some while for Mose to wake the Captain. As she waited in the parlor, Georgia looked around at the halls and spaces of the great house and realized how lonely her father must be, rattling around in rooms once filled with love and laughter. The Captain, a bit disheveled and disoriented from sleep, entered the parlor.

"Poor Papa," Georgia said, and suddenly she felt a lightness, as if her body were inside a bubble blown by a child. She was weightless and could not feel the press of earth on her mother's grave. All she felt was her father's arms and the moisture of their tears finally falling.

Although she had forgiven her father for Cherokee's death, Georgia still felt a kind of undirected anger concerning the dangers in which childbirth placed women. She was often present when Dr. Peter delivered his patients' babies, and had on one occasion served as his nurse when he performed an emergency cesarean. She was fascinated by the process, astonished at the violence of the "blessed" event. How strange that such pain could be caused by an act of such exquisite pleasure.

There were other times, usually in the night when she and Dr. Peter were close, when she became aware of a certain hypocrisy in her attitude toward the dangers of sexual intercourse. Just as she had always attacked life with vigor, curiosity, and abandon, so did she explore the possibilities of the marriage bed. She had listened to the whispered complaints of some women who found the sexual aspect of marriage a duty to perform rather than a pleasure to be given and received. At first Dr. Peter seemed somewhat apologetic about his need and its expression, and Georgia was surprised and amused that he would be so proper about a thing that Uncle Madison characterized as "so wickedly pleasurable." One of her great joys was to shock Dr. Peter and then to savor the reaction that always followed. Georgia decided she was a wanton, and she often wondered if any other people in the world did the things they did, or if she and Dr. Peter had discovered new territory, as Columbus discovered America. But always in the back of her mind, when the passion had ebbed, was the awareness that pain and death could be the price of pleasure. *Surely there must be some way to avoid the pain,* she thought. Then sometimes Georgia wondered if the danger, the possibility of death, was in some aberrant way a contributor to the pleasure. She decided no God would strike that kind of bargain. It would be too cruel.

By the time Georgia Lawshe Woods turned eighteen, just a day or two, she thought, after she had been attacked by the rogue goose, she realized with shock and dismay she now had a small flock of children hanging on her skirts and interfering with the normal rhythms of the day. After the death of her mother, Georgia had taken in her younger sister, Lovie, as her own. Then one right after another, as punishment, she calculated, for her irrepressible passion, her own children were born. The first child they named Pinckney after Dr. Peter's brother Pinckney Davidson Woods; the second, they named Cherokee, after Georgia's mother. The third child, named Georgia, they called Little Sweet. All three pregnancies and deliveries were borne with minimum complications. Yet Georgia was constantly reminded of the unfairness of her fate as a woman. "We both make love," she told Dr. Peter after little Cherokee was born, "but I'm the only one that gets big as a house and then gets stretched and torn and tortured. And you hand out cigars and accept the congratulations as if you did it all yourself. Whoever said there was justice in the world?"

When little Cherokee was six months old and Georgia was still struggling with her new role as child-mother, injustice came to call again in the person of Uncle Madison. Once again he appeared, as if from nowhere, as was his custom.

"I know it's indecently early," he said, "but we're on our way to a wonderful adventure and you must come." Georgia looked out to the road where Madison had parked his buggy. Behind it, in a mule-drawn wagon, were Mahalia, Martha Benny, and Jim. They looked as if they were on their way to church, especially Jim, who was dressed as a miniature gentleman in an outfit Georgia thought would be appropriate for an audience with the Queen. "Come, quickly," Uncle Madison said. "We're going to pay our respects to Monsieur Louis Daguerre."

The Louis Daguerre Image Salon was not nearly so grand as its name implied. Rather, it was a small, cluttered room behind a mercantile store in town, owned by an enormously enthusiastic follower of the French inventor whose experiments had given birth to the new science and art of photography. "It is an amazing process," Madison said, as he introduced the photographer, who with elaborate gestures showed them how his "camera obscura" could capture a fleeting moment in time, and transfer it to a metal plate to preserve it forever. "It is like the eye of God," he said and then, one by one, the Hawkinses, both black and white, began to pose for their portraits.

"What is this all about?" Georgia asked. There was something forced and false about Madison's excitement. It was as if he were on stage, playing himself playing himself. Mahalia and Martha Benny were silent, and they moved mechanically as they were instructed. If they had any expression at all on their faces, it was a kind of resignation. Only Jim seemed animated. He was, as usual, having a wonderful time.

"I wanted a likeness, that's all," Uncle Madison said. "Something to remember them by."

"Where are they going?"

Madison didn't answer. He turned and spoke briefly with the photographer, thanked him for his services, then led his entourage back to their wagon and buggy. "Madison," Georgia said, feeling some kind of alarm trembling inside, "what is all this?"

"It's not an easy thing, Georgia. Be patient with me. Let me explain as we drive."

They drove out from town, along a ridge road overlooking the valley. It was still early and the sun had not yet burned off the fog sleeping along the river and in the low marshes where the canebrakes grew. Georgia thought this was how Earth must look from Heaven. Below was an ethereal counterpane of pearly cloud. Each leaf, each blade of grass, was encased in mirrored prisms of moisture. The whole world was silver. The wind, denied access to the valley by the hills, tugged at them as they rose higher, and Georgia pulled in her collar more tightly against the chill. She looked back and saw the wagon following.

Madison coughed. The sound drew Georgia's eyes to her uncle and she wondered if she had misjudged him all these years. She had always thought of him as a truly happy man, at peace with himself and the fates. Only once had she glimpsed a more serious side. She had told him about Tobe's death and how when the memory of it suddenly came, she would be so completely assailed by sorrow she wanted to just "lie down and die." To her surprise, rather than comforting her, he became angry. "That's absurd," he had said. "You are a Hawkins and you should remember to act like a Hawkins. To be weak in the face of trouble is to be a thief. God gives life to be lived abundantly. If we cower, if we're timid, we take away what God has given."

She wondered then, and now, what secret challenges and sorrows this man had faced. All these years he had worn a mask to keep others safe from torments he must feel. Now, as they paused above the silver valley, she realized he was, at last, about to remove the mask.

"I'm going back to North Carolina. Back home. I wanted the likenesses to take back with me. To remember them. Three people who are very dear to me."

Georgia's mind raced. "I don't understand."

"I've drawn up the necessary papers to give them to you. Mahalia, Martha Benny, and Jim."

"Give them to me? But why?"

"Because I'm dying!" The words were spoken almost angrily. "Peter knows. I'd hoped you wouldn't be so keen on detail. I'd hoped to leave without displays of sentiment." Then he sighed, and added, "I'm sorry I spoke harshly."

"I'm sorry." Georgia was too confused to recognize the frailty of her response. Madison started to laugh and then his laughter was choked by a spasm of coughing. Georgia waited, her thoughts torn between the shock of Madison's illness and bewilderment about the gift of the slaves. She looked back and saw the three slaves sitting motionless in the wagon. She supposed they knew that she and Madison were discussing their fate.

"Uncle Madison," she said. "I don't know what to say. I don't like any of this. Why give them to me?"

"You're the only person I can fully trust to treat them right. I've always seen in you what was best in my father. The most important thing in my thoughts is that they not be separated. I know you and Peter would honor that promise."

"Why not set them free? My mother gave Josiah his freedom."

"Two women and a small boy? Where would they go? How would they live? They would just be sold back into slavery. Freedom for Josiah was a gift. Freedom for my little family would be a cruelty."

"But if you left them property?"

"It would just be taken away."

Then Georgia knew she must actually speak the unspeakable. "Uncle Madison, isn't Mahalia the mother of your children? She may be a slave, but your children should be free!"

"No law in the South would agree. If a free man and a slave woman have children, the law does not consider those children free like the white father. They're considered slaves like the black mother. Martha Benny, and Jim would be rounded up and placed on the block."

"There has to be another way. Look, I know it may seem selfish to you and unfeeling, but I've got all I can handle already! I've got my own children and Lovie. It's not fair to leave me the responsibility for three more people!" Georgia felt her cheeks reddening and she realized she had raised her voice. "Mercy," she said. "I hope they can't hear me." She looked back toward the wagon. Mahalia, Martha Benny, and Jim were motionless. Waiting as the sun melted the silver.

"You have scores of slaves. Why would three more make a difference?"

"Because you made them family!" she said. "Because you said they were dear to you." Then, suddenly, Georgia thought she saw a way out of the dilemma. "Suppose you give them to me and then I'll set them free."

"You can't. It's against the law. Anyway, Peter would have to agree, and he won't."

"Why won't Peter agree?"

"Because he knows the Devil you know is better than the Devil you don't. At least as slaves they'll be safe. And they'll have each other."

"Because I'm a woman, I can't free my own slaves? Because Mahalia's a woman, your children can't be free? That makes me wonder who is a slave on this land and who isn't. It just isn't fair."

After a long moment, Madison agreed. "It is unfair. Life often is. So is death unfair."

Georgia glanced at Uncle Madison and then followed his eyes out over the valley. The silver had tarnished now, and seemed hard and cold and soiled. She looked back to see Mahalia and Jim waiting in the wagon. They were so patient there, as if they trusted her and Madison to do what was right for their lives. For a moment she envisioned the pain Mahalia must feel. *She must know he's dying,* she thought.

"I don't suppose there's anything else to say," Georgia said softly, her voice dead and flat. "It doesn't seem to matter, does it?"

"It matters," Madison said. "Love matters. Everything human matters."

"When are you leaving?"

"As soon as Mahalia and the children are settled."

Georgia remembered the phrase Josiah used to sum up everything both large and small. "Life sure is a strange thing to live," she said. Uncle Madison clucked to the horse, and they turned and headed back along the ridge road home.

The children grew like weeds or wolves. Much of the time Georgia was so overwhelmed by the responsibilities of motherhood that she declined to do anything for fear of doing it wrong. "After all," she said, "I did all the early work. I carried them and labored and pushed them into the world. Now it's somebody else's turn." She tried to remember how her mother performed the role, but she simply couldn't recall. Cherokee had always been there, loving, mysterious, and beautiful, but strangely distant and uninvolved. Georgia thought she must have raised herself. She decided that she had turned out rather well and so the best parent was the one that parented least. But there was, she felt, something fine about watching the children at play or asleep, these living things she had made herself and had grown in her own body. When she told Martha Benny how she felt, Martha Benny expressed an opinion that had been growing in the household but had been, so far, contained. "You brought those children into this world and you sure oughta do for them more than you do. You're the mother and you oughta act like one." At first Georgia had been offended by Martha Benny's tendency to speak her mind. But she quickly learned there was nothing cruel or even mean about the criticisms Martha Benny occasionally heaped on the young, inexperienced, and sometimes unwilling mother.

Little by little, under the guidance of Martha Benny and espe-cially Mahalia, Georgia Lawshe Woods learned how to be a mother. Some of the more tedious aspects, however, like tending Little Sweet when she cried or keeping her clean, she delegated to what she called the "mother committee," Martha Benny and Mahalia and even Lovie, who was a strong young girl now with a fine aptitude for motherhood.

One responsibility Georgia refused to delegate was discipline. She made it known that she would be the one to punish the chil-dren if and when they ever did anything to merit the switch or the strap. This division of authority was a boon to the children, who soon realized they could get away with anything under the sun. Sometimes, when Martha Benny or Mahalia could stand it no longer, they spanked Pinckney, Cherokee, Little Sweet, or Jim in secret.

There were times when Georgia wondered about her feelings toward the members of her family. Of course, her love for Dr. Peter had grown immeasurably stronger. Just to think of him, as lover and husband, filled her with excitement and pride. There was also growing in her mind and heart a new perspective on her husband. As she watched him at work, she began to see him with new eyes, through the eyes of his patients who invested their trust and their lives in his hands. Her respect for him grew in pace with her love. She realized what she had felt for him on her wedding day was only a fraction of what she felt now.

There were nine members of the Woods family. Georgia con-sidered Mahalia, Martha, and Jim an inseparable part of her fam-ily, and she loved them each and all. Mahalia gave the family stability, a foundation, a sense of calm. There was often a sadness in her eyes, and wistful sighs would escape from her memories, Georgia supposed of her strange life with Uncle Madison. Martha Benny became much like a sister, and Georgia even sensed a trace of rivalry when it came to the household and the children. Martha Benny continued to speak her mind, her blue eyes flashing. As the weeks and months went by, Georgia found herself drawn closer to the beautiful, dark daughter of Mahalia. Little Jim, Mar-tha Benny's younger brother, was a delight. He seemed the per-fect little gentleman, always beautifully dressed and obedient, setting a good example for the other children. "That's because I whale the tar out of that boy when he's bad," Martha Benny said every time he was praised. "Somethin' you wouldn't know about."

By the time Lovie and Jim were ten years old and Pinckney and Cherokee were beginning to run wild through northern Mississippi, the old dream of Texas that Georgia and Dr. Peter shared began to occupy their thoughts and conversation more and more. Dr. Peter's practice had flourished and with his savings and her inheritance, they figured the time for making their dream real was drawing near. One morning, Georgia walked out to her mother's grave and did what she had dreaded to do when Cherokee was alive. She knelt by the side of the grave and she told her mother goodbye.

They came through the forest like a garden party set in motion, a hunt leisurely pursuing invisible foxes. They moved in a caravan of delicate cabriolets and broughams and buggies pulled by horses of immaculate lineage. The women and children and the house servants rode in the carriages. Georgia's own was a chaise: Its lavishly upholstered seat and slender hickory wheels had been fashioned in the carriage shops of Virginia and on the anvils of Cherokee blacksmiths. Others in the group rode in carriages made by the wheelwrights of the brothers Studebaker. The gentlemen, in flight from worn-out lands and declining estates, filled with dreams of virgin lands and the blood of highland and bog and moor, sat upon their thoroughbreds like dragoons, while platoons of slaves walked among the carriages or at the head of oxen, laboring to pull wagons laden with chests of silver and leather-bound volumes of Cicero and Shakespeare and Byron through the wilderness.

Six families moved in the column from the antebellum South toward Texas: Moore, Cox, Bridge, McKie, Donalson, and Woods—including their slaves, nearly three hundred people in all. They had lived in the community of Water Valley, Mississippi, a life of abundance and leisure. Now they moved through the green gothic solitudes like a legend let loose from a storybook.

It was noon. The yellow heat shimmered in the air as the column halted on a rise where elms formed a cathedral arch above the road. Below in the distance, toward Texas, the valleys almost smoked in the heat, and for a moment Georgia felt something tug at her mood, at her composure, at her spirit. She thought of the picnics they had spread on the manicured lawns at Water Valley, and she wondered if perhaps they were making a mistake to leave the ease and softness and civility for the hard unknowns of the frontier. She looked over at her youngest child, Little Sweet, who as usual was within the embrace of Mahalia's safe, calm, encircling arms and at peace with the world. *Is it really right to take an infant into the wilderness?* she wondered. Quickly, with practiced discipline, she forced the vagrant thought from her mind before it fully formed, and she climbed down from the wagon to join her other children. Martha Benny had spread a checkered cloth on a bed of pine needles and was beginning to prepare a noon meal. The older children—Pinckney, Jim, and Cherokee—were fighting, as usual. And as usual, Lovie, five years older than the other children, was in the midst of the trouble. She had forced a pine cone down Pinckney's pants and was now racing away, pursued by the others and a hail of pine cones. Georgia dabbed at the glow she felt forming on her forehead. "I hope they run all the way to Texas," she said, and sank onto the cloth and the soft cool earth.

"What you need to do is have them go pick a switch," Martha Benny said. "Then you need to take that switch and make it sing."

"What I need to do is none of your business," Georgia said. Martha Benny smiled, and as Georgia looked into her blue eyes she was once again struck by the illusion that she was looking in a mirror. "Don't mind me. It's just hot, and that road up there looks mighty long."

"Well, you shouldn't let them run wild like you do," Martha Benny said.

Georgia watched Martha Benny pour water into pewter cups and she wondered at the remarkable nature of their relationship. Martha was her slave, her best friend, and her first cousin. Between them there was a powerful bond of both love and blood, yet never once, through all the months, had they spoken of either out loud. Since Madison died, Georgia and Martha Benny had been constant companions, had shared secrets. The life of each was being shaped by the life of the other. They shared the same blue Hawkins eyes, the same style of speaking, the same gestures. Yet there was a gulf between them as wide as any that could exist between two young women. Georgia had long known that few distances were as close or as great as that between master and slave.

The children returned, clothes stained with elm leaf green and brown, faces flushed, breathing like steam engines, hungry, sassy, embarked on their eternal quest for trouble. "Go wash your faces in the creek and tuck in your shirt, Master Pinckney. You too, Jim. You look like a ragamuffin." Martha Benny sent them off, all arms and legs and energy. "They might as well just jump in that creek," Georgia said.

Martha Benny laughed. It was a melody, a sound like wooden bells. "There's no way those children won't jump in that creek. You know that. It's as certain as sundown." She was right, and when they returned, wet to the skin, Georgia told them to go pick a switch, and it was so uncharacteristic that even Georgia began to laugh and that was the end of that.

That evening the families camped by a clear stream beneath cottonwoods. The moon was thin and curved as a Turkish blade and there were more stars than Georgia had ever seen before. After a supper of venison and cornbread, the men told tales while mending the day's damage to horse and harness. Martha Benny, Georgia, and the children sat watching the fire dance in the darkness. Beyond the firelight, Mahalia sang a lullaby to Little Sweet, who chattered for a while and then grew silent.

"Why do we have to go to Texas?" Pinckney asked.

"We don't have to go," Georgia replied. "We choose to go. We're going to be very rich and have a great house and land reaching as far as you can see."

"We are rich. We already have land."

"But nothing like Texas. In Texas, cotton grows tall as a man's shoulder. Not scraggly like in Mississippi. Besides, it's an adventure. You're living an adventure as exciting as any you'll ever read. But it's unfinished. And we've got to go to Texas to see how it comes out."

After a while, the darkness all around began to press in on Georgia, and she began to be aware of their total isolation. Not only were they isolated in space, a handful of human beings sitting on Earth around a fire in the middle of nowhere, but they were isolated in time. For a moment she began to worry that the trip to Texas was an ending of something, a break in the continuity of their family history that reached all the way back to Admiral John Hawkins and his battle with the Spanish Armada. She wondered if the children would forget their heritage when the new chapters of their lives began in Texas. Maybe she could not make them behave. But she could, at least, give them a sense of who they were.

Georgia told the children how their great-grandfather had been a senator before he had been appointed by Washington and Jefferson to help ease tensions between settlers in the frontier states and the Cherokees and the Creeks and other Indian nations. She told them how he had spent the rest of his life opposing those who would take Indian lands, how he had eventually begun to prefer the life of the Indian, and had lived among them until the day of his death.

Georgia told the children how Benjamin Hawkins had been hated by many people in Georgia because of his friendship with the Indians. She told them how many, including Andrew Jackson, had considered him "the enemy." Only Thomas Jefferson stood by him and Jefferson, in a letter to their great-grandfather, had called the treatment of the Indians "a principal source of dishonor to the American character."

"Did he marry an Indian?" Cherokee asked. "Am I an Indian?" The other children leaned forward.

"For a long time, he lived alone," Georgia answered. "One day when he was sick, an Indian woman came to take care of him. She was the Queen of Tuckabatchee. She asked him to come live with her and be her husband."

"Did he marry her?" Cherokee obviously hoped so with all her heart and soul.

"No," Georgia replied after a moment. She paused, because she thought she could hear the sound of Tobe's drum in the darkness. "The woman he married was not an Indian. Her name was Lavinia Downs. A lovely name. And they named their children after the people your grandfather loved most. James Madison, Jeffersonia for Thomas Jefferson, Muskogee after the old name for the Creek people, and your grandmother, Cherokee. But that's another story."

"I was named for President James Madison, too," Jim announced. "There's lots of famous people in our family."

"I'll famous you," Martha Benny said. She grasped several handfuls of children and managed by physical force and threats of violence to get them into their rude beds of blankets and pine needles. Georgia kissed Lovie, Cherokee, Pinckney, and Jim goodnight, and then kissed Little Sweet, who was already asleep in a wooden cradle Josiah had carved for Georgia when she was born. Then Georgia walked to another fire, where Dr. Peter was talking with some of the other men about the route westward they would take the next morning. She stood behind him, placing her hands on his shoulders, and noticed again how powerful his shoulders were. At her touch, he turned and excused himself from the others, and they walked out of the firelight. He took her hand and they moved to a place where they could be alone.

"Would you give me a crincocreole?" he asked. It was a name they had given for the way they massaged each other when their muscles were sore or tired. After he had had a long day with his patients, Georgia would often rub the muscles on his neck and shoulders until the feeling of physical pleasure became the first stirring of passion. Then his hands would take their turn. Tonight, as she rubbed and kneaded the muscles at the base of his neck, she asked him what their life would be like in Texas. This, too, was a game they had played since they had first discovered their mutual dream.

"We'll live in a big house surrounded by lawns and orchards. All the children will have ponies and will grow up to be physicians and generals and famous artists. You and I will live to be one hundred and we'll have a grandchild for every year. The woods will be full of Woodses. It will be a dynasty renowned throughout the civilized world."

"Aren't you ever afraid?"

"Are you afraid?" He turned, concern in his eyes.

"It's just that we've always talked about Texas as if it were a place in a fable. We've never really come to grips with what it might be like. I mean, there may even be snakes in Texas."

"You're not sorry."

Georgia wasn't sure if it was a question or a statement. "Not in a thousand years." She leaned down and kissed him and the stirring began.

As the families crept westward, Georgia was surprised so many people had made their home along the way. She had expected empty frontier, great expanses of primeval wilderness. Yet here and there, along a road worn deep into the earth by wagons and horses, were homesteads and settlements, even towns where they could purchase potatoes, corn, beef, fodder, and even calico, from which Georgia planned to make a bonnet. In a way Georgia felt cheated of her romantic notion of the West as an untouched paradise she would be among the first to enter. Here were people living settled lives in Ultima Thule, the land beyond the last frontier. Occasionally, when they made camp by a stream, the men setting up tents and organizing a hunt for deer or wild turkey, a settler came by offering to sell them bacon or cheese or freshly baked pies for their supper. Georgia was surprised that many of these people were immigrants, German or Irish or Dutch. Then she would smile as she realized she was an immigrant, too.

One night, as they camped in a vacant log house in a grove of oaks, a train of eleven wagons passed and others stopped to share the camp, the fresh water, and the moon. It seemed to Georgia that all of America was moving west, and there was even talk among the men that maybe they had waited too late to claim the fertile and abundant virgin lands of Texas. That night there was music and dancing and a sense of community as strong and as close as anything Georgia had ever known. She realized these people who shared their camp were from a different world than hers. They were rough of speech and manner—yeoman farmers and storekeepers, coopers and carpenters. Here were the skills that would build the new towns and would form the foundation for her new life of privilege and plenty. Here were lives hers would have never touched in the thin blue exclusivity of Old South society. Yet, as the night grew late and the moon passed behind a dark hand of cloud, Georgia felt somehow kin to these people who were gambling their lives on a dream. The whole scene, the dancing, the homespun clothing, the flushed faces of good, strong people, the strangely sensual closeness of the cloak of the night, reminded her of a Pieter Brueghel painting of a peasant wedding dance. She felt like a village lass, a peasant free of the conventions of her class. She even wished for a moment she could cast away her shoes and dance barefoot on the earth. The thought made her blush and reach for her husband's hand. To her surprise he gathered her into his arms and they whirled away into the dancing crowd. The music of the backwoods cotillion, a curious blending of waltz and stomp, filled the night, and its rhythm matched the heartbeat of slave, commoner, and cavalier alike.

During a pause in the dancing, Georgia moved to the tent where the children were sleeping. She was somewhat surprised to find they were actually there and not away on some misadventure. They seemed asleep, dreaming, and she supposed they were tucked in for the night; still she had been fooled before. Maybe they were merely feigning sleep and would race away on some devilment as soon as she was gone. She sighed, and felt a touch of guilt that she would doubt the innocence of children as beautiful as these. Having convinced herself she had judged them unfairly, she turned away and didn't see them leap fully clothed from their blankets and run out into the night to catch fireflies as she went to join Peter Cavanaugh Woods, her husband, whose touch seemed to excite her in such a special way these nights.

Georgia stood for a moment at the edge of the lantern light. She watched her husband moving among the others, and once again he appeared somehow larger than the ordinary men around him. It was not size exactly, although he was strong and muscular. Rather, it seemed to Georgia that he stood out from his background, as if there were an aura about him that heightened his physical presence. For years now she had watched him work with his patients, their respect for him reflected in their eyes. Sometimes he let her assist him, especially with the children or with their mothers, who often needed more comfort than the little ones. Georgia knew she was good with people and could charm them out of their fear and worry. When she heard laughter in the little clinic, she believed she was not only a part of Dr. Peter but a part of his healing, too. She never loved him more than when they were side by side, working against the perils that so often plagued their community. She marveled at the miracle of healing, itself. When Dr. Peter was able to mend broken bones, tame raging fevers, heal the wounds men inflicted on each other each Saturday night in town, she felt an almost sinful pride that such a man would have chosen her to share his life. Once she had been attacked by a rogue goose near a lily pond. He had touched her and healed her, and he had been taking care of her, chasing her pain away, ever since.

That night, after the dancing had ended and the lanterns had been carried away, Dr. Peter and Georgia lay together beneath the stars. Georgia had never felt more alive, more content, more secure. She felt like Eve, as if they were the first man and woman on earth. *Whatever happens in Texas,* she thought, *I will remember this moment. This moment will be the charm I carry to keep evil away.* After a while she went to sleep and dreamed of children holding birds.

On the Sunday before they reached the Arkansas River it began to rain. They had camped a mile from Little Rock to observe the Sabbath and were, in fact, in prayer when the first huge drops fell from the sky. There was weight to the rain, almost, Georgia thought, as if God had mistaken his celestial water barrel for the one containing mercury. The worshipers, the six families and their hundreds of slaves, scurried to the shelter of their tents and wagons or to the canopy of trees surrounding the camp. At first Georgia enjoyed the freshness of the rain. It was one of those showers without wind or lightning or danger, and for a long while Martha Benny and Georgia let their children play in the deepening pools and rivulets. By nightfall the rain still fell. It was a steady, heavy, somnolent sobbing that still wept at dawn. The men decided to move on, for the nearby creek was rising, threatening flood. The sodden caravan moved onto the road, where the thin carriage wheels sank to the hub in mud. Slave and master, horse and oxen, hauled the carriages and wagons to higher ground. Never had Georgia seen such mud. Everything she touched was covered with an oily film that seeped into the carriage and into her hair and her eyes.

As they approached the river, the Donalsons' carriage began to slide sideways in the mud, slowly descending a slope as the horses danced and stumbled along, dragged downhill by the momentum of the carriage. Then like something dreamed, the carriage fell over, spilling the Donalsons into the mud. Running through the rain to help them, Georgia thought the Donalsons looked like tarbabies as they scrambled from beneath the buggy. Then she fell and was actually submerged beneath a soft canopy of liquid earth. She was more astonished at being entombed in mud than she was afraid of drowning. After all, she knew that any moment she would feel Dr. Peter's healing hands—and then there they were, grasping her shoulders, heaving her up into his arms. He brushed the mud from her eyes and she stood with her eyes tightly closed, slippery and shivering. "You have never been more beautiful," he said, and he kissed her, muddy lips and all.

By the time the caravan reached the Arkansas River, it had been raining for almost a week. The river was a swollen, undulating, roiling morass of gelatinous brown water. It was filled with trees, roots, and masses of lumber and debris swept from landings upriver toward Fort Smith, Skullyville, French Jack's, and Black Rock. On the east shore, wagons and carriages stood in chaotic formation waiting for the flood to subside. Crowds of slaves milled among keelboat masters and stevedores and roustabouts and prostitutes from New Orleans seeking their fortune among the soldiers at Port Gibson. Along the landing was a clutter of keelboats and pirogues and bullboats made fast with rawhide straps to what trees had escaped the boilers of steamboats. An old sternwheeler, belching ash and soot, strained at the lashings that held it tenuously to shore, its every available space filling with piles of freight and powder kegs and migrant families wet to the bone.

Georgia, Dr. Peter, and the children were swept down the gangplank onto the sternwheeler *Andrew Jackson,* a veteran of nearly fifty years on the western rivers. It had been built in Pittsburgh by Nicholas Roosevelt for the firm of Livingston and Fulton. Its captain, Bigelow Pennywaite, who introduced himself to Dr. Peter, was a veteran of at least that many years on the river, perhaps more. He looked a little like a banker gone wrong. His threadbare black waistcoat barely covered an immense belly. Atop his thatch of white hair, he wore a nautical blue cap of ancient issue. Because of a storm of whiskers on his chin and cheeks, there was little to see of his face, except his eyes, which were red with worry or from the bottle.

"Wasn't but a while ago, we was hauling keelboats full of Cherokees and Creeks up toward Port Gibson," Captain Pennywaite told the wheelhouse visitors. "Packed 'em three hundred to a boat and I'd tow them keelboats three at a time. That's nine hundred Indians at a whack. It was winter and the river was low and there was all kind of submerged rocks. But I'd just pour on the steam to these old boilers, and the *Andrew Jackson* would just jump over the shoals and rocks, skip up the river like a stone."

Georgia wondered if the McGregors or any of the surviving Tuckabatchees had been aboard Captain Pennywaite's terrible steamer. Had they come this way with their sacred plates and their sorrow? Her father had told her of one such steamer, the *Monmouth,* carrying Creek families held prisoner, that had sunk in the Mississippi with a loss of nearly three hundred lives. Many of them had been scalded to death by steam from the exploding boilers.

The last wagons and carriages were rolled aboard and lashed in place, and then the *Andrew Jackson*'s gangplank came rattling aboard. The rain continued to fall, the moisture polishing the river scene to a fine patina. The lamps in the wheelhouse swayed, horses screamed, the deck seemed alive and it moaned and creaked. The boilers began to thunder and wheeze like feverish giants. A child cried out in fear of all the noise and confusion. Roustabouts shouted. The boat's bell clanged, the paddle wheels began to turn, and the old *Andrew Jackson* rolled out into the river. The deck hands shouted, "Far yo'well, Miss Lucy!" and the steamboat began its battle with a river gone mad with flood.

Georgia held fast to Dr. Peter's arm as the river hurled the steamboat first to one side and then another. She, Mahalia, and Martha Benny made every effort to keep the children around them, but the press of bodies, the motion of the steamer, and the children's need to see and hear everything at once continually pulled the family apart. Mahalia held Little Sweet in her arms, and somehow the child slept through the chaos of the voyage. When the older children ran off to explore, Georgia shouted to them, threatening them with the mythical switch, and sent Martha Benny to collect them. The steamer was swept downstream sideways, sliding toward the Mississippi. Then, slowly, the bow moved around to face the racing current, and the old steamer shuddered on its wooden frames and at last began to make some forward progress. "These old boilers can hold a hundred pounds of pressure per square inch," Captain Pennywaite shouted. "Look what them gauges say now. Hundred and eighty, that's what. Most of these old boats end up blowin' sky high. But I tell you this, I'd rather fly than drown."

The captain, who seemed to relish his role as doomsayer, pointed out the most difficult part of the short voyage would be docking on the western shore. "There's rocks up there," he shouted against the noise of the river and the boilers, "and the landing is upstream from the rocks. So we gotta head up beyond the landing and back down under full power and stop dead before we hit them rocks. They may call it Little Rock up there, but them rocks ain't. They can cut this boat like a melon."

As Georgia looked down at the raging river and the terrified horses and the slaves huddled like bundles of wet bedding on the deck, she was swept with a sense of unreality. *What am I doing here?* she wondered. *How did I possibly get into this impossible situation? How can I be caked with mud, crossing a wild river with a hundred-year-old maniac riverboat captain? I should be dry and safe in my father's house.* Then she decided to will away this terrible dream. Silently, fervently, she began to pray that she was living an illusion—that she would soon wake and find herself playing the piano in the music room at Water Valley while Martha Benny served her cakes and compliments and cool glasses of lemonade. As she prayed she held tighter to Dr. Peter Cavanaugh Woods. After checking to make sure the children were there by the wheelhouse, she closed her eyes. If prayer could not save her, surely Dr. Peter could.

The captain shouted for more steam as they began their docking maneuver, backing down on the rocks with full pressure on the boilers. The great sternwheel was still, poised, waiting for the final forward rush to gain the shore. Georgia watched the needle on the steam gauge climb. Then, suddenly, she saw the children were gone. She rushed to the spot by the wheelhouse where she had last seen them. Calling to Martha Benny, she desperately scanned the sodden crowd of humanity on the decks. Then she saw them. Lovie, Pinckney, Jim, and Cherokee, along with children she didn't recognize, were climbing toward the heaving bow of the riverboat. Georgia ran to the wheelhouse door and screamed at them but the wind tore her voice away. Dr. Peter charged from the wheelhouse and began to make his way through the crowded decks toward the children. It seemed to Georgia that she was suspended in time and space. Even the noise of steam and iron and rushing water was stilled and the whole world seemed to whisper. The children rode the steamboat bow like a bucking horse, their silhouettes bold against the river. Dr. Peter struggled against the horses, and pushed through the gathered slaves. It seemed as if he were swimming through barrels of rain and flesh.

Then Georgia saw the child fall, first hurled upward, then outward, then gone beneath the river. In a moment, he surfaced in the maelstrom, bobbing, one arm high, the other holding a raft of brush and debris, the river carrying the child and the steamboat backward at nearly the same speed. But slowly the boy slipped toward the stern. Georgia refused to think whose child this could be, whether it was hers and if so which one. It was too difficult a thing to contemplate, and her mind refused to give a name to the boy who now, somehow, managed to grasp a blade of the paddle wheel and miraculously pull himself up out of the river.

Georgia rushed back into the wheelhouse. "A little boy is on the paddle wheel!" she screamed.

"I know," the captain said, and he pointed to the rocks rapidly approaching. "God only knows I know." Georgia looked back at the rocks looming out of the rain and at the child clinging to the motionless paddle wheel. She had a moment of giddy elation as she recognized that he was not her own, then was washed with dread again as she sensed what must now happen. In an avalanche of steam and thunder, the great pistons began to move and the paddle wheel began to turn and the youngster was ground down beneath the river. After one revolution, he still clung to the wheel. After the second, the boy was gone.

Somewhere on the road between the Arkansas and the Red River, Georgia began to wonder about their journey. Maybe the move to Texas had been a mistake, an awful miscalculation. They had all been blinded by their romanticism, by the myth of a noble and enlightened society in a savage land. All they had found so far was mud and mean little houses by the road and storms of mosquitoes and bad wells and night after night of boiled cabbage for supper. "I'd give a year of my life to just once sit down at a table for supper like human beings." Georgia and Martha Benny had just finished washing the family's clothes in the creek and Georgia was cleaning the mud from her knees where she had knelt on the bank. "And just take a look at my hair. I can't even get a comb through it for all the plants and varmints that live up there. I'm an absolute botanical wonder. Every conceivable species of cocklebur dwells beneath my bonnet."

"You're also lookin' dark as a berry," Martha Benny said. "Soon folks won't know who's the mistress around here."

"I don't see how it matters much. We both work our fingers to the bone. We're both about as dirty and shabby as can be. My clothes smell like they've been worn by a bear."

Martha Benny's rich, melodic laughter lifted Georgia's mood, but she felt her resolve growing stronger. She would simply confront Dr. Peter. She would insist they turn right around and go back to Mississippi. It was obvious they had made a mistake, but it could be easily corrected. Logic and good sense were on her side, so surely Dr. Peter would recognize the truth of the matter and would end this peculiar, misguided odyssey. After all, Dr. Peter and her father always did what she wanted. And the primary reason they always did her bidding was that sooner or later they always realized she was right.

Georgia waited for the appropriate moment for her confrontation with Dr. Peter. It came at the end of a hard day when one of their horses had injured a leg in the spokes of a carriage wheel.

The horse was frightened and in pain and its hooves lashed out at Dr. Peter as he tried to determine the extent of the injury. It had not rained for more than a week now, and each time the horse kicked, dust blossomed in the air and into Dr. Peter's beard and eyes. Georgia watched Dr. Peter struggle, and she felt a deep sympathy for this good man she loved. It seemed sad that a physician of his stature and abilities should be reduced to healing horses.

When they returned to their tent, Georgia saw that Dr. Peter's arm was bruised—apparently the horse had kicked him—and she washed the injury with water warmed on the fire. He looked up into her eyes and smiled. She knew now was the time to save him from himself and from a wasted life.

"Dr. Peter," she said. "It's time to go home. I want to go home to Water Valley."

He was silent for a long moment. "You can't be serious." He was still smiling, but there had been a change in his eyes.

"Of course I'm serious." She spoke matter-of-factly, tossing the words easily to his mind. "It's time we came to our senses. I'm sure when you've had time to think about it, you'll agree it's best for the family, for the children. It's the best thing all around."

"Well, well," he said, and he began to whistle a tuneless phrase through teeth closed tight.

"You're tired," she said, and she kissed his cheek. "We'll talk about it in the morning."

"We can talk about it now if you like," he said. "Now might be just the right time."

"All right. There's really not much to say."

"Except no."

"No?" Georgia was stunned.

"No, Georgia," he said again. He stood and kissed her. "Let that be the end of it."

The next day Georgia had a sick headache. She lay in the wagon, suffering terribly. Dr. Peter felt her brow and her pulse and promised she would survive. The caravan moved out and Georgia rode lying down in the bed of a wagon, bounding around like baggage. She knew absolutely that Dr. Peter was mistaken and her illness was, if not terminal, horribly debilitating. Surely travel was impossible, she thought, and she called for Martha Benny.

"If they don't stop right now, I'll die," she said. "If we don't go back to Water Valley, the children will be orphans before we get to Texas, that horrid place."

Martha Benny took Georgia's hand. "Open your eyes and look at me!" she said and Georgia did, her lids forced open by the steel in Martha Benny's voice. "Now," she continued, "you know and I know that you're healthy as a horse. You're about the toughest woman I know. So get up off your backside and take care of your babies and your good man. You might get away with this nonsense with your papa in Mississippi, but not in Texas. Set up now and I'll pull those cockleburs out of your hair."

Georgia was furious. She didn't speak to Dr. Peter until they had crossed the Red River and were deep in the pine forests of East Texas. She did not talk to Martha Benny—her slave, best friend and first cousin—until they passed Dallas.

When Georgia first saw the land on the Colorado River where they intended to make their home, she marveled that she had somehow traveled full circle and returned to Water Valley. The highwood and meadow reminded her of her father's land, where she had spent so many pleasant hours swinging on the back veranda looking out over the valley and watching the blue mists ghosting among the pines. Here the trees were not so grand, post oak, blackjack, and elm, but along the river they seemed more luxuriant than any she had seen before, more alive with emerald and jade and rainbows of other greens unnamed in the spectrum. Among the branches were songbirds, and there were grapevines hung like halyards from the heights, and enormous elephant ears spread leaves the size of tabletops. From the hills above the river, she could see what she knew was prairie, a rolling green coverlet of grass reaching, she supposed, to the end of the earth. Never had she known such space. It was a shock to feel so unencumbered by physical restraints. To walk on that blackland prairie, she thought, must be the most delicious kind of freedom.

From the very first, Georgia fell in love with the little river town of Bastrop. It was a small, thriving, comfortable little community of clapboard and promise on the left bank of the blue-green Colorado. The conversation of hammers and lumber slapping and saws chattering through the famous Bastrop pine filled the clear, sweet air. All along Church Street and Chestnut and Spring, and along the riverfront dock where the cotton rafts and steamboats loaded bales for Matagorda, and along the old El Camino Real toward Austin, carpenters were busy at their trade, building houses and churches, markets and stables, shops and even a fine hotel to accommodate the people coming west to purchase their portion of blackland prairie.

One reason Georgia loved the little town was its civic sense of self-assurance. In the town newspaper, the *Colorado Reveille,* Georgia read that Bastrop was a place that had "the most pious ministers of the Gospel, the most accomplished physicians, the most industrious mechanics, the most accommodating tavern-keepers, the most agreeable loafers, the most honest lawyers, the tallest men, the biggest babies in the State, and as for pretty women, why, God bless you, we can beat all creation." So sophisticated was this river town that the Bastrop city council had passed an ordinance making it unlawful for "any person or slave to go in the river naked in the daytime."

But what really drew settlers from Mississippi and Tennessee and Georgia to Bastrop was its vast reaches of blackland prairie, earth so rich and soft it could be turned with a wooden plow. Out from town, beyond the steam mill where the lumber for the growing town was cut and cured, beyond the old mule-powered cotton gin, was the land Dr. Peter and Georgia's father had purchased. A vast four thousand acres, it promised cotton crops that staggered the imagination. The land was a promise to be kept, and Georgia could imagine the great house that would soon rise like an alabaster temple from the fields.

But Georgia knew the great house was some few seasons away. For the moment their home would be the patched canvas tent which had served as shelter on their journey. They would live in the tent while a plank house was being built. Then they would live in the plank house until their fields began to yield cotton enough to pay the cost of the Woods Mansion Georgia had already built in her dreams. The very first day, she began to be impatient for the life the land promised, and she threw herself into the task of establishing their primitive base with characteristic energy.

The very hour the family arrived in Bastrop, Dr. Peter was summoned to treat a child with fever. He packed his medical kit and rode off toward town, leaving the campsite in chaos. Boxes and baggage, looms and farming equipment had been unloaded onto the ground, the tent half erected and billowing in a northern

wind that was rising and becoming bitter cold. There was a camp
to be made, a house to be built, a plantation to be created—and
Dr. Peter was gone. Georgia knew the demands on a physician's
time, especially in frontier towns where good doctors were rare.
As she stood amid the litter of her future watching her husband
ride away, she saw with numbing clarity what her life would be
like in the immediate future. If there was a camp to be made, a
house to be built, a plantation to be created—if there was all this
to do, Georgia now was certain it would not be Dr. Peter
Cavanaugh Woods who would get it done. Georgia walked
through the piles of household goods, pulling her cape tighter
against the wind, and glanced to where her children were throwing rocks at a mule. She called Martha Benny to her side and
asked, "Who knows how to build a house?"

As winter roared into Texas, they began to haul lumber from
the sawmill and to gather stone for the foundation of the house.
Among the slaves was a man named Ed Tom whom Georgia had
known since she was a child. He had been a carpenter for Captain
Lawshe and knew something of the housewright's art. "First you
think the house and then you do it," he said, and neither Georgia
nor Martha Benny could find fault with his strategy. Little by little, under Ed Tom's direction, the house began to rise.

Ed Tom was a slim, wiry man of average height but uncom-
mon strength. His skin was light brown, like coffee well laced
with cream. His features were regular, almost Arabic, with intelligent night-black eyes set deep beneath a heavy brow. His voice
was soft, and everything he did, despite his strength, seemed to be
done with gentle ease. Georgia grew to depend on Ed Tom and
to consider him invaluable in the creation of her new world in the
wilderness. Martha Benny spent more and more time with Ed
Tom and it was apparent he enjoyed her company as well. Yet as
much as Georgia respected his intelligence and ingenuity, there
was something about Ed Tom that made her uncomfortable.
Maybe I knew him in another life, she thought. *Maybe in that life
he was my master and I was the builder of his house and the lover
of his first cousin.*

As winter and the calluses on Georgia's hands deepened, Dr.
Peter was constantly called to the bedside of sick children. In Jan-

uary, two children came down with smallpox and died and were buried in the City of the Dead, high above the river. It was the year of the great cholera epidemic on the Brazos and every new fever brought rumor and dread.

It was in late January when Georgia began to be aware that her children smelled like something she could only describe as unholy. She had not, in fact, seen much of the children that winter. She had worked each day from before dawn until nearly midnight, trying to create order from the confusion of their sprawling tent city, and she had supposed the children were under Martha Benny's watchful eye. At first she had tried to recruit the children to help Ed Tom work on the house, but Cherokee had refused, claiming that her great-grandfather Benjamin Hawkins had indeed married the Queen of Tuckabatchee and, as great-granddaughter of a queen, she should not be required to work. Pinckney and Jim usually refused to work because they were gentleman planters. They spent much of their day lollygagging and smoking grapevine cigarettes and on warm days breaking the laws regarding nude bathing in the Colorado. It was whispered among the children that Cherokee had more than once broken that law as well. Georgia had tried to enlist Lovie to look after Cherokee, but she would agree, then forget, and Georgia's oldest daughter ran wild, much as she herself had done as a child.

Among the children, besides Little Sweet, only Jim seemed to understand the God-given obligation of children to mind their elders. But Jim, too, had an adventurous spirit and was often led astray by the others. He would bend to a given task for an hour or so, toiling for the good of home, hearth, and family. After a few minutes he would mosey off again on some high-hearted odyssey among the tents, along the river, or in town.

One night as the family closed the tent against the winter wind, Georgia noticed a small red flannel pouch hanging from a string around Cherokee's neck. As she reached for it she realized it was the source of the awful odor she had come to suspect, but refused to admit, was seeping from her children. "What in Heaven's name is this?" Georgia asked.

"Mostly horsehair and cow manure and bird bones and blood," Cherokee said. "And dirt from the graves up on the hill.

Martha Benny gave it to us. She said it would push away the sickness."

When Georgia insisted Dr. Peter confront Martha Benny about her voodoo blasphemy, she was aghast when Dr. Peter, the physician and healer, listened patiently to Martha's suggestions regarding the treatment of the growing number of Bastrop's sick children. She told him how a penny on a string prevented indigestion, and rabbits' feet worn around the neck kept away chills and fever. "Another thing," she continued, "is to drive a green stick into the ground in front of the master's house. Of course, we don't have a house, so we can't do that yet." She began to warm to the evolving discussion of the healing arts. "Another way to keep off evil spells," she continued, "is to eat butter made on the first of May and mixed with egg yolk and saltpeter."

Since Dr. Peter refused to chastise Martha Benny for her witchcraft notions, Georgia felt she must. "You can go straight to Hell for idolatry," she warned.

"I'd as soon trust a good conjurer as some doctors I know," Martha Benny said. "They come to a slave that's cut and they put on soot and molasses and spiderwebs to stop the bleeding. I saw a doctor come to a man had rattlesnake bite and he killed a chicken and tore it open and put it on the bite. Then when the chicken turned green, he killed another chicken and put it on there until the man got better. Or doctors put mashed cocklebur leaves and sweet milk for rattlesnake bite. You ask Dr. Peter. He'll tell you there's hardly a dime's worth of difference between what doctors and conjurers know how to do."

Georgia decided then and there to take Martha Benny to a revival in the hopes that her voodoo ways would be washed clean in the Blood of the Lamb.

Never had Georgia known a longer winter. Although Ed Tom completed the house before the worst cold descended, it was little warmer than the tent. It was basically two drafty boxes separated by an open hall, or "dog trot," with a long porch across the front. The wind howled through the dog trot like a pipe organ badly yet passionately played. The chimney for the fireplace was four tall posts sunk into the ground, a framework covered inside and out with clay. Georgia was constantly torn between the comfort of a roaring fire in the fireplace and the danger that the makeshift chimney could set the whole house on fire. Every waking moment and even her dreams now were filled with the fear of fire.

Clustered around the house were the shanties of the slaves, small log dwellings with clay plastered in the spaces between logs. On extremely cold nights, when the wind cut clean through the walls of Georgia's plank house, she worried about the children in the cold, mean shanties. Once when Georgia suggested the sick slave children be brought to the big house, Martha Benny said the log shanties were much more weatherproof than the big house. "Those children will do far better where it's warm," she said. It had been Georgia's plan to give this original house to Martha Benny when the plantation manor house was completed. Now she wondered if the gift would be appreciated.

Not far from the house, going out toward the prairie, there was a grove of trees called the Lost Pines. The trees covered gentle hills which rose from the vast grassy plain like a surprise, a curious remnant of what had once been a greater forest. To escape her work and worry and occasional dark moods, sometimes Georgia walked out to the grove and lingered for awhile listening to the woodwind of the pines. She, too, felt somehow like a remnant, a lost soul alone in a hard and alien world. "I was not born for this," she said aloud. "I simply was not born for this." She examined the hard, red palms of her hands. "I'll be an old woman before I'm twenty-five." Then she walked back through the prairie, away from the Lost Pines to the land where her future waited.

And once that winter, as she moved through the wide, seemingly endless pastures of grass, she knew again that sense of freedom she felt when she first saw the prairie. It was an extraordinary lightness, a feeling that she could easily fly if she put her mind to the task. She was not the girl in the Cherokee painting she had seen on the Trail of Tears so long ago, but the white bird the girl held, restrained but possessing the possibility of unlimited freedom. Maybe if she thought hard enough about it she could rise above the earth, just as Ed Tom could build a house by thinking the house and then doing it.

She was just beginning to imagine herself in flight, and was actually feeling the earth cling less insistently to her step, when she looked down at a most remarkable sight. There, before her, was a ragged, ugly ruin of a human community. Adobes of sticks and clay and weathered board that might have been an abandoned gypsy camp or the awful corpse of some ancient town sacked by Huns or Vandals. Serpents of smoke soiled the air. Mud roads scarred the prairie. A cluster of mud-brown tents spread like dirty laundry over the ground. Chickens and hogs wandered aimlessly. She could see her children, ragged and wild, running through a cold, colorless world, barren as a spinster's dream. Dark people wandered on vague, doomed errands through the ruined city, shouting words the wind whipped away. She looked down on the home they had made in Texas, and saw for the first time how ugly and primitive and temporary it was. Bedouins had finer towns, she thought. She was filled with a disappointment so bitter it verged on shame. She had worked so hard, and what did she have to show for it? This miserable rat's nest. The home she was building for her family was an insult to God's creation. She began to cry, and she pummeled herself on the breast and arms and then on her face with her fists.

When she got home she took to her bed and stayed in bed, even when Martha Benny scolded her and told her sixteen slaves had died of cholera on one Brazoria County plantation and thirty-three had died on another, and "what are your poor little troubles compared to that!"

As her children had learned, Georgia's "petite malaise," though profoundly debilitating, was always characterized by sudden, almost explosive recovery. One day she was at death's door, the next she was a whirling dervish of energy and resolve. So the children went on about their business as usual, little concerned that their mother appeared to be suffering so terribly. Only Jim was particularly concerned and he came to her bed and watched her with compassionate eyes. Dr. Peter, on the other hand, completely ignored Georgia's fits of pique. "Miss Georgia," he once told Ed Tom, "is the only woman I know who can assist me with the most difficult surgery without blinking an eye and then get a sick headache over some silly thing."

Once recovered, Georgia would make no mention of her discomposure and would tolerate no recognition by others that she had been so grievously infirm. She would simply hurl herself back into life among the living with a fervor at which others marveled and which she had long since given up trying to understand.

Spring came to the land along the Colorado in a rush of birdsong and wildflowers and spectacular renewal. Suddenly the gray, hard edges of winter eased and prairie and woodlands became vivid with color. Martha Benny said it was like "the Lord tripped on a cloud and dropped the rainbow." The air became soft and fragrant, and on quiet mornings they could hear the distant, ragged brass of wild geese moving northward on their mysterious migration.

Then they could see the geese, high above the Lost Pines and the City of the Dead, moving like a single wing through the morning light. And when Georgia rose and moved to the door to watch the sunrise she knew she would see the silhouettes of Ed Tom and the others already plowing and preparing beds for spring planting. It was a sight that filled Georgia with electric waves of excitement. On some mornings, Georgia would walk out into the fields to watch the rich, dark soil turn and she would reach down and touch the still cool earth and wonder at the life she felt trembling unseen in her hand.

As nature's miracles unfolded and the small green shoots began to appear in geometric rows, even the children felt the excitement of their first Texas cotton crop. Pinckney and Jim, who had tired of being gentleman planters and had decided to make their fortune rounding up wild Texas mustangs, turned their attention to planting again. Martha Benny had tried to dissuade them from their plans to be stockmen. "We are planters," she said, "not horse traders." Georgia believed Pinckney's high good spirits were due more to the fact that school would soon be out for the summer than to his renewed interest in the cotton crop. Then Martha Benny reminded her that Pinckney rarely went to school anyway; so summer would hardly be a break in his basic routine.

During that first Texas spring, Georgia took every opportunity to interest Pinckney in the operation of the plantation. "One day," she said, "this will be your land to pass on to your children. You've got Captain Lawshe's blood flowing in your veins." Then, as she, Cherokee, and Martha Benny carded cotton for spinning and Pinckney cleaned the new Colt revolver his grandfather had given him, Georgia told them about Captain Lewis Lawshe, war hero and one of the most successful planters in all of the South.

"You know Senator Sam Houston," Georgia began.

"Everybody knows Sam Houston," Cherokee replied. "He's the Hero of San Jacinto. Beat Santa Anna and made Texas free."

"Well, he was also a very good friend of your grandfather. In those days, back during the Creek Wars, Captain Lawshe, Davey Crockett, and Sam Houston soldiered together with Old Hickory, Andrew Jackson." Then Georgia told them about the Battle of Horseshoe Bend and how Major General Andrew Jackson was determined to exterminate the Red Sticks, a force of some four thousand warriors, mostly Creeks. "Old Hickory had been recently wounded in a duel, so his arm was in a sling, but he commanded his troops against eight hundred Red Sticks at a bend on the Tallapoosa River. The Creek prophets had told the warriors that the Great Spirit promised victory. The sign would be a cloud in the heavens." She told them how the Creeks fought fiercely from well-fortified positions, and in the middle of the afternoon a cloud appeared and Crockett and Sam Houston and Lewis Lawshe led the attack on the Red Stick fortress. Sam Houston was finally stopped by two musket balls, and Lewis Lawshe carried him from the field to safety.

"Your grandfather is a man of iron," she told Pinckney. "And his blood flows in your veins."

"So what happened to the Red Sticks?" Cherokee wondered aloud. "Were their prophets wrong?"

Georgia sighed. "It was the last battle of the Creek Wars. As victor, Andrew Jackson demanded twenty-three million acres of land be given to the United States. It was a large part of Georgia and Alabama."

"It seems strange," Jim said. "A great-grandfather fights to save the Indians, a grandfather fights to destroy them. One was an enemy of Andrew Jackson, the other fought at his side."

"My father didn't fight to destroy the Indians," Georgia said. She was not a little offended because Jim had spoken out loud thoughts that had often troubled her own mind. "He was merely serving his country. Just like Sam Houston and Davey Crockett."

"Sounds to me like he was stealing it," Pinckney said. "No wonder the damned old Dutchman's so rich. He stole all that land from the Creeks and the Cherokees."

Georgia was stunned. She could find no words that would do.

"You should whip that boy," Martha Benny said.

"Maybe it's time somebody took a whip to you, nig ..." Pinckney's words were cut off by Georgia's hand, which cracked like rifle fire across his cheek. Georgia felt the pain all the way to the center of her soul.

"I'd say it's about time," Martha Benny said, and she continued to card the cotton that would be woven into long shirts for the slave children.

Soon the cotton seedlings were about four inches tall, and the hands moved out into the fields to thin and chop away the grass between the rows. Dr. Peter continued to spend most of his time with patients, an alarming majority of whom were children. "There has to be a reason for these fevers," he wondered, and even when he was home his mind was away somewhere, seeking answers to the mystery that caused so many sad processions from town to the City of the Dead.

By late May, both Georgia and Martha Benny knew it was not just in the fields where new life was growing. They played a secret game in which they made elaborate wagers on whose child would enter the world first. Each day they compared the changes in their bodies and in their moods. They marveled at their ability to be at ease with each other when discussing things that were simply not discussed in polite society, even things Georgia could not feel comfortable discussing with her doctor husband. "One thing I've never been," Martha Benny laughed, "is polite society."

Occasionally, Georgia would feel a dark mood descending, and it usually involved the guilt she endured from striking Pinckney. She could not shake the feeling that there was some ominous trait passed down through her family. Maybe the mood swings she experienced could be traced to a genetic war between good and evil, between the compassionate generosity of Benjamin Hawkins and the hard harsh individualism of Lewis Lawshe. But then she would retreat from the thought as she would retreat from a spider, because it implied her father was evil. She adored her father. It was true he was a hard, severe, and demanding man. But she knew he loved her. He had filled her life with gifts and presents, everything her heart desired, ever since the day she was born. He had even given her thirty slaves and thousands of acres of land as a dowry. Surely this was not the act of a selfish man. Maybe the child she now carried would reflect the goodness and generosity of Benjamin Hawkins. And maybe the child-to-be would inherit his rebellious spirit, his sense of adventure. Cherokee had been blessed with this inheritance and Georgia prayed the new infant would be blessed with the same gift.

When Georgia and Martha Benny were alone, talking about the children they carried beneath their hearts, Georgia was not aware of one as mistress and one as slave, or one as black and one as white. It was more as if they were kindred spirits, two close friends sharing intimacies. The father of Martha Benny's child was Ed Tom. When Georgia asked if they wanted to be married, Martha Benny turned her head away and was silent for a time. When she turned back, Georgia could see tears in her eyes. "I love Ed Tom and I want us to be married. But he says it's bad to be tied together, because we can be untied and sold in a jiffy. He says it's better not to love too good. Not to start a family that can be pulled apart one day."

"Nobody's going to pull you apart as long as I'm alive! I swear it!" The very thought of selling Martha Benny made her feel ill with anger. "Besides, I promised Uncle Madison."

"There's things you don't know," Martha said.

"I think I do know, Martha."

"Not everything. There's things about Ed Tom you don't know." Martha Benny began to cry in earnest now. "I'm sorry," she said, "I never had a baby before. I guess I'm scared about that and I do love Ed Tom so much and I don't know what's going to happen."

Georgia held Martha Benny's hands in her own. "What's going to happen is you and Ed Tom are going to have a beautiful baby. And my baby and yours are going to grow up together. Two beautiful girls. They'll play together, laugh together. What a time we'll have watching those babies grow up to be young ladies."

For a moment, Martha Benny smiled at the shared dream, then the smile faded. "But it won't be the same. One girl will go one way, the other another way. One down a path of sunshine and flowers. The other down a road of shame and misery."

It took a moment for Georgia to realize what Martha Benny was saying, and it struck her heart like a hammer blow. She felt totally helpless, incapable of offering any word against the truth Martha Benny had revealed. For a while, she was angry at Martha Benny for speaking out loud what had always been hidden by silence. Then she felt ashamed of her anger and then terribly impotent. "I'm so sorry, Martha Benny," was all she could think of to say.

The days grew hot and oppressive. The air seemed to possess an actual substance, thickening beneath the sun. The hours passed slowly, heavily. The children of the little town continued to die. One day, when Georgia was on the front porch spinning and the afternoon was a long song without end, she suddenly decided if she couldn't find some way to cool her body and her soul, she would turn to butter and die. She left the house and walked down to the river. For a while she walked along its bank in the shade of willows, but the shade offered no relief from the heat. The shade was merely a different color of sunlight. She removed her shoes and stepped into the river and walked along the shallows. The water was not cold, not even cool, but its motion on her skin and the sound it made passing soothed and even chased away the awful heat. There was not a soul around, the river was hers alone. On an impulse, she removed her outer garments and lowered herself into the stream. It was heavenly. She became a part of the Colorado, she became weightless, and once more that feeling of lightness and freedom began to flow around her and through her and into her, as if she and the river were one. Then, she was surprised by the preposterous thought, an idea so outrageous she could feel herself blushing. *It's time I broke the law,* she thought to herself. She looked carefully around to make absolutely certain she was not observed, she removed her undergarments and hung them carefully on a branch. Georgia Virginia Lawshe Woods had decided to go into the Colorado naked in daytime.

It was a symbolic last fling, she knew. The prettiest girl in Water Valley, Mississippi, will one more time amaze and delight. *Tomorrow I'll work from dawn till dusk. I will be weary and worried and confronted by the responsibility of my family, the plantation, and an endless procession of children. But today I'm the most beautiful and desirable girl in Mississippi. And it's broad daylight and I'm buck naked in a Texas river.*

She was submerged to her neck in the gently flowing river, dreaming, blushing, thinking that this would be another of those moments she would remember all of her life, when something brushed her thigh and then her breast. It seemed to cling, like wet leaves. A chill crept down her entire body. She reached down to take away the leaves and when she brought them to the surface, she found it was a human hand, the skin floating free of the bone. Then she saw the rest of the man. His hair was bright red, but no other feature seemed human. The sound Georgia made was more a low, guttural growl than a scream, a primal sound that came from deep within her abdomen. She rushed from the water and fell to the sand. She rubbed sand on the places the dead man's flesh had touched until they were red and raw. Then she dressed, ran home, and bathed and scrubbed until she nearly bled.

It was not the first dead body that had come floating down the Colorado to Bastrop. In fact, the river carried all the refuse and waste from Austin and the other settlements to the north. Dr. Peter Woods had begun to wonder if there was some connection between the pollution in the river and the fevers that plagued the children. As the hot summer progressed and the cotton plants began to bud and flower, two more of their slave children died. One day they were fine, then suddenly they began to vomit, contort with muscle cramps, and lose control of their bowels. Dr. Peter rushed to their tents, and he made every effort to keep the children warm and forced them to swallow salt solutions. But soon, as Georgia watched, their little bodies began to dehydrate. They seemed to shrink and their faces became pinched. Their skin became dry and wrinkled, their eyes sunken, their limbs cold. "And the horror of it," Georgia would later tell Dr. Peter, "was that their minds were clear to the end."

Dr. Peter grew certain that the continuing spread of cholera among children, and now among adults, was somehow due to the contamination in the river. In his medical studies, he had read of a cholera epidemic in India, a study made by a Portuguese physician in 1563, nearly three hundred years earlier. Many of those victims had bathed regularly in the Ganges, which was also their drinking water supply and their sewer. *Could it be, he wondered, that the same conditions exist here in our own time?*

In mid summer the temperature soared, enveloping the town in a vaporous shroud. Because of the tall trees along the banks, no wind reached the river. The air seemed to boil and undulate and became difficult to breathe. By the end of July, Dr. Peter was warning people to stay away from the river. He urged everyone to use well or cistern water for drinking and bathing and the preparation of food, not water from the river.

By the first of August, a few weeks before their baby was due and the cotton harvest would begin, Georgia was shocked when Dr. Peter suggested they leave Bastrop. "This place is poisoned," he said. "We should think about selling, moving someplace new."

Georgia was adamant that they should stay. She remembered the vow she made after watching the Creek families driven from the homes. "We've worked too hard to give up now," she said. "Go out in the fields. It's like standing in the snow. Beautiful white snowballs all around, as far as you can see. You'd never leave this place if you could feel the life of the cotton."

Dr. Peter placed his hand on her abdomen, which had now grown large. "It's this life I'm worried about," he said. "The child."

Georgia again felt the power of Dr. Peter's touch and she pressed his hand against the tightness beneath her skirt. "I don't have a worry in the world," she said. "I happen to be married to the finest doctor in Christendom."

"There are things a doctor can't do."

"My doctor can do anything."

"He can move his family out of danger."

"Or he can fight the danger. I guess you can run or you can fight. It's just not in the Woodses to turn and run."

"I'm serious about this, Georgia."

Georgia felt the ice in his words and she looked into his eyes. They were tired eyes. He was exhausted from working night and day against the plague of fevers. "I'll do what you say, Dr. Peter. But, please, the harvest is so near. If we move now, we'll be ruined. Let's wait for the crop to come in, then see."

Dr. Peter left her then, walking away without speaking.

One morning Georgia rose from her bed and walked out to the front porch. It was still dark and she could see Martha Benny standing in the dawn, her blue Hawkins eyes reflecting the light of the morning star. Beyond, in the slave quarters, a woman was singing. It was already warm and there was no wind. The cardinals and mockingbirds that usually signaled the beginning of the day had not yet begun their song. Georgia walked to where Martha Benny stood, until she could feel the heat from her body reach across the few inches separating them one from the other. Inches, Georgia thought, but it might as well be miles. She wanted to embrace this good friend, to hold her close so they could share the triumph of the day. But she could only stand there beneath the morning star, listening to a beautiful hymn sung by a slave woman, and wait for Ed Tom and the work crew to move out into the fields.

"Well," Georgia said, "looks like it's going to be one fine day."

"Yes, ma'am. Fine day for pickin' cotton," Martha Benny replied. They stood in silence for a moment. Martha Benny smiled then and there was all the world in that smile. "Looks like we've made us a plantation."

"Yes, ma'am," Georgia agreed. "Surely does."

As one group of slaves moved out into the fields with their long cotton sacks, others, including many hired hands, prepared the mule teams and wagons that would carry the cotton to the gin. At the gin itself, cotton baskets made from the wild chinaberry tree and scales that would weigh the cotton were made ready. Georgia could feel energy permeating the house and the fields. It was the first day of the harvest and she had Martha Benny bake something special—caramel-sauced pound cakes and wild plum pies—in celebration.

As the harvest was progressing, Captain Lewis Lawshe arrived in Bastrop. He had written Georgia he would be in Texas to buy land for her sister Lovie and would pass through Bastrop for a visit. When she got word of his arrival, Georgia rushed to town and into his arms. She was surprised that he had somehow grown smaller. He was not at all the dashing heroic figure of her memory, although he was rather dapper in his black frock coat, ruffled shirt, and wide-brimmed felt hat. In fact, in his bright red satin vest, he reminded her of a robin. And he had grown old. Even so, Georgia felt like a girl again as they rode back to the house.

"Oh, Papa, just wait till you see my land. You've never seen such cotton." She could feel his pride and his pleasure as she told him how she had created a producing plantation from empty prairie. How strange, she thought, that I still need the approval of this little old man. As they passed the Lost Pines and rounded a hill, they could see the slaves in the distance moving through the white fields. They looked like bundles of old clothes scattered on the land.

"On the evening and the morning of the third day," Captain Lawshe proclaimed, "God created the land." Georgia recognized the professorial tone her father used when he wished to pass on a fragment of his wisdom. "Nevertheless he didn't make man until the sixth day. Now, I've always regarded that to mean that land is more important than people. You take care of the land, like God told us, and people will take care of themselves." It was not the first time Georgia had heard this theory. "There's something else I've learned over these sixty years or more," he continued. "The land is everything. Without it you are less than the beasts. There are two kinds of people in this world. There's masters and there's slaves. And the only difference between the two is land. If you lose the land you lose your freedom. God didn't say that," he added. "Lewis Lawshe said that."

During this visit Georgia noticed a strong bond between her father and Ed Tom. She had always known that Ed Tom had belonged to Lewis Lawshe before he was given to Georgia. He had always been around when she was a girl. Yet there was something troubling about her feelings for him, something vague and mysterious. During her father's visit, Georgia discerned a change in Ed Tom, a deference paid to the old planter that could have been based on fear or on love. Once she saw the Captain and his former slave walking together along the river. Their heads were close and Captain Lawshe placed his hand on Ed Tom's shoulder, either, Georgia thought, with affection or for support. Later that night, she overheard a conversation between Martha Benny and Mahalia.

"She had feeling toward him," Mahalia said. "But she was his property."

"He was a good man, wasn't he?" Martha Benny asked. "A man gets lonely."

"There was nothing else she could do, 'cept be his woman and have his baby."

Georgia walked onto the porch. Both black women lowered their heads and studied their hands. "Who was that?" Georgia asked.

"Just some woman belong Mr. Harwood," Mahalia said. "Some woman got trouble with her man."

Although Captain Lawshe readily admitted Georgia had done a remarkable job growing her first cotton crop, he was not reluctant to offer advice. At first Georgia felt an old rebellion beginning to surface, but she knew immediately that she would need the skills and knowledge her father possessed. He was a wealth of information on the intricate art of moving cotton from the field to the marketplace. Georgia and Ed Tom were excellent and receptive students. Captain Lawshe taught them how to weigh cotton accurately, how to gauge the maximum that could be loaded safely on a wagon, how to calculate the number of wagons needed, how to obtain the best river rafts and crews, how to load a raft, how many men would be needed to guard the cotton as it moved along its way, how to bargain for the best price in the cotton markets on the coast. They pored over the map to determine the best route for moving the cotton to market.

Georgia loved the sessions with her father and Ed Tom. Captain Lawshe was a bit bombastic, as always, but she could see, perhaps for the first time, the keen intelligence and competitive spirit beneath the surface. It was no surprise, she thought, that the old man had been so successful in Georgia and Mississippi. Each session left her exhilarated. She felt that she and Ed Tom were comrades in arms being briefed for a major engagement by their captain. She even began to call her father "Captain Papa," and she could tell it pleased him. Never had she loved him more.

Soon wagons sagging beneath loads of cotton bales moved from the Woods gin to the town docks. Hands wrestled the heavy bales onto rafts for the trip to the mouth of the Colorado, where they would again be loaded onto wagons for Matagorda. Some of the rafts were merely logs bound together, capable of carrying only three or four bales. Other flatboats could carry far more, but if loaded too deeply would have trouble navigating the shallows and snags downstream from Bastrop. Traveling with Reverend Cummings as an escort, Ed Tom was placed in charge of the flotilla and given an introduction to a broker in Matagorda by Captain Lawshe. Then one day the flatboats and barges and rafts were loaded and slaves with long poles began to move Georgia's future out into the river where they caught the current and began moving slowly downstream. Ed Tom, on the largest vessel, a keelboat, was the last to leave. Georgia and Captain Lawshe stood with him by the rudder as he ordered the lines cast ashore. Captain Lawshe and Ed Tom shook hands, and then the Captain turned and returned to shore. For a long moment, Georgia stood with Ed Tom by the tiller. She could see her reflection in his eyes. She studied her image in the dark mirror of his eyes, and she felt a fondness for him so powerful it took her by surprise. Quickly, she turned away and she could see her father waiting on the dock.

"Be safe," Ed Tom said.

"Godspeed, good friend," she said, and she stepped ashore.

Two sons were born into the Woods family on the night of September 9, 1853. One was named Lewis Lawshe for Georgia's father. The other, Martha Benny's son, was named Lee. Within two weeks, the fever came. Dr. Peter tried everything he knew to save the two little boys. Martha Benny drove a green stake into the ground and carried a red onion in her pocket. Dr. Peter refused the two asafetida bags Martha Benny prepared, then, when Martha Benny was not looking, he took the two pouches and with a prayer for forgiveness placed them on the pillow of his tiny son. Cholera spared Baby Lee, but it claimed Baby Lewis. Neither science nor magic could save him.

Georgia asked that her infant be buried among the Lost Pines. A brief service was held before the infant stranger was lowered into the ground. Georgia watched the earth claim her son before turning to walk back across the prairie toward her home. Martha Benny walked on one side, Dr. Peter on the other. As she walked, she felt an exhaustion flow into the very center of her being. It was not grief, exactly. After all, she hardly knew the parcel of flesh and fire that was her second son. Then she thought her exhaustion might be due to guilt. If only she had taken Dr. Peter's advice and left the poisons of the river, maybe the child would be alive and in her arms right now. Then she tried not to think at all.

After the baby's burial, Dr. Peter and Martha Benny brought Georgia into the house and put her to bed. It was obvious her reserves were depleted. But in the morning, when Dr. Peter awakened, Georgia was gone. They looked everywhere, calling. Finally, they found her out in the cotton field. She was plowing with a mule, cutting a furrow through the picked-over plants and lint-lined earth as if she were preparing the soil for a crop of winter oats or rye. They had to drag her away from the earth and off the land. Within days, the family simply abandoned the house and the gin and all the mean log cabins. They left Bastrop and the Colorado River forever.

Since leaving Bastrop and coming to the Hill Country town of San Marcos, Texas, Georgia had slipped into a river of grief, a deep turbid stream of sorrow. For days she moved through life like a sleepwalker, responding to those around her with no more animation than a plant responding to light. She probably would have taken to her bed, but as the days moved by, there developed a hard core of anger to her grief, a troubling need to retaliate against the fates.

Reverend Kerr, a circuit-riding preacher who had established the little Methodist Church in San Marcos, often sat with Georgia and walked with her on the soft green hills above the river. He talked of life and how Job cursed the day he was born because his "grief was heavier than the sands of the sea." Georgia listened to the old familiar story of Job's troubles and weariness with life and his despair, and she tried to pray and humble herself before God, but she was too angry. "I just can't pray," she told Reverend Kerr. "It's not that I don't love the Lord," she said. "I believe in His power, His love, and His presence, but I just don't feel these things. I reach out and there's nothing there."

Dr. Peter had quickly disposed of their Bastrop lands and had reinvested in land between the Blanco and San Marcos rivers. The water ran fresh and pure. The black soil was deep and rich and warm under the Texas sun. Often Georgia would walk along the San Marcos, seeking to ease the weight she carried in her heart. She remembered Madison's remark that to waste life in sorrow was to steal from God. Intellectually, she knew she should put the child's death behind her. And she tried. She would wake in the morning and say aloud: "This is the day the Lord hath made and I shall be glad and rejoice in it." She would hurl herself into her work with a passion, her mind alive with plans for the things that must be done to establish the new plantation. Then, about noon, she would remember all the labor and pain wasted in Bastrop and the image of the small grave in the Lost Pines would ghost through her mind. She would feel herself slipping back into her strange and troubled lassitude. Martha Benny watched her struggle with her darker side, and she tried what she could to bring Georgia back into the light.

"Won't be long Ed Tom'll be back with the cotton money," Martha Benny said at least once a day. "Then we're gonna have a high old time. You gonna buy ponies for all the children to ride." Sometimes Georgia thought about Ed Tom and wondered how he had fared. She had heard whispers in town ridiculing Dr. Peter for gambling a cotton fortune on a black slave. "He's a good doctor and a good man," she heard a storekeep say. "But he sure don't know nigras. How's an ignorant darky gonna make a good sale? And if he does, he'll just take the money and head up north." Georgia had approached the storekeep with fire in her eyes, but then it occurred to her that he did not know Ed Tom and could not know why she would trust him with her fortune or her life. In fact, she was not sure herself, but her trust was inviolate as truth, as sure as God's word.

During this period of Georgia's dark moods, the children, Sweet, Cherokee, Pinckney, and Lovie, kept their distance. But each afternoon Jim would bring Georgia a glass of sugar water. Sometimes Georgia found a colorful leaf or a smooth, translucent river stone on her bed or her writing table, and she knew Jim had brought her another gift. When Dr. Peter returned from his patients, he would talk with Georgia about how fertile their new land was. He liked to tell her that as soon as Ed Tom and Reverend Cummings returned from selling their cotton, they would create on their land a plantation better than the one they had before.

"Do you remember, a long time ago," Dr. Peter asked, "when you wondered what life would be like in Texas? I told you we would have the finest plantation in the state and our children would grow up to be presidents and scholars and great generals."

"Not Baby Lewis," Georgia said.

Dr. Peter gathered her in his arms. "Georgia, it's time to move on. It's time to think about life. We'll have more children."

"Not if I can help it," Georgia said, then immediately regretted the words. "Oh, Dr. Peter, I'm so sorry. I just can't think about children now." Georgia felt the tears begin and she turned away from Dr. Peter. She remembered never seeing her mother Cherokee cry, and she was embarrassed by her own tears.

With his hands, Dr. Peter gently turned her head back. "I would give everything I have to make you happy," he said. "I just don't know how to heal sorrow. There's nothing I can prescribe except time—and love."

When Captain Lewis Lawshe learned of his namesake's death and the abandonment of the Bastrop plantation, he wrote to Georgia: "My Dear Darling Daughter. How proud I am of my little slip of a girl. Who could have known when you were chasing around Water Valley without a care or responsibility in the world that you could have managed your fortune so well. There is within you a wellspring of strength and courage few possess. It is not difficult to be strong and courageous when things go well. But only a very special few can find these qualities in themselves when the world seems bent on destroying all they love. Know that I love you and think of you and will be with you every step of the way as you begin again. Those broad, white fields of cotton you showed me last month can bloom once more. Carry the image in your mind, then make that image real." Then he signed the letter, "Your loving Papa."

Georgia had to smile at the letter's final advice. "Think of the cotton fields, then make them real." It reminded her of Ed Tom's house-building philosophy. "Think the house and then build what you think." How strange, she thought, that two men like Ed Tom and her father could be so absolutely different, yet in many ways so similar.

Old Mose was the first to see Ed Tom, along with the noted horse racer, gambler, and drunk Andrew Jackson Potter, making their way through the live oaks toward the new Woods homeplace. Old Mose dropped the kindling he was gathering and ran ahead of Ed Tom's wagon shouting at the top of his voice. The word spread quickly, and by the time Ed Tom's wagon rolled into view, every living soul was out of doors celebrating his arrival. The Negroes rushed to his side and mobbed the wagon. The children danced around, asking to see the gold coins that were supposed to fill his pockets upon his return. When Ed Tom saw Martha Benny carrying little Lee in her arms, he leaped from the wagon and lifted both woman and child in the air, swinging them around as if in a dance. Then the crowd of dark forms parted as Georgia made her way forward toward the wagon and Ed Tom. He put Martha Benny down and, as he stood watching Georgia approach, the crowd of slaves grew still.

"Miss Georgia," Ed Tom said, with just the suggestion of a bow.

"Ed Tom."

"I'm sorry about the boy. They showed me his grave back there."

"You look well."

"You look fine, too, Miss Georgia."

"How was your trip?"

"Long, Miss Georgia. I didn't know Matagorda was so far."

"What's that in your wagon?" Georgia nodded her head toward what looked like a corpse.

"That's parts of your old cotton gin and Mr. Andrew Jackson Potter. He's kind of a friend of mine. Joined up with me when Reverend Cummings got too sick to travel. But now he's real sick, too. Thought Dr. Peter might take a look at him."

"What else you got in that wagon, Ed Tom?"

Georgia glanced toward Mose, who had asked the question. She was aware of the growing tension among the slaves. They followed Georgia and Ed Tom's conversation with exquisite attention, heads swinging in unison from one speaker to another. Georgia herself was almost faint with suspense. But the moment belonged to Ed Tom and she stood back to let him take the lead in revealing either the success or failure of his mission.

"Come take a look," Ed Tom said, and motioned. He moved to the wagon and began pulling a board from the floor beneath the driver's seat. There was a compartment hidden beneath a false floor. Ed Tom reached in and, with great difficulty, he wrestled from the compartment several large gunnysacks. Then he climbed up into the wagon, lifted one of the heavy sacks, and then emptied it into a washtub. The sound was like nothing Georgia had ever heard before. Like the spurs of a thousand horsemen jingling all at once. The sunlight touched the torrents of silver, and to Georgia the whole world grew brighter. The crowd sighed with wonder. The silver reflected starpoints of moving light across their dark faces. Then Ed Tom removed another sack from the hidden compartment. This sack contained paper money and promissory notes.

"This is thousands and thousands," Ed Tom said, as he jumped down from the wagon. More than anything in the world, Georgia wanted to hug her dear friend and say how proud she was and how thankful she was that he had come back safely. But, instead, she made a small formal bow and said: "It's good to have you home, Ed Tom. I'm pleased. I'm mighty pleased."

That evening, with Andrew Jackson Potter asleep after a good meal, Ed Tom told Dr. Peter and Georgia the story of his adventures. Even though cotton prices had been falling in the 1850s, Captain Lawshe's Matagorda agent had been able to get a premium price on the Liverpool market. After paying freight, expenses, and commissions, Ed Tom returned to Bastrop with more money than he ever dreamed existed in this world. But when he got to the country of the Lost Pines, he found the old Woods plantation had new owners and another slave showed him the small fresh grave among the trees.

"They told me what happened and that you came here. So I bought the cotton gin and took it apart. I figured we'd need it here. Then I partnered with Mr. Andrew to help me haul it across country."

Georgia remembered seeing Andrew Jackson Potter in Bastrop. He was, in fact, difficult to ignore. He was a small, disheveled, handsome man of scandalous reputation. He had been accused of nearly every variety of human behavior, save sobriety and celibacy, though it was widely known he was too careless and loquacious to be truly dishonest. He was, however, a victim of an overpowering addiction to games of chance. Those rare occasions when he had money in his pocket were of brief duration. He simply could not resist the need to wager his money away—or wager away the money of someone else, for that matter.

"I would think you'd have chosen a more reputable companion," Georgia said.

"Well, yes, ma'am. But Mr. Andrew is a powerful good drover. There's not a horse or a mule in the world he can't make do his biddin'."

"So you started out for San Marcos."

"Everything was fine until after we crossed the Colorado. Then everything still went fine for awhile. We moved westward over the high prairie, through bluestem and Indian grass tall as the wheels of the wagon. We passed Blanco Springs, so clear you could see shadows of the fish moving on the bottom. Sometimes we'd flush out quail and sometimes cranes so big their wings made a drumming sound in the air. Then we pulled up to Sam Ealy Johnson's place. Just a little cabin sittin' all catawumpus. Cattle wandering all around. A few good horses, some persimmon trees, and a creek. He said in summer he got good dewberries all up and down that creek. We stayed the night with Mr. Sam, there by Onion Creek. And that's when the Indians came."

Georgia glanced over at Dr. Peter. He, too, seemed enraptured by the tale. She was intrigued not so much by Ed Tom's narrative, but by the small things he noticed along the way. The dewberries, for instance, and the shadows of the fish. She felt she was actually reliving his adventure, she was with him in the wagon when he arrived at Sam Ealy Johnson's cabin. With him when the Indians came.

"Well," Ed Tom continued. "Mr. Sam is this great, tall, lanky fella. Has ears that stick way out from his head. You know how Mr. Andrew is not much taller than Miss Georgia. And together they were a sight."

"Indians, you say?"

"Yes, sir, Dr. Peter. It was like this. I stayed in a shed out back and Mr. Andrew accepted Mr. Sam's hospitality and stayed with him up in the cabin. They had a jug of home brew Mr. Sam called Mom's Mule. Made from dewberry, wild plum, and poppy. By midnight I could hear them in there cuttin' up. They were three sheets to the wind and they were cuttin' cards for Miss Georgia's cotton money. Now don't get me wrong. I had my eye on those sacks. But those fellas were in high heaven, playin' like that silver was theirs. They probably had never ever been happier than they was that night, cuttin' cards for that *big* money and drinking more and more of that Mom's Mule.

"It was pretty near midnight, I drifted off and then woke up real sudden. I swear I was woke up by the Man in the Moon. Heard his voice just as plain as day. He said, 'Get up, Ed Tom, there's Indians here.' When I opened my eyes, I saw those Comanches movin' in the moonlight. One wore armor like the old Spanish gentlemen and the other was hardly wearing any clothes at all. He was covered with scars and wore a tall silk hat. Both of them were bodacious big. Later, Mr. Sam told us the two Comanches were called Iron Jacket and Tarantula. I kept to the shadows and crawled from the shed to the house so I could warn Mr. Sam and Mr. Andrew. They were asleepin' with that bottle of Mom's Mule between them. But when I told them about the Comanches, they came awake fast, like Lazarus up from the dead. Mr. Sam bet Mr. Andrew a hundred Mexican pesos the Comanches were after the horses, and Mr. Andrew, he covered that bet and raised it one hundred dollars more."

Georgia and Dr. Peter exchanged impatient glances. "Try to keep to your story, Ed Tom," Georgia said. "Just tell us what happened."

"Well, while Mr. Sam and Mr. Andrew were betting and callin' and raisin' one another's bets, Tarantula and Iron Jacket made off with three of Mr. Sam's best horses. Mr. Sam said one of them cost more than I cost Captain Lawshe. Of course, he don't know, but that's what he said to make his point about how good the horses were."

"Ed Tom!"

"I'm makin' my way to the point, Miss Georgia."

"Well, I should hope so."

"Mr. Andrew bet Mr. Sam we could catch those horse thieves and Mr. Sam covered that bet, too. And so off we went after Iron Jacket and Tarantula. Chased them for three days."

"Where was the silver all that time?" Georgia asked.

"On Mr. Sam's table."

"You just left it there on the table? Thousands and thousands in silver and bills? What could you possibly have been thinking?"

"Tell you the truth, Miss Georgia, I believed that silver was safer on Mr. Sam Ealy Johnson's table than in Mr. Andrew Jackson Potter's pocket."

"Lord have mercy on our souls! I can't believe this!"

"Well, there might be parts that I storified a little. A little color done make the garden a whole lot prettier. But the end of the story is what counts. And the end of the story is right there in those sacks. Yes, ma'am. And that's the truth."

When Andrew Jackson Potter had arrived in Ed Tom's wagon, he appeared to be dying. At first they assumed he was merely drunk, suffering withdrawal from his encounter with Mom's Mule. Then, as his fever rose and he began to have chills and headache and moments of delirium, Dr. Peter realized his patient had typhoid fever. Andrew Jackson Potter's skin became hot to the touch and his eyes seemed to shine with an inner light, as if a fire inside was consuming flesh.

Georgia watched from the doorway as her husband sponged Andrew Jackson Potter's body and applied cold packs. For some reason she could never explain, she became fascinated with the stranger's struggle against death. Once she was drawn to the bedside and she placed her hand on Andrew Jackson Potter's forehead, and then pulled her hand away as if she had touched a candle flame.

"The word typhoid comes from the mythical Greek monster Typhon," Dr. Peter explained. "He had one hundred heads that belched fire and smoke, and he made war on Heaven to avenge the death of his brother giants." Georgia remembered the heat she had felt radiating from Andrew Jackson Potter's forehead. She understood why people might have thought fire-breathing dragons were to blame.

In the third week, the fever began to decline, yet his pulse began to weaken. "It's the natural course," Dr. Peter said. "If he survives this week, he'll recover."

As the third week passed, Georgia spent more and more time in the sickroom. She took over the task of sponging the patient with cool water, a task she had performed many times before for her husband's patients. She fed him the thick, hot broth Dr. Peter said he must have to fight the monster in his blood. During the hours she watched Andrew Jackson Potter fade in and out of consciousness, she wondered about her war against Heaven to avenge the death of her child. Once when she was sponging the patient's chest, Martha Benny caught her eye. Georgia was surprised at the obvious disapproval. It was as if she had been caught in an indiscretion, caught swimming nude in the Colorado, and in spite of herself she blushed and pulled her hand away.

As the days passed, Georgia would play a game in which she compared her husband and this stranger who had come to their door. Both were good-looking men. Dr. Peter was slender and graceful, and had about him the presence of command. Andrew Jackson Potter, even though he was so terribly ill, presented an aspect of leashed power, his compact body a tightly wound spring of steel and hardwood. Her husband was the picture of propriety and honor, a stable force in the community. Andrew Jackson Potter was a drunk, a wastrel, and a womanizer. He was a man without honor, a force bounding totally out of control. Yet he possessed a certain innocence in repose, as if here were a child dreaming of unpunished mischief. She began to believe there was something in this man worth saving. If he lived she would restore his soul to the flock and to the shepherd. She was not quite certain of her motives, but she became more and more excited about the prospect. Perhaps bringing Andrew Jackson Potter into the company of angels would be revenge enough against Heaven.

With all the passion and energy that Georgia always invested in her projects, she hurled herself into the formidable task of saving Andrew Jackson Potter's soul. Now that he was recovering, she would do for his soul what Dr. Peter had done for his body. Little by little, as she battered away at the bulwarks of his disbelief, her own faith returned. Once again, she found she was able to pray. "Dear Lord," she began. "Thank you for life and for Texas and for tomorrow. And help breathe the Holy Spirit into this poor sinner in our house." Her color returned, as did the bounce in her step, and she began to take a renewed interest in clearing more land for a spring planting.

As soon as Andrew Jackson Potter's symptoms began to fade and he was able to sit up in bed, Georgia began to read to him from the Bible. She began with passages on self-denial and the subduing of lusts of the flesh. "Dearly beloved," she read from the First Epistle of Peter, "I beseech you as strangers and pilgrims, abstain from fleshly lusts, which war against the soul." She continued with admonitions against lasciviousness, excess of wine, revelings, banquetings, and abominable idolatries. The more she reminded him of these lusts of the flesh, the more he began to miss them. By the time she got into the Second Epistle of Peter with God's promises of a new Heaven and a new Earth, Andrew Jackson Potter had fallen hopelessly in love. For the rest of his life, even after he married, his thoughts and his dreams never strayed far from this beautiful, strange woman who seemed to belong so completely to both Earth and Heaven.

"What are you trying to do to me, Georgia?" he asked.

"Lead you to Salvation," she replied matter-of-factly, as if his place in Heaven had already been reserved.

"Don't think that's possible. You'll just be wastin' your valuable time."

"I believe in the perfectibility of the human heart," she said. "I believe it absolutely. And I bet your sinful heart is just as perfectible as the next man's."

"Bet?" he asked. "What do you bet?" Now Andrew Jackson Potter, never able to resist a wager, was keenly interested. He had bet on hundreds of horses but never on a soul before. It was an intriguing notion.

"Gambling is a sin," she said. "But it's not a very big sin. So I'll bet you a horse. If the devil wins, you can have your pick of the best horses we have."

"And if you win?"

"If you win, I'll give you a horse; if I win, I'll give you Paradise," she said. She blushed crimson when his face revealed he had misunderstood, and she realized that this was the reaction she had intended. She said a prayer, asking forgiveness for luring a soul with innuendo and false promises.

That night Georgia stood for a long while by the bed as Dr. Peter was sleeping. Outside, in the night, she could hear an orchestra of sound. A soft wind breathed through the window and she could smell the sweat of the earth. All her senses seemed finely tuned and she could feel herself coming alive again. It was as if she were changing, breaking free of a chrysalis, like a butterfly. It was a feeling both sensual and spiritual. She was aroused, and from that arousal came both guilt and exhilaration. She knelt at the foot of the bed and thanked God for the day. Then she stood and let her last garment fall and she lay down close to Peter and kissed his lips for the first time in a very long time.

In the mid-1850s, the Woods plantation between the Blanco and San Marcos Rivers thrived. Each spring the cotton seemed to explode from the rich soil and hoe gangs would scatter in the fields to chop until the flowers withered and the bolls began to form and the crop was "laid by" until the cotton matured and picking began. Georgia knew just when the cotton would bloom. She would move out into the fields to celebrate each blossom and thank God for the flower's brief, fragile life. How strange, she thought, that God would create a thing so lovely yet cause it to begin withering in a single day. When she told Martha Benny about this observation, Martha Benny reminded her that all living things begin to die the moment they appear upon the earth. Georgia scolded Martha for her "gloomy" disposition caused, no doubt, by her impiety and indifference to the Word.

In 1852, Georgia gave birth to Peter Junior, a baby as beautiful and as healthy as the Hill Country itself. For a few weeks, it seemed work on the plantation ceased in celebration of the new life. The cradle Josiah had made for Georgia so long ago was once again pressed into service. Mahalia embraced her renewed responsibilities on the "mother committee." The dubious privilege of watching over Lovie, Sweet, Cherokee, Pinckney, and Jim had fallen to Martha Benny. In truth, they were hardly in evidence long enough to watch over. Lovie was a young woman now, spending much of her time with friends in town. Cherokee, Sweet, Pinckney, and Jim were running free as the mustangs of the Wild Horse Desert to the south. For a while after little Peter's birth, Jim lingered around the house watching Mahalia care for the baby, asking what he could do to help. He was so persistent that Mahalia assigned him to guard Peter while he slept and to keep him safe from goblins. And Jim was always there at nap time, standing guard. When the child would fret or cry, Jim had a magic ability to make him stop with his repertoire of funny faces and dance steps.

The year after Georgia moved to San Marcos, there had been a drought. For weeks the Texas sky had been empty as a white plate. Farmers in the area began to despair. Although the Hill Country springs kept the rivers full and flowing freely, the fields began to dry, and dust devils rose like lazy dervishes in the summer air. Georgia remembered how her grandfather Benjamin Hawkins had taught the Indians to irrigate their land, and she instructed Ed Tom to lead crews into the bottoms to dig canals from the Blanco River into the fields. For a while, the Woods plantation was occasionally ridiculed. The place was called the "Venice of Texas" and the irrigation ditches were not infrequently referred to as "Miz Georgia's water moccasin farm." Yet, the Woods land produced yields far more abundant than the land of the other farmers. Georgia had marveled at the abundant crops and also at the notion of human continuity. How wonderful it was that an idea of her grandfather's would be creating prosperity not only for this generation but for the grandchildren of little Peter.

As the years went by, Georgia and Peter bought more and more land. Soon five thousand acres were under cultivation, and their plantation was one of the most prosperous in the area. In addition to cotton, they planted wheat, barley, rye, and corn, even raised a few cattle which Sam Ealy Johnson drove north on one of the first great Texas cattle drives. Although Georgia still worked in the home and in the fields from dawn 'til dusk, she still found time to work with the women of the church and to form fast friendships with her neighbors. Among these neighbors was Sarah Burleson, the gracious widow of old General Burleson, former vice president of the Republic of Texas; the Malone, Dixon, Caperton, and House families; and also the McKies and the Coxes who had come with the Woodses in the original wagon train from Mississippi.

As Georgia put ever more land in cotton, the work of planting, chopping, and harvesting began to be more than their thirty
slaves could handle. Soon it became apparent more slaves would
have to be acquired if the plantation was to grow. Then one
morning, as if in answer to a prayer, a strange procession appeared along the road from town.

Over the horizon came a company of Negroes led by old
Captain Lawshe, his white beard flowing in the wind like that of
some Biblical patriarch leading his people to the Promised Land.
He had not written he was coming, he simply showed up that
spring morning of 1858 in company with nearly two score
souls—men, women, and children, walking, riding in ox carts,
children dancing through wildflowers rich and thick as an Oriental carpet.

As the travelers came closer and individual features became
recognizable, Georgia perceived a strange hush. Then she noticed
her people, her slaves, her friends, pause in their labors. Here an
old man leaned upon his hoe, a woman dropped the tin pitcher
she was carrying to the spring house, a blacksmith laid his hammer down in the red coals of his forge. The two groups, the Texas
slaves and those arriving from Mississippi, were being slowly
drawn together by invisible cords. It was like an ancient ritual
dance choreographed to symphonies of silence. Then she remembered these people were families: fathers and mothers, children
and uncles and lovers who had long been separated. When Georgia and Dr. Peter and the others had left Mississippi, the slaves
Captain Lawshe had given Georgia had been taken from the community with little thought to the ties that had bound them together for generations. Now, they were coming together again,
old bonds renewed.

By the spring house, Georgia saw the young woman named
Liza embracing one of the new arrivals. The man bent to speak to
a child at the woman's skirts. The child backed away, afraid of the
stranger. Were these his children? Had Liza and her man been
separated when Captain Lawshe presented Georgia her human
dowry? An old woman whose name Georgia could not remember
approached Old Mose and they walked away together toward the

slave quarters at the edge of the fields. What was that woman to Mose? Were they lovers when they were young? Was she his sister? Georgia felt a hot bite of shame as she comprehended how little she knew of these people who had been a part of her life for so many years. Then she was in her father's arms.

"There's going to be a fight," the old captain said. "Up north the Abolitionists are in a stew, just itchin' for a war. They're aiming to set the slaves free. So I thought our people would be safer here in Texas."

When Captain Lawshe had returned to Mississippi, Georgia once again began to enlarge the plantation. With the help of Martha Benny, Ed Tom, and the blacksmith Ulysses Cephas, Georgia set about creating a village for her growing population of slaves. Andrew Jackson Potter hauled in pine from Bastrop, and with additional lumber from the Burleson mill, they built rows of shanties behind the house and along the fields. Often Georgia would join in the work, helping to make the cabins comfortable, stirring large pots of water and dirt into mud for chinking the spaces between the logs.

Georgia and all the women she knew were caught up in the political controversies rising out of the issue of slavery. The newspapers were filled with editorials praising or condemning the latest speeches of Sam Houston or Stephen Douglas. But rarely did the Texas papers characterize slavery as a moral issue. Georgia had always viewed slavery simply as the way things had always been. There had always been a class of people who by virtue of intelligence and wealth and strength of character had been chosen to lead the progress of civilization. By the grace of God, she had been born into this class. She had not brought the Africans to these shores; however, she accepted the responsibility, the duty, to care for those who lacked the ability to care for themselves. Negroes were like children, she believed, needing guidance and protection and healing when they were sick and comfort when they were afraid. But there were times, when she looked into Martha Benny's eyes or when she witnessed the great joy of the families and lovers reunited when Captain Lawshe's slaves came to Texas and regretted that their grief in parting had gone unnoticed, that she had faint, vague tugs of conscience and a deep sense of foreboding. In those times she would pray: "Dear Lord, help me to care for these people and keep them safe and happy and devoted to the land and to your Name."

One evening when the McKies and the Houses and Sarah Burleson joined the Woodses for dinner, the conversation turned to the prospects of war. "I simply don't have time for war," Georgia said. "Besides, war is just something men do to escape the problems of peace, the greatest of which is boredom. There's certainly nothing boring about Texas so I doubt there's a need for war around here."

"What about the moral issue?" Andrew Jackson Potter said. "Have you heard about that new book by the Stowe woman? *Uncle Tom's Cabin?*"

You're a fine one to talk about moral issues, Georgia almost said, but caught herself in time. "Slavery is an economic issue," is what she did say. "And is war any more moral than slavery? I don't see any particular virtue in killing your fellow man." Georgia hated these conversations and how they made her say things to cover how she really felt. The problem was, she did not know how she really felt. She knew she was responsible for the lives of nearly one hundred children, five of whom were white and spoiled rotten. She had a plantation to care for with nearly one hundred horses—and a good man to love and another to save. How dare these Yankee strangers complicate her life?

Georgia had no real image of the North in her mind. The North was an abstraction, a place where Thoreau and Emerson wrote about covered bridges and conscience, and where the family's great good friend Mittie Bulloch Roosevelt lived. She thought of Mittie's last letter. The return address on the envelope was like a message from the enemy camp. "Number 28 East 20th Street, New York City." How could the fates place a girl from Georgia in such a horrible, alien place? In the letter Mittie told of her newborn son, Theodore. *Poor little chap has no chance in life at all,* Georgia thought. *Born a Yankee in the Sodom and Gomorrah of the New World.*

The year little Theodore Roosevelt was born was the year Senator Sam Houston campaigned throughout Texas as a candidate for governor. As a Jacksonian Democrat, he was running against Hardin R. Runnels, a Calhoun Democrat who played heavily on Houston's antisecessionist stand. Neither Georgia nor Dr. Peter could imagine how Houston could possibly win. Nearly all the newspapers were against him. Even the Democratic Central Executive Committee had denounced him as a "traitor-knave."

One day in July, the Woods family made a pilgrimage to Lockhart, where Sam Houston was to speak in a grove near Story Spring. The day was a furnace, as fiercely hot as only a Texas July afternoon can be, yet Houston was dressed in a long duster. His shoes were unlaced and his shirt open. He looked to Georgia as if he had slept in his clothes all summer. She was amazed that her father's old friend, a Texas hero, would appear so disheveled. However, when he spoke, when he answered the charges of "traitor-knave," he seemed to fill the whole outdoors with his voice and his presence. "Sam Houston a traitor to Texas?" he thundered. "I, who in defense of her soil, moistened it with my blood! Was it for that I bared my bosom to the hail of bullets at the Horseshoe and rode into a bullet at San Jacinto—to be branded in my old age as a traitor?"

Georgia felt a mood of sympathy flow through the audience and she, too, was touched by the passion and the indignation, and what she felt was a deep sadness about the old man. But she also knew these were new times, with new dangers, and maybe Houston's time had passed. If Houston was for preserving the Union, he was undermining the world she had struggled to build with her bare hands and the sweat of her dreams. "I will not have that world trampled by strangers or by an old man who still hears the cannons of San Jacinto," Georgia said one day to Sarah Burleson. It had been widely reported that Houston was opposed to slavery, not so much on moral grounds but because it threatened to erode the potential of the American Republic.

"For a man against slavery," Georgia heard Martha Benny say to Ed Tom, "Mr. Sam sure does have his share. I was listening to his speech with Miss Georgia. He talked against the slavers while his own slaves waited for him by his buggy. He fights the slavers and then has about fifteen slaves himself. I sure don't believe I'll ever understand white folks' politics."

One afternoon, at another political rally, Sam Houston caught Georgia's eye and they visited awhile. He asked about her father's health and when Captain Lawshe might give up his life in Mississippi and become a Texan. Sam Houston took her arm and they strolled to a group of women Georgia had noticed at other rallies. Houston introduced her to a small, intense woman with the remarkable name of Euphemia Texas Ashby King. Houston said she raised some of the finest horses in Texas.

Sam Houston gathered the two women, one on each arm. "You are my two favorite ladies," he said. "I've known each of you since you were in the cradle." Georgia wondered what the relationship was between the dark, pretty, quiet woman and the old general, but Houston was in a loquacious mood and she never had a chance to ask.

In 1859, the year John Brown raided Harpers Ferry, an act that hurled the North and South inevitably toward war—an action Horace Greeley called "the work of a madman" and Ralph Waldo Emerson called the act of a "saint"—Georgia made a final frontal attack on the arsenal of Andrew Jackson Potter's disbelief.

During the years since Andy Potter had entered the Woods family's life, he had continued to live "in the path of great wickedness." Later he would write that he had been "a moral wreck, a ringleader in sin." On the Sabbath he was often seen among crowds of revelers, drinking and blaspheming, fighting and gambling. Yet on those Sunday afternoons, when the good people of the county would gather to race their thoroughbreds, it was to Andrew Jackson Potter they turned when they were desperate to prove their horse faster than the entries of their neighbors. Drunk or sober, light-headed or heavy with wearisome burdens of guilt and ungodly passions, Andrew Jackson Potter was a horse racer of extraordinary skills.

The Woods family had become influential and respected in San Marcos, Georgia and Peter the center of a social world deeply rooted in traditional values. Consequently, there were two aspects of their lives that drew whispered speculation from the curious. The first mystery was the matter of Pinckney, Sweet, and Cherokee. They were all handsome children, Cherokee and Sweet promising to be as beautiful as their mother, but both were wild as weeds. How, wondered the good people of San Marcos, could two such stable and gracious souls parent such reckless prodigals?

The second mystery had to do with Andrew Jackson Potter. Why had Georgia and Dr. Peter befriended such an abysmal wreck of a citizen? And why did Georgia have this apparent need to reform him and not have the same need to reform her own children? Andy Potter was a constant guest, a frequent dinner companion. Often he just dropped by to hear Georgia read from the Bible. Both Dr. Peter and Georgia enjoyed his company, his wild tales, his quick intelligence, his unpredictable turns of phrase. Georgia marveled at his use of language. She said if he could write as well as he could talk he would rise to be another Longfellow.

Martha Benny viewed the friendship between Georgia and Andrew Jackson Potter as something perilous. She did not trust him and she often scolded Georgia for what she called "temptatious" behavior. "Don't you see what you're doing to that poor man?"

"I'm just trying to make him a better person," Georgia said. "Besides, what I do is none of your business."

"Just watch out you don't lose your good name before you save his soul. It's not the Spirit of the Lord keeps that poor man agitated."

"Martha Benny!" Georgia was truly angry. "What you need is a little Christian charity. I'm making progress. I know he's changing."

Martha Benny shook her head. "He'll change all right. Probably be baptized down in the river. He'd also jump off the edge of the world if you asked him to. It's not Salvation he wants. What he wants is old Captain Lawshe's little girl."

Later, when she had calmed down and examined her feelings rationally, Georgia realized there just might be some truth in Martha Benny's warning. There was a bright sharp edge of danger to her friendship and it made her feel attractive and alive. She was deeply in love with her husband and it was absolutely unthinkable that she could be unfaithful to him. But, still, when you had been the prettiest girl in Water Valley, it was good to feel the touch of eyes and to know you could alter the pace of another's

heartbeat or breathing with a gesture or a smile. Georgia was fascinated to hear Potter talk about his strange, passionate, dangerous world. She lived that passion and danger vicariously. She was
swept from her staid, safe, and proper life into a life of fast
horses, and of gamblers and harlots and sensual intrigues, and was
able to return with her virtue intact. Perhaps Martha Benny was
right. It was a perilous game she played. And it was for this reason that one spring morning just a few months after John Brown
was hanged in Virginia, she gathered her family and her slaves and
that ringleader of sin Andrew Jackson Potter, and she descended
upon the great revival down on the San Marcos River with demands of Salvation for the entire party.

It was a sunlit day and a place of extraordinary beauty, what
must have been God's original idea for the way the world should
be. The river was still as a silver mirror. Towering oaks shaded the
gathering and from the largest trees Spanish moss flowed like the
beards of patriarchs. Grapevines hanging from the highest
branches held children swinging in lazy arcs before falling, twisting into the river. Beyond the grove, a quilt of blue-eyed grass
and wine-cups and starphlox and wild petunias lay beneath the
hacks and surreys and wagons and tents of people who had come
from miles around to hear the preaching and the music. Here and
there people shared food around campfires. Others were preparing a brush arbor, and Georgia instructed Ed Tom and Ulysses
Cephas to help the preacher carry the church's pump organ down
to the river. Soon the air was filled with the old beloved melodies
and singular cadence of the well-preached Word.

When night came, the preaching continued. The campfires
glowed like the eyes of cats in the shadows, light diminishing
darkness, and Georgia could feel the saints walking by and she
knew the Spirit of the Lord was moving on the river. Georgia was
drawn to an enormous fire off where the wild plums and persim-
mons grew, and she could see the silhouettes of the Negroes as
they danced and shouted and sang to fiddle and banjo. They were
having what Martha Benny called a jig contest, the contestants
with glasses of water on their heads, each dancing as wildly as
possible, the winners the ones spilling the least water from their
glasses. Then they gathered around the black preacher to sing the

old songs. "In the new Jerusalem," they sang, "in the year of Jubilee." Georgia could see Martha Benny singing by the fire, her body constantly in motion.

Later, Martha Benny would describe what happened that night when the preacher was preaching the Gospel. "It was the most unbelievable thing that ever happened to me," she said, her blue eyes shining with grace and abandon. "I felt kind of dizzy and I lay down, and while I was laying there sin formed a heavy white veil just like a blanket over me and it just eased down on me 'til it was mashing the breath out of me. I cried out to the Lord to save me and He must have heard this miserable sinner, because in a jiffy I started shouting and shaking and I saw a white light and I could hear hundreds of bells ringing in the air." Then she placed something heavy in Georgia's hand. "It felt so good to be free of the Devil," she said. "I made this lodestone charm to keep his evil power away."

The revival lasted a week. All the great preachers of the area were there taking part in a constant and continuing round of singing and supper and preaching of the Gospel. No one left the meeting, except to feed the animals or tend those too sick to be carried in their beds down by the river under the great oaks. On the last day, the San Marcos River was filled with candidates for baptism, their garments afloat in water so clear Georgia thought for a moment she could actually see their sins washing away, floating downstream like blood from a wound. It was on the final day that Andrew Jackson Potter—imbiber, blasphemer, gambler, womanizer, self-professed ringleader of sin—was at last washed in the Blood of the Lamb.

Later that night, as Old Mose harnessed the horses for the trip home, the passionate new convert told Georgia what had happened. "I had actually gone to the revival for the worst possible reason," he said. "Some of my old comrades in vice had said they'd been converted. So I thought I'd go and see if I couldn't de-convert them with the promise of a little whiskey or a game of chance. But I started to listen to the preacher and I walked over to the arbor and he seemed to fix his keen, black penetrating eyes on me alone. And his shrill voice fell like thunder peals of warning in my ears. Peal after peal of the rolling surf telling of distant storms, startled my guilty soul."

As Potter told of his conversion, he became more and more animated and his language became increasingly florid. Georgia realized she was listening to the Reverend Andrew Jackson Potter's first sermon. Martha Benny stood apart, listening and watching the former sinner with obvious skepticism. Georgia decided she would admonish Martha Benny later for doubting Andrew Jackson Potter's conversion.

"My heart was pierced by the cold iron of sacred truth," he continued. "About me all of Israel's valiant hosts, all clad in the panoply of Heaven, stood in bright array. The guilt of a miserable life lay all its ponderous weight upon my writhing conscience. I stood there, a weeping prisoner of a thousand tears. I went forward and gave the preacher my trembling hand and just then Heaven seemed to open and pour its treasures of bliss into my willing heart. My whole being was pervaded by Heavenly power."

Suddenly, Andrew Jackson Potter swept Georgia into his arms. His lips brushed her cheek. "I feel my whole body filled with the love of Jesus," he said, as she struggled to break free of his grasp. "I've never felt such love," he continued, his voice breaking with emotion. Martha Benny rolled her blue Hawkins eyes heavenward as Georgia broke free of the former sinner's embrace.

Much later, Martha Benny confided to Georgia that some men have to be baptized two or three times before it takes. "Men have all kinds of passions and sometimes they can't tell the ones of the spirit from the ones of the flesh."

"Amen," Georgia said, thankful she had lost neither her virtue nor her horse.

One night in the late summer of 1861, when the Great Northern stage brought news to San Marcos of the Confederate triumph at Bull Run, people began to gather at the newly enlarged Moon Hotel for a jubilant celebration that would last long into the night. As Georgia watched the young people dancing by torchlight, out beneath a grove of oak, she remembered when Sam Houston had made his speech beneath those same trees. It had been in 1858 when he had been campaigning for governor against Hardin Runnels. The speech had lasted nearly four hours and that, someone suggested, was probably why Houston had lost the election.

The reason that the North had lost the battle at Bull Run was something about which Georgia was absolutely certain. It was not due to the courage of Stonewall Jackson, who received two wounds and his nickname that day, nor the heroics of Beauregard or Jeb Stuart, as the newspapers reported. Rather, she was sure that the Federals had lost at Bull Run because of the wrath of Captain Lewis Lawshe. The Great Northern stage had also brought news that a Federal raiding party had burned the Lawshe plantation in northern Mississippi to the ground. Captain Lawshe wrote: "I went to bed one night and I was worth a quarter of a million dollars. Then I woke up in the morning and I wasn't worth twenty-five cents." He had been so angry he had joined the Confederate Army. At the age of seventy-one, he fought so fiercely against Sherman and McDowell, driving their broken army all the way back to Washington, that he became a legend.

Pinckney, Jim, their friend George McGehee, and all the other young men were eager to join the fight. The South's triumph at Bull Run was so swift and complete that the young men expressed fear the war would be over before they would have a chance to take part. Pinckney had heard Stonewall Jackson's request of Jefferson Davis. "Give me five thousand fresh men and I will be in Washington City by tomorrow morning." Every young man at the Moon Hotel that night wanted to be numbered among Stonewall's five thousand. Colonel Earl Van Dorn had been named Confederate commander in Texas and the regiments of McCulloch, Rip Ford, and John Baylor were moving against Yankees in the west. Other regiments were moving south to defend Texas ports from a possible invasion from the Gulf. If a young man could not join up with Stonewall Jackson, it seemed certain there would be plenty of action in Texas.

As Georgia listened to the talk of war, she began to see her children revealed in a light she had not seen before. How was it possible little Pinckney could be old enough to go to war? But here he was, nearly as tall as his father, holding a girl in his arms, whirling through the torchlight, and Georgia could tell by the eyes of the girl that her son was now a man. And there was vivacious Cherokee, surrounded by the would-be warriors, bringing back memories of Water Valley when Georgia had been the most beautiful girl at the ball. Young George McGehee handed Cherokee a small bottle, which she raised to her lips, certainly the mustang wine Martha Benny had warned her the children consumed with secret frequency. Suddenly Georgia realized the children were children no more. But she wasn't particularly sad. In fact, she felt a sense of release. Cherokee and George McGehee slipped into the shadows. Georgia caught Martha Benny's eye and Martha Benny rolled her eyes heavenward as if to say: "I told you you should have switched those children." Georgia was tempted to stick her tongue out at her old friend, but decided a woman old enough to be the mother of Pinckney, Cherokee, and Sweet was too old for such childish gestures.

The following spring, the 32nd Texas Regiment was formed and Peter Cavanaugh Woods, physician and planter, would ever after be called the Colonel-Doctor. When the captains of the ten companies of volunteers gathered, their first order of business was to elect a leader from among them. Among the captains were veterans of the Mexican Wars and Indian Wars, but afterward, when the ballots were counted, they had elected the Colonel-Doctor their regiment commander.

Since the regiment trained at Camp Clark, a few miles outside of San Marcos, Georgia was often able to visit her husband, taking him butter and coffee and news of home. One day she came with her most prized possession, the great stallion Isaiah. "You'll be a brigadier general soon," she said, "and a general needs a fine horse. General Sam Houston had Saracen. Now General Woods will ride Isaiah." Dr. Peter thought it strange a horse named Isaiah would go to war. He said he could not possibly think of a more peaceful name.

That night, as they lay together in his tent and Georgia placed the healing hands she loved so much upon her breasts, Dr. Peter told Georgia they should not make love. "I think this war will be very long," he said. "I don't want to leave you with a child to raise alone."

"Pinckney says the war will be over within months. You'll be back in time to deliver the baby."

"I don't want you to go through another birth. It's too hard, too dangerous."

Georgia moved against him. "I'd rather love you and die than live without you holding me and touching me like this." They made love then, in a canvas tent, among horsemen who would soon ride off to a war that would seem to last forever.

They talked that night till dawn. Georgia felt his mood change as the night progressed. It was as if he had changed from lover to child. She had never seen him so troubled and uncertain. Then he talked about the terrible battle inside him between the physician and the soldier. "I made a vow to revere life and prolong it when I can," he said. "Now I've taken another vow to lead men in the taking of life. How can I be two people at the same time? Part of me wars with the other." It was a moral dilemma that would plague him through all the days and nights of the war.

As the volunteers gathered, they were required to furnish their own horses, weapons, and equipment. Most were well mounted and equipped with tents, blankets, cooking utensils, whiskey, and playing cards. Some, who had little, brought only their lives to the Confederacy. Even so, the Confederate Army, one of the greatest fighting forces of all time, required that a man pay for the privilege of dying. If a recruit had nothing, he was required to raise the money for equipment after he was mustered in.

One Sunday morning, when Georgia was visiting the Colonel-Doctor, a strange apparition swept toward the tent where the soldiers had gathered for worship. With a kind of comic grace, a huge gaunt animal with an evil countenance and legs like willow trees came gamboling out of the underbrush. It appeared to Georgia not unlike one of the more awful beasts of Revelations, something St. John dreamed on the Isle of Patmos. Atop the ugly beast was a comely young woman clutching a hymnbook and by her side, on a mule, rode Andrew Jackson Potter carrying a well-thumbed Bible and a copy of John Wesley's *Discipline*. In his belt was a six-shooter the size of the cannon of San Jacinto. Georgia learned the elegant lady was from Seguin, a young woman of dubious reputation named Pink Rosebud, whose soul Andrew Jackson Potter was intent on saving. He had brought her to attend Sunday services on one of the camels introduced and then abandoned in Texas by the Union Army a few years earlier. Georgia also learned that Reverend Potter, former gambler, womanizer, and "ringleader of sin," had been called to the ministry and had been preaching at back-country revivals for several months. Now he had joined the Confederate Army.

The Colonel-Doctor had gained a regimental chaplain and his men feared the loss of their cards and whiskey. However, Captain-Reverend Potter, perhaps recalling the joy of such pastimes, allowed the games to continue, as long as they didn't interfere with prayer meeting. Georgia noticed the chaplain approach a group of men playing cards around a fire. Rather than close down the game, he asked them "to let the Lord sit down in the Devil's place" and soon the soldiers were singing hymns of praise.

On March 26, 1862, the regiment received orders to move south to a camp on the Salado River near San Antonio. Their mission was to guard Yankee prisoners taken when the Union garrison in San Antonio had fallen to Ben McCulloch and the Rowdy King Boys of Seguin. As the troops prepared to ride,

Pinckney pleaded with Georgia to let him join the army and go with his father to war. For days he had been practicing with the old pistol Captain Lawshe had given him. He felt it was just a matter of time before his mother would give in to his arguments, so he packed, and selected a horse for the march. Much to Martha Benny's surprise, Georgia stood firm. "Pinckney Woods, don't you take one step!" There was iron in the words. "Two men from this family is enough for the Confederacy. I need you at home."

One beautiful spring morning, when the wild plums were blossoming, a great procession moved along a section of the old Camino Real toward San Antonio. The officers and men of the Woods 32nd Texas Cavalry rode from their training encampment toward the home of James T. Malone, in Stringtown, where their march to war would begin. At the head of the column of soldiers rode Colonel-Doctor Peter Woods. Beside him rode Nat Benton, of Seguin. On the other side rode Captain-Reverend Andrew Jackson Potter, his giant revolver by his left hand, his Good Book by his right. Also ahead of the column rode Sallie McGehee and the Ogletree twins, Emma and Ella. The three ladies, also in uniform, were sponsors of a farewell dinner to be held beneath the elms at the Malone home. The Confederate flag that flew at the head of the Woods 32nd had been made by the ladies of Hays County and had been presented to the Colonel-Doctor by Miss McGehee. The men were uniformly dressed in homespun clothes, cowhide boots, and tall black felt hats emblazoned with the "Lone Star" of Texas. They wore huge spurs and rode Mexican saddles with stirrups adjusted so short it seemed they rode standing up on their horses.

At first, the day of the regiment's departure was uncommonly festive. Georgia had never seen so many people gathered in one place. In the shade of the Malones' elms, long tables had been laden with food. From the trees Confederate flags and patriotic banners blossomed even more colorfully than the wild plum along the Camino Real. It seemed everyone in Hayes and Guadalupe County had come to Stringtown to pay their respects to the regiment.

Georgia felt a great wellspring of pride in her husband the Colonel-Doctor, as he rode ahead of the regiment. The beautiful

Ella Dupree Rives Ogletree had maneuvered her horse to his side and Georgia was amused to see she was wearing a feminine version of the Colonel-Doctor's uniform. "I think she's disgusting," Cherokee said. "Look how that silly girl's making eyes at Papa. Imagine a young girl throwing herself at an old man like that."

"Your papa is not old!" Georgia exclaimed with some passion. "And so what if Miss Ella can't take her eyes off him."

As the afternoon progressed, others in the crowd must have begun to harbor darker thoughts of what war and absence might mean, for a kind of quiet began to fall over the gathering. Only occasionally did the sound of laughter rise. It seemed to Georgia people were subdued, almost whispering, as they moved among the tables where the food remained, largely untouched. Georgia suddenly was very conscious of her own family. She wanted them around her and she wondered when they would be together again. There was Cherokee kissing George McGehee goodbye. Then she saw Lovie and young D. P. Hopkins were holding hands and looking into each other's eyes. Little Sweet was clinging to her father, as if she could physically stall his departure. Georgia wanted a moment alone with Peter, but she could not bring herself to send Little Sweet away.

"Hurry home to us," she whispered in his ear. "Be safe, my darling." Then the regiment formed ranks and moved out. Dr. Peter was gone. Georgia's heart nearly broke as she saw Jim mount his horse and fall in beside the Colonel-Doctor. She remembered the smooth river stones he had brought her as a child. Jim caught her eye, smiled, and waved his hat. Georgia waved and turned away, and there was Pinckney, his saddlebags packed, walking his horse toward where she stood. His eyes were filled with pleading.

"Please, Mother," he said. "If Jim can go, why can't I?"

"Because I don't want you to die!"

"And I don't suppose you care if Jim does?" Georgia almost struck her son for the second time in his life, but she was too sad to muster the effort. "Get on home, son," she said, with as much force as she could rally. And, perhaps because he was ashamed of what he had said about Jim, the closest friend he had in the world, Pinckney mounted, turned, and rode toward home. He did not hear the soldiers singing "Dixie" as the regiment marched out through sorrowful crowds of admiring women, through clouds of flags and ribbons with the band playing and tearful girls throwing kisses. He didn't see Jim riding at the Colonel-Doctor's side, on his way to war and glory while he stayed home to help his mother worm horses.

When the bluebonnets began to fade and the fine young green of the cotton crop began to emerge from the earth and the spring rains promised twenty bushels of wheat to the acre, the men had gone and Georgia did not at first feel the loss. She was immediately immersed in the work of supervising the household, managing the plantation, caring for and feeding her village, including another thirty slaves sent west by Captain Lawshe after his plantation was destroyed. In the evening, when the work was done, Georgia and Martha Benny held meditations for both children and adults and Bible lessons for her own children and the children of the Negroes. Some learned to memorize and recite verses of poetry. Ed Tom held the children spellbound with his readings from the Scriptures.

The days became a never-ending battle against the diseases that struck down both men and horse with awful regularity. Sometimes it seemed to Georgia that half the Negroes had measles. She was constantly tending to the sick. With her husband gone, the slaves looked to Georgia to heal them. After all, she was married to a doctor, so he must have shared his secret knowledge of the healing arts. She did what she could and felt terribly guilty when it was not enough. She would stay with a sick child for hours, trying to sponge away the fever. Then when a child died, and it was not a rare occurrence, she saw the overwhelming disbelief in the parents' eyes. Their mistress, this small woman who ruled their lives and was the center of their universe and in whom they had placed such infinite confidence, was suddenly revealed to be as fallible and as powerless as they. Georgia would mourn each child as if it were her own, say prayers for the parents and for strength. "I must trust to the good Lord who doeth all things for the best," she wrote to the Colonel-Doctor. And in the late night, in her empty bed, she would miss him profoundly.

If she was not tending sick people, she was often out in the pasture with Ed Tom helping care for the horses. There was constant trouble with ticks and worms in the colts. Ed Tom used calomel on the ticks and tobacco and whiskey on the worms. "If you get those worms drunk," he said, "they'll come out to repent."

Often Georgia and Martha Benny would join the women of Stringtown in the manufacture of bullets for the regiment. They would heat lead over a fire until it was molten, then pour the silver liquid into red-hot, long-handled molds. When the lead cooled, the women would shake the molds and out would roll smooth, round bullets. It was exhausting work, but it made Georgia feel closer to the war and to Dr. Peter. At the end of each day, Georgia felt as if she were carrying the weight of the entire Confederacy on her shoulders. Then, in the deep night, she would lift her pen and write: "My dearest husband. I shall never get used to you being away from home. You are missed so much. It is a serious thing to be separated from those we love dearest on earth."

In the early months of the war, when Captain Lawshe learned the Colonel-Doctor would be away for extended periods, he insisted over Georgia's objections that an overseer be engaged at the Woods plantation. When the planters went to war, many plantations with large numbers of slaves were left in the hands of the lone white mistress. The men feared that the slaves would get out of hand and a woman would not be strong enough to keep discipline and control. Although Georgia was angered and humiliated by her father's intervention, she acquiesced as a good daughter should, and the abominable Emanuel Hawker was dispatched to San Marcos.

There was trouble right from the beginning. Emanuel Hawker was a large, beefy, red-faced man with a rough manner and an inalterable regard for what he called his "responsibility." He made it quite clear that Captain Lawshe had insisted Georgia had charge of the household and Hawker would be responsible for everything else. He was pompous and almost comic in his postures of superiority, and Georgia would have been amused if she had not sensed a suggestion of cruelty in his unwavering obedience to the will of old Captain Lawshe.

Until Hawker's arrival, the management of the plantation had been shared by Georgia and Ed Tom. What was now a huge community was administered by Ed Tom. He assigned work, dealt with any problems or special needs among the slaves, attended to everything from discipline to organizing burials for the people in the quarters. He was highly respected, even loved, by his people. With Georgia's consent he even allowed certain slaves, like Old Mose, to work in town for wages.

When Hawker learned that Old Mose was earning money like a white man, he flew into a rage. He called Mose out. "If I ever hear you been off these fields, I'll whip your black skin red as an Indian!"

Old Mose complained to Ed Tom, who confronted Hawker. "But, sir, the Colonel-Doctor 'lowd some of us folks to work for wages. It's somethin' we always done."

"Boy, you see the Colonel-Doctor around here?

"No, sir."

"You see Emanuel Hawker?"

"Yes, sir."

"We do things my way now, nigger. And I'll sure as hell tell you this. If you put yourself in my way, there's gonna be one less fancy-ass nigger around here before you be seeing your fine Colonel-Doctor again."

Ed Tom decided not to tell her about the confrontation, but it got back to Georgia anyway.

"Hawker," she said, "if you so much as lay a hand on Ed Tom or anybody else on my land, I'll shoot you myself!"

Hawker was at first astonished, then he began to laugh. His laughter sounded like pigs squealing, and his face grew so red Georgia thought he was having a stroke and for a moment she actually wished he would fall dead at her feet. Yet, her anger was quickly cooled by her sense of impotence. Instead of putting Hawker in his place, she had just appeared foolish.

"Well, little lady," Hawker said, when he finally controlled his wheezing and squealing. "You surely are your papa's little girl." Wiping tears from his eyes, he turned and walked away. Georgia heard his laughter even after he had disappeared behind the horse barn.

In the fall of 1862, Georgia and Ed Tom left the plantation in Hawker's hands and made the long overland trip south to join the Colonel-Doctor below the Wild Horse Desert. The Woods Regiment had been sent to the wilderness country along the Rio Grande to guard the Mexican border. From there, the Colonel-Doctor had written Georgia a letter so loving and filled with such loneliness that she was packing the moment she looked up from his words. In the early part of the war, it was not unusual for officers' wives to visit their husbands in camp. She took Ed Tom on the journey, in part for security and in part because she didn't want to leave him alone with Emanuel Hawker. She was not sure, however, which of the men she was protecting from the other.

Now Georgia passed through the great King ranch and then on into a strange and perilous province of dunes and dry arroyos and pale colorless skies. Occasionally a wild hog would scurry from the brush or a rattlesnake from beneath the wheels, and at night when she lay in her bedroll she listened for the footfall of tarantulas. For days they would see no sign of human life except, perhaps, distant horsemen silhouetted on the blade of the horizon. Georgia would wonder who the lonely riders might be. It was said this country harbored thieves and killers and dangerous vagabonds of wide and deadly variety; renegade Comanches, wandering bandits, armed bands of Mexican revolutionaries, and assorted desperadoes from both sides of the border. As they moved into this troubled world, Georgia felt relatively safe because they traveled as a part of a great cotton caravan, a heavily guarded column of huge wagons filled with bales bound for the port of Bagdad, Mexico, near the mouth of the Rio Grande.

The Colonel-Doctor and Andrew Jackson Potter met them in the little river town of Bagdad. As she was squired around town on the arms of the regiment's commander and its formidable chaplain, Georgia was amazed at the forest of masts that rose from the brown tide of the Rio Grande. Hundreds of small, fast lighters were taking on cargoes of cotton for the ships waiting in the deep water beyond the mouth of the river. Once loaded, the ships would challenge the Yankee blockade that commanded the seas off Galveston, Sabine Pass, and Indianola. Walking the Bagdad waterfront was like taking a trip around the world and back.

Here were milling crowds of sailors and mercenaries from all nations, turbaned Arabs, Mississippi River gamblers, and ladies of
the evening, American Indians and French naval officers and
Mexican *vaqueros*. The air carried a sound like an orchestra tuning, shouts and calls and laughter in a dozen languages, the peal-
ing of bells, the rush of steam, the rattle of chains and slap of
halyards, booming barrels, bawling mules, and oxen.

"Back in the old days, towns like this were havens for pi-
rates," Potter said. "Except the ships were loaded with gold. Now
fortunes are won or lost on the cotton trade."

Andrew Jackson Potter's eyes glistened as he talked about the
gamble blockade runners took. "If I were not a man of God," he
said, "I'd make my fortune here."

"How would you do it?" Georgia asked.

"Running the blockade." Potter pointed toward the mouth of
the Rio Grande. "Out there, beyond the last dunes, the Federal
gunboats patrol up and down the Texas coast. What they're trying to do is to cut off the flow of cotton between the plantations
of the South and markets in Europe. The more successful the
blockade becomes, the better the price in Northern and world
markets and the more profit you can make." Georgia could feel
Potter's excitement grow as the old gambler began to think of the
profits waiting for the bold.

"Why, Reverend Potter," Georgia said, "I do believe you're
tempted to change your profession."

"Once upon a time I would have dreamed of piling up treasures on earth. But all is vanity. All is vanity." There was a wistful
quality to his voice, but his eyes were alive with avarice. "What
profit hath a man of all his labor which he taketh under the sun?"

"But if you weren't such an ecclesiastical fellow," Georgia
chided, "how would you do it? How would you make your fortune on cotton?"

"I'd take my cotton bales down to the Rio Grande on wagon
trains like the one you joined. A good broker sells the cotton and
converts my earnings to gold. Then I'd use the gold to buy military supplies and then sell that to the Confederate government.
I'd turn two profits on the same cotton crop. These ships in Bagdad, most of 'em are loaded with cotton bound for Yankee mills.

Some will go to England. Either way, if I could slip by the Yankees, I'd be sittin' pretty."

Toward dusk, as Georgia, the Colonel-Doctor, and the Captain-Reverend Potter watched a small lighter sail from port loaded with cotton, sharpshooters positioned on top of every bale, Georgia wondered aloud why the Woods plantation shouldn't profit from the cotton moving through the blockade.

"It's a dangerous business," Potter said, tugging on the belt that held his enormous six-shooter. "If the bandits don't get you, the Yankees will. And, then, some say it's a traitorous thing to do."

The Colonel-Doctor agreed. "The more money planters make off the cotton trade, the more land they plant in cotton and the fewer acres are planted in food crops. That's one of the reasons why there's a danger of food shortage."

"It's like trading with the enemy," Potter continued. "You'd be in cahoots with the Yankees."

"I'd be in partnership with Mittie Roosevelt," Georgia corrected. "She's a Georgia girl who's just lost in New York for a while."

"About half the ships you see out there are hired out to New York traders," the Colonel-Doctor said. "It's hard to fight them with one hand and shake hands with the other."

"But what harm?" Georgia asked. "It has nothing to do with the war. Cotton isn't gunpowder or cannonballs. It's just things people wear. Stockings, caps, and camisoles."

As night closed in on the improbable port of Bagdad, Georgia felt a need to be alone. *How strange,* she thought, *to feel this need now when I have been alone so long.* She moved to a doorway where she could see the boardwalk by the river begin to labor beneath the shadowed forms of night people. There was an oppressive stillness in the air, a brooding thing near sorrow in contrast to the almost joyous cacophony of the day. Heat trembled in the dark. The ships seemed sleeping beasts, steamers breathing threads of smoke like dragons beneath the moonless sky. Georgia shuddered. Dark painted women passed beneath lanterns and sailors swayed to the rhythm of their needs. Out in the dark, Mexican patriots plotted against Maximilian and his French army, and bandits killed for hatred and for bread. Far beyond, the armies of two nations murdered each other with abandon and children died of dread fevers. Here, the port of Bagdad was awash with ambiguity and confusion and deceit. *The world I have known all my life is coming to pieces,* Georgia thought, *and I will not let that happen to my family.* She looked out at the night and the lost people of Bagdad and she made her decision. *Let the men save our way of life by fighting the war. I'll fight my own way.*

For three days, Georgia and the Colonel-Doctor stayed alone together in a small adobe retreat above the river. Never had Georgia been more content. The fatigue and loneliness of the recent months slipped away like a discarded gown and she felt free and young and alive. It was a time of loving and peace before she would turn her thoughts to the dangerous course on which she had decided to embark.

When Georgia returned to San Marcos, she threw herself into the business of the plantation with renewed vigor. Her days were just as long and difficult as before her journey to the Rio Grande. But now she was filled with a sense of purpose and resolve she realized had been lacking before. In the past, she had simply been waiting for the Colonel-Doctor to return, living through a void as best she could. Now she was determined to actively shape what the future would be. And the future, she promised Martha Benny and the children, "will be grand."

It was in this period that she began her plans for the great house that would command the heights of San Marcos and carry her family into the future for a hundred generations. She envisioned a towering white home rising from perfumed gardens of fig, lavender, mountain laurel, and beds of mint. The Woods Mansion was to be her gift to the Colonel-Doctor. One wing she planned as a hospital. She also purchased a lot in town where she planned to build a drugstore with an office for her husband's medical practice.

The construction of the great house depended on the continued prosperity of the Woods plantation. Her herd of horses now numbered some 120 animals and they brought excellent prices from the Confederate Quartermaster Bureau. Many Southern officers rode to both victory and to defeat on horses from those Texas pastures. The price of cotton on the world market began to soar, and Georgia increased her cotton acreage and made her first tentative proposal to Mittie Roosevelt concerning a contract with northern buyers. The response was favorable, and an elaborate strategy involving the charter and double registry of vessels was created.

When the first cotton to be traded under the new arrangement was ready for harvest, Georgia encountered a major obstacle. Georgia had decided she and Ed Tom would take charge of the first cotton caravan. They both had traveled the cotton road, had been to Bagdad, and were familiar with all the dangers of the enterprise. After this first trip, Ed Tom could take another and another. Georgia trusted her old friend implicitly, in spite of her recollection that he had years ago left a season's cotton profits on Sam Ealy Johnson's kitchen table.

One day Georgia called Hawker and Ed Tom together and outlined her plan to market the year's cotton crop to northern buyers. She was mildly surprised that Hawker made no objection to the basic plan. But when she told Hawker that she and Ed Tom would be in charge of the entire enterprise, he was adamantly opposed.

"If you're dead set on this blockade business, I'll take the cotton wagons down myself. But this ain't no thing for a white lady and a nigger to do. You can't give a no-account nigger that much responsibility. He might up and take your money and head out north for the promised land."

For a moment there was complete silence in the room. All Georgia could hear was the wooden ticking of the clock that had been on her father's mantel in Water Valley. She cast a hurried glance at Ed Tom, and if she had not known him so well she would not have noticed the almost imperceptible smile dancing at the corners of his eyes. Then she looked back at Hawker.

"Ed Tom," she said, her eyes never leaving Hawker's meaty face. "You go see to that new colt in the north pasture now. I want to talk with Mr. Hawker."

Ed Tom began to leave. "You stay, boy," Hawker said. "You stay now or I'll whale the tar out of your black hide." Ed Tom paused.

Georgia was at an impasse. She was swept by a cold fury. Poor Ed Tom, her great friend, Martha Benny's husband, humiliated in front of her by this slovenly oaf of an excuse for a man. With enormous self-control she said: "Mr. Hawker, maybe you're right. But you'll need money to buy more oxen. Sit right there and I'll get it for you." Georgia turned, walked quickly to Pinckney's room, lifted the board beneath his bed where his six-shooter was hidden, removed the gun, and walked back with its muzzle pointed right between Hawker's eyes, which widened like those of an owl. "I want you gone, Mr. Hawker! Right now! If you ever set foot on this place again, I'll whip you myself in front of all the Negroes."

Hawker stood like he had been turned to stone. He began to sweat, then laugh. The Water Valley clock ticked away the moments. The smile was gone from Ed Tom's eyes. "Get out of here, you sorry rascal," Georgia said, her voice and her aim steady.

Hawker shifted. Georgia steadied the gun in both hands as she had seen Sam Ealy Johnson and Sheriff Z. P. Bugg teach Pinckney. "These are hard times, Hawker," she said. "I'm gambling my family's future on running the blockade. And you're in my way." Then Georgia pulled the trigger.

The sound was not as loud as Georgia imagined it would be. What she remembered most about the moment was how the lamp behind Hawker just flew to pieces in the air, and how Hawker's face began to tremble and contort, and how he turned and walked rapidly from the room and from the land and from his responsibility to the old planter with the insane daughter.

Georgia was so emotionally and physically drained by the encounter that, for the first time in years, she wanted to take to her bed. But she had no time. She was reckoning what it would take to get her cotton to Mexico—eight wagons each with four oxen and a driver, a supply wagon, and ample water for her caravan to Bagdad.

*　*　*

In December of 1863, after Georgia returned from Bagdad, her oldest son rode off to war. Her resistance had finally worn down. She gave him a gift of her finest sorrel, had him properly "armed, clothed, shod, and hatted" and sent his young slave to wait on him and attend to his cooking and washing on the long ride to his regiment. In a letter to the Colonel-Doctor Georgia wrote: "Pinckney is delighted with the idea of going to war, but poor child, he doesn't know what hard service is. I regret exceedingly that it has become necessary for such boys to go into the army. But I'm glad he's going in good spirits."

Although she might have spent whole days before without seeing or even thinking about Pinckney, his departure left a strange and unexpected void in Georgia's life. It was as if a stone in a mosaic had come loose, the pattern of plantation life somehow altered. There was Mahalia spinning, Nancy weaving, Sol making shoes, Leroy hauling a load of salt, Ed Tom repairing the wagons, Ulysses Cephas at his forge, Martha Benny taking care of sick children, Eddie Joe looking after the stock, Sip and Leath making ready the plow and rake, Cherokee and Sweet helping tend some soldiers recuperating from wounds or illness and the Reverend Cummings, whom Georgia had taken into her home when she learned he was dying of consumption.

Georgia was surrounded by people and activity and responsibilities, but she had never been more alone. And she also knew that another life was growing beneath her heart. She supposed it was God's way of replacing the boys that were being killed in the war. "My dear husband," she wrote, "you do not know how much I miss you and love you." She realized that the missing stone in the mosaic of her life was not just Pinckney and Jim and her husband, it was the male presence itself. She lived in a world of women and children. Little Peter was the man of the house and she wrote the Colonel-Doctor that he "was hard at work today helping the little nigs mind the birds from the wheat." Georgia missed the sounds of male laughter and the games men played, their romantic notions, their masculine posturing, their engaging sentimentality and strange opinions and loyalties. She had to smile when she thought, *All except the disgusting Mr. Hawker.*

Before the regiment moved north toward its engagement with

the Yankees in the Red River campaign, Georgia had one last opportunity to visit the Colonel-Doctor in South Texas. When she arrived, she found the regiment was embroiled in an engagement nearly as dangerous as that faced by other Confederate units to the east. It had to do, as Georgia soon learned, with the mysterious demise of South Texas pigs. Civilians who lived near the regiment's encampments complained that troopers were "shooting hogs, behaving badly, and burning fences for firewood." The Colonel-Doctor's men were accused of the crimes, their commander was severely reprimanded, and the hog-killing and fence-burning were ordered to stop. Colonel-Doctor Woods was so angered by General Magruder's reprimand that in his reply to the general he wrote that the order was so odious and "I am so thoroughly convinced of the inapplicability of the order to the regiment I have the honor to command that I can only assume your reprimand was in error and was meant for some other unit."

One morning, when Georgia and Captain-Reverend Potter had come into Brownsville for supplies and the regiment's mail, they overheard a conversation between two soldiers of Shay's Regiment, a unit bivouacked near the Woods Regiment. They were discussing an editorial in the *Brownsville Flag* that had accused the Colonel-Doctor's men of the "willful and egregious slaughter of civilian hogs."

"He's given the Woods Regiment a hard hit," said one soldier.

"Nothing more than they deserve," responded the other.

Reverend Potter was at their side in what seemed a single leap and he snatched the paper from the soldier's hands. A brief glance convinced him his colonel had been slandered and the injury to his reputation would have to be avenged. Without a further word to the astonished soldiers, he folded the paper, retrieved Georgia, and marched to the newspaper office. Georgia knew the regimental man of peace was about to declare war.

The meeting began cordially. The editor listened politely as Potter argued his case. "These men are away from home, defending our country, and it's unjust to accuse them falsely." He then demanded the editor write an article telling the other side of the story.

"You mean that the men were hungry for bacon and ham?

They killed the pigs because they were hungry and lonesome and away from home?"

"Of course not."

"But, sir," the editor said, "I cannot retract the truth. Your colonel's men are killing pigs just as sure as God made little green apples."

Captain-Reverend Potter rose from his chair. "Sir, are you calling me a liar?"

"No. I'm just saying your colonel's men are killing pigs."

"Show me those pigs. Where's the evidence?"

"I can't show you the evidence!" The editor was obviously growing impatient. "They ate the evidence!"

At this point in the discussion, as Georgia tried to restrain him, the Captain-Reverend Andrew Jackson Potter leaned over the editor's desk, slapped him in the face, pulled his massive revolver from his belt, demanded a retraction, and threatened to throw both the editor and his press into the Rio Grande. A few days later, the editor fled to Mexico, Georgia returned to San Marcos, and the 32nd Texas Cavalry moved out on a march to the Red River, where nearly three thousand Confederates would be killed, wounded, or reported missing in action.

The year 1864 was lived half in flesh and half on paper. On one level, the routine of plantation life continued with all its problems and hardships. In February, Georgia's neighbor Mrs. Caperton died in childbirth. Since her husband was away at war and the kin were unable to provide, Georgia took in little Allis Caperton. "I know you will think I've had enough children in the house, but I think this one poor little motherless one will not add much to my stock of cares."

On another level, the correspondence of Georgia and the Colonel-Doctor was constant and continuing, a torrent of ink, blood, and spirit. Each confided to the other the most private thoughts and deepest feelings. Georgia recognized her husband's anguish in regard to his participation in the war. The idea of killing human beings or causing their death was of growing abhorrence. There were even indications he considered abandoning the war and coming home. "But I would not have you give up your position as soldier to be with me. I will suffer and endure until death rather than be subject to the Yankees. Remember that your life is in the hands of an all-wise and all-merciful Heavenly Father who can and will take care of you. He will bring you home in peace and safety some day in His own good time."

When Georgia wrote the Colonel-Doctor about the coming child, his return letter came nearly a month later, delivered by Colonel Ellison's Negro. "My dear wife," he wrote, "word of our child is like a spring day in the middle of winter. I heartily rejoice and thank God for the life He is entrusting to our care. How I love you and wish I could be at your side. Try to preserve your health as well as you can. I fear you have too much to do for your constitution. I would enjoy a visit home so much. I am exceedingly wearied of the war. What outcome could possibly be worth all this desolation and death? How much more valuable I would be to the Creator if I were at your side as you give life to the world and not what I have been so recently asked to give."

The continuing correspondence from her husband, as well as reports from those who served under him, also revealed a commander of rather unorthodox style. He was often reprimanded for the lack of strict military discipline in his regiment. Although his unit was becoming legendary as a fighting force, officers and men called each other by their first names, and such niceties as salutes were rare. When his men were needed at home for plowing or to help their families, the Colonel-Doctor often let them go. Trooper Foster, the son of a Methodist minister, wrote that the men under Colonel-Doctor Woods were "the gamblingest, most profane group of men I have ever met." But they were fiercely loyal to the Colonel-Doctor, and he was just as loyal to them. Once it was ordered that his men make an attack on foot and the Colonel-Doctor refused the order. "My men are cavalry," he said. "If they attack, it will be mounted on horseback." Another letter expressed the Colonel-Doctor's chagrin that a number of generals would be visiting his command. "I suppose," he wrote, "we will have a great display of fuss and feathers—all buncombe." Georgia was not surprised that this strong good man would be loved by his troops. Years later, Andrew Jackson Potter would say: "Colonel Woods was one of the few men I know who went into the war a Christian and also came out of it a Christian."

A few weeks later, a third son was born. Although Mahalia and Martha Benny were with her throughout her labor, it was the first time a child of hers had been delivered by other than Dr. Peter's healing hands. Georgia named the little boy Frank Lawshe.

As the months went by, Georgia and Martha Benny were able to piece together from letters and news reports the movement of the Woods 32nd along the valley of the Red River. The places had such innocent names: Pleasant Hill, where one thousand Yankees perished; Blair's Landing, where General Tom Green was killed; Cane River; Monet's Ferry; McNutt's Hill; Yellow Bayou. Georgia tried to picture these places where her husband faced death. Sometimes she imagined them as spots people might go for picnics on better days, meadows with orchards and the small white houses beekeepers place beneath blossoming trees. At other times, she saw lands of deep bottomless swamp, heavy with rot and evil mists rising like the fetid breath of demons. She had to imagine her husband's world along the Red River, for Dr. Peter's letters dealt more with the landscape of the soul than with that of the river country. Sometimes his letters nearly broke her heart.

He wrote from Blair's Landing the night after General Green was killed. It was a letter heavy with confusion, sadness, doubt. "We were riding along a sandbar in the river when we saw a Federal gunboat hard aground in the sand. Tom Green ordered the men to take the vessel, charge into the river, into the concentrated fire of the enemy. He had been drinking hard and I knew what he ordered was suicide. I knew it was a trap. It would be foolhardy and lead to useless slaughter and I refused to order the assault. Our horses were under direct enemy fire. He was yelling at us to charge when he was struck down by a Yankee gunner. I will ever wonder if Tom Green, one of the greatest soldiers Texas ever produced, would be alive if I had obeyed his order. But I am comforted by the fact many more of my own men are living. Do I have the right to judge who should live and who should die?"

Pinckney told Sweet and Cherokee the horrible details of General Green's death. A canister had exploded, and the charge partially decapitated the General, his blood and brains spattering all over the Colonel-Doctor. The general was caught on his saddle horn and could not fall, and as his terrified horse whirled, parts of the general kept falling away. By the time the Colonel-Doctor could grab the reins and cut the body down, most of what had been the general was either gone or covering Peter and his horse. Sweet, the gentle lass who grew faint at the suggestion of violence of any kind, cried when the story was told. At first they thought the tears were for their father and the terrible moments he must have spent at Blair's Landing. Then she dried her tears and she said: "Those horrible Yankees! I wish they all were dead!"

In the spring of 1864, the Colonel-Doctor wrote Georgia that there was great demoralization in the army in the Trans Mississippi Department. "I fear the same among the citizenry at home," he wrote. "We are now out on a great sea of uncertainty, without helm, and I begin to fear the anchor may be lost. If so, our destruction is sure. But still I hope. If my hopes are in vain and the Yankees prevail, keep all you can out of the hands of the enemy, especially yourself."

Then came a letter from Yellow Bayou. It was written by Z. P. Bugg, and the moment it arrived, a cloak of dread began to settle over Georgia's mind. For a brief moment, she considered leaving the letter unopened or perhaps tearing it up, unread. It could only be terrible news. Why a letter from Z. P. Bugg? Why not from the Colonel-Doctor? Or Pinckney? She opened the letter, unfolded the pages, and began to read.

"I regret to write that Colonel-Doctor has been bad hurt but it could be he will live." In that one sentence Georgia experienced a sweep of emotion as wide and deep as a human can feel. She put down the letter, took a deep breath to steady the vertigo she felt, and gathered herself together for the next blow. "We was in Yellow Bayou and for the month of May it was powerful hot. The Federals had started fires and they were burning in the cedar brakes." Georgia could see the battleground, the sun a furnace hanging from white skies, the mist rising above the bayou, flames raging through the swamp. It was Dante's image of Hell. "Colonel-Doctor was out front by himself and he was hit but wouldn't fall. He charged his horse into the Yankees by himself and just kept running back and forth through their lines. Then when we seen him alone there, we came out shootin' and the Yankees lit out the other way. Colonel-Doctor never did fall from his horse. But we took him down and laid him down and did what we could to stop the bleeding. He's resting and says to tell you not to worry, and he loves you. Respectfully, Z. P. Bugg." Georgia folded the letter and wondered if it had been a kindness or a cruelty. There was so much unsaid, so much to fear. But she knew the Colonel-Doctor was alive. Nothing else was possible. Yet, she also knew he was in pain, because she could feel it searing across the miles, consuming her strength.

For five days she heard no further word. She lived in a kind of living death, the pain of his wound making it difficult for her to breathe. She considered riding to Yellow Bayou, but she was afraid she would miss the letter that said the Colonel-Doctor's wound was superficial and he was recovering and in good spirits. On the sixth day, an official report arrived, summarizing what had happened to the Colonel-Doctor during the battle of Yellow Bayou. "Severely wounded, Colonel Peter Woods dashed toward the enemy position. The sight of this lone officer hurling his life into the jaws of death inspired his men to action. Following the example of their courageous leader, they attacked, against great odds, and won the day." The report also stated a Yankee ball had entered his left hand and torn through his arm and out his elbow.

The next day a letter came from the Colonel-Doctor himself. He did not comment on his wound, except to say that it was only his hand and was not terribly serious. He confided that the official account of his action had been a bit exaggerated. "A musket ball had so frightened my Isaiah," he wrote, "that the crazed animal had run wildly toward the enemy lines. My only choice had been the humiliation of dismounting or continuing the charge. I guess I'll never know if I would have ordered the charge if my horse wouldn't have bolted."

Georgia knew her husband's war was over, both the war with the enemy and the war with himself. No longer would he be troubled by the two halves of his nature, the destroyer and the healer. His healing hand was destroyed, and the Colonel-Doctor could no longer be a soldier or a surgeon. But he was alive and Georgia rejoiced and thanked the Lord for saving the life of a great, good man.

It would be nearly a year before the last Texan, Colonel Rip

Ford, would surrender to the Yankees at Brownsville. But during the summer of 1864, as General Sherman's army approached the outskirts of Atlanta, Jim Hawkins, Z. P. Bugg, and Sam Ealy Johnson brought the Colonel-Doctor home. Because horses were required in the continuing war, they made the long, slow journey by mule. The heat was intense. To protect him from the burning sun, the Colonel-Doctor was laid in the bottom of the wagon beneath a canvas. By turns, Z. P. Bugg and Sam Ealy Johnson would lift the canvas to make sure their old friend was still alive. So shallow was his breathing that sometimes it took some moments to determine that he was still clinging to life. Although his wound had been treated in the field, Dr. Peter's arm was now terribly swollen and discolored. Sam Ealy Johnson later told how at night, when the darkness brought some relief from the fierce sun and the Colonel-Doctor surfaced from unconsciousness or delirium, he would instruct his companions on the removal of his arm. Each night they inspected the wound and prepared for the amputation. Yet, each night, they would decide to wait one more day.

At last the war-weary soldiers crossed the Blanco River onto Woods land. Old Mose was the first to see them coming. He rang the plantation bell that had once pealed from the tower of Fort Hawkins and that Captain Lawshe had saved from his ruined plantation in Mississippi. The bell sounded and sounded and sang in the summer air. From the quarters, the fields, and the house, scores of Negroes stopped their work and turned toward the east where the wagon approached. Georgia and the children rushed from the house. Mahalia lifted little Frank. "Time you met your papa," she said, as she and Martha Benny followed Georgia into the punishing sunlight.

At first, her husband was nowhere in sight. Georgia was rocked by the thought that Peter had died on the way home. Jim quickly read her thoughts. "No, Miss Georgia, he's in the wagon. He's bad, but hanging on." Georgia ran to the wagon and climbed into the bed. She raised the canvas and there was the answer to all the prayers she had prayed these many lonely months. She touched his face. It was hot as a forge and covered with grime from the road.

Georgia leaned down and kissed the Colonel-Doctor's forehead. He opened his eyes. For a moment, he stared past her into the heart of some distant dread. Then, his eyes found her. For a long interval he seemed to explore the most minute features of her face, as if seeing her for the first time. "How very beautiful," he whispered, and then he closed his eyes.

Georgia's gift to Peter Cavanaugh Woods was nearly finished and stood like some legendary castle on the brow of a hill overlooking San Marcos. Her missions to the Rio Grande and clandestine enterprise with Mittie Roosevelt had been immensely successful and, as Georgia had wished, the house purchased from the profits was grand and white and majestic, certainly among the most beautiful and commanding houses in Texas. For several months, Georgia divided her time between making the finishing touches on their house and nursing the Colonel-Doctor back to health. Although he instructed her in his treatment, she felt a curious and satisfying reversal of roles. After all these years, she was the physician and Colonel-Doctor Peter was the patient. Little by little, his strength returned. But his left arm and hand remained largely useless. Little Sweet became his constant companion, and she surprised everyone in the family with her intense interest in the war. Whenever the Colonel-Doctor, Pinckney or Jim would mention the Yankees, Sweet would grow angry. Once, after hearing Sweet rage against the Yankees, Martha Benny told Georgia the South probably would have won the war if Sweet had been allowed to fight. "I never saw a little girl get so riled up," she said. "Must be she took to heart those speeches Governor Murrah made. Speeches about women havin' to carry on the fight. Somebody oughta tell that girl the war's over."

Sometimes Georgia was shocked by the unreality of life after the war. After all the unspeakable horror and sacrifice and pain, it seemed nothing had really changed. When she had called the slaves together and had tearfully told them they were free to go, only two young men had left the plantation. The rest stayed. There was Mahalia spinning, Nancy weaving, Sol making shoes, Leroy hauling salt, Ed Tom repairing the wagons, Ulysses Cephas at his forge.

After Lee's surrender, April 19, 1865, two months passed before the Yankees turned their eyes toward Texas. It was a golden interval in Georgia's life. The center had held. The family was safe. Dear Peter was alive. Jim was back. Pinckney had returned from the war a man Georgia not only loved but admired. Cherokee was as spirited and Sweet as engagingly mysterious as they had ever been.

"We've done something fine," Martha Benny told Georgia one evening as they watched the girls pursued by suitors. "We raised those children good."

"You know full well I did the raising," Georgia snapped. "All you did was criticize and roll those blue eyes." Then they both began to laugh until tears rolled down their faces, and for the first time since they were children their hands touched and then held.

"Just look out yonder," Martha Benny said, gazing out over the grounds and up at the house and out toward the river. "I'm telling you, somebody around here sure did do something mighty fine."

On June 19, 1865, word swept through San Marcos that a General Gordon Granger had arrived at Galveston to proclaim the authority of the United States, and that Yankee troops were marching into Texas to establish their sovereignty over the defeated Confederates. Within a few months, a group of armed Union soldiers rode into town and up the hill to where Georgia and Martha Benny were picking black-eyed peas and weeding tomato vines. Old Mose appeared in the garden and announced a Lieutenant Peterson. When Georgia looked up from her vegetables, the sun was behind the Yankee lieutenant and she couldn't see his features. She was not sure how to greet one's former enemy. She stood and held out her hand. He ignored the gesture.

"It's my duty to inform you this house has been designated headquarters for the officers and men who will occupy this town." As the clipped, hard phrases fell into the garden, Georgia held up her hand against the sun in order to see who would say such foolish things. "You and your family must vacate at once. My superiors suggest you reside in the buildings to the rear of the property."

"Surely, there's some mistake. My husband will . . ."

"What your husband does is of no concern to me."

Now Georgia had moved to the side where she could see the officer's face. "Young man ..."

"Mrs. Woods, you are ordered to vacate the house by Friday. If not, you will be removed. With that said, I bid you good morning." Lieutenant Peterson turned and disappeared into the sunlight. Georgia wondered if he had been a mirage.

She felt Martha Benny reach for her arm. "What in Heaven's name can we do?" she asked. She actually felt Martha Benny's hand shaking.

"I don't know," Georgia said, "but something. That's for sure." *How quickly life can change,* she thought, as she felt her shock changing to anger. Martha Benny sank to her knees among the vegetables. "Get up," Georgia said, not too gently. "We've got to get our thoughts together. Suddenly she remembered the vow she made after Tobe had been hanged and Josiah had been driven away. "Get Pinckney and Jim," she said. "I swear, I'll never be subject to the Yankees as long as I live."

From the top of their hill, Georgia and her family watched the Union Army and State Police march into town. Georgia had been too numb to take part in the packing of the household furnishings and the burying of the silver. Now she watched the troops move like bold thieves up the hill to take her life away. No one stirred. The drums and boots of the soldiers rattled like the bones of the doomed. Then, as the troops came up the rise toward the front of the house, a shot cracked the stillness. The advancing soldiers scattered into the brush along the road. Georgia could smell gunpowder, a smell she remembered from the time she fired at Emanuel Hawker, and her eyes were drawn to the high balcony of her house, where Little Sweet was reloading a rifle to fire once more at the advancing Yankees. The war was over. The war had just begun.

In the spring of 1869, the year Ulysses S. Grant was inaugurated as president, Georgia Lawshe Woods discovered that evil really did exist in the world. Evil was a triumvirate of Yankee officers who would live in her white house on the hill and would torment her beyond her capacity to bear.

The first officer was Lieutenant Hamilton C. Peterson, the man she had encountered in her garden just before Little Sweet fired on the advancing Yankee troops. Peterson was a mean-spirited and profane eyesore of a man who had served as a private until a few months before he was assigned to the army of occupation. He was tall, angular, and loose-jointed and there was a certain imbalance about his stance, as if one side of his body had outgrown the other. His cheeks were pinched as if receding into the hollow left by lost molars. When he spoke, his words exploded in high-pitched nasal snarls liberally laced with moist expletive. His status as an officer and a gentleman was a contradiction in terms, for Lieutenant Peterson was loud, rude, and obnoxious. He had a reputation for violence and was notorious for his inability to hold his liquor. There was talk in town and among the Negroes that Peterson had killed two boys in Prairie Lea who were accused by their Unionist neighbor of stealing pigs. When they refused Lieutenant Peterson's order to come out of their house, he set the place on fire and the boys burned to death. He had been drunk, of course. There had been charges and an investigation, but the case was dismissed for lack of witnesses willing to testify.

The second officer was Morris Norwood, a former slave on the Norwood plantation, in San Marcos. How this illiterate field hand managed to become an officer in the State Police was a mystery to both Georgia and Martha Benny. "He's a powerful bitter man," Martha Benny told Georgia. "Now he's come up in the world, he's doin' his best to bring everybody else down. I don't know who hates him most, black folks or white."

But certainly the most offensive of the officers that moved into Georgia's house was Captain George Haller. A Union officer and Prussian mercenary, Captain Haller could, and in conversation often would, trace his family back to the Teutonic knights of the twelfth century. He was the new and absolute master of Georgia's world. It was his garrison of State Police and Federal units that had been quartered in her beloved house on the hill and that now soiled her linen and scuffed her fine oak floors and scrawled graffiti in the parlor and lounged indolently and insolently on her lawn. With the assistance of Morris Norwood, George Haller commanded the troops that emptied their garbage in her roses. In the beginning, Georgia had complained about the desecration of her house.

"But my dear Mrs. Woods," Haller had responded, "what do you expect? You are, after all, a conquered nation. It's only right and just you pay for the suffering you caused." His manner was oily, seemingly rehearsed and pretentious. He was of powerful build, yet there was about him a rare and remarkable absence of grace. The only thing that seemed natural and authentic about Haller was the expression of contempt he wore. It was in his eyes and pressed between his thin lips and surely into his soul.

One afternoon, after the Yankees had been quartered in her house for a little more than a year, Georgia was summoned to Haller's office by Morris Norwood. The Negro policeman had come to the door of the old slave house where Georgia now lived with her children, Martha Benny, and Ed Tom. As Georgia moved to the door, she overheard Norwood taunting Martha Benny.

"You puttin' on all them airs," he said, "like maybe you think you're white like your mistress. Well, you ain't white and you don't appear to be black neither. Maybe I'll peel you and see what color you are inside."

When Norwood led Georgia to Haller, she was received in what had been her parlor. She noticed there was a scar high on

Haller's cheek and wondered if it came from a duel or had been self-inflicted as a part of his awful masquerade. He took her arm and led her to a chair. His touch was wrong, somehow insinuating an intimacy both unthinkable and grotesque.

"I thought we should visit," he said with his poisonous smile. "Tell me, do you often wonder why your family's criminal attack on my men has gone unpunished?"

Georgia once again reeled as though the floor had fallen and her heart was left suspended in air. "That's years ago," Georgia said. "There was a war. I don't know why you keep bringing up something that happened so long ago." Although she was sure the officers did not know it was Little Sweet who had fired the shots at the approaching Yankees, she was terrified every time the event was mentioned. After the shots had been fired, Jim had rushed Sweet and her rifle from the house to hide them both in the old slave quarters. When the family had been gathered for questioning, Georgia was sure Sweet would give herself away. Without a change of expression, the girl had been as cool as a jewel thief, certainly the last person on earth anyone would consider a killer. The question of the attack on Haller's men remained a mystery. For eighteen months the secret had been kept. Since his arrival, Haller had insinuated he knew who had fired the shots and he used this supposed knowledge in constant humiliating threats to punish the family.

"Surely," he said, "you must have wondered why Little Sweet has not been arrested."

"That's ridiculous!"

"Yes, we know it was she who fired on my men from your balcony."

"You're guessing. How do you know I didn't fire the shots? It could have been anybody. A stranger."

"I think not. I think it was your Little Sweet. And the only thing that matters is what I think. If I say she is the criminal, then it's true." Haller began to pace in front of Georgia's chair. She felt her hate for the officer rise like bile. "Why, then, you might wonder, is she still in the bosom of your family?" Georgia recognized the emphasis on the word "bosom" and when his eyes followed his word she felt defiled by the touch of his eyes.

"Little Sweet knew what she was doing," he continued. "We were not at war, so her act was an act of attempted murder. A very serious crime which brings very serious punishment. However, I understand your situation. She is a good girl who acted foolishly. I respect her passion. In fact, I have come to admire the women of your South. Such beauty and passion wasted on such ungrateful men. And so I've taken it upon myself to be your protector. These are dangerous times filled with dangerous and lonely men. Well, my pretty lady, I don't need to point out that Lieutenant Peterson and Officer Norwood are great admirers of your daughters, and of you, I might add. They are passionate men who have been long away from their families. But as long as I'm here you and your daughters can feel safe. I would only ask this one thing. I have grown especially fond of Cherokee. In fact, I think of her day and night. Perhaps you could speak to her. I am, after all, a man of position and authority and she could certainly do worse."

He actually had clicked his heels together and had bowed from the waist. Then he took her hand and she rose trembling with humiliation and rage from the chair that had once been hers. She snatched her hand away and was about to speak when he touched his finger to her lips.

"Don't speak," he said, his face now hard as stone. "Don't say anything you might later regret. These are dangerous times. There are tigers in the forest and I hold the leash."

He lowered his finger, tracing a line down the curve of her breast in passing. His face rearranged itself into its mocking mask. "Good day, Georgia," he said, using her first name for the first time. There was a taste of brimstone on her lips where his fingers had touched.

For a time after this terrible encounter with Haller, she wondered if she could have been mistaken about his insinuations, about his touch. She had felt assaulted, powerless, and enormously vulnerable. His every word and gesture seemed to have a blunt edge of sexual innuendo. Each time she saw him in the yard or in town, he acted as if they had already been lovers. He looked at her as if he were laying her naked one garment at a time. Sometimes, in the bright daylight, she felt that her mind had created her assailant, that his insinuations had been imagined, that he was merely a symbol for the very real rape of her world. Then it would come to her in the darkness of the night and she would re-member Haller had touched her and she would hear the drunken voices of Peterson and the other soldiers in the night and she would know how helpless and alone she had become.

Who could she turn to? During these months, the Colonel-Doctor was in Austin trying to hammer out a new state constitu-tion. Pinckney and Jim were running cattle with Sam Ealy Johnson out in the Hill Country. Andrew Jackson Potter was off saving souls. She had encouraged the Colonel-Doctor to remain in Austin. "It's important you fight the good fight in the capital," she told him. "Now it's a political war and Austin is where vic-tory will be won." Of the men in her family only the boys Peter and Frank were at home.

Deep in the night, she would be awakened by a sharp arrow of fear and she would look out the window and see Haller stand-ing there beneath the moon, watching the house. Night after night he kept his strange vigil. Georgia would slip from bed and move through the shadows to where Cherokee and Sweet were sleeping and she kept watch on the girls as if she expected Haller might come crashing through the door. She realized then that he was not a symbol. He was flesh and blood and evil. She was afraid for herself, yet she was even more afraid for her daughters Cherokee and Sweet. It was a new experience, because she could not remember being afraid before. And when she tried to analyze the fear, she found to her surprise and sorrow it was not just fear she felt, but shame. She was ashamed of her growing powerless-ness. It was as if she were becoming an emotional invalid, para-lyzed, helpless, incapable of rational thought or action. Haller had her totally under his control. What if Haller did force himself on her or on the girls? To what authority could she appeal? She lived in a time and place when and where such an act would be con-doned, if not applauded.

During the Reconstruction years, when General Sheridan's 5th Military District ruled San Marcos and the enemy was quar-tered in Georgia's house, Texas was a cauldron of political and social chaos. The countryside was both ungoverned and ungovernable. Theoretically, Texas was under military rule. Yet it was more a rule of punishment than of law. Georgia often thought the South was being broken on the rack and was being dismembered bit by bit and forced to make restitution by repaying fragments of its soul.

Tensions between citizens and soldiers were explosively high and brief episodes of violence constantly erupted between townspeople and the occupying forces. The Yankee soldiers, both officers and men, black and white, seemed bent on humiliating the Texans, especially the planter class. Occasionally a soldier would be ambushed, beaten or killed by disillusioned patriots, madmen, or the sons of planters with vows of vengeance on their lips. There was no justice for black or white. Added to the social maelstrom were the thousands of former slaves who wandered the countryside, homeless, without work, resentful, and deeply disappointed by the reality these early years of freedom imposed. In an effort to hold political power, a bizarre coalition of carpetbaggers, scalawags, corrupt Union officials, and former slaves was forged. Former Confederate citizens like the Colonel-Doctor were denied the vote, yet their field hands were taken to the polls by the wagonload. It was, as Captain Haller had said, a violent, chaotic, dangerous time.

Since Georgia had managed to create the grandest house in the area, it was the obvious choice for the conquerors to make their headquarters. Haller and his men went out of their way to humiliate and punish her family for the alleged crimes of the Confederacy.

One night, as the spring of 1869 matured into summer, Georgia took little Frank out in the yard. It was very hot and no breeze stirred and the house had been an oven. Outside, on the hill above the river and the town, it was cooler. The planet Venus was just rising above the chimney of the great house and she could hear soldiers playing cards on the porch. One of the soldiers, apparently a loser, rose with an oath and began to urinate over the balcony into her garden. She could not look away. In the act there was a terrible fascination, as if she were watching a vandal cut the canvas of an Old Master with a knife. What shocked her most was not the vulgarity itself, but the total defilement it symbolized. It was then Captain Haller spoke from the darkness.

"Georgia." It was neither a question nor a statement, just a naked sound from the shadows. "Do you hear the tigers in the forest?"

Georgia tore her eyes away from the man on the balcony, picked up little Frank, and whirled, and it was all she could do to keep from running back into the house. Behind her, she could hear Haller laughing.

As the days and nights passed, Georgia became more and more protective of the children. Cherokee was eighteen, in the full bloom of her beauty, a voluptuous, dark woman whose smile could warm a room. She was quick to laugh and possessed of an engaging irreverence, and her eyes were alive with bright Hawkins blue. Little Sweet was just as attractive and was certainly becoming a young woman. Perhaps it was the changes within Sweet that caused the dark moods that lingered like fever for days. She would often burst into tears for no apparent reason. Her rages too were explosive, then gone in a moment, seemingly forgotten. Martha Benny claimed there were different kinds of devils in the girls. Cherokee's was a merry demon, while Sweet's fed on gloom. How strange that Georgia was more worried about Sweet than Cherokee. Cherokee had about her a certain aura of invulnerability, while Sweet was a mystery, like a beautiful, yet unfinished, painting.

Frank was beginning to reveal the same capacity for devilment that enlivened his older brothers. Georgia and Martha Benny struggled to keep little Frank away from the soldiers with their wonderful guns and uniforms. Peter Junior considered himself the man of the house in the Colonel-Doctor's absence. For a youngster, he seemed to speak in a silent language horses could understand. He reminded Georgia more of the Colonel-Doctor than Pinckney. She could tell he would be strong, yet gentle, and she hoped there would be something left of the plantation and the horses when this terrible time had passed.

In late May, Georgia received an unexpected letter from Pinckney. It was a rare treat, and an amusing one, because his hand and spelling and sentence structure reflected only marginal literacy. As she looked at the letter, she felt a breath of guilt for not having forced him to attend school more regularly. But she managed to make out from Pinckney's strange hieroglyphics wonderful tales of building his own ranch—hardship and excitement, raging rivers, stampedes, sudden violence, and the beauty of the western countryside. It was a good long letter. She loved it and found it beautifully expressive in spite of its flaws. Georgia read the letter again and again and she felt closer to Pinckney than ever before, even though he was hundreds of miles away.

One evening, as Georgia was telling her children stories about the Wild West inspired by Pinckney's letter, Morris Norwood came by to call. When Martha Benny opened the door, he forced his way into the room until he loomed before Georgia, a dark and menacing presence that nearly filled the small house. He stood there without speaking, insolent and grotesque, as if his presence required no explanation.

Georgia sent the children into the other room. "I don't remember anyone asking you to come in, Officer Norwood."

"I go where I please," he said. "I don't need no invitation from you or your uppity white nigger." He looked at Martha Benny and winked. "Fact is I got a message from the captain." Norwood sprawled into one of the few fine chairs Georgia had saved from the big house. "The captain says he knows who shot at us when we come here and he wants to make a deal. He says he wants you up in his room at midnight for a talk. I asked him why he wanted you up there and he said 'cause it used to be your bedroom and you might want to lay down in your old bed. The captain said . . ."

"Go tell your captain to deliver his own messages." Georgia was beyond fury. The whole scene was unreal and Norwood's insinuations were unspeakably disgusting. It crossed her mind she would have to burn the chair Norwood had been sitting in, and it had been a favorite, brought all the way from Water Valley.

"I don't think you want to fool with the captain. Not from what I hear he done in Vicksburg. He plain killed some civilians who fooled with him."

"I'll be careful not to fool with the captain." Georgia's voice was a flat monotone. She sent Martha Benny to check on the children.

"He sure says he wants to fool with you. And I'd like to fool with your white nigger."

"Officer Norwood, it's been so nice having you visit." Georgia stood. To her profound relief, Norwood rose as well. "Give my regards to your captain."

"I hope you and the captain do each other real good," Norwood said, moving toward the door. "I'll tell the captain you said you'd be nice."

When Morris Norwood was gone, his presence remained in the room. Georgia leaned her back against the door and closed her eyes. She was afraid now she might have to burn the entire house. She commanded her eyes not to cry and wondered how in the world Papa's girl from Water Valley had come to this.

On the last night of May, as the hour grew late and the familiar stars began to take their place in the heavens, Georgia once more drew Pinckney's old revolver from where it had been hidden from the Yankees. It was apparent from Norwood's call that Haller was ready to demand something unthinkable in return for keeping the secret about Little Sweet. Georgia was sure she knew what Haller wanted and that's why she held Pinckney's revolver in her hand. The house was quiet. Cherokee and Sweet were staying the night with Sarah Burleson. Peter Junior and Frank were asleep. Martha Benny, ever watchful, was in her room next to the children.

She had expected the revolver to feel cold in her hand but the steel was almost hot, as if the fates had warmed it up for the occasion. Looking at the gun, she wondered if she had the strength to kill Haller. She imagined herself pulling the trigger as she had done to frighten Emanuel Hawker away. She would not have killed Hawker. But she knew she could kill Captain Haller. Forcing her to meet him in her old bedroom was reason enough. Why, if the Colonel-Doctor or Pinckney could have heard Norwood's message, both Haller and Norwood would already be dead. Yes, she could kill Haller if he threatened her or the children. But what then? The Yankees would come down on her family and everybody and everything she loved would be destroyed. They would all be hanged. She realized she would have to use some other weapon to save Sweet. Something. She put the gun back in its hiding place, rose, and walked out into the night toward the house she had built for the Colonel-Doctor.

To her surprise and initial relief, Haller's manner was very businesslike. He did not insinuate intimacy as he had done before, and neither his hands nor his eyes suggested such intentions. Georgia thought Haller was being as proper as an obscene and sinister human dog could be. He came right to the point. She heard only a few words before Georgia began to regret she hadn't brought Pinckney's old revolver. Haller's words were spoken quietly in his guttural imitation of the Queen's English, and Georgia was both fascinated and repulsed by the barbarity inherent in his proposal.

"I want Cherokee," he said. "But it seems she resists my attentions. My proposal is quite simple. I will trade you Sweet for Cherokee. Once Cherokee is in my bed, I give my word Sweet will remain free."

For a moment, Georgia stared at Haller, her heart a hammer, her mind searching for an adequate response. There were no words. So she stood, walked close to where Haller waited, moved closer, very close—then spat in his face. Finally her rage found release and she began to strike Haller with all the strength she possessed. At first, Haller threw up his arms and backed away. Then he fought off her blows and grasped one arm and then the other. He threw her on the bed and she struggled to turn her face away. Suddenly, he was standing, rearranging his uniform, wiping the blood from his lips. "I like your family," he said. "Maybe after Cherokee has been with me awhile, she'll learn to love me and we'll be married. Then you'd be my mother-in-law." He laughed then, a sound like a small barking dog, then turned and left the room. Georgia had never felt more like screaming, but she was suddenly violently sick at her stomach and could make no sound.

Several weeks later, little Frank was shot while he played in front of their house. Georgia heard the shot at the precise instant she discovered Frank had left the house. It was almost as if she knew before she knew. He lay like a small scarecrow on the lawn, a crimson flower blooming on his breast.

Georgia and Martha Benny carried the small boy into the house and Georgia felt an enormous surge of relief to see the wound was superficial. She stopped the bleeding with a compress and dressed the wound before dropping to her knees. She spoke to God in a flowing, passionate litany of sobs and prayer. Later that night, when Frank was peacefully asleep, Martha Benny expressed what they all were thinking. "How in Heaven's name," she wondered, "can a little boy get shot in a house surrounded by state police?"

The next day Captain Haller came to investigate. When Georgia opened the door and saw him standing there she thought she might be sick again, but she pretended civility. After he had seen the boy and had made a cursory search for the bullet, Haller said he would make a full report. As he was leaving, he looked directly at Georgia for the first time. "A terrible thing," he said. "Such terrible things seem to happen to your family."

That evening, as it began to grow dark, Georgia decided not to light any of the lamps in the house. *Suppose,* she thought, *whoever shot Frank comes back. We would be targets he could see through the window. Could it be Haller?* she wondered. *I've got to think of something.* For a moment she was again overwhelmed with an awareness of her powerlessness. Then her resolve returned, but no plan on which to invest that resolve emerged. So she and Martha Benny, Frank, Peter Junior, and Sweet waited in the growing darkness for Cherokee to come home. She was down at the Methodist Church learning to play the melodeon. Their own piano had been requisitioned by the Yankees, and on late nights they could sometimes hear it accompany voices impaired by liquor and sentimentality. Time ticked by. Martha Benny went to bring Cherokee home, but returned to report she had already left. She was an hour late. Then two. Georgia listened for Cherokee's step. A numbing fear began to grip Georgia's soul, and when her eyes met Martha Benny's she knew her old friend, too, sensed something was terribly wrong. They sent the children to bed and they waited in a room slowly filling with dread.

"There's something evil, isn't there?" Martha Benny shivered.

"I can feel it," she said and she drew closer to Georgia in the darkness.

"Haller," Georgia said.

"We've been through bad before," Martha Benny said. "With the Almighty's help we can get through this."

Cherokee came home three hours after dark. First they heard footsteps behind the house and then the sound of a window opening. By lamplight, they found Cherokee. Her face was bruised. Her dress was torn from the neckline to the waist. At first the girl made a move to escape back through the window into the night, but then great tears began to roll down her cheeks, and she and her mother and Martha Benny were in each other's arms. They comforted each other, the three women, for a very long time.

In the quiet house, the three women talked until dawn. Cherokee told them she had been seeing Haller. The first time they met, Haller made lewd suggestions. Then he said if she told anyone he would spread rumors that she was one of those girls who teased the soldiers, led them on. When she refused to meet him, he threatened to tell people they had been lovers. Each time they met, he got more and more familiar.

"Why didn't you tell us?" Georgia asked. "We could have done something."

"Done what?" Cherokee asked. "Done what? Report him to the police? He *is* the police!"

"We could have done something," Georgia said again, feeling the futility of the words.

"I was ashamed," Cherokee said. "He's so awful. I was afraid what you'd believe." Cherokee's tears began to flow again. "Then tonight he got me on the ground and tore my dress and almost . . ."

"It's all right now, baby."

"He was so strong."

"I know."

"He told me to tell you about the tigers in the forest. What did he mean?"

Then Georgia told them about Haller's proposition and his offer to trade Little Sweet for Cherokee. She told them how she

considered killing Haller but had decided against it. She decided
not to tell about how Haller had assaulted her in his room, and
the memory of that made her understand how difficult it was for
Cherokee to reveal her humiliating experience.

"What now?" Martha Benny asked.

"We stand proud, that's all," Georgia said. "We spit in his eye.
We go about our life and let that poor, weak, pathetic man go
about his if he can."

"What about Sweet?"

"She stays in the house, out of sight," Georgia said. "Tell Cephus to ride for Pinckney and Jim. It's time they came home. I
refuse to be a victim any longer."

As Georgia waited for Pinckney and Jim, she prayed for forgiveness. *What kind of mother,* she asked herself, *would conspire
with her children to do a killing?* Then a part of her would respond: *What kind of mother would allow her children to be raped
and imprisoned?* Her anguish was like dark serpents coiling in her
heart. She once again considered killing Haller herself. But how
could it be done without bringing the Yankees down on her
household? He was too physically strong to kill with her hands
or with a knife, and a gun would be heard. Georgia knew the moment she decided to send for Pinckney, she had sentenced George
Haller to death. The murder weapon was the single simple
phrase: "Come home." Pinckney had watched General Green die
and was consumed with hatred for Yankees. When he learned
about Haller his rage would be monumental. But didn't Haller
deserve to die? He was surely beyond redemption. Haller was an
enemy soldier. Yet the Scriptures stressed the perfectibility of the
human soul. "Thou shalt not kill." It was a Commandment utterly lacking in ambiguity. So Georgia grieved for the death of her
innocence and prayed for forgiveness and that Pinckney might
hurry home from the Hill Country.

One night, early in July, Georgia was awakened by an owl.
She moved to the window, parted the curtains and there was
Haller watching, waiting, beneath the full moon. *Did he look
right into my eyes?* Perhaps it was her imagination, but she

thought she saw him bow as he had done at their first meeting. She remained in the window listening for the owl and feeling the unseasonable coolness of a small night wind stir the curtains and her hair. Quietly she removed Pinckney's revolver from its hiding place, looked in on the sleeping children, nodded to Martha Benny, and then slipped out the back door into the night.

Being careful to keep the house between her and Haller, she moved toward the distant stables. The moon knifed beneath a cloud and she walked faster, the grass of the meadow sweeping her ankles, her steps silent as whispers on the earth. The stables were nearly half a mile from the house, and soon she could no longer hear the drunken singing of the soldiers. Then she reached the stables and passed through the door. There was a smell of horses and sweet hay and something else: rage. She glanced up into the loft where Pinckney, Jim, and George McGehee were waiting, well hidden in the velvet shadows. Georgia slipped into a stall where she could watch the path toward the house. She looked out, and it was then she saw Cherokee.

The girl wore a loose white gown and for a moment Georgia thought she was a beautiful ghost who now took Haller's hand and walked with him through the wind and moon shadow toward the stables. Ragged clouds marched by the moon, and the night had a color, almost blue, as if seen from beneath the sea. Georgia wondered for a moment if she was dreaming, and when the owl called again, she knew the night was real.

Then Cherokee and Haller were at the door to the stables. After whispering something in his ear, Cherokee ran into the building, her gown billowing above her bare feet and ankles. He paused, then followed. Cherokee and the captain stood in a square of light the moon cast through an open door in the loft. She had her arms folded across her chest and was looking down and to one side. Haller reached for her and bent to kiss her, but she pushed him away and began to unbutton the top of her dress. "You better get undressed," Cherokee said. It was almost a whisper.

Haller unbuckled his gunbelt, then paused. He appeared to be listening to the darkness.

"What's wrong?"

"The horses," Haller said. He walked the few steps to a stall and looked in at the horses. In a horrible moment, Georgia realized Haller would see the horses were saddled. Haller whirled, whipped his gun from its holster, and the stable was filled with thunder and lightning. It was a numbing, all-enveloping sound that shook the earth and the stable and the soul. In the moonlight, Georgia saw Haller spin to the side, then reach for Cherokee and pull her against his body. He held her as a shield toward the source of the shots. Georgia could see dark stains spreading on Cherokee's white nightdress and she prayed the blood was Haller's. Then the firing stopped and the screaming of the horses subsided and the stable grew ominously quiet.

Georgia could hear Haller's labored breathing, a sound like a broken bellows. He had been hit. He swayed and coughed and only by leaning on Cherokee did he keep from falling. He scanned the darkness, apparently unwilling to waste his remaining bullets by firing wildly into the loft. His back was to Georgia. Carefully, Georgia walked forward until she was just behind Haller. Then she stepped to the side, pushed the pistol into his stomach, and pulled the trigger.

It was like a painting, a dark oil filled with shadow and lantern light and mystery beyond understanding. Jim Hawkins, Pinckney Woods, and George McGehee stood above the fallen form of Captain George Haller. She had seen them stand the same way as children when they had returned from the ritual of the hunt with the carcass of a javalina or a rabbit or a deer. Their faces then, and now, were solemn and drained by the incomprehensibility of death. Cherokee stood to the side, a thin cloud of white in the dark. She hugged her arms about herself as if she were cold. She was drenched in Haller's blood. He lay on the ground on his back, eyes wide, as if he had just awakened from a nightmare. Pinckney raised his gun and pointed it at Haller's head. "No," Georgia said. "He's dead enough. It's done."

Georgia looked up from the body and into the silent faces of her children. And the thing about this strange, dark family portrait she would never forget for all her days was the eyes. Georgia felt their eyes burn right into her soul. Even the dead eyes of Haller held her own in a kind of intimacy that had been impossible in life. What had been done in this stable, she knew, had been done not because it was just or right, but because it was necessary. Surely God could see there were exceptions to His Seventh Commandment. And if not, surely it was better for His wrath to be directed toward her than toward her children. Now they were waiting for their mother to tell them what must be done. Beyond the stable, on the hill, the big house Georgia had built was filled with soldiers of the enemy. But Georgia Lawshe Woods, though battered, bloodied, and heartsore, was in command.

"Bring the horse," Georgia said, "we haven't got much time." She sent George McGehee back along the path to the house to make sure the shots had not been heard. Then she helped Pinckney and Jim pull Haller's body up over the saddle, tying his hands and his feet together beneath the horse's belly. Like Cherokee, both Jim and Pinckney were now covered with Haller's blood. Georgia sent Cherokee for clean clothes. After changing, the boys were away, riding through the night to a place by the river where they had selected a gravesite. Georgia spread dirt over the bloodstains on the stable floor while Cherokee and Martha Benny searched the ground to make sure Haller's blood had left no trail from the stable. When they were sure no trace of the night's business remained, they returned to their house. Georgia put Pinckney's old pistol back in its hiding place and then went outside to pray for salvation.

Toward morning a dark storm wrapped in ribbons of light moved across the sky to the north. Being careful to keep out of sight of the great house, Georgia, Martha Benny, and the girls gathered in a grove of figs Georgia had planted when they had first arrived from Bastrop. She had planted the trees in memory of the baby she had lost so long ago and who lay among the Lost Pines. From the great house came the hard-edged sound of northerners and the easy, lilting laughter of the Negro state policemen. The women of her family stood for a moment, looking back at the stables. It was time to tell Cherokee and Sweet goodbye. There was little conversation because the plans had all been made some days ago. Cherokee and Sweet were to ride with Ed Tom back to Captain Lawshe in Water Valley. After Pinckney, Jim, and

George disposed of Haller's body, Jim Hawkins would take young Peter with him to Captain James Blair's plantation near Goliad. Pinckney and George McGehee would head up the cattle trails. Knowing that horses were the only thing of value these days, Georgia divided the horses among her children.

The new day began to glow on the horizon to the east. Georgia embraced each of her daughters. "Hurry now, it's time to go," she said. Then she whispered to Ed Tom, "Take care of my babies." Then they were gone.

In the days that followed, an intensive investigation was conducted into the disappearance of Captain Haller. Lieutenant Peterson and State Policeman Morris Norwood headed the inquiry. Rarely did a day go by that they did not order or personally conduct a search of the Woods property. Both Martha Benny and Georgia were questioned at length. After one interrogation, Martha Benny returned with blood streaming from her nose and Georgia found blue welts and bruises on her back. The night after the beating, Georgia had Old Mose take Martha Benny away.

"Just for a little while," Georgia said, as Old Mose hitched the wagon to take them back to Water Valley. "I can't imagine us being apart for long." She recalled that time long ago when Uncle Madison had brought Martha Benny and her mother to her door. "How could I have known I'd love you so?"

Now Georgia was the only conspirator left within Peterson and Norwood's grasp. She knew that they knew. It was in their eyes, and in the way they looked at her when she walked with little Frank to school. Although she had been so careful, it was just a matter of time before they came to take her away. Sometimes she wondered why they had not arrested her already. On the night of the killing, Martha Benny and Georgia had burned the blood-stained clothes Pinckney and George McGehee had worn and even the horse that had carried the blood-stained body had been scrubbed. Even Pinckney's old pistol had been thrown into a deep pool in the San Marcos River. All the evidence was gone. Yet each time the police knocked on the door, or she passed Norwood or Peterson on the street, Georgia felt the shadow of the gallows fall upon her.

When Haller failed to appear for duty, the authorities suspected foul play. His vicious treatment of civilians, especially Confederate veterans, was well known. It was not difficult to speculate he had been murdered to avenge some misdeed. Such acts of vengeance were not unusual in the years of Reconstruction. Three companies of troops were sent to search for Haller's body and to apprehend his murderers. A reward of $10,000 was offered and the State Police distributed nine hundred copies of the bounty notice. There was an extra effort to question the freedmen, who would have had a special interest in finding and convicting those who had once enslaved them. Norwood's policemen and the Union troopers went house to house, reading the bounty notice to the freedmen and promising a reward for information leading to Haller's killers.

On July 14, 1869, Georgia read the following newspaper article in the *Austin Republican*. "In Milam and other neighboring communities, many outrages and murders have been of late perpetrated upon the freedmen. Captain George Haller, a Federal officer on civil duty here, was ordered, early in June, to proceed to Milam and investigate these crimes with a view of bringing the assassins to punishment. An escort was offered him, which he unfortunately declined and he started alone. He has not since been heard from, and another officer, sent there on tour of inquiry, could not ascertain his fate. A company of troops are now on route for this disorderly region. Murders like this bring discredit and shame upon our entire state, and will continue to do so, until the people hunt these execrable assassins like so many wolves. He that harbors a criminal is a curse to the State."

Georgia put down the paper and breathed a sigh of relief. It was fortunate they had delayed laying their trap until the night Haller departed for Milam. In this way, his absence had not been officially noticed for several days, allowing plenty of time to dispose of the body. That made it seem that he had been killed miles away from San Marcos. Peterson and Norwood asserted that Haller had been killed in San Marcos, but their only evidence was that he had not said a proper farewell to them. Georgia rose and walked to the window. Again, with relief, she noticed no undue activity among the soldiers and police. But she knew it would be

a long time before the police stopped hunting the "execrable assassins like so many wolves."

One morning, as Georgia was dreaming about Tobe and Josiah and the long road the family had traveled from Fort
Hawkins, there was a sound at the door and Georgia's heart
turned to cold stone. She knew it was Peterson or Norwood
come to take her away. She knew her life was over and she could
feel the chill of the dungeon and the sound of iron tumblers falling. The door opened, and suddenly the day was golden and her
whole being worshiped in the temple of her Colonel-Doctor's
arms.

Alone later, Georgia and Peter chased memories through the
night. "Do you remember that backwoods dance on our way to
Texas?"

"We danced."

"Barefoot."

"And then we lay beneath the stars and we made love."

"I remember. I was Eve and you were the first man on earth."

"You are more beautiful to me now than you were then," Dr.
Peter said, and he asked her to dance. So they danced in the small
rude house to music in their minds. Later they made love and
they were young and alive and together again, and complete.

In the spring of 1871, Georgia watched the last Yankee soldier
leave her house to march down the hill and out of her life. Slowly,
almost fearfully, she walked up the wide front stairs, onto the
porch, and through her front door. The oak floors were filthy and
scarred. Draperies and curtains were in rags. It looked as if a bed-
lam of maniacs must have dwelled in the house. The rooms were
filled with empty crates and discarded machinery and gear and
clothing. On some walls there were messages painted, names
and dates and brief, profane essays abandoned to the wainscot
and woodwork. Georgia walked through the vacant rooms and
decided that maybe it was time to redecorate anyway. She had
grown rather tired of the subdued, subtle tones, the ivory and
creams and whites of the days before the war. She walked faster
as fragments of a new decor blossomed in her mind. Exuberant
colors. Bold, bright rooms. She grew more and more excited

thinking of the great weddings that would be held in the house. Soon Lovie, Cherokee, and Sweet would be coming back, and they would fill her house with love and life and children. She rushed to a back room filled with army cots and cartridge cases, and she threw open a window and called Martha Benny's name, twice, three times. Then, of course, she remembered that Martha Benny was gone. For a moment she felt an immense and engulfing wave of loss. The great empty house seemed to spin, and she had to hold onto a sill to keep from falling. She waited until her dizziness passed to square her shoulders and search for the broom. Later she would go to the garden to cut fresh flowers for the dining room.

By summer the house was well on its way back to its former glory. The former slaves had been given their own plots of land and the first vegetables were being harvested by the freedmen. On Georgia's land, fields of cotton, wheat, and barley created great geometric patterns upon the earth. Soon the children would come home and the family would be together again after the long nightmare of the war and the strange war that followed the war.

In August, as Georgia was supervising the placement of new floral wall coverings in the parlor, the Colonel-Doctor came home with Reverend Andrew Jackson Potter on his arm. For a moment, Georgia thought the old sinner was drunk, then she realized he was weak from illness. She hurried to his side and helped the Colonel-Doctor carry him to a guest bedroom.

"Consumption," Colonel-Doctor said. "Quite serious. But I think if he rests, he'll recover."

Georgia threw herself into the care and feeding of the former "ringleader of sin." She read to him from the Bible and supervised the preparation of his meals and she bathed his forehead in cool water when his coughing spells grew severe. In a few days, Reverend Potter was again well enough to quote Scripture and tell lies.

Here she was once again, listening to the wild, fascinating tales of Andrew Jackson Potter. From his bed he would retell the Gospel stories, Heavenly tales told in his own rich and passionate earthbound vocabulary. Georgia was sure she could listen to him talk forever. There were times, when he paused, that she wished to tell him about Captain Haller and the grave beside the river. It would be a kind of confession, a purging of the terrible guilt she carried. But she never did confess. Not when she was nursing Reverend Andrew Jackson Potter. Not after he had recovered enough to resume his preaching. Nor even months later when her temperature began to rise in the late afternoon or even when she began to lose weight and see bright red blood on her handkerchief.

Georgia knew she was dying and she was almost as angry at death as she had been at the Yankees. She was also embarrassed that she could be taken so young, and when those she loved came to see her she wanted to apologize for her ungracious, if not vulgar, behavior. Her spacious house soon filled with family. Old Captain Lawshe was summoned from Water Valley, bringing Lovie, Cherokee, and Little Sweet. Jim Hawkins brought Peter Junior from Captain Blair's plantation and was constantly at her bedside. All her children who had been scattered by Haller's death were reunited by what she now knew were her own last hours. Georgia remembered Josiah's story about the time Benjamin Hawkins called all his family and friends to his deathbed and then, having said his goodbyes, miraculously recovered. Georgia thought maybe she would survive like her grandfather and live to see the weddings of her daughters. Then she would feel life slipping away.

The last three people Georgia saw were Martha Benny, her cousin and friend; Ed Tom, her friend and half brother; and Peter Cavanaugh Woods, her husband and lover. Martha Benny's blue Hawkins eyes were awash with tears and even the tears seemed blue as they fell. Georgia kissed her husband's poor destroyed hand. Then she remembered the painting she had seen along the Trail of Tears when she was so very young: the young Indian girl holding the white bird gently in her two hands, as if she were afraid both of hurting the bird by holding it too closely and of losing it by not holding it tight enough. Georgia Lawshe Woods, granddaughter of Benjamin Hawkins, let herself become that beautiful child. She slowly opened her hands, and the white bird was free.

Idella

When Idella finished telling about Georgia's death, I could see her tears glistening in the candlelight. Somehow I had thought a medium would be, almost by definition, emotionally removed from those she contacted in that strange other world that seems to parallel our own. But here was Idella, a black fortune-teller, a descendant of slaves, weeping at the remembered death of my great-grandmother. She seemed depleted, as if she had given part of herself in the telling and was now empty as a blind man's eye. Her breathing was shallow. She was very still sitting there in the candlelight. I remember being unexpectedly uncomfortable in her presence. Somehow I felt unworthy, in the way I imagine pilgrims feel when they encounter a holy presence in the mountains. There was an almost desperate desire to please, to demonstrate a belief in her powers. Yet there was a corresponding fear that Idella, with her second sight, might see terrible things within my soul even I had never seen. But then, wasn't that why I had come to Idella in the first place? I had asked her to find what was hidden. I couldn't very well expect her to disclose only what I wanted her to see.

I asked Idella what she said to people when she looked into their future and saw death.

Idella lifted her eyes and smiled. "Darlin', we all are dyin'. Some just a little faster than others."

"If I were going to die tomorrow, would you tell me?"

"You'd know."

"I mean an accident. Something sudden like that."

Idella seemed to shrink in her chair and her long sigh made the candle flame dance. "I'm just an old woman who can see both ends of time. Don't be makin' more of these things than there is."

"How did you know about Haller?"

"A killin' is the easiest thing to know. There's nobody more willing to tell his story than a murdered person. You can hardly keep 'em quiet. They set up such a hullaballoo and clamor in the spirit world it's hard to hear about the more quiet things." She was silent for a moment as she looked into my eyes and apparently saw the traces of skepticism there. "Besides, some folks have always known." She nodded toward the river where Pink Rosebud's house of ill repute once stood on the bank. "Haller used to spend some time over at Pink Rosebud's with a girl named Precious Honey Child. And sometimes when he was in his cups he'd tell her about Miss Cherokee. Those girls over there knew he was after Miss Cherokee and they knew how that would set with your family."

"Was Ed Tom Captain Lawshe's son?"

"There's some things I promised not to say."

"Who'd you promise?"

"People dead now. A promise made to somebody on the other side is sacred."

In our family we have always known that Georgia and Martha Benny were cousins. My research had uncovered death certificates for both Martha and Jim giving their father as Madison Hawkins, Georgia's uncle. The story that Ed Tom was old Captain Lawshe's son was harder to track down. It was just something whispered between the lines of family myth. When Georgia died, and when many of the older people in our family died, at their funerals the front rows traditionally reserved for the family were filled with mourners both black and white. This mutual mourning of family has been going on for three generations. It is simply understood, a wordless, unremarked observance of a blood relationship more than a century old. How close we have been, Martha's people and mine, in spite of a gulf between us wide as the mind.

I continued to press Idella about the source of her powers, and she told me about Softfoot Willie. Every child in Central Texas who ever saw shadows moving on the bedroom wall at midnight was certain it was Softfoot Willie coming to rob the house. Yet, around town there was this feeling we had that Softfoot Willie was a benign presence, primarily because he never hurt anyone and everything he took was always returned. Euphemia's daughter Annie said Softfoot Willie was like Robin Hood, except he took from the rich and gave it back again, an improvement, she said, over the Republicans, who took from the poor and kept it.

Idella continued her story about Softfoot Willie. "You remember I said the High Sheriffs used to come and sit with me here in this room? Well, when they was lookin' for a suspect or wanted to know who done what to whom, I'd help them all I could. And over the years, the Sheriffs caught a pretty good lot of crooks that way. But they never caught Softfoot Willie and the main reason was I never told on him ever."

"Did you know him?"

"I knew him since I was a child. Born in the same settlement between here and San Marcos. And the reason I never turned him into the High Sheriffs was, we was in cahoots, me and Softfoot Willie. I guess over the years he hit just about all the rich folks in San Marcos. Then he'd hide what he stole and tell me where. When the Sheriffs came callin', I'd go into a trance and tell them where the stuff was."

"Idella!" I was astounded. "That's . . ."

"No it's not, Darlin'. We didn't diddle nobody. Everybody got their stuff back, they rubbed shoulders with the spirit world and got a good story to tell to their friends. And the High Sheriffs got reelected. I earned a little money to keep the wolf from the door, and old Softfoot Willie mooched a piece of the pie."

I was terribly disillusioned and I supposed it showed.

"I'm tellin' you this, Darlin', because I don't want you to think I'm more than I am. I have to tell myself about Softfoot Willie every once in a while so I don't get all puffed up about the little bit I can see others can't. There's some things I know for sure. Some things I don't. Sometimes you can't tell the difference between what's real and what's not. Sometimes you can't tell the difference between what's alive and what's dead. Or what's past and what's future. Or what's inside you and what's outside and only seems inside. Everything in this world is all one piece. It's spirit and flesh and past and future all rolled together, like holy dough risin' through time."

I asked Idella if she learned her fortune-telling from the gypsies.

"Darlin'," Idella laughed. "Do you suppose the eagle learned to fly from the sparrow?"

For five nights I returned to hear Idella tell the story of my great-grandmother Bettie. From Idella's window I could see the house on Court Street where Bettie King had lived most of her life, where my mother now lives and where I spent my child-hood. It once was a grand house on the road out of town, but now Seguin has grown to surround it. The house, with its white columns and flower gardens, seems to grow smaller with time. The lands, the pastures, the fields are covered now by suburbia. Only the old weathered barn still stands, partially hidden by hackberry trees. Just down the hill, by the King Branch, is the house where Euphemia Texas spent the last years of her life.

I asked Idella if she would like to come visit Bettie's house. We could look through the boxes of photographs of Bettie King's life, and perhaps she would feel the presence of the woman who lived in the rooms so long. Idella said she had lived within sight of the King place most of her life and she had known my great-grandmother well. "I don't suppose the walls of that house can keep Bettie King inside. I suppose she's as alive out here as in those rooms over there." It seemed a strange thing to say, and then I remembered what old Abraham Lincoln Miller told me one late afternoon when I was very young. I was out by the side of the house, watching Abe trim a trellis of roses. In the distance, a storm was moving across the prairie. Occasionally we could see a vein of lightning in the cloud and heard the low growling of thunder. "You know that story about Miss Bettie?" Abe asked.

I told him to go on and tell it his way.

"Miss Bettie was terrible afraid of storms. When one would come, she'd go in that very back bedroom where you live now. She'd hide in the corner and pray. You hear that thunder yonder? Well, when a storm comes, if you look in the corner of your room, you will see Miss Bettie's ghost standin' there askin' the Lord to let the storm pass on by."

I flew into the house where my mother was washing dishes. I told her Abe said Grandma King was a ghost, and when there's thunder and lightning I'd see her standing in the corner of my bedroom. I could tell this ghost story made my mother angry. "Well," she said, "I hope you do see her because she was the loveliest person you could ever know. And if you see her standing there be sure to tell her who you are."

Now I was at Idella's again. It was dark and I was about to visit a ghost I had never seen in the corner of my room or the corners of my mind. "Give me your hand," Idella said, "and I'll tell you about a good woman."

There is no way, I thought, *that Idella could know Bettie King's secret. How could she know about the terror and the wolves and the dead children?* But as the house grew still and Idella closed her eyes and the candle cast its ghostly shadows and her melodic voice rose above the sound of a distant train passing, it was with the terror that Idella began.

3

Bettie Moss King

On September 8, 1875, the master of the old clipper *Mary Celeste,* outward bound from Tangier, observed a strange silver ring around the moon as it rose above Dakar and the Cape Verde reef. In his log he noted the prevailing south wind had backed to the southeast and the glass was falling. By morning the sea had begun to rise and the sails strained under a freshening breeze.

The next day the tropical depression had been swept westward by the trade winds. A great wheel of clouds, some two hundred miles across, began to revolve around a core of rising warm air. Slowly the wheel turned toward the west, picking up speed as it passed forty degrees west latitude and moved toward Barbados and the Windward Isles. The column of swirling air rose some forty thousand feet and a band of rain began to spiral toward the storm's center. Now the seas were nearly thirty feet high with great rolling crests of spray, froth, and foam. The maturing storm hurled its fist through the Caribbean, uprooting trees and tearing down towns in Jamaica with massive tides and winds of nearly one hundred miles an hour. By now the tempest was being called "Huracan," after the god of West Indian storms.

The hurricane whipped into Galveston Bay and across Redfish Bar, then on across the bars of the Brazos and the San Bernard rivers and into the shallow brown estuaries of Matagorda Bay. In the early morning of September 16, at the thriving Texas seaport of Indianola, it began to rain. By noon the air was so filled with a deluge of rain and spray that it was difficult to breathe. The streets were flooded with huge breaking waves. Soon surge tides and terrible winds began to dismantle the town, building by building, rooftop by rooftop, house by house, dream by dream, and the people were swept away and drowned by the roiling sea.

The voracious storm turned northward, cutting a swath through the coastal prairie and uprooting ancient cypress in the river bottoms and spawning tornadoes that spiraled downward like mythic serpents from the black parent cloud.

On the Guadalupe River, near the town of Seguin, a little girl named Bettie Moss watched the black lid of day turn and tremble and groan. The air was heavy, a dark yellow throbbing with green sinews of lightning. There was a sound in the air like a stampede of Texas Longhorns, and it seemed the house squirmed in the grasp of some monstrous hand. Bettie Moss watched as a twisted cloud coiled down from the gloom. It came down, this thing, closer and closer to the earth, until it licked the woodland and trees splintered and flew into the air and into the gray mouth of the storm. It seemed the cloud hesitated in its fury, searching for some new morsel to consume. Then, as Bettie watched, the black tongue of cloud moved closer, swaying, undulating darkness, and in one terrible moment Bettie knew she too would be eaten by the storm.

Her father pulled her from the window and they rushed to join her mother and her brothers and sister huddling in a corner away from the windows in the east bedroom. They held on to each other and there was a rush of sucking wind that seemed to pull the air from Bettie's lungs. She clutched her parents with all her might and still it seemed she was being pulled away, toward the walls. There was an eerie howling all around her, the sounds of screaming children, and shattering glass and of Longhorns thundering across the roof.

By nightfall, the world along the Guadalupe was still as a crypt. The great storm had passed the Moss farm by and had moved northward to die. Bettie and her family crept from the house and they looked around as if they had been delivered, house and all, to a new world. In the gathering darkness they could see a path cut through the forest. The tornado must have come right toward their house, stripping away everything in sight. Then it veered to the west, carrying away fences, crops, corrals, trees, and the small barn where Ole Mule had been. Bettie imagined the storm had eaten her friend Ole Mule, had been sat-isfied, and then had turned to travel toward where the Braddocks lived several miles away.

When Leonard Moss saw they were all alive and uninjured and the house still stood, he bowed his head and thanked God for sparing his family. Then he surveyed the terrible damage the storm had done and his eyes followed its path to the west. "We better see about the Braddocks," he said. "I've got a bad feelin'."

"I guess you won't be takin' Ole Mule," Mollie said. "Storm already has. But you better take Bettie along. Don't know what you'll find, but two are better than one no matter what. Besides, Mrs. Braddock might need tending to and you'll need Bettie there. I'll stay with the young ones and try to make the house liv-able by the time you get back." Leonard and Nuge were sent down to the log shanty where old Ursie had lived since she was freed. They were told to ask if she needed help and to tell her the family was safe. Bettie looked out toward the Braddocks' where the storm had gone. She wished she could stay home and climb in her bed and forget the terrible sounds the storm made when it came by.

Leonard Moss gathered a lantern, his rifle, and an axe. Mollie filled a sack with bread and cheese, matches, a knife, and a change of dry clothes for both her husband and Bettie. "There'll be snakes," she said as she kissed them goodbye.

It was fully night now. The lantern cast their shadows on the saturated pasture, which was as much water as earth, islands of grass in what seemed an endless sea. Bettie watched her shadow and wished it was as large as her father's. He seemed to move so easily over the wet ground, while she had to struggle to keep up. She was afraid if her father and the circle of lantern light passed her by she might be lost forever in the night. She had been to the Braddocks' many times, but never in the dark. She decided fa-thers must have eyes that see clearly at night, like cats or owls. Fathers, in fact, had many powers ordinary people did not have. *Maybe,* she thought, *it was because God made them first.* Obvi-ously, children were made last of all and that is why they could not see in the dark and why they were afraid of it even though mothers said there was nothing there to fear. Suddenly, she found herself falling behind again and her heart skipped and thumped and she ran to catch up and she grabbed a handful of Papa Leonard's shirtsleeve to hold on.

They moved beyond the pasture and meadow into the woods. The live oaks rose like gnarled old giants on all sides. Occasionally the lantern would reveal a gash of white where a limb had been torn away by the wind. They passed a tree set afire by lightning and was still smoldering in spite of the wetness all around. Beyond and through the trees, lightning cut random wounds through the dark. Once, when the pathway narrowed through the trees, an owl screamed and in that instant before Bettie figured out it was not a fiend or an old maniac with an axe, her grasp on her father's sleeve nearly sent them both to the ground. "Storm's got the animals upset," Leonard Moss told his daughter. "Storm tears down their homes just like ours."

After walking for what seemed like hours, they heard the first wolves. The heavy air muted the sound, a chorus of sustained and sliding notes against the low, distant drumming of thunder.

They came to a spool bedstead hundreds of feet from the house. Farther along were a washtub and the kitchen table. The table seemed in perfect condition except for a table fork driven deep into the wood, the tines emerging on the underside. They heard the wolves, closer now. They moved cautiously through a ruin of shattered boards and tangled bedding. It was as if an angry giant had assailed the homestead with an axe and a maul. Nothing they saw looked anything like a house. And when they found the three children, they did not resemble the small human constructions of carbon, flame, and shadow that had been the Braddocks: Nathan, Reba, and Grace. Their bodies were crushed and torn and scattered on the earth like castaway dolls. As Bettie held the lantern high, Leonard Moss examined each child for signs of life. Certain that no life lingered, he moved the bodies together and covered them with a single quilt the storm had spared. Then they continued the search through the wreckage for Minerva and Milton Braddock. Soon they found them far from the foundations of the house, locked in each other's arms beneath a heavy ruin of timbers. Milton Braddock was dead. His wife was unconscious but still breathing.

Leonard Moss set the lantern down and motioned for Bettie to help him remove the timbers. The heavy rains had turned the field into a sea of mud, so slick it was impossible to maintain footing. The timbers would not budge. Leonard Moss grasped Mrs. Braddock's arms to pull her from beneath the wreckage but her husband's encircling arms held her fast. Leonard had to pry them loose before he could drag the woman free. Bettie wondered if it might have been better to let Mrs. Braddock sleep in her husband's arms, free of the terrible knowledge that all her family had been killed by the storm.

The three living people were alone in the light the lantern made in the center of the night. The broken woman, the exhausted man, the terrified child. "Got to get help, Bettie," Leonard Moss said. "Can't just let her die." He looked out into the darkness where the wolves were gathering. "Can't just leave 'em for the wolves."

Bettie helped her father build a huge fire from the wreckage and then drag Mrs. Braddock and her dead family into the small circle of firelight. Bettie was numb with dread. The bodies were all broken and stiff, and when Mrs. Braddock breathed, flecks of blood crept to the corners of her mouth. Bettie was profoundly afraid. "She will die anyway," she wanted to scream and she was then as ashamed as she was afraid. "Can't Mother do it?" she pleaded, knowing what the answer would be.

"There's no time to go back and get her. Anyway, she has to stay with the little children. You'll just have to do it. Keep feeding the fire. The wolves won't come near if you keep it burning high." He knelt beside her and held her and then kissed her cheek and the back of her hand. "You'll be fine. I won't be gone long. You're a strong girl and I know you can do this important thing."

Then her father was gone, swallowed by the night. Bettie was alone with the dead bodies of Nathan, Reba, Grace, and their father. Mrs. Braddock groaned, and the thought that she might wake and see the bodies of her family added to the terrible thoughts bounding around in Bettie's mind like demons out of control. What if the dead should wake? What if their ghosts rose from the mounds of flesh by the fire? What if the storm came back? And what of the wolves? She had seen the Braddocks' sheep after the wolves had feasted and she tried not to look into the night where the wolves' eyes reflected the light of the fire.

It might have been five minutes or a lifetime after Papa Leonard had left her alone when the sky opened and the rain began again. Bettie could hear little explosions of steam as the drops hit the hot embers of the fire. Although the rain itself was warm, Bettie felt her whole being grow cold with a new fear. What if the rainwater put out the fire! Already she could see the circle of firelight was smaller than it had been when her father left. Somehow, she had to build the fire up again. She remembered the fallen chimney in the wrecked house near where they had found little Grace. The roof and walls were gone but she had seen wood still stacked by the fireplace. It would be dry and already cut to a size she could carry. Bettie lighted the lantern and moved away from the fire. Stepping beyond the firelight was like leaping from a cliff, like stepping from safety into the void. As she moved toward the place where she knew dry wood would be, she began to actually see the wolves pacing in the darkness. She swung the lantern at them and saw them jump back, before glaring at her with jeweled eyes. Bettie found dry wood by the wrecked fireplace, a plentiful supply if she could only carry it back to the fire. The rain was falling harder now and the wolves had begun to circle.

Bettie knew she had to make a decision. If she continued to carry the lantern, it would take forever to carry enough wood to keep the fire going through the night. But if she put the lantern down to free both hands, her protection from the wolves would be gone. She raised the wick of the lantern to provide as much light as possible and set it high on the ruined fireplace. Now there was just a few yards of darkness to traverse between the fire and the lantern-light, only a small band of night ruled by the wolves. Bettie began to haul the wood through the rain and darkness, from one island of safety to another. At first the wolves stayed at a distance, watching, waiting, pacing. Soon they moved closer. Bettie could actually see their shaggy gray coats, their mean eyes, and their open jaws. When she stepped from the lantern light, she walked slowly and deliberately, as if to show the wolves she was master of the situation. But with each trip, her resolve and her courage began to diminish and she walked faster and then broke into a wild run for the firelight. The wolves growled and yelped and moved still closer. But little by little, as she carried more and more wood to her friend the fire, the flames began to overpower the rain. Bettie slumped to the ground by the dead Braddock children to catch her breath. They were lying on their backs and the rain had washed their faces clean and slicked their hair back. They looked freshly scrubbed for dinner rather than for the grave. Mrs. Braddock had not moved or made a sound. Bettie was sure the woman had died.

Bettie decided to make one last trip for wood. She moved to the edge of the firelight and with her heart racing and nearly faint with fear, she ran through the darkness to the chimney. As she was reaching for the last of the wood Mr. Braddock had cut and split, she was amazed to see, by the lantern-light, that the ground around her had begun to move. It was as if something beneath the earth was turning and writhing. She held the lantern closer to the ground and she realized with a horror so profound she felt bile rising in her throat, that she was standing in a roiling mass of snakes driven from their lair beneath the ground by the storm and rain. In a panic, she dropped her load of wood and leaped away from the snakes. Immediately a wolf snapped at her skirt, tearing away the cloth. Bettie screamed and leaped again to grab her lantern. She swung it around as a second wolf lunged at her, and there was a sharp pain in her arm as the lantern and wolf crashed together. The lantern came apart and a howling filled the air as the wolf was enveloped in flames fed by the spilled fuel. The flaming wolf bolted away and the pack scattered in confusion. The burning oil had cleared a thin path through the snakes and Bettie bounded toward the safety of the bonfire, screaming with revulsion each time she felt the soft, squirming bodies beneath her feet.

The hours passed. Each minute was a lifetime. The little girl listened to the howling of the wolves and shuddered every time she thought of the serpents beyond the firelight. At long last, she saw lanterns moving in the distance and familiar voices calling in the night.

How dear they were, these shapes moving in the darkness.

The stocky Agustin Flavio, the Mexican who worked with her father; the tall, angular Moses Miller from the Negro family who farmed the land just to the south; his son, her young friend Abe Miller; and her father's familiar form. She saw her father raise his rifle. The rifle barked, a wolf screamed, and the pack disappeared in the darkness. Sobbing softly, she was in her father's arms. Agustin and Moses began loading the bodies onto a cart. "Miz Braddock's still warm," Agustin said, as he gently laid her body by her husband's. Leonard scattered the fire and they started walking through the fields toward home. Abe walked very close and it was good to feel her friend that near.

In the black of night, Bettie felt she had been forgotten. Now she found herself on the outside of the unfolding drama, a character who had been briefly center stage and now was left in the wings as the women washed and laid out the dead. Mollie and Mrs. Siney Berry, who had come from the Turner farm on the creek to the east, undressed the Braddocks and washed each body with soap and water. Two of the children had compound fractures and the women gently pushed the shattered bone back beneath the skin and washed the clots of blood and earth from the wounds. Soon other neighbor women came to help prepare the Braddocks for burial. Two of Bettie's best friends, Adda Gordon and Cayloma Terrell, came with their mothers.

The Braddock children's clothes were torn and stained with blood. Since the Braddocks were nearly the same size as Bettie, Adda, and Cayloma, the three girls had gathered their own clothing for their dead friends to wear to their funeral. It was not an easy thing to do, for each girl had only one good outfit, a dress she wore only to church. But they gave them for Grace or Reba to wear to Heaven. Bettie's eyes filled with tears when her mother began to dress little Grace and she went outside where Agustin was building coffins from rough lumber.

The neighborhood folk gathered to bury the little family. They walked to the Braddock place, to a grove behind the ruins where Moses, Leonard, and Agustin had dug five graves in the soft earth. Bettie wept to think a whole family had been wiped out so quickly. Here in this place where she had played and wrestled and dreamed with her friends there was now only silence and sorrow. *Only two days ago, this place was filled with life. How quickly death comes,* she thought, and she vowed never to let it sneak up and catch her unawares as it had done to the Braddock family. She glanced toward her sister Nuge, her brother Leonard, and the baby, Frank, as if to embrace them with her vow.

The torrential rains accompanying the storm had filled the rivers and creeks to overflowing so they could not summon the preacher who lived on the other side of the Guadalupe. So when the bodies were laid by the graves, Leonard read a psalm from the family Bible saved from the ruins of the Braddock home.

"For as Heaven is high above the Earth," he read, "so great is the Lord's mercy toward them that fear him. As for man, his days are as grass: as a flower of the field, so he flourisheth. For the wind passeth over it, and it is gone; and the place thereof shall know it no more."

First they lowered Mr. and Mrs. Braddock and then the children, Nathan, Reba, and Grace. Then they covered them with earth. Bettie's father said another brief prayer and then the living walked back to the Moss farm, their days like grass, their lives as flowers in the field.

"Pet! Pet! *Pet!*"

Bettie sighed exasperatedly. She was eighteen now, and the great storm had passed long ago. Instead of wolves, her mind was full of cows. Her favorite, Pet, had not come in from the pasture with the others.

"Pet!" she called again. She rattled the feed pail, but now the cow was nowhere to be seen.

"Have you seen Pet?" she asked Frank.

"Yes, I have. Fine cow," her brother said.

"Don't be funny."

"I'm not being funny."

"I mean today!" Bettie wondered why Frank was so peculiar.

"No, I haven't seen the cow today. I can't keep track of that stupid animal every minute."

Bettie sighed again, and when the chickens and pigs had been fed and watered, she left Frank to do the milking, and went back into the pasture to find the missing cow.

She moved out beyond the corncrib and past the big oaks, and over the fence where in another season they gathered dewberries. She could hear the familiar sounds of home in the distance, her mother's laughter, the voices of her brothers and sisters, the conversation of dishes, the iron clatter of the pulley above the well. As she listened to the music of the voices from the house, she observed the absence of bass notes. Her father and brother Leonard were off in the sand and brush country of southeastern Guadalupe County hunting for wild, unbranded cattle. The capture and sale of such wandering stock had made the Maverick family rich, she had heard her father say. Henry King had ridden with them. He was the son of Euphemia Texas Ashby King. People said that just one look from her eyes could quail a bandit, but Bettie didn't know about that. She did know that she thought Henry King was the most dignified man she had ever seen.

The sun slipped behind a pillow of clouds and Bettie shivered from a chill in the air, and she thought of pumpkins and the clean fragrance of mesquite burning in the fireplace. It came as a shock to her that the long summer season was nearly over. As she walked out beyond the corncrib and past the big oaks, and over the fence where sunflowers swayed, the summers of her life came flooding back like dreams or the chorus of a half-forgotten song.

She remembered times, especially on Saturday mornings in spring, when the Guadalupe River bottoms beyond the Moss fields were filled with Apache and Yaqui scouts searching for the silver Sing Lee had taken from the Lost Tayopa Mine. Jean Lafitte was there, as well, his ship moored to a cypress tree, his cannon trained on the woods where old Henry McCulloch and Sarah McClure and Sam Houston had been seen preparing an assault. On any given Saturday, Bettie Moss might be Jean Lafitte while Adda Gordon was the beautiful bride he had captured on her wedding day. Cayloma would be an Indian princess. Nuge would be dead, killed by a Yaqui arrow.

The search for and recovery of the Lost Tayopa Mine treasure was just one of the adventures the four fast friends lived in the long golden hours of spring and summer. They would meet almost before day, when the air was still cool, when they had the world to themselves. They would disappear for the entire day, wandering the byways of their imagination. Their half-dreamed, half-lived adventures took them through the vast pasture of wildflowers that belonged to them alone and to the bull that stood in its center, the great Minotaur, guarding the way to the river. Their odyssey took them into the barn where they hid in castles of hay and into the attic where Mollie's wedding dress awaited the ladies of King Arthur's court. Bettie would be Guinevere, Cayloma became Sir Gawain, Adda excelled as Lancelot. Nuge would be dead, killed by the Black Knight's lance.

The four girls were inseparable. Bettie remembered in particular their thirteenth year. Cayloma and Adda were Bettie's age and in the same class at school, where their teacher was Mr. Nat Benton, the handsome nephew of the old Texas Ranger Henry McCulloch. Of the four girls, only Nuge, who was two years younger, was not absolutely and everlastingly in love with the dashing and sophisticated Benton, a man who not only had the blood of heroes in his veins, but had even been to the city of New Orleans.

It was difficult to say which of the girls was most attractive. Cayloma was striking, tall, with fine, near-perfect features. She walked and moved gracefully, having missed the awkward stage through which tall girls her age often pass. Adda Gordon had blonde, sun-streaked hair, and seemed beframed in a golden nimbus of light. Her small, athletic body was constantly in motion and she was nearly always smiling, as if she had a secret she wished to tell. Except for the two years' difference in their ages, Bettie and Nuge could have been twins. Both were reed-thin like their father, yet possessed their mother's regular features and warm, ready smile. Both Nuge and Bettie were unfailingly erect, their mother having warned that most of the illnesses and complaints of the world are caused by the failure to hold the spine straight, either walking or at the table. Their hair was a certain unremarkable brown, the only color Bettie knew that didn't have a name, a shade not unlike the color of the quicksand in Big Rocky Creek. Of the two girls, Bettie seemed the leader, not just because of her age, but because of a buoyancy, an energy, that animated her every move. In her bearing there was an eagerness, as if she could hardly wait for the next moment to present its gifts. Nuge was a quieter child. She seemed to contain a stillness, a willingness for the moments to pass in their own good time.

There was something in the chemistry of these four girls, a balance that made their time together a kind of music. They were each notes in a composition, one incomplete without the others. Rarely did they fight or disagree, and their moments of anger were brief and easily discarded.

When the girls were alone in their world, whether the barn, the attic, or the green hallowed stillness of the Guadalupe bottoms, they wove imaginary lives for the people they knew, especially such intriguing and mysterious people as Nat Benton and

Idella, the Negro girl they said had second sight. Idella was about Bettie's age, yet she seemed infinitely older and wiser, and often, when people in the county lost a ring or something of value, they would seek out Idella, and she would close her eyes and see the item and tell them where it could be found. The girls spent hours hiding things, then taking turns pretending to be Idella, seeking to develop her second sight.

If only they had her powers! Then maybe the future wouldn't seem so mysterious—so troubling and alluring at the same time. They often sat together, wondering what lay beyond tomorrow. Cayloma said she wanted to be an actress. "It's a way of being anything you want to be," she said. "I don't want to be just one thing."

"You'd have to leave home," Bettie said. "Go to New York, I suppose. It would be awful. Your children would be Yankees!"

"Maybe I wouldn't have children."

"You wouldn't get married?" Bettie tried to imagine a future without children.

"Maybe not. Or maybe I'd be in a family of actors like the Drews or the Booths. Oh, they had the best of both worlds! They married each other, they had a whole lot of children, and still they were famous actors."

"I don't want to leave Texas," Bettie said. She thought of her mother and her father, the wildflowers and the river, and she knew she could never leave for long. "I want to get married and have children and stay right here."

"There are other ways to live, you know," Cayloma said. "You don't have to live a life just like everyone else. Nobody's *making* you be a wife and mother."

"I know that. But it's what I want."

It had never occurred to her to be anything other than what her mother had been. She more than loved her, she admired and respected the way she managed the household and filled all the children's lives with love. *What a remarkable gift,* she thought, *to touch so many lives with your own.* What stage in New York could offer greater rewards?

As Bettie searched for the cow in the thickets by the river, she remembered how the imaginary adventures they had shared had grown less natural and less frequent as they began to feel changes in their bodies. She even knew when the turning point had been.

It was when they were thirteen. They had been taking the Gordons' turkeys to market. Adda Gordon's father was renowned for his great flocks, and each year the girls helped drive them through the fields, down Capote Road and on to the railhead in town. Before long, the turkeys had become Texas Longhorns and they were astride tough little cow ponies and headed for Kansas with Cowboy Levi Anderson's thundering herd. At great risk to life and limb, they pulled cows from quicksand and snatched calves from the gaping jaws of wolves. Soon they would arrive in town. Ahead loomed the saloon and the dancing girls and a night of debauchery. Of course, Cayloma would be the fallen woman with the stout, good heart and . . .

Bettie's thoughts skidded to a halt. Why was it so obvious that Cayloma should be the saloon girl? Then Cayloma came riding up on her white stallion, and Bettie saw, for the first time really, how beautiful she was, how her breasts shaped the cotton bodice of her dress. It was perfectly clear that Cayloma could never again be Jean Lafitte or Sam Houston or a sweating cowhand lusting for the saloon in town. Bettie felt her face grow red and she felt terribly aware of her own body. Her mind began to wonder about debauchery and all the mysterious things that waited at the end of the trail. She thought about these things with such intensity that she nearly fell off her imaginary horse.

But it was in town that the imaginary cattle drive, and perhaps her childhood itself, came to an end. As they drove the herd through the street leading to the railroad, they passed a group of boys loitering by the drugstore. At first Bettie imagined they were drovers gathered at the saloon. They called out to Cayloma, one even whistled. Then Bettie felt their eyes on her as she passed, and the horse she rode vanished and the beeves became turkeys again.

A few nights later, Bettie dreamed she had been shot by an outlaw. When she awakened, there was blood in her bed. Her mother held her and rocked her and they talked for a while. Then they cried and laughed and talked some more until it was time to get ready for school.

* * *

As Bettie searched the thickets for Pet and then moved along the creek banks, she wondered what it would be like to be married. It was hard to imagine sleeping in the same bed and touching and being together in that way Cayloma had described to her. Even the thought of a man looking at her, seeing her naked, filled her mind with confusion. For nearly half an hour, she searched and called the cow's name, but the only answer was the sharp, short bark of a coyote hunting for supper. The sound awakened a sleeping terror, and for a moment she remembered the night with the wolves and the dread began to take her over again—but then she saw Pet lying moaning, obviously hurt, in a sheltered area of bushes, beneath a river pecan.

The calf had breeched during birth. There was no telling how long Pet had been down, but she was breathing hard and no longer straining. Only one of the calf's feet had emerged. Bettie knew it was possible the calf might have died in the struggle, and she tried to remember what she had seen Agustin do when she watched him deliver a breeched calf in the spring. She fell to her knees, grasped the foot with one hand and reached into the birth passage with the other. She knew she must turn the calf. She reached for the head and touched the mouth, and was relieved when the calf began to suckle her finger. There was still life. She turned the head, found the other front leg and pulled it free. Holding both legs, she tried to pull the calf out, but it was too slippery. Then, holding the feet with one hand, just behind the joints, she guided the head with the other, turning it at an angle as Agustin had done, to prevent the hips from locking, and soon the calf was wriggling in the grass and complaining about the state of affairs in the world and Bettie felt so proud and good she wanted to shout. She dried the calf with her apron and pulled him around to Pet's head so the cow could tend her newborn miracle.

Although it had taken little more than twenty minutes, Bettie was as exhausted as Pet. For a moment she lay in the warm grass, listening to the lowing of the cows, looking up into a sky turning crimson and gold. She was trying to decide on an appropriate name for the calf when the coyote barked in the near distance, and she was again filled with terrible memories of wolves and serpents and death. But she didn't have time for that now.

Bettie leaped to her feet and ran toward home. She would get Agustin and her brothers to help bring Pet and the calf safely back to the barn. As for herself, something strange began to happen. As she ran, she began to feel more and more exhilarated. She had helped bring life into the world and the haunting memories of death were left behind. She ran along the creek bank to the low spot in the fence along the road. With hardly a break in stride, she put her hand on the top rail and vaulted across the fence in one smooth motion, and as she flew across the fence the cry of exultation and pride she felt at having saved the calf came hollering out in one great affirmation: "Yeaoow!" And when she landed, she came to a stop right in front of her father and her brother Leonard and the handsome, dignified Mr. Henry King on their way home from the brush country.

Never had Bettie seen such expressions of surprise on the faces of grown men. There was a silence that must have lasted at least half a day as the three men stared at the girl who had flown screaming into their midst from nowhere, her clothes, hair, and arms covered with blood. Her leap across the fence had carried her face to face with a very startled Henry King. They stood, staring into each other's eyes, he struck speechless by the wild, bloody apparition before him, she struck absolutely dumb by her own profound mortification.

Three weeks later, the following note was delivered to Miss Bettie Moss at her home on Capote Road. "Mr. Henry King would like to call on you next Sunday evening. Please do me the great honor of allowing me to visit with you and your family. With sincere regards, Henry King."

When Bettie told Adda Gordon about the note, Adda was certain a proposal of marriage was only a day or two away. Adda's mother and Euphemia Texas Ashby King were good friends and Mrs. Gordon had reported that Henry had been "rather impressed by a young woman who could fly and deliver calves, and he was eager to find what other remarkable talents she might possess."

Cayloma was even more excited than Adda. "Mr. King is as

rich as a man can be," she said. "They say the logs in their cabin are chinked with gold coins. The Kings have so much land, you could ride a horse all day and never see the end of it."

"And he's handsome," Adda said. "Very distinguished. Very tall and erect."

Cayloma stood tall and burlesqued the very proper and very upright Mr. King. "When you get married, you'll be the couple with the finest posture in Texas. You'll win awards at all the fairs."

"Really," Bettie said. "He hasn't even been to the house yet. Besides, he's Papa's friend. He's really coming to see Papa."

"Your papa's already been spoken for." Cayloma and Adda collapsed in peals of laughter and then began designing the outfits they would wear to the wedding.

On Sunday evening, Henry King appeared at the Moss home and Bettie decided the visit reminded her more of funerals than weddings. Never had she been witness to behavior quite so formal. The entire family sat in the living room, all her brothers and sisters wearing their Sunday best, their hands properly folded in their laps, their backs straight as pitchfork handles. Bettie's hair was twisted up in back, and the eighteen hairpins that held it in place were giving her a terrible headache. In her new long gown, corset, and high-laced shoes, she feared she would never leap over a fence again.

As the conversation moved from one topic to another—the weather, the crops, the need for a bridge at Sheffield Crossing, a new variety of grass seed from Africa that could survive the dry Texas heat—Bettie watched Henry from the corner of her eye, and in spite of herself could not help wondering what kind of choice he would be for a husband. *Is this the man I want to spend the rest of my life with? This handsome, proper stranger with the hazel eyes?* She noticed his brown hair was slightly receding, making him appear older than his thirty-four years. Although he seemed so stern, there was a tracery of lines at the corners of his eyes suggesting an unexpected capacity for laughter. Well, that was something, wasn't it?

At first, although Mollie did her best to keep the conversation flowing and lively, there were occasional intervals of silence, each thunderous and acutely painful. But little by little the silences were filled, and the tension in the room began to ease. Bettie was certain, however, that it would take decades and a series of miracles for her ever to be comfortable with the formidable Henry King, much less intimate. As the conversation progressed, she found herself trying to look beyond Henry's eyes, to see what he might be like inside. How astonishing that she was thinking about this absolute stranger as a husband. How could she even dream of being intimate with this person who sat across the table from her and seemed to be looking into her eyes?

She thought of the forbidden images Cayloma's whispers had painted of kisses and the mysteries love weaves in the marriage bed. As the conversation droned on around her, she studied Henry King carefully. "Mrs. Henry King," she said in her mind to test the sound, and then realized, with horror, that she had moved her lips and that he had seen what her lips had said. Bettie rose from the table, mortified for the second time in the presence of Henry King, and rushed to her room in abject disarray. She remained behind a locked door until her suitor had gone, comforted only by the knowledge she would surely never again see Henry King in this lifetime.

Bettie and the man she would always call Mr. Henry were married three months later in the house on Capote Road—along with Nuge, who, to everyone's surprise, had announced her engagement three weeks before to a prosperous young businessman named Tom Lay. Double weddings were rare enough in Seguin, everyone agreed—rarer still was any occasion as splendid as that surrounding the nuptials of the sisters Moss. "For two little country girls," Cayloma said, "you and Nuge have certainly done Capote Road proud."

Bettie found that being Mrs. Henry King was easy to get used to after all. In fact, Mr. Henry was kind, gentle, loving, and more than a good provider—he increased the yield of their land, built a large barn and horse lot, and purchased additional land for the farm. Sometimes, as Bettie was in the midst of baking a lemon jelly cake or training her sweet peas on the orchard fence or when she watched Henry driving his team in the fields, she would be struck with an almost Biblical sense of plenty. "He that tilleth his land shall have plenty of bread," the Good Book said. It was as if God had blessed them with the abundant gifts of the land.

For all the time spent with Henry and on her chores, though, just as important still was her time with her friends. Nuge, Bettie, Cayloma, and Adda would gather on Bettie's porch to visit and watch the world go by on Court Street, joined now by Mr. Henry's sister Annie, a woman of passionate and unconventional opinions for whom Bettie had a growing fondness.

A pink Seven Sisters rose bush climbed the back of the porch, and nearby a trellis of white-blossomed clematis filled the air with fragrance. The young friends sat in willow rockers made by a traveling peddler, and while mending and doing needlework or shelling peas or otherwise keeping their hands busy, as was demanded of a young Christian woman of the day, they continued conversations begun long ago when they were children. Nuge, Adda Gordon, and Cayloma were married now and so they talked of the men in their lives, and of the possibility of children and what the future might hold. Sometimes one of them would read aloud from a novel such as *Pride and Prejudice,* which they decided had been written specifically to be read aloud on a porch in Texas beneath Seven Sisters roses.

On other days, "The Girls" would talk about the events and people in town, and on this day in the second year of Bettie's marriage, the subject, as on many other days, was the legendary madam of the only Gentlemen's Club in Seguin, an extraordinary woman named Pink Rosebud.

The year before, Nuge's husband, Tom Lay, had been elected Guadalupe County Clerk, in which position he was privy to all the most savory and unsavory county intrigues. An election authorizing a free public school had been held, and though a number of citizens had offered land for the school, the ideal location, a site convenient to most Seguin residents, had been offered anonymously. Unable to let it be, the town fathers had delved into the county records—and revealed the anonymous donor to be Pink Rosebud. The clerk also revealed that Pink Rosebud had amassed many valuable parcels of land in town. A number of people in the community were enraged. How dare they consider a gift from a woman of ill repute?

Now a hearing had been scheduled to decide the disposition of Pink Rosebud's gift of land. Many felt the hearing was really to decide the disposition of Pink Rosebud.

"Poor thing," Cayloma said. "They're going to run her out on a rail and I think it's wrong. Pink Rosebud has just as much right to live here as anybody else. They might as well drive Belle Fulghrum, the dressmaker, out of town. Pink Rosebud's in business just like Belle."

"It's not exactly the same, Cayloma," said Bettie, and laughed. "One makes money putting clothes on, the other taking them off."

Annie felt the same way Cayloma did. "The funny thing is how silent the men are. You won't hear a peep from the men. It's all those prissy town women afraid their menfolks might wander."

"Well," Adda said, as she removed a darning egg from one of her husband's socks, "what Pink Rosebud does is wrong."

"Nobody's perfect."

"She isn't even close. She's about the most imperfect woman in Texas."

"So was Mary Magdalene," Bettie said. "And Jesus befriended her. Maybe Pink Rosebud is doing wrong. But it's not our business. It's God's business."

"So you would defend this prostitute?" Adda seemed shocked. "She's almost a neighbor. Can you imagine what goes on over there? And that new girl, Precious Honey Child? What kind of name is that? When you have children, are you going to let them play with Precious Honey Child?"

"Judge not and ye shall not be judged," Bettie said.

"Don't you sometimes wonder how they can do such a thing?" Annie wondered aloud.

"Or who goes over there," Cayloma added. "It's funny to try to imagine somebody like Mr. Grover or Mr. Heinke patronizing the place." The thought set all five women giggling.

"I guess they have to be with anybody. Even if they're old and fat." As their imaginations explored the possible pairings between Pink Rosebud and certain men in town, the results were so hilarious, and they laughed so loud and long, it occurred to Bettie their laughter must surely be a sin in itself.

When the laughter had subsided, Annie tried to bring the conversation back to its serious side. "I think we should say something. You know our churchwomen aren't like Mother or Ann Penn and they won't rest until Pink Rosebud is gone."

"Then you'll be the only woman in town that doesn't wear a petticoat," Cayloma laughed.

"I do, too, wear a petticoat!"

"I can sight you right now. Might as well be naked!" Once again the front porch was awash with merriment.

Bettie remembered a time when she had actually spoken to

Pink Rosebud. Bettie had been at Belle Fulghrum's shop, being fitted for her wedding dress. Mrs. Fulghrum had finished pinning her gown, and Bettie was turning before a full-length mirror, when suddenly Pink Rosebud swept in, accompanied by two liveried footmen. She had been riding and was dressed in a hunter's green riding habit with tight-fitting jacket, derby hat, and high-topped leather boots. Bettie had felt absolutely clumsy and terribly plain in the presence of this elegant and self-assured woman. Although Pink Rosebud was easily as old as Mollie, she had aged beautifully.

"Oh, I see I'm early," Pink Rosebud had said. "I'm so sorry. I have some errands. Do take your time." As she was leaving, she turned and spoke to Bettie. "And you look lovely, dear. Lavender becomes you. You are a very pretty girl." Then, out she swept, the footmen following, her gold earrings glistening in the sunlight, her perfume lingering in the air.

Bettie had never been that close to a fallen woman. She often saw Pink Rosebud from a distance, riding about the country alone or accompanied by strange and anonymous men. And once she had seen Pink Rosebud stepping from a carriage, in front of the Magnolia Hotel, her dinner gown a sensation, her two uniformed footmen carrying the long, long train. Never had there been a woman more mysterious. Despite herself, Bettie was fascinated by this woman, especially since the time they had actually spoken. She wondered if Pink Rosebud had an inner life, if she thought about her fall or even considered she had fallen at all. *Did she have regrets? Where was her family? What strange series of events had led this remarkable woman to her brothel on the banks of the Guadalupe? How strange,* Bettie thought. *There are so many paths to take through life. I'm taking the path of home and family. Pink Rosebud has chosen a path that is as far from mine as one can get.*

Or had she really chosen? Bettie wondered about the whole matter of choice. She concluded, with some surprise, that she had rarely made a choice in her life. She had not chosen Mr. Henry. It had just happened. He had seen her leap a fence and he had fallen in love. She had merely waited for her life to present itself, like a passenger waiting for a train. She wondered if she knew where her train was going, any more than Pink Rosebud had known where·hers was destined to go when she embarked on her journey so long ago.

On the day of the hearing, it seemed every man and woman in Seguin descended on City Park. Since debate would center on the notorious Pink Rosebud, the meeting promised to be the social and political highlight of the year. It was fortunate the county had the foresight to change the location of the meeting from the courthouse to the great outdoors so as to accommodate the crowd that had come to see what an editorial in the *Guadalupe Times* had called "the handmaiden of Beelzebub." So great were the crowds that Cayloma and Annie pretended Bettie had been overcome by the heat, and three gentlemen quickly made space. Cayloma winked at Annie, and Bettie was so embarrassed she thought she really would be ill.

Bettie looked over the crowd and saw dozens of people who had probably never been involved in public issues or any event devoted to the dubious art of politics. They were there, she knew, to see the infamous Pink Rosebud, a glimpse they hoped would be the last of this Jezebel who was threatening their homes and families. Mayor Zorn, standing in the gazebo, opened the hearing, outlined the subject at issue, and then called for discussion and presentations from the floor.

There was an immediate flurry of waving hands and raucous, shrill voices calling for recognition. Mayor Zorn pounded his gavel and demanded the meeting come to order. One voice, one presence, so dominated the chaos that Mayor Zorn had no choice but to recognize the gaunt legend that now rose and moved through the quieting crowd to the podium. There, his eyes on fire, was God's old warrior, Reverend Andrew Jackson Potter.

"I am here because there is a right and there is a wrong," the old man began in his sonorous grape-arbor voice. "And it is wrong for you to accept a gift of land purchased with the ill-gotten gains of a whore." The last word rang through the park like the tolling of a bell, followed by a plural sigh from the women.

The men, as one, squirmed. After a pause, Reverend Potter continued. "Here is a woman who fornicates for her daily bread, the most hideous insult imaginable to the God who created woman from Adam's rib. Frankly, I don't understand how you could have harbored this harlot in your midst for all these years. To tempt your husbands, to lead your children to temptation, to welcome iniquity into this good and holy city." Just as Reverend Potter was about to continue, from the corner of her eye, Bettie noticed a form rise and begin moving slowly to the front. So riveted were people to Andrew Jackson Potter and his sermon on the sins of the flesh that, at first, they did not see the woman approaching.

Bettie nudged Cayloma. "Look." Pink Rosebud was dressed in a simple black walking dress. She wore no paint and her hair was swept up in the soft waves of the Gibson Girl style that was becoming so popular. Although she moved with graceful elegance, there was nothing flamboyant in her appearance or her manner. She could have been a countess in exile or the mother of a major poet. She was tall and natural and splendid, and as she moved toward the podium, and as more and more people recognized her, a hush fell over the crowd and even Reverend Andrew Jackson Potter grew silent.

Then, Pink Rosebud and the preacher were standing face to face. Cayloma grasped Bettie's hand and squeezed, and everyone in attendance was waiting in numbing suspense, wearing their hearts on their shoulders like epaulets. For a long moment the two stood at the podium. Pink Rosebud's face seemed to be in repose, the preacher's countenance reflected a kaleidoscope of expression, first fury, then recognition, then confusion, then thoughtful curiosity. There was a moment when Bettie thought she even saw a glimmer of something soft and fond in his eyes, as if he remembered Pink Rosebud from another life a long time ago. Then to the amazement of the crowd, Reverend Andrew Jackson Potter, with what might have been a small bow, backed away from the podium and moved to his seat. Tom Lay would later say the preacher backed down because he probably fell in love with Pink Rosebud on the spot, as he had so often with available ladies in his youthful days of debauchery.

Now Pink Rosebud faced the crowd, which rumbled and moaned and sighed and rattled like an orchestra tuning. She stood there more alone than any person could be, and with her first words, the sound of the crowd diminished.

"This is my home," she began. Her voice was soft, yet firm. There was an ascending murmur and then silence again. "Everyone must live somewhere and I live in Seguin the same as you. I love this place. Whatever you may think of me, do know I love this town that has been my refuge, my port in the storm of life, and I would like to give something back in return." There was a snicker heard in the crowd, and then another, and then a low chorus of laughter. Mayor Zorn pounded his gavel. "Long ago," Pink Rosebud said, her voice raised now, above the chatter and hum of the town. "I knew long ago I could never have children. But I'd like to do something for yours."

"You can make things better by taking yourself and your harlots somewhere else." The voice was treble and terrible, like a sharp stone thrown. Other voices called insults while still others called for the decency to hear the woman out. But it seemed Pink Rosebud had spent all the courage she had to invest. She turned her head slightly to the side as if to evade the words and thoughts assailing her. But she remained erect and proud, though sad. Suddenly she looked older, and she stood unable or unwilling to move from the pillory of insult, as if she felt she was only receiving her due. Then, as Bettie saw the slight trembling of Pink Rosebud's shoulders, she was also aware of another woman who rose and moved to Pink Rosebud's side. Chepita, the Chili Queen, without a glance one way or the other, took Pink Rosebud's hand and, with one arm around her waist, helped her through the crowd and away.

That evening, as Bettie and Mr. Henry were sitting on the front porch watching the eyes of lightning bugs winking in the darkness, Henry asked why she thought Pink Rosebud should be protected.

"Just as the preacher said, there is right and there is wrong," she answered. "For once in her life Pink Rosebud tried to do something right and we wouldn't let her. And that was wrong. There were only two women in the park who showed any courage at all. One was a prostitute and the other a little woman who sells chili on street corners." Bettie ached for Pink Rosebud. But she also knew she ached for herself and her failure to come to Rosebud's defense. Before she went to sleep that night she prayed not only for the wisdom to know what is right, but for the courage to act on her convictions.

In the end the town fathers compromised. They did not accept Pink Rosebud's land, but they did not send her packing either. Her establishment continued to serve a need, just like Belle Fulghrum's shop, and an uneasy peace settled upon them all.

In July of 1890, twenty-five years after the South surrendered at Appomattox, the Confederate veterans of Woods 32nd Texas Regiment held a reunion in Lockhart, Texas. Since Papa Leonard's unit had fought with the Woods Regiment at Blair's Landing and Yellow Bayou, the whole family, including Euphemia and William, boarded the train at Seguin to make the short trip to Lockhart.

As the train rolled toward the northeast, Pink Rosebud's public hearing was still very much on Bettie's mind. She could not shake the feeling that her failure to act had been cowardice. But what could she have done? Public displays of courage were not appropriate for a woman of breeding. Men could fight wars, but women could only accept defeats. Bettie knew she would feel comfortable talking about these things with Euphemia, but she decided to wait until she had thought it through on her own.

When she was first married, Bettie had been anxious about her relationship with her mother-in-law, a woman she viewed with a respect approaching awe. Mr. Henry had told her all the old stories about Euphemia's friendships with Sam Houston and Juan Seguin. She had heard about how Euphemia had saved the Negro woman Tildy's life and her strange encounters with the renegade Comanche Tarantula. She knew about Euphemia Texas Ashby King's adventures, and Bettie was not sure she could meet the expectations of a legend. But with a glance, a gesture, with a few of her rare and luminous smiles, Euphemia had begun to draw Bettie close.

Bettie smiled as she remembered the first time she had felt a kind of spiritual bond with Euphemia Texas Ashby King. She and Mr. Henry had just returned from their honeymoon in San Antonio. Euphemia and William had organized an In Fair, a suppertime celebration traditionally held by the groom's family to honor the newlyweds. Euphemia and Tildy had baked tall cakes in dishpans. The men had barbecued a huge quantity of beef cooked on a pit overnight, next to washpots full of beans. Mollie and Papa Leonard, Bettie's brothers and sisters, Nuge and her husband Tom Lay, Adda and her beau Will Thomas, and Cayloma and her intended Felix Douglass—everyone Bettie loved had been there.

They were playing a game in which they tried to keep a feather aloft by blowing it from one person to another. Just when the Texas heat had driven the young people into the shadow of the elms, an apparition came wheeling down Court Street and onto the King property.

At first Bettie thought it was a child riding the strange new bicycle she had seen in magazines and newspapers. Then, as the rider drew near, she believed she was witnessing the unthinkable. The bicycle rider was a woman.

Bettie had been amused by the number of expressions that swept across the men's faces as they watched the remarkable woman come flashing into their midst. She was wearing the Turkish trousers Amelia Bloomer had made fashionable in the East some years before. She was tall and pretty and Bettie thought she seemed a part of the wind. She glided her machine to a stop, and with a smile bright and wide as a summer day, she announced that her name was Etta Mae Holtsenburger and that she was a traveling corset saleswoman. She claimed that her satchel was filled with the most fashionable undergarments west of the Mississippi.

Bettie had not been so embarrassed since the day she had delivered the calf and leaped the fence almost into Mr. Henry's arms. A woman on a bicycle selling underwear! Bettie could tell the men were torn between turning away from this shameless woman and being drawn closer by their curiosity and her beauty. She had seen Mr. Henry react the same way to wild animals.

There was something almost pantherlike about Etta Mae Holtsenburger, Bettie observed. Something wild and free and unencumbered by the weight of convention.

"Stay, gentlemen," Etta Mae had said as the men began to back away. "See what I've got for your ladies." The men's eyes moved from Etta Mae Holtsenburger to her bicycle and back again. "It's the perfect way for a peddler to travel," she said, noticing their interest in her bicycle. "Costs less than a horse. Easier, too. You don't have to feed it or give it water. What could be more practical?"

Soon, the women were examining Etta Mae's wares while the men lingered at a respectable distance, scuffing their feet and casting surreptitious glances at Etta Mae's bloomers and wheels. Bettie felt herself warming to Etta Mae. She felt a refreshing originality radiated from her every word and gesture. Here was a woman who made her own rules in the world. She did not depend on others for her transportation, she arranged her own. Here was a woman who did not depend on others for her livelihood. She made her own money, selling something other than her body, as Pink Rosebud did. Surely, she had never met a woman quite as self-confident or as free.

While Cayloma was trying to talk Felix into buying her a pair of bloomers, Bettie mustered the courage to ask Etta Mae about her home and family.

"My mother and father live in Cincinnati," she said. "But home is wherever I find myself at the moment. Right now my home is here. Tomorrow, down the road a way."

"What about a husband, children? I don't mean to be personal, but surely you'll want to settle down one day."

"I suppose I will. If the right man comes along. But there are all different ways to live a life. And right now, I love the life I have."

After the women had examined Etta Mae's stock of underwear, she offered to teach them all to ride. At first, the men were reluctant, but Tom Lay could not resist and he soon volunteered to try. With Etta Mae holding the machine upright and Tom precariously balanced on the saddle, the two went flying across the yard, faster and faster, scattering chickens and the In Fair guests. Etta Mae let go and Tom wobbled and careened wildly, before tumbling in an untidy heap by the barn. Everyone hurried to his rescue and to tend the damage that might have been done to his body or pride. After Tom's experience, no one else volunteered to ride the wheeled machine of Etta Mae Holtsenburger, the corset saleswoman.

After Etta Mae had gone, her presence remained like a fresh breeze in Bettie's mind. Etta Mae had gone riding down Court Street toward the future, but she left behind mysteries and questions and subjects for endless and animated debate, including the issue of whether it was proper for a woman to ride a bicycle or whether the activity promoted immodesty.

"Personally," Tom said, "I don't think women should ride."

"Obviously *men* can't," Annie said, reminding them all of Tom's disastrous attempt.

Bettie wondered what difference there was between riding a bicycle and riding a horse. She looked around at the women guests and counted at least ten who could ride a horse as well as any man. Six others could outshoot the sheriff, including Euphemia, who no longer did target practice but was as steady a shot as ever. As Bettie had listened to the very serious discussion concerning lady cyclists, she had caught Euphemia's eye and a special contact had been made. Bettie knew Euphemia had also been counting the number of women in the group who could ride as well as any man.

The train whistle wailed, and Bettie looked up, the sound scattering her thoughts. They were arriving in Lockhart.

As they rode by carriage to the reunion, Bettie was amazed to find so many people and so much emotion everywhere in the streets. She was aware of the quiet and almost physical sense of sorrow that pervaded the town as it filled with veterans mourning the recently dead. In one regiment, she learned, of the 1,089 comrades who entered the war in 1862, only 168 were still alive. And among them was the old man who had commanded the regiment, Colonel-Doctor Peter Woods, of San Marcos. He was accompanied by his daughter, Sweet Woods Montgomery, who, as a girl, had reputedly been the last Texan to fire shots in anger against the Yankees.

In the afternoon, after Papa Leonard had spoken with his old comrades in arms, he told Bettie and Euphemia about Colonel-Doctor Woods and how he was loved by his men. "He would have easily been a general but he wouldn't follow any order that would cause undue risk to his men. Not that he was a coward. He was the bravest man I ever knew. But he had an unusual reverence for life."

As Bettie watched the old white-haired man, she wondered that such a frail body could have once been capable of heroic deeds. Her father pointed out Colonel-Doctor Woods' son Pinckney and Jim Hawkins, the Negro who fought in the regiment with them. He also pointed out George McGehee and his wife, Cherokee. "It's a strange relationship, those four. Cherokee, the Negro, Pinckney, and McGehee," he said.

Papa Leonard was called to the front, where a photograph of the survivors was being taken. Bettie noticed that Jim Hawkins, Pinckney Woods, and George McGehee made a special effort to stand next to each other. She wondered what bound these three men so closely after all these years.

The next morning, on the Fourth of July, the old veterans marched from the Griesenbok Hotel to a stand that had been erected in town. The grandstand had been elaborately decorated by the wives and daughters of the former warriors. There were banners and ribbons and, high above the platform, the Bonnie Blue Flag rode the Texas winds as in the days gone by. When everyone had gathered at the bandstand, the old chaplain of the Woods Regiment, the Captain-Reverend Andrew Jackson Potter, offered a prayer for fallen comrades. After a speech by Governor Lubbock and a host of Confederate officers, including General Henry McCulloch, the old Texas Ranger who was now running for the office of State Treasurer, the entire assembly moved to the campgrounds at the edge of town, where a memorial would be held for the brave men who had fought under Alfred Howe Terry, John B. Hood, and Dr. Peter Cavanaugh Woods.

Darkness was falling on the little town of Lockhart when the people gathered at the campground and settled down on quilts beneath the trees. As it grew full dark, small campfires were lighted, but with no moon their fires seemed impotent against the night. Great shrouds of Spanish moss hung from the trees. The night was eerie and mournful, and it would have been absolutely still except for the shrill anthem of the cicadas. Bettie felt suspended in time. Even the children seemed to sense there were presences moving in the darkness beyond the fires.

The first to speak was Captain Ferg Kyle, of Terry's Texas Rangers. He drew a frequent comparison between his fallen leader and Colonel-Doctor Woods. "It was my fortune to know and to honor both the dead and the living here today. Both to a remarkable degree were stamped with that Saxon mark, blue and gray eyes and flaxen hair; both possessed with that same languid look when resting on friends; the same undaunted crest when confronting a foe. Our Terry came not from the battlefield. Your battle-scarred Woods was spared by a hair's breadth and is here to listen as he does. Of the two commanders, while we have the divergence, the wreath of the one is of cypress, that of the other is greenest laurel. Yet are we not again blended as we all weep for those of our comrades who rode down to death as gaily as every groom went forth to meet his bride."

Bettie was sitting next to Euphemia. She sensed the older woman was restless. When Captain Kyle offered his metaphor of death and the bride and groom, Bettie was shocked to see Euphemia roll her eyes and sigh. "You listen," Euphemia whispered. "Now comes the part about the southern woman."

Bettie turned back to the podium, where Captain Kyle began the close to his speech. "In conclusion, were I master of winged words I would be able to pay fit tribute to the devotion of southern women to the Cause that was lost. For themselves all comforts were denied, it was their wont to bestow all upon those whose loins had been fastened to the harness of the soldier." Bettie caught Euphemia's eye and struggled not to laugh.

Captain Kyle concluded with a story about a young man severely wounded at Shiloh. "He was in pain, near death, and someone called: 'Why did you come here?' Hear well his reply. He said: 'Mother told me to come.' The Spartan mother would have her boy to go with his shield and return to her with it or upon it."

The captain ended with a verse about fair fond brides of yesterday evening. Euphemia turned to Bettie and said, not too softly: "That, my dear, is why we have wars."

In March of 1891, Bettie was not thinking about wars and death, but about the mysteries of birth. Recently a significant drop in the size of the average American family had been recorded, and physicians blamed this phenomenon on the deteriorating health of women. It was widely held in the medical community that the move from rural to urban living was a major cause of women's diseases, especially "Hysteria," a disturbance of the womb first discovered by the ancient Greeks and named "Hysterikos." The rush and excitement of urban life also produced what physicians called "softening of the brain," and other diseases imperiling the physical and mental health of American women.

When Mr. Henry learned Bettie was "with child," he insisted they refrain from any intimate contact and she cease any physical exercise, including even the lightest housework. He had been advised by his doctor friends that exercise drew blood and energy away from the womb and from the developing child. In conversations with his minister, Mr. Henry had also been warned that Bettie's practice of reading romantic novels should be curtailed, for it might create uterine congestion or morbid mental states, which could bring about premature childbirth.

The reaction of The Girls was predictable.

"I'm astounded," Cayloma said, waving Jane Austen in the air, "that a man so intelligent and sensible could have such foolish ideas."

Annie agreed. "Sometimes I think men are joined in a huge conspiracy to make sure women stay the weaker sex."

"Well, men are stronger," Bettie said. "Can you plow a field? Or cut down a tree with an axe?"

"You bet your life I can!" Annie insisted. "So can you. Every woman in our family can. It's just we've been told all our life we can't. Men would rather we look pale and delicate."

"I really don't care to plow a field, thank you," Cayloma said. "Or chop down a tree. Or lift an anvil. I'm perfectly willing to concede those chores to our better halves."

Reluctantly, Cayloma closed the book Mr. Henry had warned against and she picked up her crochet. She was making a crazy-patterned afghan from scraps of thread. When she had first shown Bettie the emerging haphazard, aimless pattern, Bettie had said it matched her personality perfectly.

"I don't know if it's ignorance or meanness or what," Annie said, "but just think about this. When a person is pale, you generally think that person is ill. But for women, it's fashionable to be pallid. We're encouraged to cultivate the appearance of poor health. So men give us all this white powder to cover our faces. It's supposed to be a beauty aid, but actually it just makes us look sick."

"That's just fashion," Bettie said, as she finished mending one of her husband's stockings.

"And who makes fashion?" Annie asked. "Men, that's who. Everything they do is designed to make us appear inferior. They dress us in about thirty pounds of clothes that are so tight we can't breathe, sit, or bend over. Bound up like that we can't do anything. So they can say we're helpless. They make us wear corsets so our waists look more ladylike and our breasts and hips look more alluring. As a result we get broken ribs and all kinds of injuries. So they say we're weak."

"It's like the Chinese women binding their feet. There's permanent damage."

"Just imagine what kind of damage corsets do. I read that corsets can cause collapse of the uterus. It's so common that doctors are prescribing pessaries. Imagine having to wear one of those contraptions inside your . . ."

"Annie, really."

"It's true. You know it's true. First, they make us wear a corset on the outside so tight it collapses our uterus. Then they sell us pessaries to wear on the inside to straighten it out again! One hand sells us poison and the other sells the antidote."

"Annie," Cayloma said. "You don't even wear a corset."

"That's right. I refuse to be manipulated by the salesman and the doctors. And when I have my child, I'm going to be very careful whose advice I take. Especially men doctors who want to try out all their new modern inventions on my body."

Bettie put down her sewing. "Can't we talk about something else? Why don't you read, Cayloma?"

"And risk hysteria? Not on your life."

"I don't think you're being reasonable," Bettie said. "About men, I mean. You can't blame everything on men. Look at Mr. Henry. No man could be kinder. No man could have more genuine concern for the people he loves."

"I'm sure you're right, Bettie."

"Thank you."

"But I would ask you this," Annie said. "Your Mr. Henry advised you against exercise. Isn't that what you said?"

"Well, yes. He did."

"And what do your heart and your mind tell you would be one of the most beneficial things you could do for the health of your baby and for your own health? Do you think it's to adopt an unnatural and confining state of inertia? Or do you think it's to adopt a natural life of activity and motion?"

"So, do you want me to go dancing? Do somersaults across the lawn?"

Annie laughed. "I wouldn't be surprised if the next book of advice for young mothers doesn't have a chapter prescribing just that. There's a theory in support of just about everything else. Why not dancing and somersaults? The whirling dervish approach to childbearing!"

After The Girls had left, Bettie remained on the porch. She thought about the life she carried inside. She tried to imagine a face, a smile, the eyes of the infant whose motion she could hardly wait to feel. She wondered at what instant consciousness would come to her child. Where was that consciousness before? Was it in the stars somewhere or in Heaven? Where was the child's soul? Were there now two souls in this body? Seldom before had Bettie looked so deeply into the mysteries she had considered only in church or when she watched the miracle of a starry night or felt Mr. Henry's heart beat against hers in the charged privacy of their room. Now she thought not necessarily about God, but about life. She continued to attend church with Mr. Henry, and she read and studied the Scriptures each morning when she arose, but neither the pulpit nor the Gospel satisfied her need to know where her child's soul had been before it would waken in her womb. While such ethereal notions accompanied her waiting, so did more earthly concerns: would Mr. Henry think she was ugly and would he love her when she was big as Billy Horse? "You only grow more beautiful, day by day," he had said last night, and because of either kindness or passion he had broken his rule about physical intimacy. But still she wondered.

After a while, a cold wind began to rise. To the north, dirty clouds hung in the air like soiled laundry. It was apparent the false spring was over. Bettie shivered and went inside. Then, shutters began to pound and the lamps were set dancing by the cold drafts from beneath the windows. She could feel the old fear begin to stir somewhere in the shadows of the house, and could imagine wolves prowling in the dark corners of the room. For a while she tried to fight the terrible fear rising like a flood around her, but it entered her, as if through the pores and apertures of her body, and she was violated by a savage terror.

She ran to the bedroom, and rolled up into a ball in her bed, closing herself as tightly as possible. She could not leave the bed, she knew. There were coils of snakes on the floor and wolves were waiting in the darkness of the hall.

For two days the wind howled and Bettie remained in her room, hating herself for her weakness, yet powerless before her fear of the storm. Each time the wind screamed, or a shutter slammed, or hail hammered upon the roof, or a tree branch clattered against the eaves, her terror became actual physical pain. She would call out and Mr. Henry would come hold her and rock her like a child in the horrible embrace of a bad dream. Behind her tightly closed eyes, the faces of the wolves grinned and leered.

Bettie knew they were the emissaries of death and something dreadful was uncoiling just out of sight.

The third day after the storm began, spring returned and brought the warm sun again. Bettie crept from her room, weak, embarrassed, and ashamed, yet thankful that her prayers of delivery had been answered. Somehow she had survived another storm. She went out on the front porch half expecting the world to be in ruin. But what little damage had been done had already been set right. It was as if there had been no storm at all. Bettie questioned whether she could have dreamed the entire episode, including her very real feeling of impending disaster.

And then, at dusk, as Bettie came onto the porch to watch the sunset, she saw her friend Abe walking toward the house. When he saw Bettie, he stopped and remained standing there, dead still.

"Abe?" Bettie felt a numbness begin to move across her mind. "What is it, Abe?"

"It's your mama, Miss Bettie. She's bad sick. Your papa already went for the doctor," he said. "Your mama just keep shakin'."

Within minutes, Bettie was on her way with Mr. Henry and Abe to the Moss farm. As they rushed through the growing darkness, Bettie willed herself to fight off the slight vertigo she had felt since she had seen Abe coming down Court Street toward the house.

The Moss farmhouse was filled with the wives of tenants and with Mollie's children. Her own terrors pushed aside, Bettie quickly restored some order. She sent the children out to play or to their chores. Thanking the neighbors, she asked a few to stay and watch the children and the rest to go home to await word. Then, she turned toward Mollie's bedroom. She could hear her mother coughing behind the door.

Mollie's chill had subsided, only to be replaced by a punishing cough. Her breathing was shallow, her pulse rapid, and she was afire with fever. The cough was terrible and frequent. It was as if she were coughing little pieces of her life away. Bettie went numb with shock when she saw flecks of blood on the sheet. Mollie's eyes were red and ringed with shadow, as though she had not slept for days. Her lips were blue. She looked small and frail as a child. Bettie held her mother's hand and prayed the coughing that racked and twisted Mollie's body would cease and that Death would find some other door to enter.

Mollie's pain was so great, the grip of pneumonia so strong, she could not speak. Each time she tried, the spasm would come again, making speech impossible. Mollie's eyes were filled with pain and disbelief. Bettie kissed those eyes, then did what she could as she waited for the doctor. But what could she do? She raised the window to bring in fresh air. She lifted Mollie's head and tried to make her drink as much water as she could bear. It was obvious much of Mollie's pain was in her side, perhaps from the strain of coughing, so Bettie prepared a mustard poultice to relieve it. She administered a dose of calomel. She tried to wash away the fever with towels soaked in cold water.

As Bettie worked at the bedside, she chattered away, telling Mollie about The Girls and their lives and about the names she and Mr. Henry had chosen for the new baby. Only once did Mollie respond. There was a moment when a stillness came, like a holy blessing, and Mollie pulled Bettie's head down close to her own. "I have loved my life," she whispered. "I just wish the end of it wasn't so hard." After a moment of labored breathing, Mollie spoke again. "Take care of the little ones." Then the coughing began and a part of Bettie's heart was broken forever.

When the doctor arrived, Mollie was already dead. And all he could offer was prayer for this joyous woman who was taken at the age of forty-three to brighten an unknowable world as she had brightened the one she knew.

Now, not yet twenty-one, Bettie was not only expecting her first child but had fallen heir to five of Mollie's children as well. Leonard and Frank, the two older brothers, remained on the farm with their father. But John, Edward, Kittie, Mildred, and Ola came to live with Mr. Henry and Bettie on Court Street. They would remain for the duration of each school year, then return to spend the summers on their father's farm.

Out of the blue, Bettie's dreams of becoming a young woman of leisure, of attending performances at Klein's Opera House, of helping organize the Seguin Village Improvement Society and the Shakespeare Club and Garden Club, of enjoying the many balls and dances held by the better families of Seguin, of spending long, lovely afternoons with her friends—these dreams came asunder beneath the weight of duty and of love. Just as other married women her age were beginning to move out of their homes, Bettie was forced by circumstance back into hers. Cayloma said Bettie was the only woman in recorded history to have had quintuplets even before going into labor.

Bettie shouldered the responsibility of her family without complaint. In fact, many were the times she took great pride in her ability to create order out of potential chaos. She organized the family chores, established rules of acceptable behavior for the children and strategies to assure those rules were followed. Mr. Henry's stern and formidable countenance was often enough to dissuade errant behavior. It was rarely necessary to command a misbehaving child to do the unthinkable: to go in the yard and pick a switch. The process of finding and cutting the switch, stripping it of leaves, and anticipating the sound and the terrible sting of this monstrous device was nearly as punishing as the switching itself.

It was Cayloma who first pointed out that Bettie was the central figure in a community of family, friends, and tenant farmers that was, in number, almost the size of Gonzales, Texas, or at least the size of Luling. Once she even counted them out on paper. There was the immediate family, her father and seven unmarried brothers and sisters. There was Mr. Henry and Annie. There was Euphemia and William. Then there was Nuge and her husband, Tom Lay, as well as her dear friends Cayloma and Adda and their husbands. And on the King land were the Negro tenant farmers; Abe and Lucinda Saphronia Miller, Walter Walker, Jack Williams, Em Bean, John Franklin—and their families. There was Jack Hicklan, a descendant of Granny Boyd's slaves, and Albert McClure and his family, descendants of the McClure slaves. By actual count, Cayloma summed up, Bettie was the maternal focus of at least fifty-eight souls.

In addition to the young women Bettie had known since childhood, two others became part of her close circle of girlfriends. Both were school friends of her sister Kittie. The first was a rather serious young woman named Mary Lou Lannom, the other, Jennie Scott, Mary Lou's exuberant opposite. Jennie and Mary Lou were constantly at the King house and Bettie found enormous pleasure in their company.

The child who would always be known as "Bettie's little girl Virginia" was born on a midsummer's night in the year 1891. As the child was placed in its mother's arms, Bettie was certain she saw Mollie's soul moving through the window, a golden chimera somehow enveloping the child, then passing within. In that brief moment of joy and exhaustion, she was absolutely sure life was eternal and the transmigration of souls explained everything unknown to the human heart. She looked down at the infant's face, beautiful as a Dresden doll, the child that she and Mollie and Mollie's mother had made, and she knew instantly all there was of life and death and Heaven. It was a knowledge she would carry inside like a secret, an awareness of a life principle she would never discuss with the preacher who came to dinner one Sunday each month or even with Mr. Henry or Cayloma. God revealed Himself that midsummer night and what He revealed was continuity and kin and the flow of one human life into another. It was all very clear in that brief moment she first held Virginia in her arms, and for the rest of her life Bettie would try to bring the insight back through the veil time unfolds before the truth.

In 1894, when Little Virginia was three years old and Mr. Henry had replaced their outdoor privy with one indoors, Bettie's small, complete, isolated world on the Guadalupe was invaded by alien forces just as inconceivable and fully as troubling as the new pipes rumbling and rattling along her walls.

Running water was just one of several changes sweeping the little town of Seguin in those middle years of the 1890s. Most of the streets had been paved and a mule-drawn streetcar carried mail, freight, and passengers from the train depot down Austin Street around the city square downtown and back again. There was even some talk of an electric trolley. Thomas Alva Edison's dream of artificial light was a reality in Seguin, and at night the city glowed like a constellation of stars had fallen to earth. Bettie now had a telephone. Her phone number was 258 and she talked with one or more of The Girls each night after the supper dishes were cleared away.

Bettie was fascinated by the growth and progress of the town, by the rushing crowds and lively activities, the new stores and buildings which seemed to grow taller every day. She loved the bustle and drama of the railroad depot, the harsh, labored breathing of the steam engines, the hollow wail of the train whistle, and the frightening, thunderous squeal of the wheels when the train stopped to disgorge its travelers and drummers and all the assorted pilgrims of the new day.

Marvelous labor-saving technology had come to Seguin. But along with running water, the telephone, and electric power came a gray flood of solemn and impoverished pilgrims. They came along the railroad tracks or through the woods, like jobless, hopeless refugees, survivors of some distant disaster. Ever since the school hearing and her failure to come to Pink Rosebud's defense, Bettie had welcomed anyone who was hungry or in trouble or in need to her kitchen.

"You know why all those men stop here?" Mr. Henry asked Bettie. "It's because of the secret sign. The first time you gave one of those hoboes something to eat, he marked our fence with a sign only hoboes can read. Now our house and your kitchen are known in camps along the railroad tracks from here to California."

Bettie felt she was merely doing her Christian duty. "After all," she responded to those who warned her against opening her door to hoboes, "the Bible says, 'Be not forgetful to entertain strangers, for thereby some have entertained angels unawares.' " Now, hardly a day passed when at least one vagrant wanderer did not stop at her gate.

One day as Bettie was watching Mr. Kishbaugh measure the fireplace for a new mantel, a remarkable visitor came to call. Mr. Kishbaugh had built some fine buildings in town, but in these hard times he had agreed to build the new mantel in exchange for bacon, butter, and eggs. Bettie was talking with him about the mirror he was fitting above the mantel when it caught the reflection, through the window, of a stranger coming through the gate toward the house. He was a tall, angular apparition, dressed in an exaggerated Western costume—breeches, leggings, a fringed buckskin coat with Mexican coins for buttons, and a large black sombrero. His shoulder-length dark hair and wild unkempt beard were streaked with gray.

From the front porch Bettie told the strange visitor to go around to the back door. "You'll see there's a wash basin and soap and a clean towel. When you've washed, come on into the kitchen." Bettie never feared for her life and limb when the hoboes came to her house, but she was concerned about disease. In addition to a cauldron of fresh water, she kept on her porch a brand of lye soap so strong that Cayloma said it was dangerous. Mr. Kishbaugh continued his measuring while Bettie went to the kitchen to get corn bread, a slab of ham, beans, and a tomato for her raggedy guest.

Up close, the stranger looked even stranger than from a distance. He wore a fur cloak and a string of Indian beads around his neck. He was so tall he had to stoop to walk through Bettie's kitchen door, and his voice was so deep and resonant it made the kettle dance on the stove. After introducing himself, Carl Browne told Bettie he was a general in Coxey's Army, a huge band of unemployed workers who were marching on Washington to demand relief for the poor and the jobless. They were followers of Jacob Coxey, a flamboyant reformer and prophet of discontent, who believed the unemployed should be put to work building roads and that Washington should simply print more greenbacks to pay their salaries.

The hordes of desperate men streamed eastward by foot and by rail. Many actually seized trains, riding the coaches as if they owned the railroad. The Southern Pacific Railroad called it train robbery. The Mayor of San Antonio threatened to shoot them all, causing Texas Governor James Hogg to intervene and stop the massacre.

Bettie was well aware of Coxey's battalions of hoboes, tramps, and honest unemployed. Their march to Washington had been accompanied by dozens of reporters and their escapades were highly publicized.

"General Coxey will be president one day," Carl Browne said, as he tasted a glass of clabber. "And I'm not just saying that because I married his daughter. He's the only one that can give this country back to the people."

"It's been my impression the people already own the country."

"It may look that way from here where you own your own farm. But not in the cities where the masses are destitute." Carl Browne pushed his plate aside and sat up in his chair, as if to deliver a sermon. He was nearly as tall sitting as Bettie was standing. His voice, though deep, had an unexpected softness. "Why is it," he continued, "that those who produce food are hungry? And those who make clothes are ragged? And those who build houses are homeless? And those who produce nothing own everything? These are the questions that General Coxey asks and that must be answered."

"I think you overstate your case, Mr. Browne. I don't see

people homeless and hungry here in Seguin. Just those passing through."

"Don't you think these are worthy of your concern?"

"That's why you're at my kitchen table, Mr. Browne."

Carl Browne dropped his eyes and placed one hand over his heart. "I sincerely apologize, ma'am. You've been kind and I've been thoughtless. But it's been a long, difficult journey."

He told Bettie about the army's ride from California, packed into coaches and boxcars like sardines, tormented by police and rangers and railroad officials. "At one place they'd pack us on a special train just to get us out of town. Then at the next stop they'd throw us off the train to keep us from getting to the next town. We were thrown off the train in El Paso, out into the desert like common criminals, without food or shelter from the sun."

"Did you have tickets?"

"Of course not, ma'am. These are destitute men. Without jobs. Without funds."

"I'm not destitute, but if I got on a train without a ticket, I'm sure they'd put me off."

"It's symbolic, ma'am. But you must admit our cause is just."

As Bettie began to clear away the dishes she said, "I believe people should work. It's a rich country. I don't see why people shouldn't have enough to eat and a place to stay."

"That's the sum of it, ma'am. It surely isn't right the way things are."

"I suppose you'll be headin' on to Washington?"

"Yes, ma'am. Soon as I can get the price of a train ticket. It seems the authorities here agree with you on the matter of our fare. There are no free rides, it seems." Carl Browne pushed back his chair and stood. "I'd like to pay for my meal with work. Maybe there's something around here I could do?"

"I can't take work away from Everett, my regular yardman. But I'm sure you can find something. There's lots of work in Seguin and on the farms around."

"Is that Everett?" Browne nodded his head toward Kishbaugh, at work in the parlor.

"That's Mr. Kishbaugh, the carpenter."

"A good and noble trade. He's a fortunate man. I'm sure he's being paid generously."

"Well, I suppose so. Bacon, eggs, and butter are hard to come by."

"Well, ma'am, forgive me, but that's hard wages for a craftsman. Maybe times are tougher around here than you think."

"I wouldn't scoff at bacon, eggs, and butter," Bettie said, angered by Browne's remark. "I probably spent far more hours raising those hogs and chickens and churning that butter than you've spent doing honest work all year."

"That's the whole of it, ma'am. I'm being denied the right to do honest work."

It was then Carl Browne reached into the pocket of his breeches and withdrew a gold watch. "Speaking of gold, ma'am, I have here an heirloom that belonged to my grandfather. I'd like you to have it. In return, maybe you'd find it in your heart to loan me funds to purchase my ticket to Washington. The cause is just, ma'am. We've got to let the politicians in Washington know there are people in this country who want to work but can't find jobs. Jacob Coxey says it would be so simple. Provide funds for public improvement—roads, bridges, levees to control floods— projects that would need the manpower that's now idle. It would be good for the country and good for the laboring man."

"I don't want your watch, Mr. Browne."

"The farmers and working men of this country are the victims of theft on a grand scale. The railroads, the politicians, the robber barons of the East, are taking money from our pockets and food from our mouths."

"I always know what time it is, Mr. Browne. I don't want your watch." Bettie's voice contained a note of finality. She busied herself, hoping Browne would recognize it was time for him to go.

As the visitor moved toward the door, he said, "The world doesn't stop at your kitchen door, Mrs. King. People are suffering out there. You can't just look the other way. To ignore suffering and injustice is as bad as causing it. The result is the same."

Bettie moved to the shelf by the stove where she had hidden

her small crockery pot of butter-and-egg money behind the coffee grinder and the salt and pepper. She poured it out on the table.
"This cash is money I earned, Mr. Browne. I saved it after selling
the butter and eggs you speak so lightly of. It's handy for emer-
gencies. For educating my children." She put some of the money
back in the pot and handed the rest to Browne. "I want you to
take this. Then buy a ticket to help you on your way to Washington. When you get there tell them here's a woman in Texas who
can see beyond her kitchen door."

After the man left it took several hours for Bettie's heart to
resume its normal cadence. She wasn't quite sure if she was angry
or ashamed of having given the Coxeyite money out of pique
rather than compassion. "It just isn't fair," she said aloud to the
empty kitchen, "for a total stranger to accuse me of some terrible
crime." She was even less certain of what terrible crime she had
committed or had been accused of committing. She hadn't taken
money from Browne's pocket or bread from his mouth. In fact,
she had filled him up with clabber, corn bread, and ham. She
composed imaginary answers to the stranger's charge, answers
that made her seem a good and generous woman. "I've never
turned away anyone in trouble or hungry or in need from my
land," she told an imaginary listener. Then she remembered what
Browne had said about the world not ending at her kitchen door.
She remembered Pink Rosebud standing alone before the city fathers. The difficult thing, Bettie realized, was knowing where the
line was drawn between her world and the outside world. Everything that happened on Mr. Henry's land was her affair. But the
boundary was not very finely drawn.

After the Coxeyite's visit, Bettie began to look around more
carefully at her community. Were there wrongs here that needed
to be made right? Was this really the best of all possible worlds?
For the first time, she began to realize what happened to many of
the transients who passed through her kitchen. The angry ones,
like Carl Browne, usually moved on, but those without hope often stayed, becoming residents of the old dilapidated two-story
hotel between the Kings' home and the courthouse. Although a
prominent landmark, the old Mission Hotel was essentially invis-

ible and was rarely mentioned in polite conversation. In that money panic year of 1894, the hotel was filled with transients, the jobless, the homeless, and the lost. Then, one hot fall day, a drummer named Schlotsky riding a train from San Antonio brought smallpox to Seguin.

As the epidemic spread, the stricken with no family to care for them were taken to the Mission Hotel. There, in the darkened rooms, the transients languished under the care of Bessie Pauline, the Negro who worked for the jailer and cooked meals for people in both the jail and the Mission Hotel. Now that the epidemic was raging, the old hotel was so crowded, Bessie Pauline was overwhelmed and had given up even trying to prepare enough food for the new inmates. Many of the rooms of the hotel opened onto two wide porches across the front of the building. Abe told Bettie one day he could hear from within the moaning of the dying when he passed. Bettie lay awake all night thinking about the awful sounds Abe heard and imagining the horror that must lurk in those darkened rooms. She wondered, *Have some of those desperately ill and dying people sat at my zinc-lined kitchen table, drinking my buttermilk, talking about their wanderings and their lives?*

During the height of the epidemic, The Girls sat on Bettie's front porch talking about what Abe had heard and seen at the Mission Hotel. "There are people in there dying," Jennie Scott said. "Dying in those rooms alone." It seemed unreal to be sitting on the porch, surrounded by pink Seven Sisters roses, talking about death. Nuge had recently had an eleven-and-one-half-pound baby boy, and she was nursing little Harry as they talked.

"Abe said he saw one man try to get away," Jennie continued. "He said a sheriff's deputy caught him and took him back and locked him in a room. Like a jail. Then, later, Abe saw them carry the man out with some others who had died. Abe said the man finally found a way to escape."

"They go in there to take them to their graves," Mary Lou Lannom said. "Why don't they go in there earlier with medicine? Why don't they help Bessie Pauline with food? Maybe they wouldn't have to take them to the graveyard."

"Why don't we go there?" Bettie asked.

"Because it's not right to put your family at risk for a stranger."

There was a stillness on the King front porch. The women
looked within, struggling with easy questions and hard answers.
All Bettie's friends were active in the work of the church—they
were Methodists, with the exception of Jennie Scott, who was
then a Presbyterian. When the poor farm had burned down, they
helped raise money for the repairs and for new bedding, clothes,
and furnishings. Jennie was especially active in providing services
to shut-ins and had been named Cheer Chairman of the women
of her congregation. Rarely a day went by that she failed to visit
the old and the sick. But this was different, they agreed. But,
then, how different? The people in the Mission Hotel were strangers, yet somewhere, at one time or another, they had loved and
been loved. Bettie wondered, *Isn't this the heart of the meaning
of charity, making the great leap between helping someone you
know and helping a stranger?*

One early morning, Bettie rose before the sun and she walked
to the home of old Mrs. Neal across the street from the Mission
Hotel. Mrs. Neal was on her deathbed, and Bettie and her friends
were taking turns caring for their friend. In dawn's shadow, Bettie
looked across the road at the hotel. She knew she had passed this
spot perhaps hundreds of times, but if someone had asked her to
describe the hotel she could not have done so. It was little more
than a large ruin of weathered pine and concrete. Two dead oaks
cast skeletal arms up against stark walls. It was as if the trees and
the hotel had died together, in some kind of unholy pact. Bettie
tried to imagine how the hotel might have looked when new. She
looked for some remnant of elegance, some echo of music or
voices or the ring of silver against crystal. But nothing was left to
suggest this had been anything but a dying place. The streets were
empty. The town was still.

Then, down the road, Bettie saw a closed carriage come and
stop before the ruined hotel. Two figures emerged, a woman and
a man. The man carried an armful of parcels and they both hurried onto the lower porch. Being careful not to be seen, Bettie
moved closer. She saw them opening each door, sliding plates of
food into the darkness, then quickly closing the doors again.

They worked rapidly and efficiently, first on the lower porch, then on the balcony above. Clearly it was something they had done before. There was something stealthy about their movements. In another time at another place they could have been cat burglars. For a while, they disappeared from view, obviously placing food in rooms to the rear. They emerged from behind the hotel. As the man helped the woman back into the carriage, she noticed Bettie watching. She paused and nodded. Then Pink Rosebud climbed into the carriage and was gone.

All day, as Bettie and Abe's wife, Lucinda Saphronia Miller, worked in the garden, Bettie was tormented by thoughts of the Mission Hotel. Of all the Christian women in Seguin, only two outcasts, a Negro cook and a harlot, actually were doing Christ's work. But what could she do? If she were to join Pink Rosebud at the Mission Hotel, she would be an outcast as well. It was not her place. She asked Lucinda Saphronia about Bessie Pauline.

"She's doing all she can. But it's killing her. Even with Miss Rosebud, it's too hard."

"What does she need?"

"Mainly food. There's not enough for the jail, let alone the hotel."

Bettie looked around her garden and toward the house. There was enough food to feed Coxey's Army. The cupboard was overflowing with quart jars of tomatoes, buckets of green beans and potatoes, shelves stacked with cornmeal and five-gallon crocks of hominy. Hanging from the ceiling of the smokehouse were hams and sausages. Her garden had fresh corn, turnips and collard greens, yams and okra.

"We surely do have plenty of food here," Bettie said.

"We surely do." Bettie noticed Lucinda Saphronia was wearing the beginning of a conspirator's smile.

The next morning, Bettie rose before the sun and helped Lucinda Saphronia hitch the mule to the wagon. Then they loaded the wagon with sacks, crocks and jars of food, her strong lye soap, and fresh linens. In the still darkness, they drove to the Mission Hotel kitchen to deliver their cargo of comfort for the sick and the dying. As they made their way down deserted Court Street, Bettie had a vision of Precious Honey Child and the other girls preparing food and washing bedding and clothing after the last of their guests had departed and she smiled at the image. She looked across at Lucinda Saphronia and the two of them smiled so wide their smiles turned into laughter. Bettie found she was floating in a kind of pure happiness. She felt light and good, rebellious and faithful all at the same time.

When they arrived at the Mission Hotel, Pink Rosebud emerged from the back door. She walked toward the wagon, wiping her hands on an apron worn over her gown. Bettie was once again struck by how beautiful Pink Rosebud was, as though she had stopped by the hotel on her way home from a ball. Yet, as she drew close, Bettie could see she was exhausted. Pink Rosebud leaned against the side of the wagon, looked up at Bettie, and smiled.

"Good morning, Miss Bettie."

"Good morning, Miss Rosebud."

Pink Rosebud glanced into the wagon. "All this ..." Her voice broke and she grew silent.

"It's not much."

"It's everything," Pink Rosebud said.

Bettie helped Pink Rosebud, Lucinda Saphronia, and Bessie Pauline unload the wagon. They worked quickly and silently, taking the food and supplies into the kitchen of the old hotel. When they entered the gloom of the interior, Bettie was assailed by a great, raw, raging beast of an odor, a smell Bettie recognized as despair. She wondered if this despair weren't more contagious than the disease that filled the rooms and pressed the life from the doomed and dying tenants.

As it grew light in the east, the last of the provisions had been unloaded. Bettie and Pink Rosebud stood looking at the hotel.

"I've got to go," Bettie said.

"I know."

"I wish ..." Bettie had wanted to say she wished she could stay and help, but she knew she didn't actually know what she wished.

"We can only do what we can," Pink Rosebud said. "You'd better hurry home. It's getting light."

While the epidemic lasted, Bettie and Lucinda Saphronia carried several wagonloads of food and supplies to the Mission Hotel. All that time, and for weeks afterward, Bettie was certain she could be taken by the plague. Even though she had only been in the kitchen and not in the rooms of the tenants, she worried about infection. Each day, as she examined herself carefully and washed her hands and body with the dangerous lye soap at her back door, she was amazed that she remained free of contagion. Part of her was enormously free and joyous. Her work with Pink Rosebud made her feel somehow closer to God. Yet, when these feelings of euphoria came, she was ashamed that her joy was at the expense of the suffering people at the hotel. She was confused about these feelings and perhaps this was one reason she never told a soul about her sunrise missions with Pink Rosebud. If she had told any of The Girls, she would have had to explain what she herself did not understand. As far as she knew, Lucinda Saphronia, Bessie Pauline, and the girls who lived with Pink Rosebud were the only ones who knew she had left her land to make a difference in the world beyond her kitchen.

As Bettie orchestrated the shifting patterns of lives in her household, choreographing the family dance, she and her close friends continued to gather on her porch to pass those times of day when their attention was not demanded elsewhere. Bettie hungered for these precious intervals. They offered a kind of continuity to a life that so often seemed to progress by fits and starts, the activities of one day having little in common with the days preceding or following. She was so deeply involved with the lives of her children and younger sisters and brothers and the families of her tenant farmers that her relationship with Cayloma, Nuge, Adda, Jennie, and Mary Lou had a quality of romantic fiction, and she could hardly wait to hear the latest chapters in their lives. As the years went by, she began to sense how their lives diverged, like railroads leading to a distant city along different routes. They had been so close she had always assumed their experience and fates would be close as well. But now, on the porch, as they talked of their days and their loves and as she became aware of the sorrows and disappointments their silences expressed so eloquently, she realized that as much as they loved one another, their lives were drawing apart.

One spring morning in 1896, as The Girls met on Bettie's front porch to talk and sew and catch up on one another's lives, Nuge announced that she and Tom might be moving from their ranch in the Chihuahuan desert.

"Tom's got his eye on a new place," Nuge said as she worked on her Texas Star quilt. "Closer to the Rio Grande. He says this time he's going to make the desert bloom. My Tom says you can take the sorriest land in Texas, irrigate, and make it prime cattle country."

"Tom Lay has always been a dreamer," Cayloma said. "If you could put a dream in the bank, Old Tom would be the richest man alive. It must make life exciting, never knowing what kind of adventure he's going to dream up tomorrow."

"My Tom's a dreamer, all right," Nuge said.

"I remember the stories he used to tell," Annie said. "He could make you see what wasn't there."

"He still can." Nuge's eyes never left her busy needle. Bettie was once again amazed at Nuge's skill. Her quilts were wondrous creations. In a day when quilting was judged by the number of stitches to the inch, Nuge was unexcelled. Her patterns, especially her Texas Star quilts, were studies in precision, balance, and symmetry. Over the last few years, Bettie had observed that Nuge's quilts expressed the very qualities that were lacking in her marriage. When she and Tom Lay were married, Tom had built a house in town and from his prosperous family he had inherited 482 acres, with 250 being prime farmland. Then, Tom dreamed of a thundering herd of cattle. Surely being a cattle baron was a more noble calling than being a dirt farmer. He sold the town house and his fertile farmland to buy a thousand acres of dry ranchland on the arid Mexican border. The ranch failed, the land too poor to support enough stock to make a profit. Tom sold that ranch and purchased another near Kingsville that he felt held even more promise than the first. This new ranch also failed, probably doomed from the start. Cayloma had said it was a pity Tom's land was not as fertile as his dreams. Each failure prompted a larger gamble, with a greater chance for another. Each time Nuge visited Seguin, she had a new homeplace to describe, always smaller, always further from Tom's dream than the last. Nuge excused Tom's gambles with their life and never indicated anything but unconditional love and support for the man she had married.

"Well, it should be exciting. Going to a new place." Bettie looked up at Adda's face to see if the remark was patronizing or sincere. "Seems like I'm going to live my whole life in the same old place."

"Can we help you move?" Jennie asked.

"Oh, no," Nuge answered. "We'll do fine. Tom's got it all worked out." Bettie wondered if there was anything left to move and she was saddened once again by how thin, almost gaunt, her sister had become. Her eyes were shadowed and less inclined to rest comfortably upon the eyes of her friends. Her silences were so terribly revealing. Will Thomas had once surprised the Lays with a visit, and he later told Adda their house was just a shack, a disaster. Bettie marveled that fate had been so cruel to her sister. They had been almost twins, so much alike, had fallen in love with two wonderful men, had married on the same day in a double wedding. But one man had been substance, the other shadow. *Happiness is not always a matter of choice,* she thought, *it's often simply chance.* There was one moment, on the porch, as Bettie studied the shadows in her sister's eyes, when she wished Nuge would leave this man who was making her life so hard. But the unthinkable thought passed, and in the embrace of the love of her sister and friends, Nuge created the harmony and order lacking in her life in the most beautiful quilts in Texas.

"Well, I'm not going to stay here and grow old in Seguin," Jennie said. There was in her voice that particular excitement that precedes an announcement.

"Well, I declare. I suppose you've found the fountain of youth?"

"Something better. I found the finest, handsomest man in Texas. He loves me and I love him and we just might be taking a trip."

Every one of The Girls looked up from their sewing, eyes wide with curiosity and disbelief. "What man?" they all asked at once. If Jennie had been seeing a man they'd have known. "What man?"

"The right man," Jennie said, her eyes filled with stardust, youth, and innocence. "He's staying at Mama's place." Jennie's mother ran a fine boarding house on Austin Street. It was popular among drummers and traveling businessmen who stopped in Seguin for lodging and for the legendary meals Jennie and her mother served at their table.

"A stranger?"

"Not anymore. Not since last night. After I met him, we went out on the back porch and talked. It was so beautiful. I met him at dinner and by midnight we knew we were in love. He proposed and I accepted."

"Jennie!" Cayloma reminded her that four hours was a rather brief courtship. "You don't just meet a man at dinner and agree to marry before the dishes are dry."

"You'd have to know him. He's so special."

"I can't believe this!" Cayloma said. "What is he, some kind of traveling salesman?"

"So what if he is?" Jennie said, a bit provoked, even peeved, at the reaction to her news.

"A traveling salesman," Cayloma laughed. "They make jokes about traveling salesmen."

"Jennie!" Bettie was having a hard time keeping her composure. "You can't do this! You just can't marry a stranger!"

"What did you know about Henry when you married him? Wasn't he a stranger? I really don't see the difference. We all marry strangers. Mine just happens to be a stranger for a little shorter time."

Bettie was torn between supporting her friend's obvious happiness and protecting her from what was so obviously a mistake. She had always recognized in her beautiful and seemingly poised friend a curious and unexpected insecurity. Jennie and her father, a prominent physician, had been inseparable, and when he had died, just a few months after the death of her younger brother, Jennie was devastated. Bettie asked herself if Jennie was trying to make up for the love she had lost in her family. She also wondered about this four-hour courtship. But Nuge and Tom Lay had known each other all their lives before they were married, and look how that marriage was hurting Nuge. Maybe four hours was plenty.

"Well, at least tell us about him," Annie said. "Maybe his name would be a good place to start.'

"You did ask his name?" Cayloma inquired.

Jennie sighed and turned away. "I don't want to talk about it anymore."

Bettie felt an outpouring of love for her beautiful, usually sensible friend. "You have to admit, Jennie, you've taken us by surprise. If we didn't care for you so much, we wouldn't be so concerned. Give us a little time to get used to the idea. But you've got to promise to give it a little time, too."

"Who I'd like to see run off and get married is Annie or Mary Lou," Adda said, changing the subject slightly.

"That'd be the day," Cayloma said. "Annie's too headstrong and Mary Lou's too finicky." Bettie smiled at the accuracy of Cayloma's assessment. For nearly a year, Bettie had tried to maneuver a match between her brother Leonard and Mary Lou. She was constantly creating strategies to throw them together. On one occasion, when all the young people were at a party, including her brother and Mary Lou, Leonard Moss described his ideal woman. It was obvious after a few emphatic phrases he was describing exactly the woman Mary Lou was not and could never be. Even Bettie had to agree it would be a match made very far from Heaven.

"I can't even imagine being married," Mary Lou said. "It's not that I don't want to be. I can't even picture it in my mind."

"You're too choosy," Bettie said.

"What choice do I have around here? Maybe an itinerant preacher or one of those boys who loiter in front of the saloon they made from the old Sons of Temperance Hall? Maybe a blacksmith?"

"There's nothing wrong with a blacksmith."

"Why live your life with somebody less than you deserve? I'd rather live alone. Then if I feel I need male companionship, I can have it."

"Mary Lou!"

"I'd rather have my beaux and be the topic of lively gossip than bear a lifetime of unhappiness."

As they talked, Bettie looked around at her circle of friends, and she recognized how they each brought certain qualities to the group. Of them all, Mary Lou was the most independent. When Mary Lou's father had grown older and sicker until he was unable to take care of the family farmlands, Mary Lou had taken over more and more of the responsibility of running the farm. Bettie had often seen her supervising the tenant farmers, negotiating with merchants, selling the produce of the land—all activities generally considered the province of men. She had an amazing knowledge of the Bible and was probably the only woman in the county to hold an office in her congregation. Yet unquestionably, Mary Lou was one of the most feminine women Bettie had ever seen. She was slim and lovely and wore dresses with embroidery, delicate lace, and bouquets of ribbons and bows. She was obviously very appealing to men and attracted lots of them. She often had boyfriends, yet when their attentions began to threaten her independence, she simply sent them away. Bettie had decided her reluctance to marry could be traced to her father. Mr. Lannom was every woman's ideal. He was very distinguished-looking, intelligent, and loving. No man could measure up to such a father, certainly not the boys who drank and gambled away their days at the saloon in the old Sons of Temperance Hall.

Bettie's eyes shifted to Annie. Here was another case of an unusually attractive woman. She was tall and poised, a talented artist possessing a flamboyant energy that made her always seem in motion, even in repose. Unlike Mary Lou, however, she intimidated men and managed to scare them away by the droves.

"I can picture being married," Annie said. "I can picture the man. Problem is, I haven't got the faintest idea where to find him. He sure doesn't live around here."

"Maybe he'll be coming to dinner at Jennie's," Cayloma said. "Seems like some pretty good men come through there."

"Stop it," Jennie said, still angry.

Annie was almost always polite and could converse gracefully on any subject in any group. But her tongue could cut like a blade and she had a presence so formidable that most men seemed to shrink by comparison. Bettie concluded that it would be a rare man who could tame this red-haired, creative, unconventional woman. And it was this very man who Annie King was waiting for.

"I'll tell you about the man I'm looking for," Annie said. "It's someone you all know. I'm looking for a man as strong and loving as Henry King, as adventurous as Tom Lay, and as intelligent and giving as Felix Douglass."

Cayloma laughed. "If Felix weren't quite so giving, maybe

we'd have something left for ourselves. Maybe we wouldn't be so poor."

Of all Bettie's friends, Cayloma turned out to be the luckiest in love. Her marriage to Felix Douglass appeared to be ideal in nearly every respect. They were still like two children, the quality of their love unchanged since they'd been courting. If anything was missing from their marriage it would have to be money, for Felix was a schoolteacher devoted to teaching. To Felix there was no higher calling, and he believed it was a profession far more important than politics. "Politics," he once told Bettie, "is the art of persuading people to ignore facts. Teaching is the art of persuading people to understand them."

Both Cayloma and Felix came from affluent backgrounds. By their families' standards, Cayloma and Felix were poor. Yet Cayloma was so much in love that she found her poverty at worst inconvenient and at best amusing. "Poverty must be in great demand these days," she told Bettie. "It must be, or else there wouldn't be so many poor people in Texas."

The afternoon passed. The day was warm. Sometimes whole minutes went by without a spoken word. Bettie watched her friends sewing, and occasionally when they looked up from their hands, they smiled at each other as if to acknowledge the gift of the other's presence. It was such a passive scene, Bettie thought. *We could easily be done in needlepoint, framed and placed on the wall. Yet right here within my friends there are battles between hope and sorrow, desire and regret raging in the silent arenas of their minds.* Jennie's desperate quest for love, Nuge's yearning for stability, Mary Lou's demands for independence, and Annie's search for the perfect man. When they were children, they had talked about these things openly, without embarrassment. Now that they were grown and mature, their conversation tripped along on the surface of things, not braving the depths where pain could be felt or caused or known. Bettie looked at her beloved friends and pondered what would become of them. She thought of suggesting they walk down the street to Idella's house and ask her to predict their path through the labyrinth of the future. She thought about it for a moment, shuddered, and reached for the darning egg in the basket by her feet instead.

A few days later, as Bettie prepared the younger children for bed, the telephone rang. Bettie believed she could tell from the sound of the bell whether the caller had good news or bad. This time, however, the bell had an unfamiliar sound.

"Jennie's gone," Cayloma said. "Her mother said she just left."

"Where? Didn't she say? No note?"

"Nothing. She didn't take very much. Just a few things. A change of clothes and some jewelry."

"Well, then she's coming back."

"I don't think so."

Jennie was gone indeed, leaving a troubling void in Bettie's life. *How completely unpredictable the world can be,* she thought. The lovely, sensible Jennie Scott, pillar of the community and both the Methodist and Presbyterian churches, had run off to Columbus, Texas, with a man who sold felt hats from town to town. Jennie was there one day and gone the next. Bettie had seen Jennie's intended only once, and he was indeed handsome and mysterious, and was precisely the kind of man she had imagined the romantic lovers of the Brontës to be, perhaps Heathcliff. No wonder physicians warned against reading romantic novels. Surely Jennie had fallen victim to Hysteria, the most common consequence of this dark activity. Jennie Scott had given new meaning to the concept of loving strangers.

Shortly after Jennie ran away with the felt-hat salesman, Felix had a terrible accident. He was riding to school when a rattle-snake frightened his horse. The mare ran wild through four fences and then threw Felix headlong into a fifth. Since the Civil War, the barbed-wire fence had been festooned all across the land like a necklace of razors. Between the Douglass home and the school, there were twelve such fences to be crossed or maneuvered around. The first four killed Felix's horse, the fifth nearly killed Felix.

Until Felix's wounds healed, Bettie spent much of her time with Cayloma at his beside. The cuts healed slowly and imperfectly. It was obvious Felix would be terribly scarred for life. As the days passed, Bettie also began to sense that the scars had cut deep beneath the surface, and that something of Felix's spirit had flowed out through the wounds. She knew it was something Cayloma realized as well. One day they would speak of it, but not now, even in the privacy of the porch and the arbor of Seven Sisters roses.

It came as a relief when, two weeks later, Bettie left her friend's convalescent room to join Mr. Henry on a long-scheduled trip to Columbus, Texas. Mr. Henry was there for an agricultural conference, and Bettie had arranged to visit her friend Sis Townsend, who lived downtown, about four blocks from the courthouse. Little did she know what else she would find there.

Down the street from the courthouse was the famous Stafford Opera House that had opened in 1877 and had staged performances by many notable actors, before falling on hard times. The Opera House was on the second floor of a building that included a bank, a store, and the owner's home beneath. When the owner had died, his widow had not liked "all that noise and all those acting people upstairs" and had closed down the Opera House. It was now used only occasionally for local piano recitals and school plays. The town itself had begun to decline, primarily because of the violence that had killed its sheriffs at frequent and regular intervals. Henry warned Bettie not to walk to the Opera House alone and not to talk to strangers on the street.

Hoping to find at least something of the Opera House in its glory days, Bettie and Sis Townsend, guided by the tall courthouse tower, walked the few blocks to the Opera House. As they approached the theater, Bettie saw a woman huddled in a doorway. It was hard to judge her age—her hair was unkempt, and her clothing in disarray. Her face was in shadow and her eyes downcast, but Bettie could not shake the feeling there was something familiar about this pitiful presence. At first Bettie's heart went out to the woman who seemed so lost and alone. Then she recalled Henry's warning about strangers on these violent streets and she began to walk on by, trying not to look as she passed. Then something made her turn back, and suddenly it was as if her heart had been torn apart by teams of horses.

"Jennie?"

The woman pulled her collar up and turned away. Then she began to run. "Jennie!" Bettie ran after the woman, who slowed, began to sway, and collapsed against the wall of a building. She slid down the wall to the sidewalk, her face turned to the rough red brick. Bettie knelt by Jennie's side and encircled the girl in her arms. Jennie began to cry, and Bettie could see bruises beneath her eyes and a swelling on her lip. "Jennie, what did he do?" Bettie tried to turn Jennie's head so she could see her battered face, but Jennie struggled against her, trying to hide against the bricks. Then it was as if all Jennie's strength had fled. Her body relaxed and she seemed to wither. "I'm so ashamed," she said, and did not speak again until Bettie and Mr. Henry had put her to bed in their hotel.

Bettie swept up the wreckage of her friend and took her home to Seguin. "Arthur said I was born for the theater," Jennie confided. "He promised me a part at the Opera House. I would be a star in a James O'Neill production. But the Opera House had closed. As soon as he left Seguin he turned mean and left me, and I was too ashamed to come home."

Bettie nursed Jennie back to health and helped contrive a story about her adventure with the hat salesman in Columbus to spare at least some of her dignity. She also made sure Jennie was back helping her mother at the boarding house. *She'll be all right,* Bettie thought to herself, as she watched her friend serve the drummers their dinner. *She'll be all right.*

In the summer of 1903, Bettie made a journey east on the San Antonio & Houston Railroad, a pilgrimage to the old family home on Peach Creek where Euphemia had been haunted by Santa Anna's army and the wailing of the widows of the Alamo. Bettie, Little Virginia, and baby George joined Euphemia, Tildy, and Annie at the depot where they boarded a train for Gonzales. Annie had sewed a beautiful embroidered dress for Little Virginia. Bettie, whose most creative handwork, according to Annie, was her perfect buttonholes, was somewhat miffed, but her resentment was soon forgotten.

At the Gonzales depot they were picked up by Sarah's daughter Mollie Jones and were driven by buggy to Peach Creek. And there, on the porch, in the shade of the Sam Houston Oak, was the legendary Sarah McClure Braches. Sarah embraced her old companion Tildy. Bettie was astonished that the women looked as old as God. It seemed to her that Sarah must have shrunk, like an old cotton shift after a lifetime of washings, and she was curious how a woman so thin and small could have fought so bravely against the Comanches. When the old woman rose to greet her sisters, she grew no larger, and it was obvious she was lame—the old tale Bettie had heard as a child of Sarah's wound from a Comanche arrow must really be true—and today the old woman walked only with the support of Tildy, whose life she had saved at this very spot so long ago.

For a moment, as Bettie moved into the old mansion with its fine furnishings and its grand piano, its silver and servants, crystal and candelabra, she seemed to be moving back in time, with everything in the house maintained exactly as it was in the last days of the Texas Republic when Comanches lurked beyond the meadows. Here were the Ashby girls—Sarah, Euphemia, Fannie, Mary, and Jane Isabella—women of the legendary Texas Rangers who had carved a nation from the wilderness. They were gaunt, tough, and lean as Longhorns—all except Fannie, who was round as a melon and so short and heavy that her buggy was equipped with extra steps so she could manage to pull herself aboard. Although in their eighties, Sarah and Mary still enjoyed their pipes. Bettie figured the sisters probably enjoyed their whiskey, as well.

How strange that the five sisters and Tildy were together again in the house. They had embraced like children and now chatted comfortably with one another and giggled and teased. When Euphemia scolded Fannie for building her home on the high hill overlooking Sarah's house—a hill that had been Euphemia's secret place for dreaming as a child—and Fannie hotly defended her right to build her house anywhere she pleased. Fannie actually balled her fists, and Bettie saw that even among five women whose combined ages exceeded three hundred years there could still be sisterly rivalry.

All afternoon the five sisters picked over the past like raptors, ravenously consuming scraps of time and memory. They talked of great revivals and of dead children and of the comings and goings of the men they had loved. They recalled the humor, irony, and absurdity that had touched their lives, and they laughed and sighed and wiped their eyes. They talked of the house and wove tales around the events that transpired in each room. They talked eagerly, leaning forward, the words almost hurried as if each brought life into the house and into the corridors of their minds. Sometimes they disagreed and argued, Fannie would ball her fists again and Euphemia's eyes would flash and Mary's face would flush with polka-dot heat and Jane Isabella would draw herself up straight and erect and defiant. *How amazing,* Bettie thought, *after all these years the passion is still there.* The five old women had survived so much. Sarah alone had buried eight of her nine children. They had endured wars and death and cruelty and every dread missile the dark horseman of the Apocalypse could hurl. They more than endured. They loved and fought, knew anger and compassion, were filled with the full range of the emotions they had felt when they were young. *There is something in us,* she thought, *a flame, that does not change through time, that is as alive when we are old as when we first opened our eyes to this world.*

In the afternoon the family sat in the shade of the venerable Sam Houston Oak. Bettie held Little Virginia's hand and hoped the child could remember this day in all its detail so she could tell her children about it. As the women talked, the cows came close as if to eavesdrop while they grazed.

"Remember when Juan Seguin herded his goats and cattle by here?" Euphemia said, gesturing to the wide pasture before the house.

"The McCullochs never liked him much," said Jane Isabella. "Believed he was a traitor."

"Nonsense!" Euphemia's eyes were flashing again. "How can you still believe that? Why do you think our town is named Seguin?"

"Well, he was a Mexican. And it appears to me that's who we were at war with."

"Juan Seguin was the most faithful friend Texas ever had," Sarah said. "A good-hearted man."

"It's public record," Euphemia added. "The legislature restored his pension and all his rights. History will show he was a patriot."

"History sometimes gets things wrong," Jane Isabella said. "Like Santa Anna. Just ask Sarah about his mama."

"Some swear it's true," Sarah said. "But when I brought my slaves from Kentucky they kept talking about Santa Anna's mama being part Negro. They said his papa was a French plantation owner there named Sainte Anne. Mrs. Sainte Anne was not his wife, but his slave. They had a son named Antoine. Antoine grew up and went to a military academy in New York and he got caught stealing and they sent him home. When the authorities found out his mother was a Negro, he was afraid he'd be sold back into slavery. So he stole a horse, clothes, money, and pistols and rode off to Mexico where he would be accepted as the Santa Anna our family knew."

"That's a fantasy or idle gossip," Fannie said.

"Maybe not," Sarah said, a bit offended that Fannie would scoff at a tale that just might be true.

"I don't believe it for a minute. Not even a second."

Bettie was spellbound by the conversation beneath the Sam Houston Oak. The sisters talked of history as if its great characters and events were simply things that happened on their way through a normal day.

"I suppose this old tree will still be here when Virginia and baby George have grandbabies," Euphemia said. "Seems like yesterday Sam Houston rode into this yard on that big white horse."

Sarah drew on her pipe and the blue smoke rose about her eyes. "I thought if anybody was immortal it was Sam Houston," she said. "I was sure he'd live at least as long as this tree."

"William and Henry McCulloch saw him when he was an old man," Euphemia said. "It was during the Civil War and Mr. Sam was sitting on his porch in Huntsville. William said when the soldiers marched by, the young ones jeered. They viewed him as the old man who opposed Texas secession from the Union. The old soldiers who had known him in the Revolution either averted

their eyes or they turned to salute their old commander out of respect for what he did for Texas. William said he didn't know
whether to feel pride or sorrow."

"Well, they're all gone now," Sarah said. "Juan Seguin lies in
an unmarked grave across the Rio Grande in Nuevo Laredo.
Santa Anna died in poverty and disgrace for inviting the French
into Mexico as conquering rulers during the War Between the
States. Sam Houston was a warrior who had seen too much of
war. He was probably the greatest hero in Texas history, but on
his headstone they just put his name and the date. They didn't
even put Rest in Peace."

Tildy had been listening quietly to the others, her eyes moving from one sister to another. "You remember Joe?" she asked.
"The man with us on the way to the Brazos?"

"He was the slave of William Travis. The one who survived
the Alamo with Mrs. Dickerson," Euphemia said. "I doubt if
we'd of made it through the Runaway Scrape without Joe."

"He was on his way to Alabama to see the Travis family,"
Tildy continued. "Goin' back to tell them the last words of Colonel Travis. And he did just that. But he was still a slave and the
Travis people treated him so bad he ran away and came back to
Texas. Started a farm and a family near Austin. Come freedom he
didn't take the Travis name. He was just Joe, I suppose, 'til he
died."

"It sure is strange," Euphemia said. "Of all of 'em—Travis,
Bowie, Seguin, Houston, and the rest—it looks like Joe was the
only one to live long and die with his good name. Even if he did
have just one."

In the late afternoon, the conversation turned to the subject
of Mary's divorce. Bettie had never known anyone who had been
divorced. She assumed Mary's divorce must have been one of the
first in Texas. She had never heard this story before and Bettie
was fascinated as the shocking tale unfolded beneath the pale
summer sky.

"I still think about it," Mary said. "How ashamed I was. I
shouldn't have disobeyed Papa. I should have gone on to Kentucky like Papa said."

"You had no reason to be ashamed," Jane Isabella said. "There's no shame in wanting to be with someone you love. Even less shame in leaving him if he turns mean."

As Mary's sisters continued their half-century-old support of the sister who might have been the Republic's first divorcée, the details of the scandal were revealed. Back during the days of the Republic, when Santa Anna's army was marching toward Peach Creek, John Ashby decided to take Mary, Fannie, and Jane Isabella to Kentucky where they would be safe from the approaching army. Mary, however, refused to go. She had fallen in love with Mr. John Smothers, a man who had been one of the original three hundred settlers in Stephen F. Austin's colony and owned some two leagues of land and forty head of hogs along the Lavaca River. Mr. Smothers was more than twice Mary's age, and when Mary's father became aware of his intentions he refused to allow him to call. The young girl then ran away with Mr. Smothers, and since there were no preachers in the vicinity at the time, they were married in bond.

"How can you really know a man?" Mary wondered aloud. "How can you love a man who hurts you?"

"You couldn't know," Euphemia said. "You can't see inside a person's heart."

Bettie was moved by the tears that now began to fill Mary's eyes. "What hurts is that I could be so deceived. How could I have been so blind?"

Sarah reached out for her sister's hand. "You should be proud. Not many women would have done what you did. Most would have stayed, too afraid to leave."

The sisters talked about the day Mary decided she had had enough abuse. After a particularly violent quarrel, she left under the protection of a man named John Greenwood, the local justice of the peace. Then Henry McCulloch, who was sheriff at the time, hand-delivered the divorce petition to Mr. Smothers.

"I'll never forget the wording of that petition," Mary said. "It read, 'John Smothers continually attacked his wife with physical blows and malicious epitaphs of reproach and slander which decency forbids public mention.'"

"Well, you've made yourself proud," Sarah said. "You held on to your dignity, a fine passel of children, and your land. Not many women in this world can claim that."

Eight women and a little girl gathered around Sarah's table for supper. The talk lingered on the past and Bettie knew each of the women was mindful of the absence of the men with whom they had shared this table and all those years. Indian fighter and legal scholar Bart McClure; Civil War hero General Henry McCulloch; Sarah's second husband, the studious and highly respected Charles Braches; Euphemia's first and only love, William G. King, youngest of the Rowdy King Boys; Fannie's husband, Major Roderick Gelhorn, who took off his hat to no man and who brought the first Jersey cow to·Texas; the long-dead and much-criticized John Smothers. Bettie felt they were all somewhere near, just beyond their reach. Yet she also realized how much life these women had lived after their men had passed on. They had grieved their loss, then had lived again, changing, growing, becoming whole once more in a different way.

After supper they all moved outside again, through the pasture to the grove of oaks where the family graveyard waited for the harvest of time. The old women moved slowly, like phantoms, through the heat and the sound of bees, Sarah leaning for support upon Tildy and Euphemia. Bettie and Little Virginia fell in behind and watched as the women laid fresh flowers on the graves. Bettie was so moved she began to cry.

"Mama, are you crying because you're sad they're dead?" Virginia asked.

"No, my sweet. Because I'm happy they're alive."

Bettie and Little Virginia held hands and watched the six old women. Bettie had no sense of the women as separate. They were touching and seemed a single being, a community of hand-me-down souls, ancient and holy, still strong and alive as the oaks growing from this hallowed family soil.

In the year 1904, Euphemia Texas Ashby King went to sleep one night and died while dreaming. There had been no illness, no time for farewells. She was buried in the family cemetery where lay five Texas Rangers, her brother William Ashby, Granny Rachel Boyd, former slaves and servants, her firstborn baby girl, two sons, and her beloved husband William G., the youngest of the Rowdy King Boys, who had preceded her in death by hardly a year.

The evening before, Euphemia had come up from her house to sit with her son Henry and Bettie on the front porch. She had talked about her childhood friend Matilda Lockhart who had been captured by Comanches and died of shame. Euphemia had shown them a mourning bracelet made of black glass and a lock of Matilda Lockhart's hair. Bettie felt the making and wearing of hair jewelry was morbid and was surprised a woman as practical and stoic as Euphemia had saved her friend's hair all these years.

Then Euphemia talked about a time, when she was a little girl, when she lay down in a secret place, in a bed of clover, and watched a hawk flying overhead, and she knew she was at that moment utterly and completely happy. She had no pain anywhere in her body and no discomfort in her mind and she had told herself then she would remember the moment as long as she lived. "I remember it now," she said that night on the porch. "I can smell the clover and almost hear the wind in the wings of the hawk." When it grew late, Henry walked Euphemia home and made sure she was settled for the night. In the morning, when Bettie rose to prepare breakfast for her family, the Negroes had already begun to assemble. They stood silently at the back door with bowed heads, and Bettie knew Euphemia was dead.

Euphemia's body was washed and dressed, and laid out in the living room of the new house. The yard filled with people and all the rooms were crowded with family, friends, and flowers. The constant flow of mourners included people from the church, friends of a lifetime, strangers who were curious about the legend of the first Anglo woman born in DeWitt's Colony, Texas. Under Annie and Mary Lou's direction, the Bible class ran shifts preparing and serving food, washing dishes, accepting food and flowers. They made a record in the memorial book of who brought what, to assure the pots and pans and bowls would be returned to the proper owners.

All night long, in pairs, the men kept vigil. In another room the women read the Bible, shared memories, comforted each other in the house where death for the moment dwelled. Occasionally someone would be moved to speak aloud of some special incident in Euphemia's life, some critical or frivolous moment when her life touched theirs. Dozens of Negroes, remembering how Euphemia had stood for their families, often alone against the prejudices of the day, came to pay their respects.

Then, on a clear morning, after a long Methodist tribute, the people of Seguin carried Euphemia's casket to the cemetery beneath the oaks on the highest point of the King land. Jane Isabella and her grown children were there; and Mollie Jones, Sarah Ann's daughter, had come in from Gonzales. Bettie saw Cousin Kizzie Outlaw, who had come all the way from Moore Station. There was Mayor Zorn and the carpenter Mr. Kishbaugh and his wife, Kittie, the child of Mahala King, who had been reared by Euphemia. Drucilla Lockhart Phillips, sister of Euphemia's friend Matilda, stood among the mourners, and Bettie remembered her last conversation with Euphemia about Matilda's mourning bracelet. How strange that Euphemia would have remembered her young friend on the eve of her own dying day. Of course, Tildy, a very old woman now, was at the gravesite with her friend Idella, as were Abe Miller and his wife, Lucinda Saphronia, and all the families whose lives had been eased by the cool strength of this good and just woman.

The small fenced cemetery reminded Bettie of an island in a sea of rolling pasture. The oaks towered above the fertile shore, like soft green mountains rising. It was very still and filled with a sense of the past. Some of the older headstones had tilted and were crumbling; they were not carved from the fine hard Georgia granite used in more recent years. Among the graves was that of Euphemia's first baby, Mary Jane, and Bettie felt a special sadness for the child who had no chance to live before she died. *So this is the other shore*, Bettie thought, *where I will be one day*. Euphemia's open grave was deep and dark, seeming to reach to the center of the earth. *What a very strange entrance to the Celestial City, as if we were all invited to Heaven through the back door. We go through the servants' entrance*, she thought. *After all we are all servants of God.*

Bettie turned away as the first shovel of dirt dropped with its awful unmistakable sound on the wood box below. Slowly, quietly, the mourners, both black and white, moved down the hill and away from the island in the field. When Bettie moved a short distance from the grave, she turned back, thinking perhaps something was left unsaid, something about Euphemia that must be out before the last shovelful fell. It seemed too quickly completed, this last tribute to Euphemia Texas Ashby King. She had been a pioneer and a warrior. She had hurled herself against the times and had changed the lives around her. Her life was heroic. Where then, Bettie wondered, were the parades, the medals cast in bronze, the tributes carved in stone to inspire generations to come? Euphemia was heroic, but she was a woman. There was no band with its drums and fifes playing "Come to the Bower" or "Bonnie Blue Flag." There was only the dull dread drumming of earth on wood.

Bettie saw one last mourner come to the hill and stand before the grave. Pink Rosebud dropped a flower into the partially filled opening and then knelt on both knees in prayer. Bettie's mind was filled with the astounding contrast between the woman who died and the woman who mourned. How absolutely different could two lives be? They had lived as neighbors for most of their adult lives, yet Bettie was certain they had never spoken. No cup of sugar borrowed, no greetings passed on holidays, no shared hours mending or in worship or in delivering babies or laying out the dead. Why, then, did the harlot pray at the passing of an old woman of unblemished virtue? Bettie watched as Pink Rosebud stood again in a motion both graceful and proud. Two strong women were there on the hill—one stood tall, the other lay in repose. Then Pink Rosebud moved out from under the shadows of the oaks and down the hill toward the river. As she was passing close by, Bettie felt compelled to speak.

"Please wait, Miss Rosebud," Bettie said, her inflection almost a question. She searched her mind for a way to express her feelings, how much she cared that Pink Rosebud was in her life. But all she heard herself saying was, "How very nice of you to come."

The woman paused and turned. She looked into Bettie's eyes. Her expression contained a mystery that would haunt Bettie the rest of her life. It was an odd blending of anger and sorrow and curiosity.

"Everybody loved Miss Euphemia," Pink Rosebud said, and then neither spoke for a time. Bettie heard the express from San Antonio whistle its approach to the depot.

"I wanted to say goodbye," Pink Rosebud said, at last. "She was my neighbor."

Then Pink Rosebud turned and walked toward home and it was the last time Bettie ever saw her, for the notorious madam left town the next day and never returned. She abandoned her houses and her gowns and her vast land holdings and simply disappeared without a forwarding address or a trace. All her girls, including Precious Honey Child, were last seen drinking cocktails with traveling salesmen on the late train to San Antonio.

For a long time Bettie thought about Euphemia and Pink Rosebud. She concluded it was somehow important that these two friends, whose only contact in all those years had been a nod in passing, would give in to fate's pressure at the same time. Pink Rosebud was driven out of town, Euphemia was taken under it. Both were gone; one despised in life, the other respected in death, each surely embraced by the love of God.

In the few years following Euphemia's death, the King house became a crucible of renewal. A whole cycle of life was beginning anew. First Kittie married Charley Fisher, and they started a store in Temple, Texas, the town where they had gone to school. Then Mildred married Clifton Fleming, nephew of the man who had owned the famous Billy Horse years before, and they moved out on the Capote Road near Papa Leonard's place. Ola, the youngest of Bettie's sisters, married Ferdinand Biediger and moved to the little town of Moore Station, on the railroad line between San Antonio and Laredo. Each time the flowers and wedding decorations had been cleared, another sister and her man stepped to the altar. "Reminds me of those magic bottomless trunks at the Glasscock Circus," Cayloma said. "One of those trunks that keeps dispensing an endless supply of clowns."

One late fall afternoon, Virginia and her little brother, George, were playing out in the brush near the Brenner farm, across the creek from Papa Leonard's place. In a particularly beautiful and lonely part of the woods, they came upon an unfinished house, the planks and timbers freshly cut. Soon, after reporting the house to Bettie and Henry, they learned the house was being built by Bettie's brother John as a gift for his bride, Jessie Elkins. But the work had halted when the bride's father, the formidable Parson Elkins, had refused to allow John to see his daughter ever again. The preacher had called him "an undesirable and a heathen," because he played cards and drank with the boys and was generally thought to be far beneath the station of the parson's daughter. John had been crushed and had abandoned the house. He had stayed clear of Leesville for more than a week, which was a lifetime, in his view, without Jessie.

Bettie was hurt, shocked, and furious, in roughly that order. She was hurt that John had not told her about a thing so important in his life, shocked that he played cards and drank with the boys, and furious that "that old fool of a parson" would consider her brother unworthy or un-Christian.

"Well," John said, "he's right. She is much too good for me."

"That's just not so! You're as good as anybody in this world."

"You haven't seen Jessie."

"I certainly haven't!"

"She's real pretty and good and perfect."

"Certainly has an ugly father," Bettie said. "What does Jessie think of all this?"

"I'm sure she loves me. She said so. Or at least she didn't say she didn't. And she yelled at her father when he ran me off."

"Well, if you want the girl and she wants you," Bettie said, "it's God's will should be served, not the parson's."

"Now, Bettie, don't do anything rash," Mr. Henry said. "I see that look in your eye."

"Well, God's will sometimes takes a while to move along. He's got an awful lot of folks to look after and a lot of lives to organize. I'm just going to give things a little push."

A few weeks later, John Moss rode up to the Elkins place. The parson looked up from where he was working a team behind the barn and shook his fist at the boy and bellowed that he be gone. John urged his horse forward, carefully keeping some distance from the enraged man of God. Brother Elkins leaped from his team, and as he came around the barnyard corner, he saw Jessie running from the house, her raven hair flying, both hands struggling with the satchel that held her pitiful dowry.

"Don't you dare go!" the parson shouted, and he ran after the girl faster than John knew preachers could run. John swept his intended onto the horse and thundered away just inches ahead of the flying, now cursing, parson.

At the main road, Frank Moss waited with a buggy. John and Jessie climbed in, and Frank mounted the horse, and they raced away to Seguin and to the King home on Court Street, where Bettie had kettles of hot water ready for the couple to freshen up. Bettie helped Jessie comb and brush her long, black hair and loaned the girl talcum to dust her lovely face. Jessie's eyes were bright and her excitement infectious, and in this first few minutes of their hurried acquaintance, Bettie grew to love the girl, and even supposed that, if pressed, she might have to admit Jessie could be too good for her often wayward brother, especially now that he had admitted to drink and cards.

Not only had Bettie heated kettles of water for the young couple, she had also made arrangements for them to be bathed in The Word. She had invited Brother T. J. Dodson to stand by with his Bible. Then, before the mantel in the King home in Seguin, Mr. Henry stood by John, and Bettie stood by Jessie, and the marriage was solemnized according to Baptist ritual. At 9:00 P.M., just three hours after Jessie had been spirited away on horseback, John and Jessie were man and wife and Bettie tasted the sweet and sinful joy of social vindication.

Meanwhile, much to the delight of Bettie and The Girls, Annie finally found a man who met the strict requirements she had set for any male she might consider as a husband. Apparently no man in America could pass muster, for she selected a New Zealander named Charlie Colville. Bettie and her friends thought he must have the strength of Paul Bunyan to win the heart of their Annie. "Or maybe the strength of his blue ox," Cayloma suggested, and she and Bettie spent hours on the front porch sewing and mending, and trying to imagine a man with strength of will and character enough to manage life with their good and dear friend.

Annie had met Charlie on a visit to her brother John's place in Roswell, New Mexico. They then returned to Seguin to be married. It was a small family wedding in the "new" house that William and Euphemia had built next door to their old log cabin.

Bettie's older brother, Frank, married Miss Daisy Konde, daughter of old Mr. Konde, who had gone south with William King and Leonard Moss to round up and brand cattle gone wild in the days following the Civil War. Bettie and Mr. Henry held an In Fair for the couple, and the house was filled with friends, neighbors, relatives, music, and the lively dialogue of joy.

Bettie never really got to know Daisy very well, though. Within a year, her sister-in-law lay screaming in these same rooms, giving birth to a child. Throughout Daisy's awful labor, Bettie held her and washed her burning face with cool water and whispered that everything would be all right. A few moments later, Daisy was dead. Bettie wished she knew more about this girl than that she had been sweet and frail and died hard.

Although Bettie was no stranger to death, Daisy's funeral made a profound impression on her. As a girl she had lived through the deaths of the neighbors in the tornado, and she had mourned the deaths of her mother and of Euphemia, and of the many other relatives and friends who had shared her journey through time. She understood that these were part of life, to be mourned for sure, but to be survived. Now, watching her brother weeping at the graveside of his young bride of only seventeen, she knew she had lied to Daisy in the same way she had been lied to all her life. *Things will not always be all right.*

Things began to go very, very wrong. Cayloma's husband, Felix, died. He had never really recovered from his encounter with the barbed-wire fence. Cayloma sold their house and moved to San Marcos, where she opened a small rooming house for boys. Annie's husband, Charlie, the indomitable New Zealander, died suddenly of a heart attack. Charlie had come into their lives like a brief, bright star. Now, just as quickly, he was gone. Tom Lay, Nuge's husband, pursued the downward spiral of his dreams in a mean hovel on the harsh skirts of the Chihuahuan Desert. Nuge continued to cling bravely to some kind of order and propriety as they fell. Both of Mary Lou Lannom's parents died and she was working dawn to dusk keeping the farm together, refusing to be burdened by what she considered the "overwhelming disadvantages" of wedlock. Only Bettie and Adda Gordon Thomas had been left relatively unscathed by the wounds and carnage of the years. *Things don't always turn out all right*, Bettie thought, as she, too, suffered the unspoken loss her friends shared.

"It's like we were in a war," Annie said. "We marched straight ahead into the enemy fire, like those British soldiers in their bright new uniforms, straight ahead, standing tall, our steps keeping time with the drum and the fife. And then we began to fall. One on our left, one on our right. But we marched on, stepping over the fallen."

And here we sit, Bettie thought, *the survivors, doing our tatting and embroidery, just as if nothing had happened. Except for the scars on Jennie's face, we are the same as we have ever been. We smell the same Seven Sisters roses and the trees in the yard look exactly the same this year as the year before.* With the possible exception of Annie, the philosopher, Bettie knew none of her friends would reveal their innermost feelings in a group. They had all confided individually to each other and in one-on-one, intimate talks had shared their dreams and their pain and their fear.

Now, together, they could carry on a long and passionate conversation without a word, or with words of little significance, and express volumes with their eyes and in the powerful intervals between the words.

"The wind has shifted to the south," Bettie said, glancing at the tops of the trees.

"I need to clean the grass from around the peach trees," Adda Gordon said.

"If it rains, the road will be very bad," Mary Lou said. "The ground will be so wet I won't get any work done at all."

Bettie listened to the ticking of knitting needles.

Then the silence was broken by Nuge. "What is the point of it all?" she said. She had stopped sewing and her back was rigid, her hands curled tight, her eyes closed. "This isn't the way it was supposed to be."

"Will went to the river and grafted some grapevines," Adda Gordon Thomas said. "Tomorrow we'll set some posts for a trellis." Then, after a moment, she quoted a passage from the Book of St. Luke. " 'Behold, I give unto you power to tread on serpents and scorpions, and over all the power of the enemy: and nothing by any means shall hurt you.' "

Again, there was a charged silence. Bettie perceived a difference in the wind. "There's rain in the air," she said.

"I'm going to marry again," Jennie said, and every head turned to regard the speaker with astonishment. "His name is Maurice. He stays at the hotel. He's a drummer." Jennie's fingers fairly flew over the pattern of her quilt. She was smiling so broadly her old scars were hidden by her dimples and the laugh lines of her eyes.

"Oh, for Heaven's sake," Cayloma said. "You can't mean it. Tell me it's just a bad joke."

"I know what you're thinking. But this time it's going to be wonderful. He comes from a fine family in Gonzales. They're coming to visit us Sunday. You'll see for yourself."

"Well, my, my, my," Annie said. "Will wonders never cease? I guess that's the point of it all." And she leaned over and kissed Jennie on her bruised cheek. For the rest of the afternoon, all The Girls could talk about was Maurice and Jennie, their courtship, where they would be married, what she would wear, where they would live, and how happy Jennie would be in this world where women had power enough to diminish serpents, scorpions, and the dark, dread knights of fortune. Bettie hoped it was true.

Then one morning in 1910, after Halley's Comet had passed over Seguin, Bettie prepared for a party at Adda Gordon Thomas's house. She selected a suit in current fashion, a freshly ironed blouse, and gold earrings to match her gold-handled umbrella. Her hair was neatly pinned. She removed from a shelf in her wardrobe a bonnet and gloves to protect her skin from the late August sun. George was in school and Virginia had gone with Annie to a chrysanthemum show sponsored by the Village Improvement Society. As Bettie stepped onto her front porch, she thought she heard someone calling. She went around to the west fence to see if someone had driven up the carriage driveway. Her neighbor, Sue Holley, was there, shouting that Mr. Henry had fallen from the cotton wagon and seemed to be badly hurt.

Bettie felt a numbing cold clutching at her heart as she ran down the hill toward King Branch, where it was said you could hear the footsteps of the dead at night. She cast away her gold-handled umbrella, and as she ran it came to her in an odd burst of recollection that she had been running full out when she first met Mr. Henry as a grown woman. Bettie could see old Granny Holley folding a blanket over something by the road and then she could see it was Mr. Henry, still and crooked, lying amid scattered cotton bales and the wreckage of the wagon.

Idella was there with Granny Holley, and two men from Baxter's Blacksmith Shop were bringing back old Charley and Old Sleepy, the mules that had broken free when the cotton load shifted and the wagon had overturned, throwing Mr. Henry down beneath the heavy bales. Although it was less than two hundred yards from her porch to the King Branch Bridge, it seemed miles to Bettie's racing mind, and at every terrible step she thought of the many men she had known who were ruined or killed by accidents on the farm. But she knew Mr. Henry was too strong to be among these broken men and surely, she thought, as she grew near, the grotesque bend his leg made in the road was a trick of the light and her eye.

Mr. Henry's eyes were closed. He didn't move. Bettie fell to her knees in the road and loosened his collar. She removed the jacket of her suit, rolled it tightly, and gently lifted his head to slide the jacket beneath it. Granny Holley returned from her house with a solution of water and whiskey and sugar that Bettie tried to spoon-feed to Mr. Henry while they waited for Dr. Stamps to come see what could be done. Most of the medicine ran from Mr. Henry's mouth onto the suit jacket she had selected for Adda Gordon Thomas's party. For a moment she wished that she were there, helping Adda serve lemon tea cakes and that Mr. Henry was on his way to the cotton compress with his harvest and that the incident on the haunted bridge was merely a runaway morbid thought, a nightmare, a bad dream. Then she heard Mr. Henry's breathing and she longed to cuddle him up and hold him, but she was afraid to even touch her husband for fear he was broken too badly to be healed or even helped by her love.

Soon Dr. Stamps arrived, all bluster and efficiency, asking for rags and napkins or a handkerchief to tie Mr. Henry's broken leg so he could be moved. By now a small crowd had congregated, and Abe Miller quickly removed his shirt for Dr. Stamps to use as a binding. The doctor removed the blanket, revealing the awful angle of Mr. Henry's leg, and as he lifted the two legs together to bind them to a wagon-board splint with Abe's shirt, Bettie thought she could actually hear the bones grinding against each other and she prayed that Mr. Henry would not soon awaken. *Sleep,* she prayed, *sleep through this for a while.* She remembered saying the same prayer, long ago when she was a girl, so that Mrs. Braddock might not wake and suffer the pain of seeing her dead children after the storm. Involuntarily, Bettie glanced skyward to see if black clouds were clustering, and her old feelings of dread all fused with a terrible new one.

Someone brought a shutter from the barn. The men carefully rolled Mr. Henry onto its surface and he was carried up the hill toward home. One arm hung loosely down and Bettie held that hand as they walked. Near the house, his hand closed on hers convulsively and she saw he had awakened.

"I'm being carried home on my shield," he told her. He said nothing more until he was placed on the dining room table, where he looked up at Bettie and said, "I'm so sorry."

Dr. Stamps had summoned Dr. Beasely and Dr. Graves to help him set the bones in Mr. Henry's leg. They poured ether on a wad of cotton and held it to his nose. Three men held him down as Dr. Stamps began his work. Mr. Henry stared at the ceiling and Bettie wiped away the sweat flowing from his brow. At one point, as Dr. Stamps was binding Mr. Henry's leg to a splint weighted with bricks Mr. Henry called out, "Oh, dear God!" and then he slipped away. For one terrible instant Bettie thought he had died, and she wished for the chariot of Jesus to come and sweep her away as well. Then she heard Dr. Stamps giving his orders for Mr. Henry's care, and she realized he was prescribing the kind of attention dead men do not require.

"There's a very good chance he'll recover," the doctor told Bettie, after several men had lifted Mr. Henry from the dining room table and carried him to the bedroom. "He's strong and healthy as a horse. If he doesn't get pneumonia he'll probably live through this. I think the thigh is the worst thing. It's a bad break that will heal slowly. He won't be himself for a long time and it's hard to tell how well the bones will mend. I can't find anything else broken, but there might be something inside we can't see." As he talked, his hands and fingers probed her husband's body, pushing here and bending there, and Bettie wished the doctor would go away now and leave them alone. She knew it was unreasonable, but as the doctor droned on she grew to dislike him intensely, as if he were the cause of Mr. Henry's pain, not the agent of its relief.

"Only time will tell," Dr. Stamps continued. "Time is the very best doctor. Better than me, for sure." He repacked the tools of his trade and went away, and Bettie was left alone with a man who hurt so bad she thought she would die.

Bettie pulled a chair up to Mr. Henry's bedside. She sat down and she waited. "Why me?" she said to herself, and felt a tug of shame because what had happened had not happened to her but to Mr. Henry. She listened to the traffic on Court Street and looked out the bedroom window toward Euphemia's house across the way. She thought of Euphemia and Sarah and all the King women who had pulled chairs up to the bedside of pain. "I will get through this," she said. She began to rock and plan dinner for the children, who would be coming home from the chrysanthemum show before long.

As Dr. Stamps had predicted, the break where Mr. Henry's hip met his thigh did not heal quickly or cleanly. When it became apparent he would not walk without pain, he carved a cane and fitted it with the gold handle of the umbrella Bettie had broken on her frantic dash downhill to the site of his accident on the King Branch Bridge.

Each morning, after the family had finished breakfast, the hands would gather for coffee on the bench behind the kitchen stove and Mr. Henry would tell them what work was scheduled for the day. Bettie was there, of course, filling their cups with fresh, hot coffee, passing out buttered biscuits, and listening to the men talk. She absorbed Mr. Henry's knowledge of the seasons as the earth absorbs the spring rains. After the hands had harnessed the mules and filed back to the fields, Mr. Henry returned to the front room, where he sat in the huge rocking chair that had been a gift of Governor Ireland. He visited with old friends, like County Commissioner Will Blanks, who came often to see how he fared. They told tales and talked about the news and politics and the weather. Then, leaning on his gold-handled cane, Mr. Henry rose and walked out to the back yard, where he could watch the workers cut cornstalks, or repair wagons, or haul firewood, or shell seed corn, or harrow the ground for millet, or curse the grasshoppers in the orchard. The effort caused such obvious pain that Bettie herself grew faint with the thought of it, and she had to fight to resist the temptation to persuade him to stay in the house. She was terrified he would fall and break the hip again, and that would be the end of him. Occasionally Abe helped Mr. Henry into the wagon to ride out and supervise the workers. That was when he was most like the Mr. Henry of old, the stern, good general watching over his men and keeping them safe and productive. But Bettie could see that these forays into the fields cost her husband dearly. She knew how the pain exhausted him and how he fought against that pain until the exhaustion was so great he would be driven back to his bed or into the Governor Ireland rocking chair to rebuild his strength and his spirit.

A few months after Mr. Henry had begun to walk with the aid of his cane, Bettie and Annie were sitting on the front porch when Little Virginia, now seventeen, came bounding up and settled into a rocker with all the grace of a newborn filly. Bettie doubted she herself had ever been as energetic as Little Virginia, certainly never as young. She seemed all legs and elbows and alacrity, leaning forward into life as if impatient for the next moment's arrival. Today, as she rocked, she wore a secret smile. But Bettie could tell it was a secret Virginia would not, could not, long keep. She was right.

"There's something important I want to say," Virginia said. "But don't tell Papa. At least not yet. Promise?"

"You know I can't promise such a thing."

"Well, at least don't tell him until Will talks to him. You can promise that."

"Virginia King, you aren't ..."

"Out with it," Annie said.

"Will Bergfeld asked me to marry him and I said yes!" The words hit Bettie like a soft hammer, and when she looked up from her sewing she saw a very young child looking back, her eyes filled with adventure and delight. For a moment she thought she had been awakened from a nap by words she could not quite understand.

"I'm sorry? I didn't quite hear." She knew, however, that she had heard and she would later wonder why her initial reaction was shock and her second was sorrow. After all, Virginia had been seeing Will for a year or more. She was almost the same age Bettie had been when she married Mr. Henry. But that was different. Things were different then. She speculated as to whether her sorrow had anything to do with Virginia at all. *Maybe I am mourning the loss of my own youth.*

"Mama!" A cloud passed behind Virginia's eyes. "Please say something!"

"It's hard," Bettie said, feeling the tears come. "I just didn't think it would come so soon."

"Please be happy, Mama."

"Oh, she's happy," Annie said. "Just give her a little time to get used to the idea. After all, Will Bergfeld is a little wild. Not exactly every mother's first choice."

"He is not wild!"

"Why, all of Seguin has seen him drive his motorcycle like a daredevil," Annie said. "Life is dangerous enough without such foolishness."

"Mama?"

A thousand thoughts ran through Bettie's mind, a thousand reasons why her baby should not marry. But none of them, especially that Will rode his motorcycle too fast or that Virginia was too young, made any sense at all. She thought of her mother, Mollie, and how she must have felt when she had married Mr. Henry, and she wiped away her tears, held out her arms toward Virginia, and said: "Come."

Virginia bounded up and folded down with Bettie in her chair, and Bettie rocked her child for the last time.

Once again the King household was thrown into a frenzy of controlled confusion. It was decided the wedding would be on Christmas Day at the King home. As Bettie and Annie set about to radically redecorate the entire house, they talked about the wisdom of their daughter and niece choosing for her husband a man renowned for riding his motorcycle wildly along the country roads and for shooting rattlesnakes as he passed at high speed. Bettie insisted, and she made Virginia promise, that she would not accompany Will Bergfeld on any of his daredevil antics. For weeks before the wedding, the house was filled with friends and family and painters transforming the conservative parlor with a color scheme that the Seguin newspapers would call "a tasteful blending of pink and white" and that would make Mr. Henry complain he had somehow been imprisoned within a wedding cake.

On the night before the ceremony, Mr. Henry confided to

Bettie a fear that had grown in his heart as the wedding had approached. For years, watching his beautiful little girl grow into a woman, he had pictured the day of her wedding and how proud he would be to walk down the aisle at her side to give her hand in marriage.

"Someone else will have to do it," he told Bettie. "I'm afraid to. What if I were to fall? She is so beautiful and I walk so ugly."

"Virginia knows how you love her. She'll know you're at her side, even if you're not physically there." Bettie could feel his indecision and she did not know what to advise. No one can feel another's physical pain or measure the limits of the struggle against it. She could tell that Mr. Henry felt removed, even isolated, from the wedding preparations, as if he had no role and was only a distant spectator to one of the most important events in his daughter's life. Fate was denying him a very special moment in the life of a father. "One way or another, you'll be there," she told him. "You'll be there and she will know."

On Christmas morning Mr. Henry rose and did battle with his pain, but even with his enormous strength and indomitable will he could not walk far without collapsing onto his cane for support and leaning there on his cane waiting for the numbing agony to pass. Bettie watched his struggle, and she held him tightly when he made his decision.

In the afternoon, Helen Bartels, the maid of honor, beamed as "To the End of the World with You" was played and Virginia, wearing a chocolate-brown velvet suit and a pearl-and-diamond lavaliere, a gift from the groom, and carrying a bouquet of white carnations, came into the parlor on the arm of her grandfather Papa Leonard Moss. Bettie had never been so proud and she would have been very happy if she hadn't known how badly Mr. Henry wished to be at his daughter's side. As Virginia passed her father, she paused and kissed his cheek before proceeding on to the fireplace mantel banked with flowers. It was the most beautiful gesture Bettie had ever seen, and she wondered, as she watched Mr. Henry's face, which of them was most proud of this daughter they had made together.

* * *

As the years went by, war threatened in Europe, and Bettie was thankful it was so far away. In Seguin, Mr. Henry completed his service as finance chairman of the church, and because of his injury he participated in only the less demanding activities of the church and his lodge. Each day, after reading the mail, Mr. Henry rode to the fields in his buggy to assess the progress of the crops. He talked with the hands, asking for their opinions and offering advice from his reading of the latest farm journals. Usually Bettie rode with him, and as her understanding of his work grew, she had less and less time for The Girls.

In the afternoons, it was a common sight for those driving down Court Street to see Mr. Henry on the shady side of his front porch reading his paper, or propped back with his chair leaning against the porch post and his newspaper tented across his face. Annie remarked that Mr. Henry was like a human sundial: you could tell the time of day by where he had positioned his chair to escape the summer sun. Sometimes, after lunch, Bettie would lay a mat down on the front hall floor, where she would rest for an hour. Lying out flat on her back with her head toward the door, she was near Mr. Henry and could hear him if he called. She loved this hour of pleasant inactivity. Unlike Henry, she did not sleep, for sleep made time pass too quickly. Rather, she would close her eyes and open her mind to the world around her and time would flow by slowly and sweetly and she would be swallowed up by the afternoon. She heard the life of the town; the blacksmith's truck rattling by, or the iceman, and sometimes the song old Sing Lee, the laundryman, sang as he carried notes between children in love. She listened to screen doors slamming down at Granny Holley's, and she heard the voices of the children playing chase and the train heading off somewhere, its whistle wailing an invitation to the imagination.

Bettie cherished her afternoon repose primarily because repose in her life had become so rare. She had thought life would become easier and more leisurely when the battalions of youngsters and her own children bivouacked in the way of her life marched away to homes of their own. But her day was still filled to overflowing. As Mr. Henry was less able to manage any difficult physical chores, Bettie was more and more involved in the day-to-day operation of the farm. And in many ways she longed for the old days when cotton was the money crop, because it was so basic, while today it seemed their problems multiplied with the number of crops they raised. Bettie spent more and more time outside, enlarging the garden, supervising hog killing, taking charge of the orchard. Although the farm continued to prosper, Bettie felt it was no longer growing as it had when Mr. Henry had been more active. He continued to study new methods in farm journals and at the annual County Fair, but he no longer seemed interested in acquiring new land or new equipment.

Each time the farmhands went to the Cantu farm to cut firewood, they took enough for Tildy to keep her old bones warm over the winter. After Sarah died, Tildy had come to live on the King Place in a little house near Rosie Bean and her son Johnny.

Bettie sometimes joked that she was turning out to be as good a farmer as Mary Lou Lannom, who was fast becoming an old maid while still cultivating her lands as her father had.

Mary Lou reminded Bettie of a strange phenomenon that sometimes occurred among the local Mexican families. La quedada, Bettie thought, *the one who remains. Mary Lou is* la quedada, *the daughter who never marries, the one on whom all others depend, particularly the parents as they grow older.*

Without fail, every Sunday evening, promptly at seven, as predictable as the coming of night itself, Mary Lou found the time to ring up Bettie on the telephone. Often there was no reason for the call except to say hello. But one of Mary Lou's peculiarities was that she never said goodbye. When she considered the talk finished she simply hung up, often leaving the other party speaking to the empty wires.

Mary Lou was not alone. Bettie's telephone was a clearinghouse for all the news and information concerning the life and times of Seguin, Texas.

One day Annie called with the terrible news that Will Thomas had died. After the initial shock, Bettie's thoughts turned to Adda.

"What will she do? How will she manage those three children?"

"What can she do?" Annie asked. "Take in sewing, I suppose."

"We survive," Bettie said. "Mama Euphemia used to say most Texas men had three wives. The first and second wives died in childbirth, or were just bone tired and worn out before their time."

"We must be a very tough crowd," Annie said. "They should send us to France. The war would be over a lot sooner."

When the British liner *Lusitania* was torpedoed by a German U-boat and went down with 128 Americans aboard, the call for America to enter the war grew to a clamor. The talk on Bettie's front porch and on her telephone centered on the unexpected clash between President Wilson and his Secretary of State, William Jennings Bryan.

"Did you hear Bryan resigned?" Mary Lou said, as an opening to one of her 7:00 P.M. phone calls.

"It's a shame," Bettie said. "Bryan might have kept us out of this war. He did everything he could. But Wilson is bent on a war. Trouble is, it's our boys who'll have to fight." After pressing her point still further, she waited for Mary Lou to agree, before realizing she had hung up, in mid-conversation, some moments before.

All along Court Street, Bettie could feel a gathering mood for war. Flags began to appear in colorful profusion and a spirit of patriotism grew. The old soldiers who had fought the Comanches, the Apaches, and the Yankees, or had been with Winfield Scott in Vera Cruz, or had made that wild ride with Teddy Roosevelt up San Juan Hill, began to feel the old and violent lure of battle. The young boys who had never heard a shot fired in anger began to group on corners to contemplate the ancient and compelling mystery of war.

One day Adda called and told Bettie, "Quick. Hang up your phone and go look out your window!" There, along Court Street, was a parade of people carrying signs and banners. "Death to the

Kaiser," the signs read. "Kill the Huns." At the front of the parade was a flatbed truck with an effigy of the Kaiser strung up beneath a gallows. When they had passed by, Bettie returned to the phone.

"Who are they?" she asked.

"From Leesville. They don't have German families there. So they've brought their hate here."

Later that day, in front of the courthouse, the Kaiser was hanged in effigy. Prejudice against the German families grew. One of the most respected Seguin preachers, a man of German extraction who preached his sermons in German, killed himself rather than face the humiliation and hatred he could not understand.

By the end of July, 1917, the sons of most of The Girls had gone into the service. Bettie's son George, Nuge's son Harry, Annie's son Myron, Adda's son Oury, Virginia's husband Will, Rosie Bean's son Johnny, had all been taken to the depot and carried away by the train. By the time The Girls returned from the depot and settled on Bettie's front porch, the train had already crossed the trestle over Dead Man Creek and the whistle could no longer be heard. "Well," Annie said. "They killed most of the men. I guess now it's time for them to have a shot at our boys."

"Who's they?" Cayloma asked.

"Whoever it is that makes these wars. I didn't make this war. Did you? Somebody did. I want that person delivered to me here so I can spit in his eye!"

"Wind shifting to the south," Adda said.

"What's the war for?"

"Democracy," Bettie answered.

"A word?" Annie said.

"A principle," Bettie replied.

"What difference does it make to the dead?" Annie was angry and thoughtful, and the others were quiet in respect for her anger and her thoughts.

After a while, Bettie asked: "Do you think, somewhere over there, some women like us have just sent their boys off to war? Maybe sent them on a train to the front? And they asked themselves what it's all for?"

"To make the world safe for tyrants," Cayloma said. "Maybe that."

Bettie rolled her eyes, as she sometimes did when Cayloma refused to take important matters seriously. It was a thing she had learned from her children. "Do you think they want their sons to go to war? Of course not. I can see them on a porch like this, good Christian women who love their children and would rather die than see them hurt. Why can't we talk with these mothers and work things out?"

Adda caught the spirit of the argument. "When the war people come with their flags and their slogans to carry our children away, we would just join hands and say: 'Get on out of here 'cause nobody's coming to your damn war.' "

Bettie smiled and sighed, and they all looked off toward Dead Man Creek, but they could not hear the cry of the whistle of the trains taking their sons to war.

The war against the Kaiser did not come to Seguin, but the influenza epidemic that began in 1918, the same year the war ended, did. Early in 1919 Mr. Henry and Bettie were hit, as if by the Kaiser's gunfire, and were driven to their knees and to bed. They prayed for each other and for George and for all the people who were dying, and for an end of God's anger toward their own. Virginia, who now had two girls and was pregnant with a third child, was living at Bettie's house while her husband served with the Matagorda Bay shore defenses. She simply could not cope with the demands of nursing so many people. To help out, Rosie Bean moved into the plunder room and took over the many household chores, caring for the stricken family with patience, kindness, and competence. Mr. Henry's fever raged for days. Bettie's chill grew more pronounced and she felt as if every muscle in her body was shaking.

With the coming of spring, the King family began to recover. One sun-blessed morning, Mr. Henry and Bettie took the buggy out into the newly turned fields. Bettie reached over to take Mr. Henry's hand. The joy of seeing the earth waiting for the seed and for life to start anew made her confident the bad days were over. "I think we've put this dreadful war and this awful winter behind us," she said. For the first time in a long time, she wanted to sing out loud, simply to express her happiness.

Then Mr. Henry's hand grew tense. Bettie followed his gaze to the mules hitched to the back gate of Em and Rosie Bean's house. As a farm woman, she knew there were only two reasons a man stopped plowing this early in the morning. Someone was either hurt or sick.

"I'll see to it," she said, knowing she could run into the house and out before Mr. Henry could struggle out of the buggy. When she reached the door, she saw Em was holding Rosie in his arms. Rosie's face was frozen, like stone.

Em saw Bettie in the door. "That long black car came from the army. They said our boy Johnny is gone." Bettie helped Em get Rosie to her bed. "Miss Bettie, could you please call Dr. Davis to come. Rosie's been mighty sick, and now this."

Although she had worn a soft cotton mask to protect herself from contagion, Rosie's constant attention to the Kings and other neighbors and friends had worn her down, and she was exhausted and weary and ill. When word came Johnny had been killed Rosie took to her bed, and died. Em told Bettie, "I think she just gave up so as to cross over and join her boy."

After the war was over, and the old Texan Colonel Edward House had helped President Wilson work his plans for a just and lasting peace, all the sons of The Girls came home. Johnny Bean was buried in France.

During the years following the war, a kind of normalcy settled over Bettie's life and her land. Sometimes now it was Bettie who instructed the hands in the morning before the big wood stove. Mr. Henry would be there with his books before him, but it was Bettie who scheduled the work in the sorghum patch or with the north crop or in the bottoms where there was good firewood to be chopped.

Bettie's home continued to be the center of the life of a great extended family and rarely a day went by without visitors. The town was changing fast and it now seemed to Bettie there were more automobiles than cows. She was alarmed that the town had quickly swallowed the King farm whole, and that their place, which had once been on the edge of town, was now closer to its center. But there were some things that did not change fast enough to suit her. The forces of bigotry were once again forming in Seguin and Bettie would find herself in the vanguard of those who opposed them.

Each year on Independence Day, the Farmer's Alliance hosted a public celebration in the wooded park where the Capote Road Bridge crossed the Guadalupe River. Nearly everyone in town attended the eagerly anticipated all-day affair. It was a time for families to renew their friendships, to reaffirm their love of liberty, and to discuss the latest political issues. In 1922, the issue on everyone's mind and lips was Congressman Harry Wurzbach, the first Republican congressman since Reconstruction to represent Guadalupe County and the only Texan in Congress to vote for the Dyer Bill, a law that made lynching a criminal offense.

Bettie and Mr. Henry drove out to the celebration in their 1919 Dodge automobile. As they moved toward the Capote Bridge, Bettie balanced a bowl of peach cobbler in her lap and tried to will Mr. Henry to slow down to a respectable speed. "I think twelve miles an hour is entirely too fast," she told her husband, the wind in the open car tugging at her hair and cooling the cobbler. Since his accident in the cotton wagon, these high rates of speed made her nervous.

"I really think you should learn to drive," Mr. Henry said. "If you knew how easy it is, you'd be more comfortable."

"I can't imagine why I'd want to do that. Driving's a man's job."

Just beyond a rise in the road, they came upon a team of mules driven by Sal Ray Boyd. The wagon was loaded with watermelons and large wooden barrels of lemonade. Sal Ray's daughters, Rachel, Aileen, and Nancy, were struggling to steady the barrels on the wagon. The four Boyd women had been hired by the Farmer's Alliance to help serve watermelons and lemonade at the picnic. Bettie was once again impressed by the Boyds, not only by their beauty, but by their strength as well. A descendant of Granny Boyd's slaves, Sal Ray's husband had died shortly after the youngest girl's birth. Yet Sal Ray had managed to raise her daughters alone and to make a stable home for her family on a small plot not far from the King land. They raised much of the food they needed and they made extra money catering and serving at parties, fairs, and public celebrations.

Just as Mr. Henry was preparing to pass the Boyd wagon, a Ford flew by, its wheels spinning, its horn blaring. Bettie recognized Dewey Rouche, owner of the livery stable, as he called out to Rachel, Sal Ray's eighteen-year-old daughter. Dewey Rouche was well known for chasing after Negro women.

When they arrived at the Capote Bridge, the grounds were lined with wagons, buggies, and automobiles. People stood in small groups or sat on the hoods of automobiles or on quilts beneath the trees. Children chased each other through the crowd or swam in the river. Soon the Boyd women arrived with the lemonade, and the men of the Farmer's Alliance helped them wrestle the barrels to the serving area where tables were spread with food. Each family had brought one dish and a dessert. The men of the Farmer's Alliance had cooked barbecue all night, and they began to sell heaping plates of beef and pork. Rachel Boyd and her daughters ladled lemonade from the barrels and sliced wedges of watermelon. Bettie and Henry spread a quilt on the riverbank.

A rocket arched into the sky and they heard a fusillade of firecrackers. "Mama Euphemia said they didn't have fireworks when she was a girl," Bettie recalled. "They just banged their hammers on anvils and horseshoes at the blacksmith shop."

Bettie looked out at the crowd. "Well, I love Independence Day. It's one day a year everybody gets along."

"Don't be so sure," Mr. Henry warned, only half joking. "The political speeches have yet to begin."

After lunch, Bettie saw Darden Wurzbach, wife of the congressman, walking along the river. Bettie invited her good friend to join them for the speeches. Darden was an extremely attractive woman with dark hair and dark eyes, and with an intensity in her manner that Bettie found intriguing. She seemed constantly on her guard, perhaps poised to defend the controversial actions of her husband. As they moved through the crowd toward the platform, Darden whispered to Bettie her concern about the speeches. "Some people here are very angry at Harry. It's not just that he voted for the anti-lynching bill. It's a speech he made to an all-Negro audience in Washington. Harry just said all people are equal in the eyes of God, no matter what the color of their skin. I've never seen people so angry about truth."

The speeches soon began. Each of the politicians up for election that November had been assigned a specific amount of time to speak. The first on the platform were those officials running for state office. Then came the two candidates for the U.S. Congress. Bettie could feel the excitement and tension building as the time grew near for the congressional candidates to speak. She was not at all pleased to find herself standing behind Dewey Rouche and some of his unsavory companions.

Among the first candidates to speak was a man named Hertzberg, who was Harry Wurzbach's Democratic opponent. As challenger, he spoke first. Harry, a short, stocky man with quiet, almost peaceful eyes, sat patiently waiting his turn. Hertzberg lost little time launching into an attack on his opponent's "peculiar and unhealthy" views on race. As Darden had predicted, Hertzberg was infuriated by Harry Wurzbach's vote for the anti-lynching bill and the contents of the congressman's speech to the all-Negro audience.

"Just imagine!" Hertzberg shouted. "You good people may find this difficult to believe, but Congressman Wurzbach believes that there is no difference between a white woman and a colored woman except the color of her skin. And my friends, the greatest outrage about this poor excuse of a man in public office is that he writes letters to a Negress just like she was a white woman!"

As Hertzberg was awaiting a reaction to his revelation, Rachel Boyd walked by with a pitcher of lemonade. Dewey Rouche stopped her and put his arm around her. "You must be the gal the congressman writes his love letters to," he said quite loudly to Rachel and the crowd, and he pulled her to him in a suggestive embrace. As if by automatic reflex, Bettie raised the gold-handled umbrella she was holding and she thrust the pointed end into Dewey Rouche's ribs. Dewey released his hold on Rachel and swung around with his fist poised. In a firm and steady voice, Mr. Henry said: "Dewey, I'd like for you to get out of my sight. And I better never see you set foot on King land as long as I live."

Dewey looked at Bettie, then at Mr. Henry and the cane on

which Mr. Henry leaned. "Maybe you won't live all that long, old man."

Bettie was so angry she raised her umbrella again for another blow. Mr. Henry said later she looked like the Count of Monte Cristo preparing for a duel to the death. But before she could strike, Sheriff Neubauer intervened. "Settle yourself down and move along, Dewey," the sheriff said, as he and a deputy helped him do just that.

Bettie's heart was making such a commotion that she missed the rest of Hertzberg's speech. She noticed Rachel wiping spilled lemonade from the front of her dress. "Are you hurt, Miss Bettie?" Rachel asked.

"No," Bettie said. "Are you?"

"No, ma'am. I'm not hurt this time."

"Look at poor Harry," Darden said. "He just has to sit there and take all those things that awful man says. It's bound to hurt. I don't care if they say it isn't ladylike for an elected official's wife to sit next to her husband on the platform. From now on, I'm going to be right there next to Harry." Then Darden left to do what simply was not done. She sat next to her candidate husband to share both his honors and his wounds.

On the way home, Bettie's heart was still hammering away and her thoughts and feelings were in a whirl. She was astounded at the violence she had discovered in herself and she was angry. *How can people say such terrible things?* she asked herself. *How can people be so cruel? What if I hadn't had an umbrella? What if the umbrella had been a sword? What if the sheriff hadn't passed by? What if Henry hadn't been there?* She thought of that now and the thought was both painful and confusing.

As they turned onto Court Street, Bettie at last began to grow calm and she decided that maybe it was time she did something about people like Dewey Rouche and the Klan and that terrible Hertzberg. She didn't know exactly what, but if she got the chance—well, it would be more than a cane in the ribs this time.

Within days, Bettie had her chance. One Sunday evening, there was a special song service at the Presbyterian Church. Bettie, Mary Lou, Annie, and Jennie were sitting in the front pew, to be recognized for their work providing new bedding for the

needy. While the quartet was singing "Nearer the Cross," a robed
and masked messenger walked up the center aisle and handed an
envelope to the minister, Reverend Thomas Griffiths. As the
Klansman turned to face the startled congregation, Bettie saw a
dozen or more other robed and masked figures move into the
church and down the side aisles. A hush settled over the congregation. Bettie could feel the fear moving in the church and she
could see it in the eyes of the worshipers. Reverend Griffiths
cleared his throat and opened the envelope. Bettie saw the minister remove a letter and what seemed a substantial number of
greenbacks. The minister reached forward and placed the money
in a collection plate, handed the letter to Deacon George Vaughn,
and asked him to read it to the congregation.

"Whenever a man of sterling integrity who is a servant of the
lowly Nazarene distinguishes himself by unceasing devotion and
righteousness, it is fitting that some expression of commendation
and gratitude be made in recognition of his valuable service and
as a token of appreciation.

"We believe that as it is a custom to honor, decorate with
medals, men of war who have distinguished themselves by acts of
conspicuous gallantry and bravery in battle, so should the warrior
or leader in Christ's cause likewise be honored for untiring devotion and services in His cause."

The letter was signed by some kind of peculiar title Bettie
thought sounded very Eastern, exotic, and un-American. As Deacon Vaughn handed the letter back to the minister, the Klansmen
began passing out leaflets. Bettie was appalled to see they were
urging the election of the hatemonger Hertzberg. "I must say we
are honored by this most generous gift," Reverend Griffiths said,
with a slight bow to the Klan leader who stood right next to
Bettie's place on the front pew. Bettie was sure she noticed the
sour smell of cheap whiskey coming from beneath the man's
robes. "We should consider the gift as appreciation for what all of
us in God's house have done." Then the preacher asked them to
join him in prayer. Bettie was again appalled to hear him pray for
the Klansmen who worked so hard and "at great personal risk to
cleanse the community of usurpers and the unrighteous."

Bettie looked toward the front of the church, where Jennie

Scott Hodges was sitting at the organ. Their eyes met and Bettie felt the heat of her friend's anger searing across the space between them. *The very arrogance of these people,* she thought. *First they try to control the political system, then the judicial system and now they're even trying to control the church. How dare they come into our sacred place with their hate!* Bettie turned and looked back at the congregation. She met Annie's eyes and could tell she was outraged as well. In the midst of the minister's prayer the Klansmen started to distribute campaign literature. Bettie's eyes were drawn to a sound that did not belong at all to the moment. Mary Lou was pounding a staccato rhythm on the back of a pew with a hymnal! From the rear, another woman began stamping her foot with the same rhythm. It was loud and disruptive, and the preacher looked up from his prayer, but continued in praise of the Klan. Jennie began playing loud and dissonant chords on the organ. Again, the same cadence, the rhythm building and growing insistent and imperative as more and more people joined in the drumming and pounding.

The preacher stopped his prayer and asked, then shouted, for quiet. The Klansmen nervously moved from one foot to the other and exchanged glances from beneath their hoods. Betty thought they were deciding whether or not to leave.

Bettie looked down and saw the Klan leader's robe was only inches from her foot. As he took a step to leave, she put her heel hard on his robe and pressed down with all her might. The Klansman tried a hurried retreat. But with his garment trapped by Bettie's foot, his hood pulled away and the Klansman was revealed to the entire congregation. The pounding rhythm ceased and it was very quiet. Then a woman giggled. A chuckler joined in.

"It's only Dewey!" someone exclaimed. Now raucous laughter filled the sanctuary like an anthem. "It's only Dewey!" Dewey Rouche ran from the church, followed by a chorus of guffawing and catcalls and whistles and by the other Klansmen, unsuccessfully seeking to retain their air of menace as they departed.

Deacon Vaughn and several others moved to the front of the church and spoke quietly to the preacher. Jennie began to play "A Mighty Fortress Is Our God" and the people began to sing as fervently as they ever had. Reverend Griffiths was escorted from the church, and despite his "unceasing devotion and righteousness" Bettie and The Girls refused to attend the church again until the presbyter found cause to send him to Ada, Oklahoma.

It was difficult for Bettie to say whether Jennie's second husband abandoned her or she abandoned him. Jennie had been so devastated and humiliated when she had been abandoned by her first husband, the handsome felt-hat salesman, that she rarely went on the road with her second salesman at all.

When he packed his trunk of wares and headed toward Gonzales or San Antonio or to the towns along the border, Jennie usually found reason to remain in Seguin with her mother. It seemed to Bettie the marriage finally just withered away, like a muscle seldom used.

Shortly before Jennie fell out of love with her second drummer, her mother sold the hotel and bought a store building on West Court Street, which she divided into three houses. Jennie, her son, and her mother lived in one and they rented the others to people for little more than promises each month. In the terrifying years since the death of her doctor husband, Jennie's mother had been increasingly enveloped in a kind of grayness, like a plant kept too long from the sun. Jennie had to take over more and more of the responsibility of their survival. Sometimes when Bettie saw her old friend, who had once been so beautiful and affluent and had twice been so exorbitantly in love and twice abandoned, struggling just to survive, her heart nearly broke. But Jennie was like a cork in the flood, buoyant and light and resilient.

Nearly every week, Bettie took Jennie and her mother gifts from the garden, and at hog-killing time she gave them pork and sausage. Jennie's father had amassed an extensive and valuable library, and each time Bettie took food, Jennie gave Bettie a book in return. Some were first editions and collector's items. For a while Bettie had been concerned that Jennie, out of pride, would refuse the gift of food. But there developed a kind of living game between the two women, with no discomfort when nourishment for the mind and food for the body were exchanged.

As the years went by, Jennie continued to wear the clothes that had been stylish when she first astounded wandering drummers with her beauty. Now they were sadly threadbare and out of style. Jennie was terribly afraid of automobiles and when Bettie saw her walking all over town in her antediluvian fashions, she realized her friend was becoming an eccentric. She was shocked at the changes time and poverty could bring to those she loved. In many ways, Jennie remained much the same as always: alert, loving, a caring and active member of her church. But who was that woman Jennie had climbed inside? That woman who leaped in fear at the sound of an automobile horn and wore old-fashioned clothes purchased at church rummage sales?

After Charlie Colville's death, Annie had at first assumed his responsibilities as partner in the Smith-Colville Grocery business. But Charlie's partner ignored her suggestions and advice, even the fact that she was a partner. "It was just a matter of time before he ruined us," Annie said. "I couldn't bear to see all Charlie's work go down the drain." At the first opportunity, she sold her half of the business and invested her money in a number of new companies like American Telephone and Telegraph and General Motors.

Cayloma, like Mary Lou and Annie with no husband to lean on, was making it on her own in a man's world. The boarding house she operated in San Marcos after her husband's death had become a favorite among students at Southwest Texas State Teachers College. Like Jennie and Mrs. Scott, who had managed to profit from trading property and from renting rooms and serving meals, she had found one of the few ways a woman alone could succeed or even survive in Texas. Adda, who took in sewing, and Pink Rosebud, who took in men, had found the other two ways.

One early morning, the day after some of Cayloma's student boarders had performed in a school play entitled "This Thing Called Love," a fire somehow started in the kitchen of the roominghouse. At about 1:30 A.M., Cayloma was awakened by the heat and the smoke. "I opened my door, and the flames were racing up the staircase and down the halls and they were being sucked into the rooms. It was like winds on fire. I remember screaming and running and seeing these fireballs and then realizing with horror they were burning people running through the flames, jumping through the windows like Roman candles."

Six of the boarders were severely burned and most suffered broken bones from the leap out the second-floor windows and the balcony. According to the *San Marcos Record*, the fire alarm was turned in too late for local firemen to save the house. Although frightened, neither Cayloma nor her son was badly injured. But Cayloma was out of a job temporarily and she returned home to Seguin and to her friends, to mend and to make plans for the future.

On Cayloma's first evening back in Seguin, Bettie and Mr. Henry invited Cayloma and Jennie, Jennie's son, and Jennie's mother for dinner. When they were seated, Bettie asked Jennie to say the blessings. As Jennie began to thank God for sparing Cayloma from the fire, her deaf mother, supposing Bettie had meant for her to lead the prayer, also began praising God for Cayloma's delivery. So heartfelt was Jennie's prayer and so deeply did she concentrate on the Lord that both continued their simultaneous prayers. "It was a battle," Cayloma later said, "between the deaf and the devout." Before too long, Cayloma was back in business. It was absolute proof, she would say, of the power of prayer.

Bettie's third grandson was born in the King home on Court Street during that strange season in American social history when the nation was fascinated with the boy King Tut who had been unearthed at Luxor, Egypt, a few years previously. Cayloma teased Bettie with the supposition the new baby would be named Tutankhamen King. They did not reach quite so far for a name. He was called George Henry King, after his father and grandfather.

There were times, when little George Henry was nestled in his cradle, when Bettie would creep into the back room to watch him sleeping. Sometimes she would stay so long she pulled a chair close to watch in comfort the subtle changes of his face as he dreamed. She realized why great painters had never been able to capture the beauty of an infant. They change, she thought, with each breath, with each twist and turn of their dream. Annie, who was a fine painter, had once said with her typical irreverence:

"There has never been a painting of Baby Jesus any other mother but Mary could really love. And on the basis of the paintings of the infant Moses it's a wonder he made it out of the bulrushes."

On these nights with George King, the thought came to her that she had never stayed like this to watch her own children sleeping. Too often there were too many other, more pressing, things to do, and she simply had not had time. Her love for this child was so intense it alarmed her. The awful opposite of love, fear of its loss, lingered at the bottom of her heart, dreadful and repressed. Cayloma suggested it was thanksgiving she now enjoyed. "Here is a child you can love without worrying about making it mind. Making a child pick a switch really complicates love."

As Bettie grew older, her fear of storms did not pass away. She had hoped the years would change this troubling, even humiliating aspect of her life and she would grow out of it as a child grows out of a particularly annoying habit, like bedwetting. Her strange affliction was one of those unspoken mysteries that some families experience but do not mention beyond the walls of the house and her own family certainly did not mention the mystery in Bettie's presence. She was sure The Girls talked about it constantly among themselves and that her children did as well. Sometimes she felt like a person with epilepsy, subjecting her family and friends to a loving yet fearsome vigilance and when the thunder rolled in the distance she would hide as much to avoid their eyes as to avoid the storm. Sometimes she would decide to sit down and reason the thing out, like the intelligent, practical woman she was. But when she tried, her mind simply would not stay still and focused. It was like trying to catch one of those greased pigs at the fair: The harder she tried to grasp the thing, the more easily it slipped away.

One summer afternoon when Cayloma and Bettie were shelling peas on the front porch, clouds began to build to the west and the wind freshened and the day grew dark and lightning made a tracery of vivid veins in the cloud. Bettie began to grow restive and her fingers hesitant. Cayloma said, "Tell me what's wrong."

"I'm frightened."

"Of what?"

"I don't know."

"Please, Bettie. I want to know so I can help." Cayloma
turned in her chair, took the bowl of peas from Bettie's lap, and
grasped her two hands in her own. "Share this with me," she said.
"Tell me why you're afraid."

"Something bad's going to happen."

"Something bad always happens. Only dead people don't
have bad things happen to them. Are you afraid of death?"

"No."

"Of the storm?"

"Yes."

"But what about the storm?

"It's hard to think. I'm afraid." Bettie swallowed the numbing
dread rising like bile. "I'm just afraid. I don't know why."

The first large drops of rain fell and the wind swept the dust
from the barnyard and the tops of the trees were set in motion.
"If you don't let me go . . ."

"You'll what? You'll die?"

"No."

"What, then?" Cayloma leaned forward, her hands tightened,
her dark hair pulled from its pins by the wind.

"I'm afraid." Bettie had begun to weep, yet she did not pull
her hands away. "I'm afraid of being left alone." Now there was
thunder rumbling and the rain became a solid wall. Bettie trembled and sobbed and her cries were like the howling of an animal.
Cayloma lifted her friend from the chair and half-carried her inside and put her in bed. After removing Bettie's shoes, she covered her with Euphemia's Texas Star quilt and she lay down
beside her and sang to her until the storm and Bettie's terror had
passed.

In February, 1932, one of those magical early springs swept
into Texas on the wings of a balmy southerly wind. Windows
were thrown open and Bettie plundered the plunder room for
blankets and quilts to be aired in the fragrant sunlight. As usual,
the house on Court Street was a magnet for visitors, including
Henry's old friend Will Blanks, and with the help of Abe Miller
they brought the Governor Ireland chair out on the porch, so Mr.

Henry could be out in the healing air and talk politics with the former county official. They talked of the mounting number of unemployed and of Hoover and the likelihood he would be defeated by Roosevelt in the November elections. They talked of troubles in Germany and the famine sweeping Russia. Bettie could see Mr. Henry was tiring, yet it had been some time since she had seen him so interested and alive and seemingly free of pain.

In the late morning, Sue Holley brought Mr. Henry a mess of greens from her garden. Annie came by with flowers and news that Amelia Earheart had announced she would fly nonstop, alone, across the Atlantic from Newfoundland to Ireland. Little George Henry and his best friend Allen Hoermann came leaping onto the porch claiming that they had seen the mythical Peachtree, the wild old kook who lived in the Guadalupe bottoms. Cayloma dropped by with her new Kodak. She asked George Henry to pose beside his grandfather so she could take a snapshot. Bettie called her friend aside. "Let's not take a picture of him now," she said as she looked at the shadow of the man she married. "Let's remember him as he was." The visiting continued and people came and departed in a continuing parade throughout the morning.

Just before noon, old Idella passed with her grandchild. She looked up toward the porch, and then inexplicably she turned and hurried away as if she had seen something frightening on Bettie's porch. "What a strange woman," Annie said as they watched Idella pulling the little girl along toward her house.

After lunch, when Mr. Henry had returned to his room to rest and the noontime dishes had been dried and put away, Bettie and Annie returned to the front porch. They looked across the side lawn to the house where Euphemia had lived for so many years.

"Do you know why our bedroom is on the wrong side of the house?" Bettie asked.

"Wrong side?"

"Everybody's master bedroom is on the side of the house that catches the breeze. But not ours. Mr. Henry put our bedroom on the side that faced Euphemia and William's house so he could hear them if they called out in the night."

"Now I sleep in Euphemia's room," Annie said. "If Mr. Henry calls, I can hear."

Betty was unexplainably overcome with thoughts of Mr. Henry. What a good man he was and how strong he had been before the accident and especially after. Everywhere she looked she could see something his hand had caused. "Mr. Henry built this house with his two hands." Bettie was filled with the marvel of it. "It's more than a house. It's a place where people are born and die and where they bring their lives to be mended. Think of all the people whose lives have centered on this house Mr. Henry built with his hands and on his mother's house next door."

Annie viewed the house with her artist's eye and after a while said: "The Arabs say there are four things a man must do in his lifetime. He must love a woman, have a son, build a house, and write a book. I suppose my brother has done three of those things as well as any man who ever lived."

Bettie did not sleep that night in the bed she had shared with Mr. Henry so many years. After a busy day, he was sleeping soundly and she was afraid her movements would trouble his slumber or bring pain to his dreaming. She slept in the back room among the toys Mr. Henry had made for his grandson to play with on his frequent visits.

In the night, Bettie was awakened by a dream that Mr. Henry had died. She rose, walked to their room, and knew he was gone. She stood for a moment, looking down at his face in the moonlight and the face she saw was beautiful. It was the beauty of the child newly embarked from Heaven to Earth and filled with the memory of God's face. Now her husband had returned and he was remembering. Bettie sighed and walked to the window. Softly, she called Mr. Henry's name. Annie heard and she came up the hill. Watching her coming, Bettie started a mental list of the people who must be called and the things that must be done.

South of the Atascosa River, the road leads south toward Piedras Negras through land as stark and barren as a skeleton's dream. When Nuge had talked about their land near the Mexican border, she had said it was desert and Bettie had pictured the great golden dunes of the Sahara. But the country she passed on the way from her sister Ola's house in Moore Station to Nuge's ranch was not at all the desert she had expected. As far as she could see was a great pasture of silver and purple cenizo reaching into the distance. She had not expected color in a place so bleak, but the land was wrapped in a rainbow of blues, greens, and grays, subtle and tentative, as if the primary colors, all but the brilliant yellow of the prickly pear blossoms and the crimson fingertips of the ocotillo, had been driven to ground by the heat. Here and there dust-devils walked through the land and the hollow iron complaint of windmills mocked the few cadaverous cows that passed by, casting almost no shadow at all on the sand. Occasionally the road passed the ruin of a doomed adobe restaurant with its ubiquitous cold-drink sign, and Bettie supposed it was once the dream of some desert family who had given up on the land and tried to harvest the highway instead, luring cars with their bright sign and the promise of a few moment's respite from the sun.

Ola drove her Pontiac coupe. As they motored south, Bettie thought about Mr. Henry and how she wished he was with them now on what she had come to consider a mission of mercy. He would know just how to repair the fences, round up the stock, and do what had to be done to stay Nuge's ranch on its slow sure slide back to the womb of the desert. Since Henry had died, her thoughts of him were generally wistful, a kind of bittersweet

longing. Grief had not been the cutting blade she had expected
and she supposed it was because of the time Mr. Henry had lain
broken in the road by the bridge at King Branch. She had grieved
all those years for his pain. Now that the pain was gone, she was
left with more relief and longing than sorrow. Besides, life went
on and now her attention had turned to the needs of her sister
Nuge, who lived in the desert like a Bedouin on a failed ranch
north of the Rio Grande.

They arrived at the cutoff Nuge had indicated on the map and
turned westward along a dirt track through the sage and chaparral. They passed through streambeds dry as old skillets. Brush
raked the bottom of the car and slapped the grill and Ola steered
with her whole body like a sailor caught in a storm at sea. They
passed clutches of skinny cattle brooding in the brush, and twice
jackrabbits leaped from their path and bounded away. Bettie assumed the country was highly cherished by rattlesnakes.

The ranch where Nuge and Tom Lay lived was hardly more
than an extension of the earth itself. The house was a weathered
shack built of rough boards from scrub oak and the inferior pine
that grew along the slope of the mountain across the river. Its
roof was tin. The outbuildings and fences were made from the
dry hulks of ocotillo. A large metal windmill rattled and clattered
in the breeze, but it broadcast that hollow, sorrowful sound that
promised little flow.

Nuge stood watching them approach. She looked so helpless,
yet somehow so incredibly strong, standing there alone on the
earth, waiting for fortune to halt its headlong downward spiral.
Tom was away seeking to sell leases and drilling rights to the new
oil barons who frequented the hotel lobbies in Fort Worth and
Dallas. Nuge had been left with the unenviable, probably impossible, task of keeping the ranch alive until the next rains or a
buyer or a driller came. "It's hard to imagine they were once
wealthy," Ola said as she wrestled the Pontiac around a suicidal
armadillo. "Tom has managed to parlay their wealth into disaster.
Look at this place!"

In her visits to Seguin, Nuge had never been apologetic about
her circumstance, nor was she now as her sisters unloaded the
booty they had brought from town. Bettie brought canned vege-

tables from her garden, peach tree seedlings, and cuttings of Seven Sisters roses. She also brought the money Nuge was due from the stores in San Antonio where her Texas Star quilts were popular. "Who would have thought of Texas Star quilts as a cash crop," Ola said, knowing this income was all that kept her sister's ranch going.

Bettie found Nuge's home in surprising order. It possessed the Spartan neatness of a well-organized encampment, though in several places she could see the pale white Texas sky through cracks in the walls. Nuge kept the doors and windows open, but it was still very hot inside and when their conversation lagged Bettie could hear a choir of insects she imagined were gathering for an invasion of the house come nightfall.

Bettie's mission of mercy to the border country resulted from Hoover's economic policies and from Tom Lay's mistaken strategy that the more cattle he ran, the more prosperous the ranch could be. Both policies were ruinous and would have been even if Hoover ran the ranch and Tom Lay ran the country. There had been grass on the Lay ranch, and other ranches in the area survived in the ongoing drought. But Tom Lay's pastures were overgrazed and their cattle had begun to starve. The market price for the animals was at an all-time low, the income less than the cost of moving them to market, so there was nothing left to do but hold them and pray for higher prices.

Bettie had run her own farm for years, so she came south with ideas far more suitable to the Guadalupe farmlands than to the parched, dying ranchlands above the Rio Grande. She had planned a garden, an orchard to supplement Nuge's income, chickens and perhaps some pigs to reduce their dependency on the market in town. The problem was more immediate. Some water remained in the tanks, but the windmill was pumping air and the cattle were so hungry they were dying. The women had to find a way to keep them alive until Tom struck it rich or until it rained. Bettie reckoned the prospect of either was very slim.

Nuge had a plan. "The Mexicans burn prickly pear when times are hard," she said. "If we sear the cactus in a fire, we get rid of the thorns. Then those cows will eat the cactus like it was the finest fodder."

The cactus was abundant, but the work was too slow and their fires too scattered to easily tend. It seemed they would never build enough fires to feed the starving animals. All day Bettie and her sisters refined their plan. The next morning, before the sun grew too fierce, Bettie and Ola went out into the desert with machetes and they hacked the fat green ears of prickly pear from the plant. Being careful of the terrible thorns, they loaded the pieces of fleshy cactus onto a wooden hand cart and wheeled the cart back to a place beneath the tin roof of a shed where Nuge had built a fire in an open chamber of river stone. After skewering the pears on iron rods, Bettie and Ola laid the roads across the fire. As they turned the rods, the flames burned the thorns from the pears. Then, when the pears had cooled, they were fed to the cattle. It was still a slow and laborious process. There was plenty of dead mesquite from the arroyos to keep the fire burning and there was enough prickly pear to feed all the cows in Texas. The bottleneck in this otherwise perfect process was picking up the firewood and the prickly pear and hauling it all across the burning sand to the fire. The three sisters, in their bonnets and aprons, leather boots and gloves, worked on through the heat of the day and into the night. "I'm too old for this," Bettie said. "What are three old ladies doing out here in the desert anyway? I should be rocking on my porch and playing with my grandchildren."

That night, Bettie saw the desert sky for the first time. The air was like fine crystal and there were more stars than she imagined Heaven held. She was so tired she could no longer feel the pain her old bones must be suffering. She was so tired, in fact, she felt almost giddy, and then she felt she was immortal and could drift away to that gossamer cloud of stars at will. *A night sky like this makes the labor of the day worthwhile,* she thought. She looked over at Nuge and saw her sister was lost in the night sky as well. Bettie knew now why Nuge had never left the desert country. She had plenty of reason to leave and ample opportunity. But she stayed and she fought to keep the land alive and, perhaps, her reward was the night, when the stars came down like jewels from the dark.

On the morning of the second day, Bettie was awakened by the bellowing of Brahma bulls. In a territorial dispute, a neighbor's bull had torn down the barbed-wire fence and was trying to butt through the plank pen occupied by the Lays' bull.

In an explosion of rage and motion, the two fierce opponents were threatening to tear into each other with their hooves and deadly horns.

Both bulls were easily as large as locomotives. Nuge snatched a rope hanging on the wall and rushed out into the cattle yard.

"Stop that!" she yelled at the bulls. They did not even glance her way.

Bettie was horrified when she realized her sister was actually going to walk up to the crazed Brahma.

"You can't!" she shouted.

"Nobody'll buy a beat-up or killed bull!" Nuge hollered back.

The runaway bull halted, astonished to see her there. He stopped trying to break down the fence and lowered his massive head and bellowed in fury at her. The bull lunged toward Nuge, snorting and pawing the earth. But Nuge stood her ground and as he lumbered toward her, it was no great chore to cast the lasso over his head. A split second later, Nuge was down flat on her back and the bull was straddling her and swinging his great head of horns back and forth.

Later, Bettie would say she did not remember exactly what happened next. She just recalled a series of images filled with the color of terror and a kind of awful anger. Ola said Bettie shrieked terrible things at the bull before yanking off her apron and flinging it and slapping it in front of the bull's face. The Brahma charged the apron, and according to Ola, Bettie simply stepped aside with the grace of a matador. Nuge leaped to her feet, grabbed the end of the lasso, and then working together, half pulling, half dragging, the two women managed to coax the bull to an empty cow pen and slammed and bolted the gate. It all happened, the women agreed, in about forty seconds.

That night, as the three women nursed their pains and watched the stars blooming in the night sky, Bettie pointed out a constellation she thought to be Taurus, the Bull.

"Papa Leonard used to know all the constellations," she said. "I'm sure that's Taurus."

"What were you feeling when you fought the bull?" Ola asked.

"Rage," Bettie said.

"Weren't you afraid?"

"I was just plain mad," Bettie said. She tried to remember what Papa Leonard had told her about Zeus and Europa and Taurus, the Bull. Papa Leonard had died a few years before and she missed him terribly. She believed that Papa Leonard was one of those constellations and she tried to find his face in the stars.

In four hard days, the women had burned enough prickly pear to keep the herd away from starvation. On the fifth day, Tom Lay returned from Dallas with the news that Texas John Nance Garner had been selected for the second place on Roosevelt's New Deal ticket and there would be relief for the farmer the next year. On the seventh day it rained. The three sisters sashayed in the rain until they were soaked to the skin, and from where he watched on the porch Tom Lay wondered if they had any sense at all.

In October of 1932, as the presidential election grew near, Bettie King began to consider voting for the first time. Annie was horrified to learn that her sister-in-law had never been to the polling place, and had even gently criticized her to her face. More than once, Annie said: "If you don't vote, you don't have the right to complain about the government you get."

"Well, I don't," Bettie would answer over her sewing, and Annie had to admit it was true.

Bettie had almost voted the year the Klan had invaded the church, but she had decided that the vote of one woman would not even touch the power of the Klan. That was something men would have to do. Then, after her experience in the desert with Nuge and Ola, Bettie did begin to complain, at least in her mind, about the way men ran the world of politics. She had always thought politics was an activity that happened in another world entirely. Government was a game men played when they were bored or greedy or between wars, and the laws they passed had little to do with the day-to-day lives of the people. "Hoover just doesn't live in the same world we do," Bettie complained to Annie. "His policies don't have anything to do with real people living real lives. That's why we're so bad off in Texas. It's why Nuge can't sell her cattle."

As the Great Depression deepened, Bettie began to feel her hold on her life and her land begin to slip away. She had always considered herself protected from the ebb and flow of the national economy, but the Great Depression overwhelmed some of the Seguin banks where Bettie kept her savings. Besides a small account at the Nolte National Bank, her only other savings were in the jar where she kept her butter and egg money. Before he died, Mr. Henry had stored cotton in a warehouse in town, but now, with prices plunging, that cotton was nearly worthless.

To help keep the farm afloat, Bettie took in roomers in her once-grand home. She rented the plunder room to one couple and the bedrooms to men working the newly opened Darst Creek Oil Fields nearby. Bettie allowed several people to live in their cars on her property. She rented them space by the garden faucet and the chicken house faucet. Another man slept on a cot on the porch. None of the hard-time tenants were allowed to use the indoor toilet; they had to go back where the old outhouse was still standing.

So gradually did her fortunes turn that Bettie was not quite sure when she woke up to the fact she was poor. She had the land, of course, but the land could not put her granddaughter through college nor provide funds to repair her house, which seemed to be coming apart around her. The roof leaked, some shutters were loose and a few had been blown off by a recent Norther. The beautiful white coat of paint was gray and flaking. And now the yard was filled with old cars and desperate people. But there was plenty to eat and she had her friends and her family and surely these hard times would pass as all the others had. Maybe Roosevelt and John Nance Garner would bring prosperity back from wherever it had been hidden by Hoover.

In November of 1932, Bettie met one of the lesser-known candidates for President of the United States. His name was Jacob Coxey, the man who had led Carl Browne and the Coxeyites on their march to Washington so many years before. Jacob Coxey had arrived in Seguin with characteristic flair, traveling in a red patent medicine truck covered with campaign slogans and patriotic flags and bunting. An insistent calliope blared Sousa marches when Coxey was not shouting out praise for his Cox-E-Lax medicinal concoction or shouting down those whom he claimed had sold their souls to the "coupon clippers." Mary Lou said Coxey was a populist run amuck. "He's for all the right things," she said, "but there's no way he could be elected. How could you vote for someone who named his son Legal Tender?" Annie also said she could not vote for a candidate who had garnered the support of the American Martian Society.

A few hours after arriving in Seguin, Coxey's patent medicine wagon came rattling up in front of Bettie's house. Coxey looked carefully at the front fence and at the gate before walking up to the front door and knocking. Bettie came to the door.

"Mrs. King?"

"Yes?"

"Jacob Coxey. I was asked by a dear friend to give you something. Do you remember Carl Browne?"

"It's been years. He was on his way to Washington."

"He said you were very kind. A true woman. Told me you gave him money for his train ticket to the capital."

Bettie remembered the Coxeyite and how he was so tall he had to stoop to come through the door. She recalled his outlandish outfit and how she had refused the gold watch he had offered.

"Mr. Browne is a hard man to forget."

"Well, he's gone now. Passed away some years ago. But he told me if I ever passed this way to give you this." From his pocket, Coxey took a gold watch and handed it to Bettie.

Bettie took the watch and turned it over in her fingers. "My lands," she said. "Do come in, Mr. Coxey. I'll fix us a fresh pot of coffee."

Jacob Coxey's private persona was not nearly so flamboyant as the one he revealed to the public. He had a kind, intelligent, almost cherubic face with eyes alive with humor. He wore an old-fashioned stand-up collar and silver-rimmed spectacles. Bettie saw the face of a dreamer rather than a man of action. As they shared the pot of coffee, the visitor talked about Carl Browne and how he had remained a faithful Coxey lieutenant for many years.

Coxey told her that Browne had returned to California to build a flying machine. "He thought it was going to change the world and it looks like he was right. Here I've spent my life trying to change the world and I haven't changed a thing. Maybe I should have turned to aviation instead of politics."

"Maybe it's time for another march on Washington."

"I'm too old to march," Coxey said. "But I'm not too old to run. And you're right about the need. When Carl Browne and I marched on Washington in 1894 there were three million unemployed. Today there are five million out of work."

"I've got most of them here on my land. Coming to my kitchen for food."

"Well, I'm going to see they're put back to work." Coxey rose. "I suppose I can count on your vote?"

Bettie paused a moment too long, trying to decide how she could tell him she could not vote for a man who named his son Legal Tender.

"Well," Coxey said, moving toward the door. "Could I interest you in a bottle of Cox-E-Lax?"

When the patent medicine truck was gone, Bettie walked back to her porch and sat down in one of the few rockers with its cane seat still intact. She looked at the old cars in her yard and at the peeling paint on the front porch columns and then at Carl Browne's gold watch. *Maybe I'll have to make a march on Washington,* she thought. *How can I leave the world in the hands of fools like those?*

After she quit chuckling to herself, she began to think about her voting, if not marching, and what it might mean. She thought back over the things in her life that she had experienced, that had opened her eyes to a world in need of change. She thought about Carl Browne at her kitchen table and the dying vagrants at the Mission Hotel, and the Ku Klux Klan coming into the church. She thought of all the women forced to take in washing or sewing or be whores in order to survive in a man's world. And she thought about Nuge and her ranch. Nuge had struggled heroically against her troubles, and all she needed was a little help from the rest of us. Somehow, as she thought about Nuge, the definition of government changed from "them" to "the rest of us." Coxey's plan was a way to get "the rest of us" involved in helping those whose farms were failing or who could not get a job or whose children could not afford an education. *Maybe Euphemia and Annie were right, maybe "the rest of us" can make a difference in this world. Coxey's problem was the messenger, not the message.* Then came the stinging memory of her failure to come to the assistance of Pink Rosebud at the school land hearing, and her inner argument was decided.

Early in the morning on the first Tuesday in November, 1932, Bettie walked down Court Street, straight and tall, and with the singleness of purpose with which she encountered all her responsibilities. When she got to the courthouse she voted against Hoover and for John Nance Garner of Texas and Franklin Delano Roosevelt of New York. As she walked home again, she knew at last what Annie meant when she said she was never more happy and proud than in the few hours following the casting of her ballot. On March 4, 1933, Roosevelt, with Bettie's enthusiastic assistance, became President of the United States.

When Jennie's marriage to her second drummer failed, she was left to raise her son alone. He was called Junior. As Bettie watched Jennie struggle to keep the boy fed and clothed, she thought it was terribly ironic that a boy named Junior would have no father at home. Jennie's son was darkly handsome, as beautiful as his mother had been, but he was quiet and thoughtful, even a brooding child. Jennie adored him and she focused her whole life on this son of the dashing drummer she had loved for a brief, tragic season.

Junior had been close to Mr. Henry. They had often talked for hours on the front porch. Now that Mr. Henry was gone, he frequently came with Jennie for Sunday dinner.

Often in the spring and summer, Jennie, Junior, Annie, and Bettie packed a picnic lunch and followed the path past the old mill trace to the huge oak that branched out over the bend in the river. Here the water was so crystal clear you could see the fish darting between the rocks and the river fern. Bettie, Annie, and Jennie would spread the quilt in the quiet Eden of the King land to visit while Junior fished. He was an excellent fisherman and often caught a good string of fish for supper. Sometimes Bettie brought her grandchildren, usually George Henry, and Annie would invite her grandson Lynch. When the little boys were with them, Junior became the quiet teacher who showed them the secrets of the woods and the river: how to bait a hook, how to find the best fishing spots, where the swamp rabbits made their burrows. He showed them the difference between poisonous snakes and the harmless snakes and where the dangerous sinkholes were in the river.

The women watched the boys play and they tried to imagine what they would do with their lives. "These three are special," Annie said, as she watched them fishing. "It's not just because they're our boys, either. Just look at them. Have you ever seen three more handsome youngsters?" Bettie agreed and she felt very loving to the other women and she wished Mr. Henry was alive to see how strong and tall his grandson was growing.

When the Great Depression had come and the banks closed, Jennie told Bettie she was heartsick because the money for Junior's education was gone. "Somehow, I'll find the money," she said. Bettie knew Jennie had always been resilient, but she was seeing a maturity and sense of resolve she had not observed in her friend before.

Jennie managed to scrape up enough money to send Junior off to college. After finishing the first semester he began looking for a job. He traveled to Houston, San Antonio, and then out of state, riding the rails, living the life of a hobo. But all he found were other desperate men and boys seeking work, and he came back to Seguin despondent and defeated. One day he came to return some books Mr. Henry had given him to read. As they talked on the porch, she could tell Junior was nearly in tears. "I'm a worthless son to my mother," he said. "She keeps trying to make things work out, and I just keep dragging her down."

"Things will change," Bette said. "These bad times will pass. I remember the hard times before. But people survived. Things got better."

"There's no work."

"Maybe you should go back to school. An education would be a good thing to have when things turn better."

"It's too big a problem for Mother. I just don't know what to do."

Bettie had never faced a person who seemed so completely whipped by circumstance. "Failure is something that happens at the end of the road," she told Junior. "You've hardly even started. You've got a whole life ahead of you. Just try the best you can. Nobody who does that can ever be a failure."

The phone rang shortly after dark. It was Jennie. "Bettie, Junior went to catch a mess of fish for supper, but he hasn't come home. Did you see him pass your house?"

Bettie had not seen Junior go by. "It's not that late, Jennie. Give him a while more."

At midnight, Junior had still not come home, and by now Bettie ached with a powerful sense of foreboding. And in her mind she went back over what she could have said or done to bring the boy out of his depression. She put on her sweater to walk the two blocks to Jennie's house. *How many times have women waited through the night for their children?* she asked herself. *How many times have women comforted each other into the morning hours as they tried and failed to create perfectly logical reasons for the unexplained disappearance of a child?* Bettie and Jennie waited.

The next day, it was Abe's son Adolph who found Junior's body in the river, just down from the King land where the current had cut a backwater from the riverbed. Junior had drowned in a familiar shallow where he had fished and waded countless times.

A few weeks after Junior's awful rendezvous in the river bottoms, Annie's grandson Lynch and a number of other Seguin boys went on an outing to a place on the Guadalupe called Dam Number Five. It was only five miles from home, but it seemed an undiscovered and mysterious wilderness. One time, when George Henry was visiting Bettie and they were talking on her front porch, he told her about some of the things they would do at Dam Number Five. They often talked, these two, and Bettie cherished the times they shared. Although Bettie would normally have disapproved of some of the things George Henry and his adventurous friends did when they were away by themselves, she had decided it was not her place to criticize and so George Henry was quite open about their escapades. Bettie also knew her disapproval might destroy the wonderful bridge she and the boy had built across the generations.

"It was really cold," George Henry said, "and there was ice along the edge of the lake. We had our BB guns and my friend Clifford had a .22 rifle and some ducks flew over and we decided to shoot one and cook it for dinner. So, boom! Down comes the duck and it lands way out in the water. Well, so we had this deck of cards and we cut the cards and the loser had to go out in the ice-cold water to get the duck. Lynch lost and so he stripped down and he swam out there with nothing on and got the duck and brought it to shore. While he was getting the duck, the rest of us got this big fire going. We got warmed up and plucked the duck. It took us hours to get the pinfeathers out. But we cleaned and cooked the duck and had him for supper."

On this night, the boys rode their bicycles down to their camp at Dam Number Five. They set up the wood and canvas army cots, struggling as usual because the canvas seemed much too small for the wood frames. Next they decided to set up a blind near the water's edge and wait for that hour before dark when the animals came down to drink. Maybe a deer would come by. Between the camp and the tall grass where they planned to hide and await the dusk was a fence. Lynch led the way beneath the fence and turned to watch George Henry follow with the rifle. As George Henry passed the rifle through the fence and started under, there was an explosion and the smell of cordite, and Lynch said, "I sure hope I wake up from this soon." He sat down beneath a tree and George Henry unbuttoned his shirt to see the hole the bullet made. It was right in the center and seemed much too small to kill a boy as big as Lynch. But Lynch never waked from his nightmare, and he died beneath the cottonwood by the water's edge at Dam Number Five.

Later that evening, after Lynch's body had been delivered to the funeral home, both families clung to one another in Bettie's parlor. The boys explained how the accident happened and how it was just one of those unexplainable things. Their words were little comfort to Annie, or Lynch's mother, or to George Henry who had fled to his room, his face ashen and rigid with shame and guilt and terrible remorse.

Lynch's father and George Henry's father, who were like brothers and had been inseparable since childhood, stood looking down at their hands and searching for any words that could comfort the other. At last, after comforting Lynch's mother, the two men went out into the dark to talk. As she watched the two men leave, Bettie felt a hand on her arm. She turned and it was Annie. "George Henry needs us," Annie said, and the two grandmothers moved into the back of the house where the boy was suffering a private hell they knew would be with him the rest of his life.

In the few years before Pearl Harbor and America's entry into World War II, Bettie's house overflowed with her nephews. Four of them, Joe, Acey, Leonard, and Eugene, the sons of her sisters and brothers, filled the bedrooms and even slept on cots set up in the living room. A fifth young man, Virgil Halm, also boarded at the King house. All the young men were single and worked at jobs in town. Bettie loved having "her boys" around and it was good to have so much life and commotion in the house again. She also liked having her nephews there because they were a good influence on George Henry, who loved to come visit and listen to the tales of his cousins. Bettie believed it had been the companionship of the cousins that had helped George Henry deal with the guilt and grief he felt after the death of Lynch.

Each day after school, George Henry would pass by the farm and if the mules were not working in the field, he was to stop and make sure they were fed and watered. George Henry also delivered milk for his father's dairy, and he raised his own prize-winning dairy cows which he entered in the Future Farmers of America Fat Stock Show each February. Bettie was very proud of her industrious grandson. Once, when the high school principal said George Henry was only capable of average grades, Bettie bristled. "If you had to get up at 4:00 A.M. every morning to deliver milk," she said, "you wouldn't make straight A's either."

In the fall of 1942, George Henry entered college at Texas
A & M University, in College Station, Texas. His cousin Bill
Bergfeld, another of Bettie's grandsons, had been accepted the
year before and had told George Henry all the romantic tales
about the Cadet Corps and their military traditions. In letters to
his grandmother, George Henry wrote of his plans to enlist on
his eighteenth birthday. He wanted to volunteer for the Marines
and "help pay back Tojo for what he did to the boys at Pearl."
Bettie praised his patriotism, yet advised that he stay with his education and wait until he was called.

In the winter of 1942, Bill Bergfeld's entire Corps at Texas
A & M was activated and began their long journey to North Africa to enter the fight with General Patton against Field Marshal
Rommel. George Henry returned home to persuade his parents
to sign his enlistment papers, and on his eighteenth birthday he
and his friend Allen Hoermann said goodbye to their friends and
families and boarded the train for San Antonio where they joined
the Marines.

Bettie had never realized how round the world really was.
Time was a wheel turning and the same spokes kept coming
round, familiar and predictable and personal. War had taken the
boys away again. It seemed to Bettie they had been through a war
just the other day, and here one came around again. She remembered the day her son George and the others had marched away
to fight the Kaiser, and now their sons were on their way to fight
over that same soil.

Bettie followed her grandsons on the battle maps published in
the newspapers and through their letters. She tried to imagine at
which island or which woods or field or river crossing they
fought and slept and wrote their letters home.

During the Christmas season of 1944, she received two letters
from her grandsons. One was from the European theater of war
and the other from the Pacific.

"Dear Grandmother," George Henry wrote. "My morale has
been kept high by receiving letters regularly from you. You can't
imagine how a fellow overseas looks forward to each mail call.
We usually have mail just before dark and it sure makes the night
feel friendlier when we hear from home. We had a little Christ-

mas cheer out here. We had a large Christmas tree all decorated with lights, also Christmas banners strung up along the regimental street just like dear old Seguin used to have."

Nothing in the letter provided a clue where George Henry might be. However, Bettie felt the reference to a "regimental street" suggested he might be safely behind the front lines. The letter from her grandson Bill, describing how he spent New Year's Eve, was not quite as comforting.

"I was on guard New Year's Eve to usher in the New Year. I was sitting in a dugout next to my machine gun watching the fireworks of both sides. Machine guns were firing, mortars and artillery and flares illuminated the sky and the anti-aircraft guns seemed to set the heavens on fire. It was a beautiful sight to see." Bettie was sure she had never read anything so sad.

"After midnight," his letter continued, "I thought I heard a piano playing. I thought for a minute I might be hearing things. The music was coming from Jerry's side of the lines and when the music stopped a man said: 'Greetings to the men of the 363rd Infantry. This music is for your entertainment.' He played another song and then he said, 'How long has it been since you've had a girl in your arms? An American girl I mean, not one of these Italians.' We found out later it was a radio program called 'Berlin George and Sally' the enemy broadcast to break down our morale. It would play for about 15 minutes each night before our artillery would find the range and we wouldn't hear any more until the next night."

It seemed to Bettie the censors had not been very efficient and it wasn't difficult for her to tell where Bill Bergfeld was fighting. She wondered for a moment whether she should be more concerned about Bill's exposure to the artillery or to the arms of the Italian girls.

In one letter, George Henry wrote that four Seguin boys had met on an unnamed Pacific isle halfway around the world from the Guadalupe. Allen Hoermann, Max Bergfeld, Jr., George Henry, and his friend Virgil Halm met several times and had established what they called "Texas Night" somewhere in the Pacific command.

Each afternoon, Bettie would sit on her porch and pray for

the Western Union boy not to appear. As the war progressed, the women of Seguin began to understand a certain pattern to the unthinkable. From her porch, Bettie could see far down Court Street. But about halfway to town, there was a rise, and anyone coming from town emerged from behind that rise like a mirage. When the Western Union boy appeared from behind that rise, the hearts of the women stopped and they existed in a kind of half death as they waited to see which way the boy turned and to whose house he delivered his telegram. But there was a terrible complication to the pattern. If the message was brought by a boy on a bike, it almost always meant the soldier was wounded or missing in action. But the women knew when the long dark car came, the message was death. So Bettie prayed she would not see the boy on the bicycle, but she also prayed that if a message must be delivered it would be by the boy and not the long dark car.

Then one afternoon as Annie and Bettie were talking on the porch, Bettie looked up to see the distant form of the Western Union boy rise from the road. She stopped breathing and watched as the form grew larger and the number of houses left along the road grew fewer and fewer. Now Annie was watching, too. The boy turned on King Street and Bettie stood and sighed for there were only two houses on that road. Her grandson Bill lived in one, her grandson George Henry lived in the other. The boy got off his bike and walked to the door of George Henry's house. The two old women embraced and Bettie began to pray. "Thank you, God, for sparing the boy. Please bring him home now. Enough is enough."

Although his wounds were severe, George Henry did not come home that year. He was healed in the hospital and sent back to the war. He would not come home for nearly two years, and then only after the long dark car had come to call.

George Henry's body was brought home on the train from San Antonio on a Saturday at sundown. The cars had begun lining up by the depot before noon and by midafternoon they were three or four deep facing the track. The day was cold and the sky was the color of dishwater. Bettie waited in the back seat of the Goetz Funeral Home's Buick, bewildered as to why it took so long to bring a small dead boy from San Antonio. While she waited and tried not to think, Allen Hoermann, George Henry's friend and companion in arms, came by and leaned in the Buick's window to tell her how sorry he was George Henry was dead. "He was my friend," he told Bettie, "and one of the bravest soldiers I ever saw." Allen had tears in his eyes and he seemed so lost that Bettie asked him to sit with her awhile and tell her about how George Henry died. That she would ask such a thing surprised her, but she was intimately familiar with his birth and how he lived, and she needed to know as much about the end of his life as the beginning. Allen Hoermann climbed in the car beside her and they talked as they waited for the train.

"We left San Diego on a luxury liner," he said. "The *Lauraline*. Beautiful. Carpets that thick, mirrors all over the wall, and elevators from top to bottom. They had these huge silver coffee urns. The only problem, there was ten guys in every stateroom. Some two thousand Marines including me and George Henry. We crossed the equator and they had this ceremony and we got certificates to say we were Shellbacks or something. After we landed in New Caledonia, George Henry and I got separated there for awhile. He was in Roosevelt's Raiders and I was in Edison's Raiders. But then I saw him again at Guadalcanal."

It had begun to rain and Bettie watched the drops on the windshield coalesce and form rivulets running down the glass. The funeral home driver started the engine to turn on the wipers and they made a sound like the heartbeat of a dragon. The windows fogged and the world outside grew unreal while Bettie listened to the boy talk about the life and death of his friend.

"When we got to Guadalcanal, the fighting was mostly over but there were plenty of Japs around the island. And there were these native people, and they loved American money. They'd do anything for a shiny quarter. We'd say to this one: 'Japs, yeah, Japs. Go get Japs.' So he would take off and in a few hours come back with an old gunny sack over his shoulder. And then he'd dump the bag and three or four Jap heads would roll out. All that for a shiny quarter."

Bettie remembered the family story about Sarah and the doctor who brought a satchel of preserved Comanche heads to Peach

Creek. It was so long ago, back in the time of the Indian Wars, still all these years later men were still collecting the heads of their enemies.

"I saw George Henry shot and he fell over and he said, 'Oh, my God!' and I said, 'George, wake up!' But he wouldn't and they carried him away. That was in the Russell Islands and we were hacking our way through the jungle, on our way to capture Mundo Airfield. Up in the air there were these Japs tied in the palm trees and when they shot George, I kind of went crazy and I kept shooting up into the trees. But the palm trees were sometimes a hundred feet in the air and the Japs were up in the foliage in the top. But when you shot them they didn't fall because they were tied up there and you didn't know whether they were dead or not, so you had to just keep shooting and shooting until . . ."

"But that wasn't the battle when George Henry was killed."

"Yes, ma'am. He was killed trying to take Mundo Airfield. We were shooting into the trees and then I saw him shot and he didn't move and there was blood everywhere and they carried him off."

"I was told he was killed in Okinawa."

"No, ma'am. That was much later."

"You saw him shot, but he was only wounded. They took him to the hospital and then put him back in and he died in Okinawa."

Allen Hoerman looked into Bettie's eyes for a long time. "You're sure?"

"Okinawa's in the official notification. And he wrote me letters until 1944."

"I'll be damned," Allen Hoermann said. "It's like he died twice. Okinawa. That was at the last, he almost made it through." Then they sat quietly, waiting for the train and Bettie tried not to think about the significance of the two extra years George Henry had lived after his friend saw him shot. And she tried not to think of how close he came to lasting out the war.

"I'll be damned," Allen said, again. "You can imagine how I felt. I was sure he was dead. If I had known he was alive I would have been the happiest person on Earth." His eyes filled with

The day after Bettie's seventy-fifth birthday, the following item appeared in the *Seguin Enterprise.*

"Friday the 13th of this month was the birthday anniversary of Mrs. Henry King, one of Seguin's most respected and best-loved citizens. A group of friends decided that a surprise party was in order. So, headed by Mrs. Felix Douglass, quite a number of ladies surprised Mrs. King by invading her hospitable home on East Court Street that afternoon. However, these invaders were cordially welcomed by a very gracious hostess."

Bettie had never heard "Happy Birthday to You" sung with such prodigal harmonies. But it was good to have her five old friends together again on the occasion of her birthday, even if their birthday song did sound, as Annie would remark, like "Shakespeare's sweet bells" jangled out of tune. "If music is the voice of Creation," she added, "we've set the Lord's work back some."

Six elderly women sat at the dining room table, sharing a cake Annie had baked in the morning. As Bettie glanced around the table, she noted that these same six women had been celebrating one another's birthdays for more than sixty years. She looked from one beloved face to another. She saw in their faces the girls they had been when they all were young and spending whole Saturdays playing imaginary games in attics, barns, and the Guadalupe bottoms. There was Jennie in her sad Gibson Girl blouse that had been stylish some forty years before. Cayloma was there, and Annie and Adda, and her dear sister Nuge, with the enormous diamond earrings she always wore no matter how far poverty drove her down. And there was Mary Lou in her bright feminine ribbons, fashionable silk, and ladylike lace. She watched tears again and they ran down his cheeks like the rivulets on the windshield. "Now I don't know what to feel."

"Feel thankful you're alive," Bettie said, and she patted his hand.

The rain fell more steadily now, but through the fogged glass Bettie could see people climbing out of their cars. Even through the closed windows, she could hear the train's whistle wailing. She opened her door and the funeral home man helped her out and she could see the train moving slowly into town from the west. The people stood in the rain, the women dressed in black, the umbrellas a dark garden blooming from their hands. The train came in slow until it reached the North Austin Street Crossing and then it stopped in a cascade of machine sound, pooled then into silence. For a while nothing happened; it was as if the town had been visited by a ghost train and no engineers or brakemen or redcaps would tend to its arrival. Then, with a grating sound, the door of a boxcar slid open and the people could see the single casket in the center of the car. It was draped with an American flag. Two Marines standing by the casket saluted the family and then the men in the family rushed forward to help the Marines hand the casket down from the train and carry it to the hearse.

On the way to the First Methodist Church South where her grandson would rest awhile before joining all the generations in the family graveyard beneath the live oaks on the hill, Bettie allowed herself the rare luxury of tears. She thought of Mollie and of Mr. Henry and of George Henry. *It's just that I've made this trip so often,* she said to herself. Then she squared her shoulders, wiped away her tears, and prepared to bury one more dead child. Outside it was growing dark, and the town of Seguin was washed clean and silver in the rain.

her friends as they ate Annie's cake. She even caught Cayloma licking icing off the bottom of the candles. *How many candles have we lighted,* she guessed, *to mark the passing of the years?*

They moved to the parlor and talked of their children and their grandchildren. They spoke of how times were hard again and of how a neighbor of Mary Lou's had starved to death because she was too proud to ask for help. Bettie told them how she missed the mules, now that Abe was using the tractor. She talked about Abe and Lucinda Saphronia's seven children and how all but the two oldest had graduated from high school. They talked about how all the High Sheriffs still went to Idella to help them solve their mysteries and to find out who did what to whom. They talked about Lady Bird's radio stations and Lyndon's chances against Hardy Hollers for another term in the House of Representatives. Cayloma recalled the treasured mementos she had lost in the boarding house fire. She showed them a photograph of the old DeLaney school sent to her by Professor Nat Benton, with whom they had all been madly in love when they were girls.

Although the six women were in almost constant contact by phone, now that they were together in one place Bettie was warmed by a closeness, an affection, and a sense of peace that nearly brought tears to her eyes.

As the afternoon passed, they began to talk of those who were not there. Of all the children, husbands, and lovers they had lost. They remembered Felix Douglass and Mr. Henry, Tom Lay and Will Thomas, Charlie Colville and Jennie's dashing drummers. They remembered the children killed by steel, by grief, and by the waters of the Guadalupe. They touched the surface of memories with their words, told the old stories of Euphemia and the days of the Republic. But as they talked Bettie knew each of them was left with the same overriding and bewildering question. *How can it be we have survived when all the others are gone?* Bettie thought of all they had suffered, the pain and poverty, calamity and death, loneliness and injustice and guilt. Yet, here they were, battered and bloodied by the years, survivors now sitting safely in the parlor. It was as if they had been touched by the wand of a guardian angel and made immortal. Bettie decided there must be some inner chamber God placed in woman where she can go to be safe from the storms fate hurls her way. And she decided it must be a chamber made of boot leather and steel.

The afternoon passed and their words moved safely along the surface of their lives, but Bettie knew they all shared her incredulousness at being alive. A comfortable interval in their talking came and for a moment the six old women sat, silently looking inward, feeling the bond they had like silk wrapped round them. Then it was Mary Lou who asked the question. "Do you think it's possible we might live forever?"

"We've got a very good start," Cayloma said.

"Sometimes I run out of things to do on a Sunday afternoon," Adda said. "I'm not sure I could fill forever."

"Would you really want immortality?" Bettie asked.

"Maybe for a little while," Nuge said. They laughed until the tears came. Then they talked about Little Virginia's husband Will Bergeld, who had lost his Ford dealership during the Depression and was now working for a highway construction firm in Uvalde.

Cayloma had arranged for a photograph of The Girls, and late in the afternoon the photographer Leon Kubala arrived with his wonderful array of photographic equipment. They gathered in a group and after elaborate posing, Mr. Kubala snapped the picture. Bettie retrieved the photograph she had taken with Cayloma when they were twenty years old and Mr. Kubala studied the old print and positioned the two friends in the exact pose they had struck some fifty-five years before. Bettie wondered what would become of it in the years to come. She reckoned as long as the image lasted, "The Girls" would remain alive and Nuge's practical desire for at least temporary immortality would be achieved.

Much later, after her friends had gone, Bettie sat alone in her house listening to the sounds it made. She walked through the rooms, one by one, and she remembered the lives each had held. As she moved through the old house, disquietude settled around her. What would happen to this house when she was gone? What would happen to the Governor Ireland chair, and the cane with the gold handle, and the table where Henry's broken leg was set and where the family celebrated Papa Leonard's ninetieth birthday? What of the parlor where there had been so many marriages and where all their plans for the future had been made? She wondered, *What will become of the memories that dwelled in these rooms?*

The thought came to her suddenly that there were things about the future she must know. The house had protected her family in the past, held them safe from storm, war, and plague. *But who will protect the house in the long years when I will be sleeping with Mr. Henry beneath the oaks?* Bettie walked out onto the porch. There was a chill in the air and she shivered and pulled her shawl more closely around her shoulders. *What will happen to the King land?* She had seen the town encroaching now for years, swallowing up old homesteads, spreading its cement skirts along the Guadalupe. *What will happen to the fields where Euphemia played and the barn where Nuge, Cayloma, Adda, and I pretended to be beautiful strangers?* She sat down in a rocker and she could feel her home seem to fold around her, safe and comfortable and alive. *What, I wonder, will happen to my house?*

The thought crept into her mind like a small, unfamiliar animal, a bit wild and wary, and she first tried to shoo it out by humming a melody. But after lingering outside her mind for awhile, the thought came back, irrepressible and exciting. *Idella. She will know. What I seem to have lost is the future,* Bettie thought. *And Idella can find things lost.*

It was growing colder and the wind swept autumn leaves down Court Street toward the King Branch Bridge where passing traffic made minor maelstroms of their reds and yellows and browns. Bettie crossed over Court Street to the river side and walked the short distance to Idella's house. Idella was standing in the door. Bettie wondered how long she had been waiting there, letting cold air into her house. She decided Idella had seen her coming in her mind. That was, after all, what people said she could do.

"Afternoon, Miss Bettie," Idella said.

"Afternoon, Idella."

Idella's house was rather dark. There was a scent of lavender and candle wax in the front room and the house seemed to muffle the sounds of Court Street traffic more efficiently than her own house. Bettie wondered if Idella was ever concerned about what would happen to her house in the future. Then she realized Idella already knew, and that was why she had come visiting the fortune-teller in the first place.

When Bettie told Idella why she had come, she felt embarrassed, like a child asking for something only adults could have. But Idella made her feel comfortable and assured her that curiosity about the future was a natural thing all people share.

"People are the only ones of God's creatures who care about what comes. We've figured out how to control just about everything. But we can't control the future. We look at it like an enemy we can't conquer. But in my mind, the future is the best friend we got. It never will come back and haunt you like the past can."

Idella asked Bettie to sit with her at a table where a candle burned and bled wax like lava from a small volcano. Then Idella asked for Bettie's hand. A moment passed, then another. Idella's hands were soft, not warm nor cold. But there seemed to be a life in them, a tiny vibration, and Bettie felt as if Idella's hands might be asleep and tingling as her own hands often did at night beneath her pillow.

"I see your home," Idella said. "Columns white as alabaster. A little boy playing in a sandpile in the yard. A man carefully tending his tomato vines. Wildflowers and a rose garden behind the plunder house. I see a young woman living there who looks just like you, and a little girl with Hawkins eyes growing up to be a woman in your house. I see cousins' club suppers and wedding receptions and tea parties for elegant ladies. I see people coming by who will do things to change the world. I see senators, governors, and people making important decisions. A President of the United States will be welcome in your home. I see more children who look like Euphemia playing in the yard and more children who look like Mollie and your Papa Leonard. You're a mighty lucky woman, Miss Bettie. Your house will outlive your great-great-grandchildren."

"What else do you see?"

Idella wrapped her hands around one of Bettie's more firmly. Her eyes were tightly closed. "I see animals in the dark."

Bettie attempted to pull her hand away, but Idella's grip tightened. "Wait, Miss Bettie. If the house is to be safe, you must face this thing in the dark."

The candle flame flickered and Bettie felt the coming of her fear, like a beast in the twilight. Once again she tried to pull her hand away.

"Miss Bettie, I can help you. Let me help you get rid of the wolves."

Bettie shuddered. "You see the wolves?"

"I see a little girl alone by a fire. It's night. She is terrified. There are dead children in the firelight. There is something else in her heart. What I see is hatred. Her father has left her in the dark with the dead and with the wolves and she hates him for being so cruel."

"But I always loved Papa Leonard."

"Of course you did. If you didn't love him so much, you wouldn't have carried this hatred around so long."

"I don't believe . . ." Bettie searched her very soul and could not find a trace of hatred. The thought that she would hate such a good and loving man made her feel ill. She put the hand Idella was not holding to her forehead. "I feel woozy."

"How, exactly?"

"I feel faint. Like I'm swooning. Like the world is closing in."

"Like a storm is coming?"

"Yes. Like that."

"And you're afraid? Afraid of being left alone?"

"Yes."

"Like when your father left you alone with the dead and the wolves."

"Yes."

"Listen to me, Miss Bettie. I have known your Papa Leonard all my life. I know things he never spoke to another living soul. Things he didn't even tell Miss Mollie. About wolves. About when he was a little boy coming into Texas. He was no more than nine years old. Your papa's family and the others were German immigrants. They'd come to Texas to make a new life. Except when they got here they were set ashore and abandoned. They had no food and there was a killin' fever. They started up the trail, sick and starving, and your papa had to watch everybody dyin' around him. They fell by the trail and were buried in shallow graves by those too weak to dig a decent grave. At night the wolves came. And that little boy could hear the wolves fighting over the bodies of the dead."

As Bettie listened to Idella's voice, she found that she was weeping. The tears had an unfamiliar feel and at first she was not sure what they were as they fell to the table. She could actually hear the sound they made on the wood.

"First Papa Leonard's little brother died. Then his mama. Before she was buried his papa died. Your own papa and his brother, Johann Christian, buried their folks by the trail. They tried to make the graves deep, but they were just little boys, too weak and sick to dig. And the others were going, about to leave them behind. They had to leave their folks there by the trail in graves hardly deep enough to protect them from scavengers. When they got to the Guadalupe River, your papa was too near dead himself to go on.

"One hundred thirty-four miles those little boys walked. Your papa was took in by a family named Oliver and raised by their slave Aunt Urcey. She told me that every night he was at their place, your Papa Leonard slept ugly listening for the sound of the wolves fighting over his mama and papa's bodies. So you see, Darlin', your papa just couldn't leave those Braddock people to the wolves. Papa Leonard was a good-hearted man. He didn't leave you alone out of cruelty, but out of trust and love."

Bettie could not stop crying now and the tears continued to run down her face. "I didn't know."

"We children never know the torments of our parents. We can't know the wolves they fear."

"But the hate you said you saw . . ."

"Ain't no more hate, Miss Bettie. It up and leaves when you say its name."

For a long time, Bettie sat with Idella at her table. They did not speak. Only after the candle burned out did Idella release Bettie's hand. From the distance came the sound of thunder.

"I believe we're in for some rain," Idella said. "You best run before you get soaked."

When Bettie left Idella's, night was settling over the houses along Court Street. She hurried to her door and into the quiet of her house. She thought about calling Cayloma, but decided to quilt instead.

The night came down like a shade. Bettie was alone in the house and the rooms were filled with echoes and shadows. The wind rose and its voice was like the distant howling of wolves. Through the windows Bettie could see lightning cracking the dark. The house began to moan and move as if alive. Bettie felt the old deep dread clutching at her center. She felt the approach of vertigo, queasiness, and something else, terrible and undefined.

Her terror of the storm drove her toward her room where for all the years of storms she had cowered behind her bedroom door. Then she thought of Idella, stopped, and turned. She returned to the parlor. With some effort she pulled the Governor Ireland chair to the center of the room. She sat down, straight and tall as a broomstick. She waited. The wind pummeled the house like a fist. Shingles were blown from the roof and a window was shattered by a board torn loose from the trellis. Rain slashed in through wounds the storm had made. As the wind howled Bettie listened to the sounds of the storm and to all the voices carried on the wind.

They whispered to each other for some time—the old woman, the house, and the storm. Then they grew still. Near morning, Bettie's family rushed into the house expecting the worst. They found Bettie sitting tall in the Governor Ireland chair, rocking gently, quilting a Texas Star.

Idella

There is no season more beautiful along the Guadalupe or in the Hill Country of Texas than the week before Easter. Winter's tyranny is vanquished by warm spring rains and easy sunlight, and wildflowers bloom in the meadows and along the roadsides as if in joyous anticipation of the Resurrection of Christ. I asked Idella if she would like to go for a ride. Maybe we would wander down Capote Road and to Peach Creek and through the landscape of her memory. I don't know why I was surprised when she assented and fetched her old feathered hat and her shawl. I suppose it was because I'd always associated Idella with her river, as if it was from the waters of the Guadalupe her second sight was drawn and to leave it would diminish her powers.

We stepped from the darkness of Idella's house into the April sunshine. I helped her into my rented Volvo. Idella seemed fascinated by the knobs, switches, and controls and she twisted in her seat, looking all around. "I love your automobile," she said. "I haven't been riding in an automobile since they started making them in colors." I reached over to fasten her safety belt. "No need for that," she said. "I see no accident up yonder. As long as we don't go by Uvalde. There's one waitin' up by Uvalde."

We drove around the old Magnolia Hotel where Pink Rosebud, Ida Helen, and Precious Honey Child cast their earthy spells, past the Mission Hotel, past the Los Nogales, the adobe building owned by Juan Seguin, and on out Court Street toward the south. We crossed King Branch Bridge and I could tell Idella was listening for the footsteps of the dead. On the left was Euphemia's "new" house, where Annie's grandson now lived, and then up the hill was Bettie's house, where I grew up and where Virginia Woods, my mother, now lived. A few blocks beyond, on the left, was the cluster of oaks where Euphemia, William, and many family members and Texas Rangers were buried. Beyond were shopping centers and the cluttered outskirts of Seguin, spread haphazardly on King land.

We turned right on King Street and then left onto Capote Road. This was the route Santa Anna had taken from the Alamo to seek out and destroy Sam Houston's little army. The earth was rich and dark, rolling away from the Guadalupe, crossed and recrossed by creeks where Mollie and Papa Leonard's children played and prowled.

The Guadalupe River crosses Capote Road just before Gonzales. When we arrived at the spot, Idella asked if we could stop. We pulled to the side of the road, got out, and walked to the bridge railing where we had a view of the river. "Up there," Idella said, shading her eyes from the morning sun, "just a little way, is where the Comanches stole away little Matilda Lockhart. See that stand of pecan trees? That's where it was. The children were pickin' mustang grapes right there."

We crossed the Guadalupe and drove down into Peach Creek. I told Idella the land was still in the family, four hundred virgin acres, just as it was in Euphemia's time. We passed beneath the venerable Sam Houston Oak and drove up to the house. I turned off the engine and helped Idella out of the car and into the yard. We stood before Sarah's great white house as pilgrims stand before a temple.

"Glory be," Idella breathed. "What time has done."

"It's been empty so long."

"Houses need people. When the people leave, the house begins to die."

There was something skeletal about the old house. The white paint was gone, the wood weathered and stained by the square rusted iron nails that somehow managed to hold the house up beneath its sagging roof. A few siding boards were loose and broken. In spite of its neglected state, a sad kind of elegance remained. The house was like a church where no one prayed anymore or a temple forsaken and abandoned by the gods once worshiped there.

"This house needs fixin'," Idella said.

"It would take a fortune. We're trying to get the State interested. There's so much history here to preserve."

We had hoped to enter the house and explore the rooms, but boards had been nailed across the doors and downstairs windows. Maybe it was just as well. We did walk through wildflowers and a few wandering cows to the small fenced graveyard where Sarah Ashby, Bartlett McClure, Charles Braches, and so many of her family were buried. Rising from the cemetery were two immense live oaks. I imagined they had grown so much larger than the surrounding trees because they were nourished by my ancestors.

From Peach Creek we followed the route Euphemia, Sarah, and the toddler Little Johnny had taken on the Runaway Scrape. We passed Big Hill, where Euphemia and Sarah had their encounter with the Comanches and where Fannie and Roderick Gelhorn built their home. All that remained of the Gelhorn place was a lone chimney. We drove to the Lavaca River and through the woods along the Navidad, where the women executed the looter and Little Johnny died in Euphemia's arms, then northwest to Plum Creek, where Bartlett McClure fought the last great battle against the Comanches. We took Highway 71 north to the Lost Pines and The City of the Dead and the charming little town of Bastrop itself, where we found the Colonel-Doctor's pharmacy and office had been gutted by fire, the front door boarded shut. We tried to find where Georgia, Martha Benny, and Ed Tom had established their first plantation, but Idella said she could not feel the place, that the land by the river was silent about the past.

We took Highway 20 a few miles south to Lockhart. When we passed the Greisenbok Hotel, Idella pointed out it was where the Confederate Reunion had honored the Colonel-Doctor before his death. Minutes later, we passed Staples, where the Woods Regiment trained and the beautiful young Pink Rosebud came riding into camp on a camel at the side of Reverend Andrew Jackson Potter. We took the old Austin road back toward San Marcos, crossed the Blanco to High Prairie, where Ed Tom and Sam Ealy Johnson chased Iron Jacket and Tarantula after gambling with Georgia's cotton money. We emerged from a grotto of waterfalls and fern into the spare, rocky terrain of the Hill Country. On the right was a field of prickly pear, an astonishing display of pinks, yellows, and whites. I pulled the car to the side of the road.

"I see trouble in them prickly pear," Idella said. "Trouble that crawls and stings and sticks. If you don't mind, I'll stay right here and leave them snakes and scorpions alone."

From the car, I could see the shack in the center of the field, framed by the deceptive beauty of the cactus blossoms. It was falling down, of course, its roof sagging, its doors and windows long taken by time and the seasons. It was the place where Martha Benny Hawkins and Ed Tom nursed old Captain Lawshe through his last days until he died in his nineties, cradled in the arms of his elderly son. About a mile south, on a knoll, was a Negro cemetery where Ulysses Cephus, Martha Benny, Ed Tom, and all the slaves named Hawkins, Lawshe, and Woods were buried.

As we approached San Marcos, even from a distance, I could see the hill from which Georgia's mansion once dominated the town. The house was gone now, had been swallowed up by the campus of Southwest Texas State, the college where Sam Ealy Johnson's grandson Lyndon and Georgia's grandson Wilton had gone to school together. We drove past the San Marcos River, filled with students presenting their pale young limbs to the first ultraviolet of springtime, cavorting in waters that had baptized Andrew Jackson Potter. We drove up the hill the Yankees had ascended when Little Sweet attacked them from her balcony, and we paused awhile on the crest where the house had been and the stable where Georgia and the children had lured Captain Haller to his death. As we drove back down the hill, we passed the First Methodist Episcopal Church. Idella said the bell in the belfry had once hung at Fort Hawkins in the time of old Benjamin Hawkins. "Captain Lawshe brought that bell all the way from Mississippi," she said, "after the Yankees burned down his plantation."

We took Highway 123 out of San Marcos, past Geronimo Creek and the Navarro *estancia* where the White Dove had surveyed his lands on a pure white horse. We crossed the railroad tracks where the train had brought George Henry King's body back from Okinawa. Soon we were driving back along Court

Street and to Idella's house on the Guadalupe. She asked if I
would enjoy a glass of iced tea and I said I would.

We sat in the shade of several large elms that arched over
Idella's back porch like the nave of a cathedral. We could see the
river, slate green and deep, moving through scrims of sunlight and
shadow.

"How far you figure we went this mornin'?" Idella asked
when we were settled with our tea.

"Not far. We were only gone a few hours."

"Imagine that." Idella seemed to be watching the sunlight on
the river. "We rode in that new car from Santa Anna to the war
with Japan. We passed by whole armies and nations and wars. We
rode that automobile hundreds of years and through hundreds of
lives and we got back hardly before the sun was high. Imagine
that. Everywhere is here. The past was just down the road."

As I sat with Idella listening to the Guadalupe say its name—
Guadalupe, Guadalupe, Guadalupe—I felt more at peace than
ever before or since. My senses seemed heightened. I could feel
the touch of even the slightest breath of wind, hear sounds that
must have been buried in the noise of my life before. There were
shades of color along the riverbank and in Idella's eyes I could
swear I had never seen before. I found myself absolutely calm and
easy and enchanted by each component of the world around me.
What was this spell, I wondered, this high, this sense of complete-
ness?

"What's happening, Idella? Are you doing this to me?"

"No, Darlin', it's not me. It's just you found what you came
to find. That's all. Nothin' all that much about it. You're not just
pieces any more, you're a whole cloth. A Texas Star quilt God
made with pieces of your grandmothers."

I wanted to stay on Idella's back porch forever, to revel in this
new feeling of aliveness and to feel the flow of the past through
my veins. But Idella rose and she seemed fragile, and almost
transparent in the early afternoon light. "It's good you came,
Queenie," she said. "And I loved the ride in your automobile."
We embraced and Idella was like a waif, a leaf, a chimera. As I
held the old woman in my arms, I looked down into the Guadalupe bottoms and I thought of Peachtree.

"Whatever became of Peachtree?" I asked.

"Oh, he's around. They're all around. Like I told you, everybody that was still is. To call them, you just say their name."

When I last saw Idella, she was standing on her porch above the river. Her lips were moving and she was smiling. As I walked to the Volvo I thought I heard an owl. I turned and Idella was gone.

Author's Notes

1   As Idella predicted, Bettie's house would be filled with life for generations to come. After Bettie King's death, my parents, Virginia and Wilton Woods, my brother Wilton, and I would move into the house at 920 Court Street. We hosted many important people in our home. These included Governor John Connally, Congressmen Jake Pickle and William Patman, State Senator Walter Richter, U.S. Interstate Commerce Commissioner Willard Deason, Lady Bird Johnson, and the thirty-sixth President of the United States, Lyndon Baines Johnson. Virginia Woods continues to reside in the old King Homeplace.

2   Euphemia's home, at the corner of Heideke and Court Streets, the "new" house replacing the old log cabin she and William built on the site when they were first married, still stands. It is currently occupied by Aunt Annie Colville's grandson, William King Colville.

3   Pink Rosebud's abandoned properties in Seguin were sold for taxes.

4   The Reverend Andrew Jackson Potter died in the pulpit while preaching a sermon in Lockhart, Texas.

5   Juan Seguin's body was returned to Texas from Nueva Laredo, Mexico, in 1976, and was reinterred with honors in Seguin.

6   The debate concerning whether Georgia's mother, Cherokee, was the daughter of the Queen of Tuckabatchee still rages in the family. Willie King Coleman, age ninety-four, Georgia's granddaughter, insists her grandmother was an Indian. Daddy Jack

Montgomery, however, the 102-year-old son of Sweet Woods, is adamant Cherokee is just a name and his grandmother's veins did not flow with Tuckabatchee blood.

7   Chief Iron Jacket, of the Tunumas Comanches, was killed in a skirmish shortly after the Battle of Plum Creek. Sheriff Z. P. Bugg lived on to become the great-grandfather of actor Robert Redford.

8   There is still no monument to the women and children who lived through the Runaway Scrape, no road sign commemorating the five thousand who escaped Santa Anna and arrived at San Jacinto or the hundreds who died along the way.

9   In 1944 the aged Jacob Sechler Coxey was invited by President Roosevelt to Washington, D.C. Coxey accepted the invitation. Fifty years after the march of Coxey's Army, Coxey delivered the speech he had written in 1894 from the Capitol steps.

10   The ruins of Fort Hawkins still stand in Macon, Georgia, and the fort is slated for restoration in the near future.

11   Cherokee Hawkins Lawshe is buried on the site of the family home in Water Valley, Mississippi. No trace of the home itself remains.

12   The remains of Joanna Troutmann, who sewed the first Texas flag, were moved to the state cemetery in Austin, Texas. The Troutmann home still stands near Knoxville, Georgia.

13   The Ocmulgee Indian mounds where Georgia played as a child are now a part of Ocmulgee National Monument, near Macon, Georgia.

14   The body of Captain George Haller was found on Elm Creek in Milam County eight months after he was last seen alive. According to the *Dallas Herald,* March 19, 1870, "his body was riddled with balls, but his papers and money were untouched."

15   A large monument containing a memorial to Colonel-Doctor Peter Woods stands at the east entrance of the Hays

County Courthouse, in San Marcos, Texas. Georgia, Dr. Peter, and Captain Lawshe are buried in the San Marcos City Cemetery.

16 What became of Peachtree remains a mystery Idella Lampkin took to her grave. She is buried in the graveyard of the Capote Baptist Church, on Capote Road.

Acknowledgments

True Women is the joyous accomplishment of my family and many friends who provided the interviews, research, and access to letters and historical papers. For the marvelous tales and recollections I wish to give the following particular thanks:

For *Idella Lampkin*—her granddaughter Sara Harris and the Seguin Chief of Police Leroy Schneider. For *Euphemia Texas Ashby King*—her great-grandson William King Colville, Katie Lay Hurt for the Beard family letters, the Daughters of the Republic of Texas, Donaly Brice, Michael Green at the Texas State Archives, William Richter, Ralph Elder, Trudy Croes at the Eugene C. Baker Texas History Center, and the Gonzales County Historical Commission. For *Sarah Ashby McClure Braches*—her great-great-grandchildren Emily Anne Derounian and Hartwell Kennard for the diaries of Charles Braches, the *Gonzales Inquirer*, the Seguin Public Library Genealogy Section, Sandra Mauldin, and Dorcas Baumgartner. For *Juan Seguin*—Alfonso Rincon, Charley Eckhardt, the Seguin Conservation Society, Los Nogales Museum, the papers of Willie Mae Weinert, and the Sterling Memorial Library at Yale University. For *Jane Isabella Ashby McCulloch*—her great-great-grandson Dr. Larry Waldrip. For *Polly Gordon*—the papers of Polly Hollamon Bergfeld. For *Georgia Lawshe Woods*—her granddaughter Willie King Coleman, her grandson "Daddy Jack" Montgomery, and her three great-granddaughters Bette Woods Wehner, Mary Nell Spak, and Dorothy Woods Schwartz; also Mary Lou Coleman, Frances Stovall, Dr. Robert Montgomery, Dianne Wilcox, Sam Lawson, Joy Gold, Patty Dalton Arnold, Katherine Ferguson, Mary Anne Welch, the *San Marcos Record,* and the Tula Wyatt Papers of San Marcos

Public Library. For *Colonel-Doctor Peter C. Woods*—the papers of Wilton G. Woods, Allan Duaine for the papers of his father, Carl Duaine (author of *The Dead Men Wore Boots*), the letters and first-person accounts of Emma Woods Thorpe collected by Clifford Woods, the diaries of O. A. Fischer, the autobiography of the Reverend Andrew Jackson Potter, the Julia Idelson Library, and the Lyndon Baines Johnson Library. For *Martha Benjamin Hawkins and Ed Tom Lawshe*—their granddaughter Johnnie Rutledge and their great-grandson Paul Rutledge, Jr. For *Bettie Moss King*—Mary Louise Orr, Virginia Woods, Maxine Halm, William A. Bergfeld, Jr., Henry Edsel Bergfeld, Leonard Moss Fisher, Leonard Fleming, Joe Fleming, Burton Biediger, Katie Brenner Carter, Virginia Pybus, Nelda Kubala, and the *Seguin Enterprise*. For *Abraham and Lucinda Saphronia Miller*—their daughter Elizabeth Miller. For *Daisy Moss*—her daughter Daisy Thomas. For *George Henry King*—his mother Nellie King, his brother Donald King, and Allen Hoermann. For *Mary Lou Lannom*—her niece Gladys Engbrock. And for *Darden Wurzbach*—her niece Mabel Fayant.

For the interviews that provided information on the history of African-Americans in Seguin I thank Leonard Merriweather, Pinky Wilson Applewhite, Lizzie Miller White, and Henry Franklin Wilson.

I also want to remember those who contributed and who are now deceased: Ella Langley, Arden Reed Sparks, Karl O. Wyler, Sr., and Harry Gordon.

The following helped in many different and significant ways: My attorney and agent, Robert B. Barnett; my editor, Neil S. Nyren, Vice President, Publisher, Editor in Chief, G. P. Putnam's Sons; my brother, Wilton E. Woods; Kay Banning; Bea Bragg; Edith Firoozi Fried; Patricia Henry; Maurice Heller; West Lee King; Susan Berresford; James A. Joseph; Frances R. Bagwell; Tracy Pepper Lydick; Shirley Welk Fredericks; Anne L. Schwartz; Cissy Weidner; George McAlmon; John Fainter; Virginia Kemendo; and the Board and Staff of the El Paso Community Foundation.

A very special thanks to my children, Wayne Wilton Windle and his wife Mary Jane, Virginia Windle Shapiro and her husband Randy, and Charles Kendrick Windle; to all others who helped along the way; and, with love and gratitude, to the wonderful people of Seguin, Texas.

BETTIE MOSS KING HOLDING
GREAT-GRANDDAUGHTER JANICE KING WOODS

Seguin

1831~1946

Euphemia
Texas
Ashby

William
King

King

Henry
King

King

Bettie
Moss

Bergfeld

Virginia
King

William Bergfeld

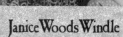

MATERNAL

Virginia
Bergfeld

Janice Woods Windle